COMPLICATED

OLA TUNDUN

Storm

To request permissions, contact the publisher at rights@stormpublishing.co

Ebook ISBN: 978-1-80508-315-3
Paperback ISBN: 978-1-80508-317-7

Cover design: Leah Jacobs-Gordon
Cover images: Shutterstock

Published by Storm Publishing.
For further information, visit:
www.stormpublishing.co

ALSO BY OLA TUNDUN

Roommates

Complicated

To every single reader and reviewer who gave Roommates a chance. I feel very privileged to share this journey with you.

ONE

CALEB

'What you said last night sounds a lot like she sexually assaulted you, mate,' Tim says solemnly. 'I think you might need to see someone about that.'

I'm jerked back to consciousness from the food coma Em's spectacular Christmas dinner has triggered.

Tim takes a sip of whisky to warm himself up as we sit quietly under the dark night sky in his chilly garden.

'I can assure you that I wasn't assaulted by the five-foot-one Singaporean heiress I spent more than two years shagging enthusiastically.'

I wish I hadn't told Tim now. I'd actually come over looking for Em a few weeks ago, only to be confronted by Tim, who recently started assuming full responsibility for his three sons one weekend a month to give his wife, Em, some downtime. The most I'd been able to share at the time was that I'd slept with Melissa, the said heiress, and I felt like shit. Since then, Tim has been digging for details at every opportunity. Late last night, after too many beers, I told Tim and Em all the details about Melissa and my last encounter; including how difficult it was to say no.

'You need to tell Ariella, Caleb. Tell her everything,' Em whispered before she kissed my cheek softly and left the room to go to bed.

If what I said could stun Tim and Em into silence, then goodness knows how Ariella will take it. Even now, Tim is struggling to look at me. I can tell he wants to say something.

'Out with it,' I prompt. He might as well get it off his chest.

'Hasn't Ariella noticed that something is wrong?'

'A little. I've been keeping my hands to myself, but she may have her own reasons as to why,' I admit guiltily.

'I hope she doesn't think it's her fault.'

'She might.'

'Caleb, what are you doing? You can't punish her for someone else's crime. It's Christmas Day. Have you even called her?'

'I wished her a Merry Christmas this morning when she called.'

'Do you actually love this girl or was what you told Jack and me bullshit?'

'Of course I love her.' I feel the familiar choke in my throat as intense sadness overwhelms me.

'Mate.' Tim reaches over my shoulders and pulls me into a rough and quick side-hug. The tear falls before I have a chance to catch it. We sit in silence while I pull myself together.

Tim breaks the silence. 'Why don't you fetch us the whisky, and give Ariella a call while you're at it? It'll make you feel better.'

I'm dialling before I stand.

'Hey,' I say softly when she picks up.

'Caleb! I'm so glad you called! I was going to phone as soon as dinner was over like I promised but we got a little carried away!' She chuckles down the phone.

The excitement in her voice immediately lightens my heavy heart and I find myself laughing along with her.

'You're supposed to be in emotional agony missing me, not getting carried away with what sounds like *maybe* too much Christmas cheer?'

Tim was right, this feels good.

'Maybe? I'm certain I've drunk my weight in champagne and I've had to undo all the buttons on my jeans. I've got a proper bulge!' She laughs.

I bet she's stroking her belly right now. Bloody hell. I'm in love with this girl.

'Also, I have news... Zach proposed to Isz!'

'No!' The last time I'd seen Ariella's brother and his girl-friend was at lunch in their parents' home. Isszy and I had left together, and she'd looked perilously close to dumping him.

'Yes!'

'What did Isszy say?'

'She said since nobody else is asking, she might as well say yes. For now.' Her laughter reaches through the phone and wraps me with joy.

'That could have gone either way.'

'I know, right?' She laughs again and I join her. 'How are things over there?' she asks.

'Great! Em cooked for five thousand, Leo and Seb loved their gifts from you. Alfie was upset we didn't get a picture of Santa but got over it before his first present was unwrapped. I got his first Christmas hug.'

'That is so sweet! Will you give everyone a hug and Alfie a special little squeeze from me?'

'What about me?' I tease.

'You can have all the kisses and hugs you want when we get back home,' she whispers. I don't deserve this girl.

'Can you come home now?' It may end, yet again, with crip-pling anxiety and me stopping things before they go too far again, but she makes me brave enough to try.

'I'm so sorry, Caleb, I'd love to but I can't. I promised Isz that I'd help her start planning tomorrow. I can wrap up early here and see you in the evening?'

Disappointment, mixed heavily with relief, floods me. I won't have to try tonight.

'Stay and help Isszy. Let's stick to our original plan.'

'But I want to come home early to be with you.'

'It's just one more day. We'll be fine.'

'But Cal—'

'There's the whisky! Tim and I are getting wasted in the garden. I thought I'd say hello while I hunted for the bottle.' I try to sound upbeat.

'I'm glad you did,' Ariella responds, deflated.

'I'll see you on the twenty-seventh. Sleep well, Aari, I'll call in the morning.' I blow a couple of kisses down the phone and hang up quickly. I know what's coming as I return with the bottle.

'Manage to speak to her?'

'Yeah. Everything is fine.'

Tim looks at me, unsure. I beckon his glass over and fill it before mine.

'If you lose that girl, Caleb, you'll regret it,' he warns me gently, looking at the stars above.

'I know,' I agree as I take a sip of my drink. Its warmth flows over the knot in my stomach.

I want to tell Ariella, but the risk of losing her is too great.

TWO

ARIELLA

'Remind me, are we together or just friends?' Caleb asks in the glass elevator hurtling up to Zachary and Isszy's engagement party, thirty-nine floors above London's streets.

'We agreed we'd go with just friends.'

'Should we though? Almost everyone here will have an ex,' he says, leaning in to kiss my forehead just before the lift doors open.

'Aari!' Isszy screams as she spots us, turning away from the group she is speaking with.

'Mrs Mason, commiserations,' I joke, hugging her tightly.

'Silver lining, we're finally going to be sisters. I love you!' A tipsy Isszy tightens her arms around me.

'I love you too!'

I am ecstatic that Zachary and Isszy are engaged. My brother adores Isszy but he can be challenging; so Isszy loves, tolerates, but lets him get away with nothing. They are perfect for each other.

'You brought Caleb! Wonderful.' She beams warmly at him. 'Tonight is your night. Most of the single girls are huddled over there and single guys are in short supply at the moment.' She winks at him.

Caleb rubs his hands together gleefully while throwing me an exaggerated look of excitement, before he disappears off into the crowd. I chuckle as Caleb's inner extrovert explores its playground.

'Jas is already here,' Isz whispers, referring to my ex-fiancé. 'I know it's not ideal that he's best man, but maybe this is an opportunity to mend things?'

A wide berth is probably a better suggestion. 'No need to worry, Isz, Jas and I are good.' I do my best to convince her.

'There's still trouble in paradise then?' Franco, our childhood friend, joins us with a sympathetic grin. 'I never thought I'd see the day. I'd already picked the lamp post we were going to tie Jasper's naked and drunk butt to on his stag. I never expected to have to look at Zachary's arse first. What did he do?'

'I'd rather not...'

'You might want to come up with something, because I won't be the last person to ask. When Jasper arrived with a girl that wasn't you earlier, the whole room went into meltdown. There she is, the blonde in the shiny dress.'

Franco points his tanned finger to a stunning blonde in a skintight dress, sipping on a martini and throwing her hair back in slow motion.

I feel jealousy rising as I watch the girl at the bar, laughing and engaging easily with the group of guys surrounding her. I knew that Jasper would move on, but I hadn't prepared myself for this. I have to snap myself out of it.

'You wouldn't happen to know where Zachary is, would you?' I don't wait for a response before I sift through the crowd.

Zachary isn't difficult to locate. I find the densest population of men at the party and I correctly guess that he is in the middle of them.

'Zach! I've offered Isz my commiserations, yet again,' I tease. 'How are you feeling?'

Zachary pulls me away from the group surrounding him onto a banquette seat nearby. 'Very, *very* lucky.'

'You should.'

'Are you going to be okay being maid of honour with Jas as best man?'

I tell him what he needs to hear. 'Sure!'

'Scrappy, there will be some discomfort involved. You need to be ready for that. Take tonight – he's shown up with a hot, clearly aristocratic, unobtainable knockout; and you turn up with... Caleb.' Zachary nods his head in the direction of Caleb, who is joyfully knocking back synchronised flaming tequila shots with three women. Good ol' Zach. Dishing out the truth, hot and cold, twenty-eight years running. 'It's not a competition. I like Caleb. He seems fun and all, but are you sure you don't want to rethink this whole situation?'

'Zach, Jasper has moved on. I'm happy for him.'

'I don't understand how something so solid could fall apart so quickly.' He sighs heavily.

I look in my brother's eyes. I'm not sure if he is talking about me or worried for himself, so I channel Mommy.

'I think that we only regret the chances we don't take, but you and Isszy are not a chance. You're meant for each other. Whatever happens, I will always be here for you, the same way that you are for me. And, I promise to be just as appalling a sibling as you are.' That makes him laugh and I give my brother a hug. Only then does he let me go.

I politely greet old friends and dodge Jasper questions before descending one floor below from the private space into the public bar to hide from the party. I claim one of the spare stools at the bar, order a drink and quietly relish my anonymity.

'You too?' I freeze. Jasper.

'Hello, Best Man,' I respond without turning around.

'Hello, Maid of Honour,' he whispers playfully in my ear before taking the stool next to me. 'What are you drinking?'

'Caipirinhas.'

'Interesting. Same again for the lady and I'll get a Ron Zacapa XO. Neat,' Jasper tells the barman.

I'm too nervous to look at him, so I keep my focus elsewhere.

'Am I making you nervous?' he asks kindly.

'No,' I lie.

'It feels like I haven't seen you in yonks, Scraps, but you still take my breath away.'

'Jas...'

'This was supposed to be us. Now we're sitting here, too nervous to touch one another,' he says quietly.

I playfully poke him in the ribs and he jumps. 'There. Consider yourself touched.' We both chuckle and all I see is my best friend.

'Shall we hide down here together and keep each company?' He smiles, gently stroking my cheek, and it makes me feel a little uneasy. We're both here with other people.

'Aren't you here with, in Zach's words, "The Knockout"?' I hate how spiteful I sound.

'Ariella Mason, are you jealous?' Jasper laughs.

'Of course I am.'

'Sophia is just a friend.'

'You mean an ex-girlfriend from university, don't you? I remember her. She resurfaced quickly.'

'Don't you dare, Ariella. I hadn't seen her since graduation. And remember, *you* left me.' He jabs his finger on the bar in front of us and I notice the barman glance at me, then at an angry Jasper. 'I'm sorry... I don't know what our new rules of engagement are. I've been worried sick since we were last together and we... but I didn't know whether to get in touch.'

'Why? We chatted over Christmas.'

'"Merry Christmas Jas" written under a dancing Santa GIF isn't chatting, Aari. Besides, we were irresponsible. You could be pregnant. Not that I'd mind. In fact, a big part of me has been hoping that you are.'

'I'm not, Jas.' Tears well in both our eyes. 'I'm sorry for all of this. I wish... I hadn't felt so empty.'

I was an emotional mess that night. I stood between the safe but hollow comfort of Jasper and the frightening, unpredictable precipice of falling into Caleb. When Caleb and I established a 'cooling off' period to tell Jasper about us, I thought I wanted Caleb. The Jasper that opened the door the evening I went to tell him was the boy I remembered loving my entire life. He was so wildly different to the man that he'd become that I felt an uncontrollable need to be sure. Safety or adventure. Assurance or unpredictability. Fear or bravery. Choosing him or choosing myself. Jasper or Caleb. So, I reached for Jasper. It confirmed what I already knew. I'd lost my heart to Caleb.

I knew that telling Caleb what happened with Jasper that night could destroy us, but hiding it from him certainly would; so, I took the risk and went with the truth. Things with Caleb are by no means perfect right now because of the pain I've caused him, but the price I am currently paying is worth moving forward with complete honesty.

'You don't feel empty with Caleb though, do you?' It stings, but then he takes my hand in his. 'Scraps, can we—'

'There you are!' We both whip around and see Sophia, standing with her hand on her hip, radiating happiness. She walks over to Jasper, plants a slow kiss on his lips and, somehow, manages to gracefully lift herself onto his lap and drape her arm around his neck, all in what looks like slow motion.

'Just a friend' my derrière. Sophia casts a look that makes it very clear to me she owns Jasper, while he looks like a child who's been discovered doing something very naughty. She crosses her legs as she balances on his lap, while he steadies her with his hand on her hip. All I can do is stare back at what looks like an Annie Leibovitz portrait; they look exceptionally beautiful together.

'Hello, Sophia, we've met before. We went to university together.' I smile and stretch out my hand.

She hesitates before she takes it. 'Pleasure to meet you.' She returns a cold smile that dismisses me before she turns to Jasper.

'Speeches are about to begin and they have Zach's parents on video, calling in from their holiday. Luckily, Caleb asked me to try down here.'

Jasper flinches at his name. 'Caleb?' he repeats accusingly.

'You must have missed him. Darling, we must have him over for dinner and set him up with Meaghan, he is just her type. Tall, devilishly handsome with a streak of bad boy; and he is single.'

'Guys like that are always single, Sophia,' Jasper responds, looking pointedly at me.

'He's actually very sweet. When he found out that I didn't know anyone, he kept me company before he got dragged to the dance floor by some girl who has been following him around all night. You'll like him. I'll introduce you after the speeches, but right now we have to go.'

She descends from Jasper's lap just as gracefully as she situated herself.

'You coming, Ariella?' Jasper asks, unable to meet my eye.

'Sure.' I grab my purse and my bar tab card. I am going to need it immediately after this.

THREE
CALEB

I knew that the engagement party would be a bloody nightmare. Everybody there would know Jasper and Ariella's extensive relationship history, so it made sense to label ourselves as friends; and we weren't wrong. As soon as we arrived all eyes fell on us, but Ariella was too busy wrapping herself around Isszy to notice.

They were a good, lively crowd, endlessly offering to buy bottles of extra champagne or a round of drinks from the top shelf, even though all the preselected food and drinks were free. They also loved to gossip. I could get used to hanging out with a whole bunch of rich kids with generous spending habits and a love of the scandalous.

By the time I saw Ariella reach Zachary, I'd been fed so many juicy and inaccurate snippets of the Ariella and Jasper saga that even I began to believe that the whole break-up was much more exciting than it actually was.

Just when I was ready to slip 'I was there. It was tedious and boring.' into the conversation, someone pointed out Jasper's new, smoking hot, obviously loaded, body-to-die-for, girlfriend Sophia. I have to concede that Jasper isn't too shabby at snagging incomparable women. I, of course, went over to introduce myself, because it would be rude not to. It didn't take her long to lace her arm through mine and declare me her 'new bestie'. What can I say? I've got a heart of gold.

It pleased me no end that Jasper was moving on. Then again, I had thought he was doing exactly that a couple of months ago, until I nipped over to Singapore for five minutes and he was all over Ariella, yet again.

Speaking of Jasper, for someone that was apparently there with someone else, he wasted no time appearing from nowhere to follow Ariella away from the party. That was when I decided to make his blissfully ignorant date my party bestie. Unfortunately, Dahlia and Hugh, Ariella and Zachary's parents, called in by video for the speeches a little early. Jasper and Ariella were nowhere to be found so I shot a text to Ariella's mum asking her to stall. Like a pro, she filled the delay, starting with me.

'Look at all of you!' She glowed through the screen. 'Caleb, where are you?' Hugh Mason grimaced, walked away from the camera, grabbed a broadsheet and started reading, obscuring his face and chest from the rest of us. Nothing's changed there then.

I love Ariella's mother much more than I ever loved my own, and she is the perfect accomplice if you want to get up to some mischief. Her chatter kept the room distracted while I sent Sophia after Ariella and Jasper. There was no way I was going down there. Sophia was happily smug when she returned, clutching possessively at an embarrassed Jasper's arm as Ariella followed behind with downcast eyes. A few people next to me chuckled that they 'always do this', while others expressed pity for Sophia. I was pissed off.

I get straight to it as soon as we get home.

'What happened between you and Jasper tonight?' I ask, tossing my keys into the bowl.

'Nothing. I slipped away for a bit and he showed up. We talked.' I catch her hands trembling slightly as she sits on one of our bar stools and starts taking off her shoes. I'm making her anxious. I soften my tone instantly.

'I should have been with you.' I crouch to help with her shoes.

'People would have been suspicious.'

'Unlike their suspicion when you disappeared with Jasper?'

'I know how that looked. I'm sorry.'

'You should send him away next time.' She doesn't answer. 'But you won't, will you?' I arrange both liberated shoes neatly by the stool base before I stand.

'Caleb, Jas—'

'You still love him.'

She silently shrugs her shoulders before nodding slightly.

'What hold does this guy have on you, Ariella? What am I missing?'

I watch her take a deep breath. Here it comes.

'I don't think I will ever stop loving Jasper, Caleb. But I think I love him the way I love Zachary, Isszy and my parents. Sophia did make me a little jealous tonight, but I also want, more than anything, for her to make him really happy.'

'And I'm just supposed to accept that, am I?'

'I know you're still upset about what happened last time with Jas, but I want to be with you, Caleb. If we can find a way to get past it, I don't want us to hide any more. We could tell Zachary and Isszy. Mommy already knows, but we'll have to tell Daddy – what do you think?'

I was not expecting Ariella to hand me everything I want.

'I'm not saying this because Jasper is now with Sophia, but it definitely influenced it. They came out together and the world didn't end. Why can't we do the same? Maybe you can be my date to the wedding?'

'I got a few offers tonight, so you might need to convince me,' I tease, as I reach for her fingers.

'I won't be trying to seduce you again if that's what you're asking. There is only so much rejection a girl can take.' She shoos me with her hand before she stands to pick up her shoes.

'When did you try to seduce me?'

'Last week. I asked if you'd like to take a shower. You said "back in a minute" and left me on the couch.'

'I thought you were telling me I was stinky. Your seduction technique needs work. You should have joined me.'

'I haven't been your favourite person recently, so I didn't think you'd want me to.'

'You've been my favourite everything for a lot longer than you think, Aari.'

I close the gap between us. I know I've been hurting her deeply with my distance. Truthfully, I've been unable to touch her since Singapore because, whenever things start to get intimate, all I can see is Mel. On top of me. Climaxing. It fills me with a revulsion so intense that it makes it almost impossible to breathe.

'If we decide to do this, what's next?' I ask, shaking the thought.

'We can tell Zach and Isz this weekend and the next stop after that is probably Sunday lunch? Daddy can't kill you with witnesses around.'

I laugh at her smiling apologetically. 'As long as your mum is there, I'll be fine.'

It's Ariella's turn to laugh.

'Let's be clear, Caleb, I'm the witness. Mommy likes you and she will definitely feel sad if Daddy kills you, but she won't think twice about helping him dispose of your body and then, confidently ask "Caleb who?" when the police pay them a visit. She will always pick Daddy.'

Ariella's description makes me smile. I want that. 'It will be worth the risk if I fall in love with you,' I joke.

She shifts away uncomfortably. 'Caleb, you haven't decided whether we should tell everyone yet. Maybe we should clear that hurdle before anything else?' She's nervous.

'I've decided. Tell the world. What happens if I fall in love with you, Aari?'

She shuts her eyes as she inhales deeply, then lets out a long slow exhale.

When she opens her eyes, she walks quickly to the kitchen, then grabs a pen and our sticky notepad. Her and those bloody sticky notes. Someone is going to have to tell her that nothing good ever comes when she reaches for them. She scribbles on it and enters my bedroom, asking me not to follow her. She returns shortly after.

'Goodnight, Caleb,' she says before she hurries into her own room.

I'm in there like a shot, participating in a treasure hunt at almost two in the morning. I look in the obvious places. Nothing. Then, I look in the less obvious places. Behind the blinds, under the bed, in my drawers, beside the shower. After ten minutes, I am still looking.

'Where is it?' I say as I barge into her bedroom, startling her as she makes her way to her shower.

'Go to sleep, Caleb.' She smiles, entering her bathroom and shutting the door.

'Give me a hint!'

'Go to sleep!' she calls from the other side of her bathroom door.

I go to impossible places. Bottoms of drawers, behind the loo, between my hanging shirts. For something that she promised hasn't been hidden somewhere impossible, it is proving pretty impossible to find. I eventually tire myself out and sit on my bed to think about where it could be. I lie back and there it is, on the ceiling above my bed. Cheeky. I stare at it for a little longer before I reach for the ceiling and finally muster the courage to take a look.

I'm not ready to say it, but I think I'm falling in love with you, Caleb. I completely understand that you don't feel the same way after what I did, but I hope one day that may change. Aari x.

I want to run to her room, get in her bed and fall asleep holding hands like I've craved these past few months. I want to tell her about my last visit to Singapore as I hold her close, breathe her in and tangle my legs with hers. I'm ready to run the gauntlet of her anger, disappointment and hurt, because I know there will be forgiveness on the other side. With her note, Ariella is diving into us, head first. The only problem is, I don't understand why.

Playing with 'the loadeds' tonight was fun but I can see why Dahlia Mason kept her home as normal and humble as she could. It's the same reason that Hugh Mason protected Ariella fiercely, kept Jasper close and made sure Zachary kept his practical, and often inconvenient, brutal honesty. The bubble they created was intentional.

Everyone at the party was all right, but it was impossible to get away from the men comparing their ridiculously expensive performance cars and investments. One of their friends picked up the entire engagement party bill, meant for Zachary and Isszy, right in front of me, like he was paying for a packet of crisps. He didn't even look at the total before he jabbed in his PIN, laughing that Zachary could use all the help he could get if he insisted on being a lawyer with a conscience.

This is the universe she moves within. Money, access and entitlement. I can't imagine ordering twenty bottles of Krug Grande Cuvée for my friend's engagement just for 'choice', like another friend did tonight. Tim and Jack, who are like brothers to me, might get a couple of pints and a pat on the back. Maybe. If Jack has a party like that for Lou, his temperamental ex-fiancée recently demoted back to girlfriend, I am drinking the bar dry and not parting with a penny.

If I step out into the world with Ariella, this is what I will be stepping into. I'll be the one who can't afford the Lamborghini. The one with the off-the-rack suit. The one with the smart-watch rather than the crazily expensive chronographs they wear. They are the kind of crowd that will notice that I don't belong to a members' club, I don't have a family ski resort and I definitely do not go on holidays 'just because'. Almost every-thing that I have, love and own is contained within these four walls. I check all my bills for discrepancies, twice, I've adjusted the hot water to come through the taps for a maximum of four hours on weekdays because these energy bills aren't going to pay themselves, and I rely on work travel for any international fun.

The only edge I have is that I know how to have a good time. It was fun to hold the room tonight with the women, but to them that is all I will ever be. Fun. Like I was to Melissa.

She may be quiet about it, but Ariella is accustomed to a standard of life that I will never attain or be able to give her. I've seen the bills from her butcher and grocer. It's about the same as she pays in rent. Sometimes, it's more – and that's without adding in the Chelsea fishmonger she's recently discovered.

Yet, she has chosen me. Against all odds. It's euphoric, knowing that I've won the fight for her; especially as I'm so used to fighting for everything. My job, my house, my life, my future; and to fight for someone who I didn't realise I wanted, who I now know I needed, was thrilling. It has been challenging, painful, enjoyable, and has ultimately ended with me feeling, for the first time in my life, like I really matter to someone.

Now that I am about to commit to being her boyfriend publicly, I can't shake Jasper's words when I told him a few months ago that I might be falling for Ariella. Especially after tonight. I am too far behind and in too slow a vehicle to catch up with Ariella's life. And that feeling of being inadequate isn't going anywhere.

So, I lie in my bed, alone, and awake most of the night, trying to think of ways to break up with Ariella Mason.

FOUR

ARIELLA

In the morning, I throw the covers off and jump in the shower to calm my nerves. After the note I left, I'm too scared to see him this morning.

I need to talk to someone. Even though I know the ultimate suggestion will be to dump Caleb, peppered with bits of useful advice, I hit the number 3 on my keypad and hold. It doesn't take long to hear her voice.

'Hey, Aari!' Lara greets me croakily. My beautiful, wild and delightfully naughty best friend's voice immediately makes me happy.

'Go back to sleep. I can call back later.' I chuckle.

'Nah. Awake now. Just need to free my arm,' she grunts. 'Ah, there. What's up?'

'I did something really stupid.'

'Please don't tell me that you have finally caught something, you've been ignoring the itching for weeks and it's now a bigger deal than it initially was?'

'No, Lara.' I can't help smiling. I relay last night's events through her peeing, flushing, brushing her teeth and drinking something from her fridge.

'You do know that you two fools can announce your relationship to the entire planet and you're still going to have the same problems, right?' She laughs.

'Things weren't this complicated with Jasper,' I complain.

'But you don't want Jasper, do you? Caleb clearly isn't going to indulge your secretive nonsense, so you're going to have to learn how to communicate. I imagine he's as thick as bricks, so you're going to have to spell out everything you have swimming around in your head. He'll listen and take it seriously, because it's you.'

'So, I did the right thing? Letting him know that I'm falling in love with him?'

'Absolutely not. The only thing you should be doing is gathering your stuff, making a break for it and thanking the universe that you survived disease-free. I hope. However, if you're not going to escape, you're going to need to make sure that you're on the same page.'

'I'm a little scared.'

'And I'm mortified. I can't believe you've got me giving you hints and tips that will lead to his happiness after all the time I've invested praying for his downfall. Seriously though, go for a walk, clear your head and decide if this is what you want.'

'That's not a bad idea, because I'm not sure I can face him yet.'

'Before you go, can I suggest that when you guys become official you keep his ego crushed and regularly dangle the possibility of being dumped in his face?'

'No, Lara.'

'Just saying that strategy has its benefits. Love you.'

It's early. Maybe he isn't up yet. I can sneak out for a little walk on Hampstead Heath. After a long, calming shower, I pull a fleece over my head, slip on my Converse hi-tops, grab my phone, pull my headphones over my ears and take a quick peek. The coast is clear. I tiptoe across the living room and make it to the front door. When I open it, I smack right into a sweaty and panting Caleb, fresh from a run.

'Hi,' he greets me breathlessly, scanning me from top to bottom. 'Sneaking off somewhere?' He smiles that smile I can't see past and my worry almost evaporates.

'Just for a walk.'

'Are you walking to hide from me?' he asks softly as he moves to lean against the counter.

'Last night was... overwhelming.'

'I know, but please don't be afraid of me, Aari. Talk to me. The only way we are going to get through this is to be completely honest with each other. Want to go first?'

I shake my head.

'I'll start then. Honestly, I've hoped for a while that some day your feelings will be the same as mine, but now that we're here, I realise that I have no idea how to be someone's boyfriend.' He makes the word sound foul. 'I spent all night trying to work out how I was going to live up to what you and everyone around you expects of me, because all of them, including my own friends, expect me to fuck this up. But I want to try. I will go through the judgement, the expectations, the obstacles, all of it, for you. But I need you to be absolutely sure that you want to be in it, completely, with me. If you're not ready, I need to know. Do you want to do this, Aari?'

I have seen him at his best, at his worst, at his most tender, his most brutal – and it doesn't change anything.

'I do. I really do.'

Caleb leans forward and kisses my forehead softly before he pulls me into a warm hug. Just as I put my hands on his waist to hug him back, he pulls away.

'I liked your plan yesterday. Let's tell Zachary and Isszy. We can tell your parents when they get back. After that we can feel our way through. What do you think?'

. . .

After Caleb showers, changes and we have breakfast, we go over to Isszy and Zachary's home. They take the news much more positively than I expect, with Zachary pointing out that Caleb might want to write a last will and testament before he tells Daddy. Isszy, after being horrified at directing Caleb to the single women the night before, looks genuinely pleased for us. When Jasper is mentioned, we respond that he has known for a little while. We spend the rest of the day and evening with Zach and Isz, hanging out, making me feel like Caleb and I have always been together.

I flop, exhausted, on the couch when we get back home.

'That wasn't so hard!' I smile.

'No!' Caleb exhales with relief. 'Ice cream?' he offers from the kitchen, opening the freezer door.

'Yes!' He returns with the almost-finished tub and two spoons and we sit on the couch eating in comfortable silence.

'Do you know when I first caught myself looking at you longer than I should have?' Caleb asks, licking his spoon.

'Day one? When you thought – it moves; I'd shag that?' I poke, attempting his light Liverpudlian accent and laughing. This feels good.

'No! One, that was a terrible accent. Two, stop talking to Lara!' He smacks my thigh lightly with his cold spoon. 'It was a Saturday morning when you stumbled out of your room for breakfast. You were grumpy, your curls were wild and your hair was absolutely everywhere. You were wearing your faded Yosemite Sam T-shirt, some ugly shorts, and you had a weird half-wedgie. You looked hungover and ridiculous but I couldn't understand how you could look so beautiful when you were obviously doing your best to look the exact opposite.'

I laugh; it could have been any Saturday morning in my first few months living here.

'I love those pyjamas!'

He rolls his eyes. 'I know. I have grown to like them too. After that, strange things started to happen.' He looks embarrassed as he scratches his head.

I chuckle. 'What strange things?'

'I first noticed in San Francisco. I went out to dinner with... a friend.' He swallows nervously and I immediately know to which kind of 'friend' he is referring. 'Just before we left the restaurant, a song came on and all I could think about was you in your pyjamas with your hair in your eyes having breakfast, smiling at something funny I said to take the piss out of you. It pretty much ruined my evening. It took me ages to find that song and now it's your theme song in my head.' He laughs at himself.

'What song is it?' I immediately worry that it's a derogatory 'booty' song because, let's face it, it's Caleb.

'I'll play it for you.' He whips out his phone, and before long the flat is slowly filled with Mac Miller's 'ROS'.

We sit there listening quietly for a little while, before Caleb pipes up again.

'That's when I knew something was very wrong. I called you that night.'

'That phone call?' I remember. Caleb called to give me details of what I should do and people to call in an emergency, should anything from the plumbing to the lights go off. He had been extremely unhelpful as he took the time to describe, in detail, a load of scenarios that were unlikely to happen. I remember I had been a little impatient, as it was all written down anyway and it wasn't a call I wanted to have at four in the morning.

'Yup, that phone call. I didn't know what it meant at the time, but I knew it wasn't good.' He smiles sadly.

I climb onto Caleb's lap, place my knees either side of his thighs and face him. His eyes are a pool of sadness. I lean forward slowly to kiss him lightly. He doesn't kiss me back but I persevere until his lips eventually start moving in rhythm with mine.

'It's a beautiful song, I love it. Thank you for sharing it with me. Goodnight, Caleb.'

When I climb off him to go to my room, he doesn't try to stop me. We have done a lot today; he just needs time. I strip off and walk into the shower to let everything wash over me. If this isn't right and we change our minds, it is not too late. I'll be the butt of Zachary's jokes for ever, but no real damage will be done. I grab my towel, wrap it around myself and step out of the shower with heavy eyelids. Sleep will come easily tonight. I enter my bedroom to find Caleb sitting at the end of the bed staring at the floor. He looks so dejected, it's painful.

I tap him on the shoulder. 'You okay?' I ask, rubbing his back.

'I'm not sure. I have so much in my head that I want to share with you, Aari, but I can't because I don't want to lose you.'

I kneel in front of him so that our eyes are level. I have to try again. 'Caleb, I'm really sorry about what happened with Jasper when you were in Singapore. I know you say you've forgiven me, but I know how hurt you still are. I can feel it.'

'Aari, I should be apologising to you.'

'You did nothing wrong,' I whisper. 'It was all me. I really wish I could erase that week.'

'Why don't we just forgive and forget everything up to this point?'

'And start again? Are you sure?'

'I am. Can I stay over?' He may be asking, but he seems conflicted.

'Only if you really want to.' Staying over is a leap and I don't want to push him. I know I have a lot of trust to regain.

Without a word, Caleb stands, undresses and walks into my bathroom. When I hear the shower come on, I pull on some

24

underwear and a vest before I get into bed. We can take this slowly.

When he emerges, he pauses to take a deep breath and exhales slowly, before joining me under the covers.

'Are you sure about this?' I ask.

'Yes, come here.'

Abstaining while we figured things out had been a good idea when it was floated by Caleb, but I'd felt the limitations of our decision pretty quickly. We need this to get back on track, but it has to be at his pace. I get caught by surprise when I feel Caleb's fingers graze the base of my belly, and my body tingles as he runs the route up between my ribs, past my breasts right up to my mouth. I've missed him. I feel for his free hand and intertwine my fingers with his, to let him know I want to keep him close.

'It's been too long,' he whispers.

'It has.'

'Where would you like to start?' he asks shyly. Wait. Is he nervous? I know what to do.

I've missed the way his body feels against mine, so I wrap my arms and legs around his before I lean in to put my lips on his. I have missed this so much. I miss the touch of his hands, the smell of his hair, the taste of his skin. Our kiss becomes more intense, with him breaking it off to explore. He leaves a trail of kisses as he works his way down the side of my neck, stopping to leave his mark.

'I've missed branding you here.' He chuckles before kissing the base of my neck a bit harder. I feel it between my legs and instinctively lift my hips. I've not only missed his kisses but, as his last hickeys faded, I began to feel naked without them. I love seeing the memories of his mouth on me.

'Good.' He smiles at me, admiring his work. 'I think my work is done there.'

'I don't think your work is ever done, Caleb,' I moan. My

back arches in response to his gentle touch, but when he pauses I know something is wrong.

'I'm sorry I let you down, Aari. I'm sorry I haven't been myself. I need you to forgive me.'

I fold my boyfriend into me. 'You didn't—'

'Please just tell me you forgive me?' he pleads sadly.

'Of course I forgive you,' I reassure him.

'Good, because I'm going to take your clothes off and we're going to revisit some of our old hits. It's going to be a little awkward at first because while I know the songs, remembering the chords might be a little tricky.'

'I remember your chords perfectly,' I offer playfully as I see parts of the Caleb I remember start to resurface after weeks of hibernation.

'While that may be, my little show-off, I'm in charge tonight.'

The sound escapes me before I know what I've done.

'Did you just squeal with delight?' Caleb asks incredulously before we both burst out laughing.

'You've ruined me, Caleb,' I declare, mid-laughter.

'No, you've ruined me. I love you, Aari. You make me feel safe.' Before I get the chance to respond, his mouth closes in on mine and, this time, his kiss is filled with promises of certainty that his body confirms when it follows.

FIVE

CALEB

Ariella Mason is going to be the death of me. The plan for Saturday was to go for a run and tell her that we weren't going to work out. We're too different and the odds are stacked against us. For starters, she was raised surrounded by love. I was dragged up, clinging to anything that ensured my survival. And aside from our cavernous class and wealth gap, there's Melissa.

I couldn't tell her about what happened on the last trip to Singapore without telling her the real reason I am so successful at work and how long I had an ongoing affair with someone I knew was engaged to someone else. I'm not the man she thinks I am and she deserves better, but looking at her face, full of hope and belief in me, when I returned from my run, made me believe that I can be. There and then, I committed to doing whatever it was going to take to be that man, for her.

So, we head to Zachary and Isszy's and I find myself grinning like an idiot and doing 'boyfriendy' things like stroking her leg and playing with her hair. It's all new territory and bloody scary, but none of it was more terrifying than having to face Ariella last night, when we were home alone.

Since I came back from Singapore, I've been pretending

everything is normal, when it feels anything but. Keeping our hands off each other for a while was my idea; and because I'm an absolute bastard who doesn't deserve to be happy, I let her believe that my withdrawal was because she slept with Jasper. Her sleeping with Jasper hurt, but I understood. The truth is that I've spent the last few weeks disgusted with myself, having nightmares, waking up to vomit in the middle of the night; and, most worryingly, I was petrified of bursting into tears if Ariella touched me. So, I stayed as far away from her as possible.

As soon as I stepped into her room last night, the debilitating panic I'd got used to feeling intensified, as the detailed memory of my last night in Singapore came rushing back. I really wanted to come clean but I couldn't find the courage. Her concern as she touched me, when she emerged from her bathroom in that napkin she calls a towel, forced me to push through the fright and commit to making all my bullshit up to her. Giving me the space that I wanted, to take the control I needed, when I froze, was the best thing she could have done for me. It was time to make her believe that all was forgiven and completely forgotten, because simply, I can't lose her.

We slipped back into each other so easily, it was hard to believe I'd forced us apart for so long. Muscle memory was on my side. By the time I let her go to sleep just before dawn, she was so grateful, I heard her mumble, 'thank goodness' into her pillow.

We're back, folks.

I spent Sunday chasing her around the apartment. When she escaped into the shower, I wasn't far behind. I rediscovered the joy of undressing her and committed to re-exploring every inch of her and inspiring her giggles and gasps full of pleasure. Every time she self-consciously covered her mouth because she thought she was being too loud, or when she hid her eyes behind her palm during embarrassed laughter, it just made me fall deeper in love. I'd forgotten who we became when we were

28

together. By Sunday night, as we sat half-naked ravenously eating sushi, we coursed through each other's bloodstreams again.

The next couple of weeks are a dream. We settle back into each other, work is great – with an unexpected surge of projects from Singapore – and coming home to Aari's smiling face is all I could ask for. I have to admit that I was wrong about monogamy. It's not a trap; it's magical with her. The contacts on my phone have been cleared, my relationship status on social media changed, dating apps and associated profiles have been deleted. I even got Ariella a picture of both of us in a frame to put on her work desk. When she explained that she needed her desk clear, I put it in my office instead. I want everyone to know that we belong together because we know sides of each other that no one else can imagine. The Ariella everyone at work gets is quiet and efficient. My Ariella is blindingly radiant. And funny. And witty. And charming. And brave. And daring.

And there is still a lot to discover – for example, guess who likes a morning surprise? Considering I am usually full of surprises when I wake up, her particular fondness for this is a win-win. She is still a little embarrassed about certain things we may try, but that is just a matter of time; and if that time never comes, that is fine too – as long as we're together, nothing else matters.

The one thing I have finally managed to get her to stop hiding is Shark Week. I'm still struggling to nail down an exact pattern for her monthly cycle, but I've got a rough idea when to have hot-water bottles ready for her crampy tummy and stock up on her French cacao truffles. They're great to toss in her mouth from a distance, when she is feeling extra bitey.

I find it comforting that while we have our own lives, we also have the security of knowing that we will always be there for each other when we get home. I have signed more stress-inducing kids up for the weekly Muay Thai class I teach because seeing how committed Ariella is to supporting the shelter she cooks for makes me want to do more 'good deeds' too. Now that I have extra time liberated from swiping and dating, I see Tim and Jack more often. They may still be suspicious of the fact that I am actually behaving myself, but I don't care. I'm happy.

Aari is enjoying yoga, taking on more complex projects at work, and is cooking more, which, thanks to the extra training I am doing, is great news. She reminds me that I matter every time she checks in with me when she is going to be late, and always asks how I am or if I need anything, because I want to know those things too. I adore the way she washes my hair and puts her hand over my heart every night before we fall asleep. I have never had that. I am elated with this new life – but also worried because her parents are back and I'm going to have to face Hugh Mason. I'm not sure how many people would want to willingly piss off an ex-SAS soldier, but I would, for Ariella. I conveniently put him in the back of my mind. I have more pressing matters.

'Move in with me,' I whisper into her ear as she gets under the covers after her shower.

'I already live here.' She laughs, confused.

'You pay rent and you have your own room. Let's get rid of both those things,' I suggest, softly kissing her earlobe.

'I like paying rent and having my room,' she whispers back, before she plants a kiss on my nose. It's sweet.

'I want you more than your rent.'

'This way, you can have me and my rent. You're winning here, Caleb. You're not going to find anyone else foolish enough to pay twenty per cent above asking.' She moves her hand to stroke my back. I melt when she does that.

'But—'

'Caleb, please understand. I like being responsible for myself. I'm only just learning how to do that. I'd never paid a utility bill or needed to budget for myself until I moved in with you. I know you hate it when I bring up Jasper but...'

'Fine, I'll concede for now but it won't be the last time I ask.' I move to hover over her.

'I know.' She smiles and pulls my face down for a kiss. Ariella's lips touching mine sends shivers down my spine. I lower myself down slowly and cover her body with mine.

'I am hopelessly in love with you,' I catch myself whispering into our kiss.

'I love you, Caleb. You make me feel free,' she responds for the first time, wrapping her legs around mine. Her tongue slowly and softly reacquaints itself with mine. This is so her, delivering deeply heartfelt words that change everything without drama and fanfare.

At that moment, I know. I belong to her. I don't want to be anywhere she isn't, and I will do anything to keep her happy, safe from harm, and mine. Anyone who attempts to interrupt that is going to be faced with a hell of a fight.

SIX

ARIELLA

I am smitten. I'd been in love with Jasper for so long, I had no idea that the world Caleb and I inhabited could exist. There is freedom, challenge, adventure, surprise, laughter and naughtiness in loving Caleb. Most importantly, there is the comfort of complete safety. He has the magical ability to quieten my busy, anxious mind, and being by his side, as he throws open the doors to a world that I have spent my life either hiding or being protected from, makes me brave enough to discover parts of myself that I didn't know existed. He has somehow managed to make me find more of me.

While Jasper may have been steadfast, Caleb is my playmate and co-conspirator. He is unpredictable, passionate, and delightfully childish when he's in the mood. The other morning, I found out that he has little names for my body parts. My nipples are 'the girls' because, according to him, it would be unfair to pick a favourite, even though secretly he knows it's the wonky one, because apparently she tries harder. My left bum cheek is 'Cheeky' because tapping it supposedly puts me in the mood, and the right is 'Chuckles' because tapping it makes me laugh.

We've created a fun little bubble unlike anything I have experienced. He has his life, I have mine, and where we intersect is exciting. Caleb can hold me in place with just a look, that dirty laugh is my favourite and all he has to do is brush past me for my body to sing. He knows it too. He is acutely aware of the power he has over me and has no qualms wielding it and shaping my responses. I have no qualms either because, even when he is being dominant, he is so gentle. I trust and appreciate him most whenever we try something new because he checks in constantly. He always starts by putting on his serious face.

'You have to tell me if you don't like it, okay?' Once I've agreed, he follows it with his dirty smirk. 'Also, tell me if you do like it; so, either way, let me know.'

Caleb fills our weekends with weird supper clubs, concerts, comedy shows, obscure art galleries, fun activities around London, absorbing Sunday pub lunches with his friends – and we once got locked in a room with a zombie. Fun but absolutely terrifying.

Caleb even recruited Lara for the afternoon to help him find a dress for me when we were invited to a club night by his friend Jack, to celebrate his girlfriend Lou's birthday. While I was happy Lara and Caleb were spending time together, I spent the entire time expecting one or both of them to return covered in blood. I was only able to relax when Lara sent me a text message.

> When he's not trying to shag you, Caleb can be fun.

The backless skater dress they'd selected was tinier than I was comfortable with, which made me think that they were perhaps better apart.

That night at the club, he carefully introduced me to each person who came up to us as his girlfriend; to which the returned expressions were of shock, confusion, a conspiratorial wink or a laugh. Caleb just smiled, held me closer and planted little kisses on my nose. It was a lovely opportunity to see Caleb's friends, Tim and Em, again, who seemed genuinely happy for us.

'So, is it true love?' Em asked warmly, beaming at me, when the boys were at the bar grabbing our drinks.

'We're just taking each day as it comes. Caleb keeps me... occupied.'

'Ariella.' Em moved close and gently covered my free hand with both of hers. 'Caleb is in new territory here and he has a way of making things seem fine when they aren't. Please be careful with yourself and with him. I really want you both to work out.'

I got it. She cared deeply about Caleb, but she'd also seen hearts broken.

'Coat off, dance time,' Caleb announced to my horror when he returned.

'I don't know...'

'I do.' He laughed as he pulled me up, relieved me of my coat and escorted me to the dance floor just in time for one of my favourite songs, Temper Trap's 'Sweet Disposition'.

'You look delicious in that dress.'

'I wore it for you. I'd do pretty much anything for you.' I shrugged.

My boyfriend stopped, held my face in his hands and kissed me so deeply that some of the people around us started clapping. Then Caleb and I danced the night away, song after song, with our bodies in constant contact, as everything and everyone around us seemed to disappear.

Caleb and I became so lost in the music and each other that, eventually, Tim and Jack had to come over to separate us. It wasn't until he was pulled away that I realised that Caleb's mouth had been at the base of my neck, branding me, with his hand almost indecently near the top of my thigh. I had so much desire coursing through me that we were going to have to leave. I pulled him by the collar of his shirt.

'Take me home, Caleb.'

We hopped in one of the black taxis queuing up outside and gave our driver a borderline indecent eyeful all the way home. Feeling guilty, we tipped him heavily.

Caleb and I couldn't have been home for more than fifteen seconds before I was on the living room sofa, my underwear was on the floor, and he was inside me. It didn't take long after that for me to shudder and for him to follow before he collapsed on top of me.

'Come on. Shower with me,' I said, still out of breath.

We took great care washing each other down before we stepped out and did our teeth. As I put on my knickers and vest, Caleb pulled open one of my bottom drawers, took out some boxers and slipped them on casually.

'Hey! That's my drawer!' I pointed and laughed.

'It's the smallest one of six drawers you're not using so...' he defended himself matter-of-factly.

'How do you know how many drawers I am not using? Are you quietly moving in?' I chuckled.

He picked me up, threw me on the bed and jumped on after me. He pulled me into him, wrapped his body around mine and rested his chin on top of my head, as I leaned against his shoulder. It was a little uncomfortable but I didn't care.

'Tonight was incredible. It felt so good to have you there with me, Aari. And that dress. I know wearing it took some bravery, but I was the one that had to stop myself from biting you in public.'

I hit him playfully before I ran my finger across his back suggestively. He rolled his eyes and looked at me.

'Yes?'

'Perhaps it's my turn to do the biting?' I hooked my finger on to the strap of Caleb's boxer shorts and gave it a soft pull before looking for his consent.

'Fucking hell, go on then.' He smiled and I covered his mouth with mine, as I thought about where I'd like to place my first love bite.

'Holy fuck, Ariella. You are a very naughty girl, and it's all my fault.' Caleb spoke hoarsely into his pillow the next morning.

I burst out laughing and looked over. He had one eye open and a cheeky grin on his face.

'I'm scared of you,' he complained with a smile playing on his lips.

'I'm scared of me too!' I laughed through yawning.

Yes. This was right. This was me.

SEVEN

CALEB

Ariella's mother opens the door and regards both of us with some surprise. I don't understand why, since she is expecting us.

'Hello, you two, come on in. You're looking very chirpy, Caleb,' she welcomes us warmly, before pulling me into a hug.

'Hi, Mommy. I missed you guys! Lunch smells amazing.' Ariella leans in and gives her mum a kiss while Dahlia is still hugging me. It feels nice sandwiched between them.

'Hi, baby. You look... different.' Dahlia lets go of me and sizes her daughter up approvingly.

'Different how?'

'Just different. Brighter? Lighter? More confident? I don't know, but I approve.'

'Mommy, the sun got to you!' Ariella laughs nervously and clears her throat.

'Maybe. But I am fairly certain something, or maybe someone, has got to you too.' She calls us in with her hand as we walk into her home.

I will never cease to be amazed by the home Ariella grew up in. It is such a far cry from my childhood. She had parents who loved her, a brother who cared and a best friend who spent his entire adult life trying to give her what he thought she wanted. Even when things are tense, as I'd witnessed previously, it's still full of love. I find myself never wanting to leave.

'Mommy, where's Daddy?' Ariella asks.

'I think he is outside somewhere. Go. Find him. Caleb, you can come and help me.' With that, Dahlia Mason effectively splits us up.

I more than like Ariella's mum. She makes me feel like my well-being is important to her. She is naturally maternal, but not in that nice, cosy, wouldn't-hurt-a-fly way. She is strong, warm, mischievous and funny. She's also deeply protective of her family, and you wouldn't want to mess with her.

'I need a potato peeler,' she instructs, smiling.

I follow her into the kitchen, where she has just finished frying off some bacon lardons. I reach for one and she smacks my hand away with a tea towel.

'Wash your hands, heathen,' she reprimands me, laughing.

I make my way to the sink, roll up my sleeves and wash my hands, then pull up a stool opposite her on the other side of the kitchen counter. Only then does she offer me a single lardon at the end of some tongs, while rolling her eyes and shaking her head at me like I am a little boy. That single act of telling me off and then rewarding my good behaviour, like she would with one of her own kids, makes me feel like I belong. She arranges a bowl of washed potatoes, a peeler and a pot of water in a neat line.

'Thank you, Caleb.' She nods as she starts peeling carrots opposite me. 'Apart from the obvious, what exactly are you doing to my daughter, Caleb?' She asks with an innocent look on her face.

Bloody hell, Dahlia Mason doesn't mess around, does she?

'Nothing,' I respond, trying to fight the smile spreading across my face.

She puts her carrot and peeler down temporarily to watch

me lose. 'You poor fool.' She smiles, shakes her head and continues peeling.

'Is it that bad?' I ask.

'Yes. You've got it bad. I don't know how she does it.'

'Genetics.' I raise my eyebrows at Ariella's mom. She picks up the tea towel and swats me on the arm.

'Ow.'

'Shut up and stop flirting. Peel.'

I catch a mid-sentence laugh. 'So, does Jasper still go running with Mr Mason?' I try to ask casually.

'Every other Sunday. Without fail. No more sneaky breakfasts though. Have you thought about how you are going to deal with Jasper?' She keeps her eyes on the carrots. I know she sees him as her son, so I have to tread carefully.

'I have to find a way to come to terms with the fact that she still and always will love him. I just have to accept it.' Irritation fills my voice. 'In spite of everything, I like the guy. He was the first person I told that I had feelings for Ariella. Right there in your back garden, shortly after he decked me. I just can't help thinking that if he couldn't make the grade, how on earth can I?'

'I'll kill you if you tell anyone I said this, but Jasper is kind of...' she looks around as if to make sure no one is listening, and whispers, 'boring. No one wants to be good *all* the time.' She looks surprised at her own words.

Just then, I see Ariella. There she is, in front of me, years from now, and I know that, if by some miracle I'm by her side, I won't take a moment for granted.

Dahlia picks up her peeler and points at me. 'Don't get boring, Caleb. Break some rules, take some risks, live the best life you can. However, if you hurt my daughter, I'll lure you to a dark street with no CCTV and run you over with a plate-less truck.'

I say it before I think it. 'I'm in love with her, Dahlia.' When I admit my feelings, my emotions get the better of me.

'You hopeless thing.' She drops her peeler and vegetables, wipes her hands on her apron and comes around the counter to give me a hug. I am dreading it when I see her approach, but as soon as she puts her arms around me, she feels loving; and I feel acceptance.

'I'm rooting for you, Caleb. I genuinely am.' She gives me a smile so warm, I feel like I can conquer anything with her on my side.

'Gin?' she offers.

'Yes!'

She makes us both gin and tonics as we carry on cooking together. I watch her face as we work and talk, and I know I want to be part of this family. When we finish cooking and set the table, Dahlia asks me to fetch Ariella and her father.

'Hello, Caleb,' Hugh Mason murmurs as he walks in and stands behind his chair. I hear and feel his deep disapproval, but I am also absolutely positive that he has no idea why we are over for lunch. He may suspect my intentions, but there is no way that he has a clue about what is going to go down.

'Afternoon, Mr Mason,' I reply cautiously. Ariella gives me a reassuring smile as her mother asks us all to sit.

'How are you, Ariella?' Dahlia asks casually to kick us off. I know it's a loaded one.

'I'm really well, Mommy. Work is great, I'm back at yoga, I'm attempting desserts again and finding more time to read. I'm running twice a week on the Heath too.'

Mr Mason smiles. 'I didn't know that, Aari! That's great. But you shouldn't go running alone. Jasper will probably come with you if you ask; he's been putting me through my paces.'

I bristle at the name and stare at my plate, but I am more worried about what Ariella is going to say next. She is either going to sidestep the suggestion, indicating that she will consider it, which will relieve and annoy me, or she's going to tell the truth, which will also relieve me but put me in the firing line. She can't win.

'I go running with Caleb,' she responds, pointing at me with her fork.

Hugh Mason grunts. 'You could use that time to see Jasper more. Just because you're not in a relationship any more doesn't mean you still can't be friends.'

'We are friends, Daddy, but he has Sophia now, and I don't think it's a good idea to occupy the periphery. It may be a little bit too soon.'

'They were here the other day for lunch and I understand why you might want to respectfully keep a distance.' With that, Ariella's dad drops it, thankfully.

'What about you, Ariella?' Dahlia pipes up, smiling at her daughter. 'Anyone on the horizon?'

Oh shit. Ariella looks at her mother with panic in her eyes and Dahlia returns a knowing 'Isn't that why you're here?' expression. Ariella's bottom lip disappears into her mouth before she puts her hands in her lap.

'Well, I've been hanging out with Caleb quite a bit...' she starts.

'Dahlia, give her a break. She needs some time.' Hugh Mason turns to Ariella. 'No need to rush into anything, sweetheart. Ignore your mother.' He beams lovingly at Ariella. Great. Now she is going to have to tell him because saying nothing is effectively lying to him. Ariella looks like she is about to throw up. I have to step in front of her to take the bullet.

'Mr Mason.' I swallow. 'Ariella and I have been friends for a while now...'

'You haven't been friends *that* long, Caleb,' he responds, putting a roast potato in his mouth. He doesn't even look up from his plate.

We both look at Dahlia with 'this is your fault' written on

our faces. She rolls her eyes and sighs like she has given up on us.

'They are trying to tell you that they are dating, Hugh.'

'No, they aren't.' He looks up at Ariella. 'Are you?'

She suddenly finds something really interesting to look at on the ceiling, so he turns to me. I decide to man up and prepare to get decked in the process. Hugh Mason's fist is huge, so it's going to hurt.

'Mr Mason, I have a good idea of what you may think of me. The way I have behaved in the past has been pretty awful. When I first met Ariella, I very much doubted we would be friends and somehow that happened; and our friendship has grown to a point where we feel like there could be more, and we'd like to see if it's possible.' I take a swig of water and also find something really interesting to look at just behind his ear.

Hugh Mason puts down his cutlery and stands up. His wide, muscly, six-foot-four frame dominates the end of the dining table.

'Sit down, Hugh,' Dahlia says gently.

'I can't... I *won't* sit here and have him tell me that he has conveniently fallen in love with Ariella. I understand why she may think she has feelings for him. She is still vulnerable, clearly lonely and emotionally fragile. She has just broken up with her fiancé and is probably adjusting to being on her own. Of course he has fallen for her. Look at her, she's incredible. They are both just two single people who happen to be living under the same roof. If they weren't, would we be having this conversation? They worked together for years on the same floor and he didn't even know she existed until she moved in. Now he wants to explore more than friendship? Of course he does. Our daughter deserves better; not just some bloke that just happens to be there, trying his luck, when she's at her lowest!'

Wow. Hugh Mason even has me questioning whether or

not I am a predatory creep. I conclude, without any further help, that I am.

'Hugh Mason! Don't be so insulting.'

'I know his type.'

'Why do you have such a problem with him?' Dahlia asks her husband.

'His behaviour has been appalling!'

'He's owned that.'

'He went off with that girl, knowing she was with Jasper.'

I put my hand up slowly in my defence.

'Put your hand down, Caleb. He slept on her couch and Jasper, if you remember, was too busy chasing Ariella all over my birthday party.'

'I don't like him and I don't trust him.'

'You don't have to. You just have to give him a fair shake and try to get to know him.'

'I don't need to.'

'Yes, you do. Your daughter is going to need you to.'

It is like watching a tense but calm tennis match, where the players recognise and respect each other but no one is going to drop the ball; even though we all know that the Serena Williams of this match is Dahlia Mason.

'He's not good enough for her.'

'Funny, that's what my father said about you,' Dahlia says with a smirk.

'That was different.'

'Was it?'

'Yes. They didn't know me.'

'Please, answer honestly, Hugh. Do you think that if they had known you before you met me, they would have liked you?' She raises an eyebrow. It's immediately obvious that we are in private territory here. It sounds like Hugh Mason was a less than ideal choice for Dahlia. I enjoy that fact a little more than I should.

'This isn't about us.'

'Exactly.' Dahlia smashes the winning shot. I look at my shirt, trying to suppress and hide the smile spreading across my face. Hugh Mason just got owned. Dahlia is a fucking queen. He sits down with a face of thunder.

'Baby,' Dahlia starts in a voice so soft that I feel thirty years of love wrap around him. 'You've been in Caleb's seat. You were attacked because of me. I abandoned my family for you. The people on your street threw rocks at me and your family dragged me out of your house by my hair when you brought me home.' She absent-mindedly traces a finger across her eyebrow over a faint scar that I hadn't noticed before.

I see Hugh Mason in a new light. I'm certain he thinks I'm an idiotic downgrade from Jasper, but that isn't why he's grumpy, mostly. He fought for Dahlia. He fought against everything for her. I now see a man who would do anything for his wife and family, and understand in that moment that the bar is higher than I could have imagined. This is the man I am going to be measured against. He isn't just tough – he is fuelled by love and driven to protect. He made his own way, even when his world turned its back on him. I feel the respect I have for him swell.

'We went through that, Lia, so she didn't have to face what we had to.' All the anger has left his face and body and I know that we are eavesdropping on a private conversation.

'No, she was always going to face it, my love, and we both know that there's more to come. We went through all of it so that she wouldn't face it, *from us*. Get to know him. Be there for her if it turns out that you're right. But also, be open to being wrong. Don't let us be them. Please.'

I catch Ariella wiping away a silent tear. Hugh Mason also notices his daughter in that instant and goes so quiet, I can almost hear his heart break.

'Okay, Caleb.' Hugh Mason stands up and stretches out his hand.

I stand up and take it. 'Thank you, sir. I promise I won't let you or her down.'

'Don't make promises you can't keep, Caleb. Just promise you will do your best and we'll start with a clean slate.'

'Understood.'

'Good. You now know what you are going to have to deal with.' He tips his head towards his wife lovingly. 'You can't promise a damn thing.' The second he smiles, all of us laugh.

As we sit down, I mouth a thank you to Dahlia and she gives me a warm smile, then restarts the conversation by asking us about Zachary's engagement party and in turn fills us in on their holiday. Ariella's father eventually relaxes, listens and contributes to the conversation. True to his word, he stays uncritical and engaged.

After lunch, Ariella and her mother go for a walk out to the garden while I help her dad with the dishes. As soon as the sliding door shuts behind them, Hugh Mason turns to me and puts his hand on my shoulder.

'My young friend,' he starts, looking not the least bit friendly. 'I want to make myself perfectly clear. Ariella is like her mother – you are innocent until proven guilty. You will have guessed that I am nothing like that but, to keep them happy, you are getting a pass. You so much as make her lip quiver and you will be dealing with me.' He lets go.

'No disrespect, sir, but frankly, I am much more frightened of your wife.'

Hugh Mason's mouth twitches into a smile as he utters the words, 'good girl' to himself. He pats me on the back.

'You're not as stupid as I thought. Pass the bowl.'

EIGHT

ARIELLA

I am not sure whether to kiss or strangle my mother, as we make our way to the rose bushes she has conveniently decided need a little trim.

'I know you want to strangle me right now, but you needed to just tell him.' Mommy breaks the silence as she stops to inspect her roses.

'I know, Mommy. I just could have used some more time.'

'Sweetheart, what were you waiting for? You've changed. It's glaringly obvious. Your back is straight, your chest is out, you're much more confident and you look like you've... grown up!'

'Grown up? You only saw me a couple of months ago.'

'I'm not stupid, Aari. When you were with Jasper, you walked around like you were still waiting to have your cherry popped!'

My mouth springs open.

'Don't look so shocked. I had a life before your father, you know. Whatever Caleb is doing to you, it's working. I like this version of you.' A mischievous grin crosses her face.

'I have a version?'

'Oh yes, you do. Daddy's little girl has been dispatched and replaced by a vibrant, radiant young woman; and I'd bet my last penny that it has something to do with Caleb being good in bed.'

'MOMMY!'

'Oh shut up. That crap may work with your dad but it doesn't fly with me. I've seen the way you look at each other.' She laughs her dirty laugh and waves her hands. 'Don't worry, I won't tell.'

I immediately wonder what she and Caleb were talking about in the kitchen when they were alone.

'If you're worried, Caleb was an absolute gentleman earlier and I was a responsible mother, not the dirty old lady you're speaking to now. So how do you feel about him?'

'Caleb is...' I try to think of the right word. 'Challenging.' I feel the smile spread across my face.

'I'll bet.' She smiles too. I don't want to say any more but I can't help myself.

'I love him, Mommy, but I'd be silly to ignore who he was for so long. Caleb does some odd things when he is upset and I don't want to get hurt.'

'So you're holding back, like you did with Jasper.'

'I didn't hold back with Jasper.'

'Aari, no one saw what you pulled with Jasper coming because you're terrible at communicating. Jasper had the patience and tolerance to deal with you. Do you think Caleb does?'

'No, he can be... confrontational. It's uncomfortable,' I complain.

'I'm liking Caleb more by the second.' My mother chuckles.

I often question whose side my mother is on.

'Oh, don't pull that face. I can't gossip about Jasper's new girlfriend with you if you are looking at me like that. It takes all the fun out of it.' She winks.

'She's graceful, beautiful and hasn't walked out on him...' I state the obvious.

'Yes, but Daddy didn't like her.'

'Daddy doesn't like her because she isn't me. Did you like her?'

She pauses because she knows she has been busted. 'She's got perfect manners, is exceptionally polite, has zero chance of putting a foot wrong. She's besotted with Jasper and she sounds like she's ready for babies, so she isn't going anywhere unless Jasper tosses her out. The only reason he might do that is if you decide to return to him, and I think we both know that isn't going to happen. Once he realises that it's truly over, I think he might marry her.'

'They're already in marriage and kids territory?' The last time I spoke with Jasper, he still wanted to work *our* issues out.

'It's time to let him go, Aari.' My mother sits down next to me and rubs my back.

'I have. It's just the thought of someone else having children with Jasper is... unexpectedly crushing.'

'You're only finding it hard because Jasper has only ever really belonged to you. He may have started as Zachary's friend, but you're the reason he came to live with us all those years ago.'

I look at my mother for an explanation. She sighs and looks back at the house, to check if Daddy is coming.

'When Jasper found his father after he shot himself, he didn't speak to anyone apart from you for a very long time. Not his mother, not me, not Daddy, not Zachary, not his counsellor. With you, though, he was a little chatterbox. You were both constantly whispering, so we all took advantage of reaching him through you, because he was a little boy who needed us. I hated that we let you be the conduit because, sometimes, we forgot that you were a little girl who needed us too. I'll never forgive myself for that.'

Mommy wells up and sighs deeply.

'After that, you both occupied a space that no one else could reach. It seemed harmless at first, but after a while I noticed that your decisions were heavily influenced by Jasper and his feelings. When he was happy, you were. When he was sad, both of you were nowhere to be found. You only wanted to play games he wanted to play. You only wanted to do things he wanted to do. You followed him to university, for goodness' sake, and when you fell out, you closed the door to everyone. You didn't even come home for the holidays. You just stayed away. There's just no way your relationship with Jasper isn't one of the major triggers for your panic attacks.'

I feel my throat tighten and I attempt to take a deep breath. Mommy immediately places one hand on my chest and one on my back. I start to cry, letting my mother lead my breathing.

'You've always looked after Jasper, Aari, and he you. I love Jasper with all my heart but, when he first told me he thought he was in love with you, all I wanted to do was get him as far away from you as possible, because when you were together his needs being met was your sole purpose. You've never made space for yourself.' My mother sighs heavily before she continues.

'Just in case you haven't realised it yet, you didn't leave Jasper because you didn't love him any more. You left Jasper because you decided, at some point, to start loving yourself.'

I am sobbing so uncontrollably that all I can do is keep breathing.

Mommy continues. 'Let this girl love him, baby. Without the baggage, the duty and all the sacrifices you've both already made. She'll adore him and put up with all his crap. She'll have his babies and stay at home raising them, without complaint. It's what she wants, and what it seems that he needs.'

I nod. It's time.

'So, they're official.'

'It's moving a little too quickly and Daddy is devasted, obviously, but yes, I like her for Jasper. Both families are already going skiing together. Her dad has hired The Alpina in Gstaad for a week. We got invited but declined for obvious reasons. Daddy almost broke ranks on that one, but he course-corrected. See? We're not bad parents.'

'You and Daddy should join them. It would mean so much to him and—'

'Sorry, Dahlia. Aari, it's getting late,' Caleb interrupts.

The sun has almost set and the garden is getting darker and colder.

Mommy gets up from where we are sitting. 'You're right. It's time for you two to get going.'

Caleb's relief envelops us both as he folds me into him on the train back to London. He is happy, light and surprised at not only escaping Daddy with his life, but with some form of reluctant acceptance.

'Can we just celebrate the fact that I wasn't killed by your father and I have a girlfriend?' Caleb laughs as he kisses the top of my head. He gently lifts my chin, tilting my face up to his. 'I actually have a girlfriend.'

Caleb takes one look at my forced smile and his mood deflates immediately.

'Tell me.'

'I'm sorry to do this right now, but I need to see Jasper.' I watch him watch me.

'Okay.' That's it from him.

'Okay?'

'I love you. I trust you. If you need to see him, then that's what you need to do.' Caleb shrugs, looking into the distance.

'Will you come with me?' I can see that he definitely doesn't want to do that, but he nods anyway.

'When?'

'Now?'

He holds me tighter, but stays silent until our black cab pulls up in front of Jasper's home.

'I'll wait in here, if that's all right,' he whispers, kissing my head before I open the door to step out.

I know he's hurt, but this needs to happen tonight. I gather all my strength as I approach the front door and press the bell.

'Aari?' Jasper asks cautiously as he opens it.

'Hi, Jas.' I give him a small wave.

'Er... good to see you. Would you like to come inside?' He looks nervous. Sophia must be there.

'No, thank you. I won't be long. Can you come out for a second?'

'Yes, of course.' He hastily grabs a jacket from the entrance coat rack and steps outside. He shuts the door quietly before putting it on, and follows me down the front steps of his home. 'Is everything all right? It's pretty late,' he asks, checking the door behind him.

'I want you to know that I am happy for you, Jas.' I can't help the tear that rolls down my cheek.

'Scraps...' He reaches out and I take a step away from him.

'Unless you can make it sound at least half as insulting as Zachary does, I'd be really grateful if you don't call me that any more.' I hear my voice crack and see the pain in his eyes, but continue. 'We have to end the uncertainty surrounding us. It's unfair to everyone.'

'Then come home...' He takes a step forward and I take another one back.

'I am not coming back, Jas. Please don't wait for me. I hear Sophia is wonderful and she makes you happy. Please don't mess it up.'

'But she's not you.'

'No, she's not. She's better. She's ready. She's clearer. She knows that she wants the same things you do. Mommy thinks that she's going to make you happy and, truth be told, I'm really happy for you.'

'Jassie!' A chirpy Sophia opens the front door, singing her pet name for Jasper. I see her expression change and darken when she spots me. She rearranges it just as Jasper turns around.

'Hey, Fi. It's just Ariella. I'll be there in a sec.' He smiles warmly at her as I offer her a small wave and smile from behind him. I watch her force a smile and shut the door.

Jasper and I look at each other for a second and then burst out laughing.

'Jassie?' I chuckle.

'I know.' He laughs while he shrugs. 'It makes her happy.'

'Then keep her happy.'

'I don't want to lose my best friend.'

'You won't, but if we don't really move on, it will destroy us. I want you to be able to tell me that Sophia met my parents and that they love her. I want to be able to tell you that Mommy threw Caleb and me under the bus today and saved us at the same time. I don't want to lose my best friend either,' I plead.

'Goodness, Scraps, I love you.'

'And I love you, Jas. That's exactly why I really need you to help me to love her too.'

Jasper pushes his hands deeply into his pockets and takes a big inhale as he looks into the night sky, before he sighs it out. 'Consider the line drawn.'

'Thank you, Jas.'

'I'd better get back in.'

'See you later, Jassie. Give my love to Fi.' I chuckle.

'This is going to be a nightmare.' He smiles back at me as he hurries into his home.

I watch him go in and shut the door before I walk back to Caleb and the waiting cab.

'Thank you for letting me do that.'

'You told him you loved him.'

'I did. Right before I told him I needed to love Sophia too.'

I reach for his hand and he pulls it away.

'Do you have any idea how huge today was for me? I went to declare myself to someone who detests me, knowing that I would have to commit to be the best of something I have never been before, for someone who I know loves someone else. The least I expected was for this to be a Jasper-free day. Instead you hand me front row seats to your ongoing emotional saga. I can live with you loving him, but I'm not sure how long I can keep setting myself on fire to keep you warm, Ariella.'

'I'm sorry.'

Caleb grunts, moves away and says nothing all the way home. I know I need to make it up to him as soon as we get in.

'Would you like to—'

'I'm just going to go to bed, Ariella. It's been a long day.' He walks into his room and slams the door. Just as I decide to leave him alone because his emotions are raw, I remember Mommy's earlier warning. I don't want to make the same mistakes, so I force myself to walk into his room. He's in the shower so I enter his bathroom, shut the loo and sit on the lid.

'I'm stupid, insensitive, selfish and I'm sorry.' He says nothing and I keep talking. 'Jasper reminds me, whenever we speak, that he is still waiting. He needed to know that I am not coming back. Ever. I also wanted to give him and Sophia my blessing, because I don't want anything holding us back. I'm in this with you, Caleb. I am all in.' I wait. Nothing.

Just as I start to leave, Caleb's head pops out of one end of the shower wall with a wide grin.

'Drop your clothes and get in here.'

I strip and run to join my boyfriend, faster than I have ever done anything in my life.

'I'm a soft touch when it comes to you.' He smiles before he

53

pulls me close. I feel a sense of completion as I join him, knowing that things will only get better from this point on.

That knowing is eviscerated the next day as I sit next to my best friend Lara, opposite our boss Harrison. His huge desk is between us as we wait silently for our other boss Christopher to join the meeting. Harrison Ivory and Christopher Bow are the owners of Ivory Bow, the international marketing and communications agency that Lara, Caleb and I work for. Harrison's charming, magnetic and fun personality is essential for his responsibility over sales and business development at Ivory Bow, while Christopher oversees all the operations with his quiet, steady and thoughtful approach.

'You look like you're about to throw up,' Lara whispers, keeping an eye on a fuming Harrison, who is rage-typing on his keyboard.

'This isn't good, Lara. Why aren't you—'

'Less chit-chat, you two,' Harrison scolds. I shrink in my chair and Lara just rolls her eyes like he is being dramatic. 'Let's keep the conversation to a minimum until Chris gets here, shall we?'

I nod, wiping my sweating palms on my jeans. Thankfully, Christopher doesn't keep us waiting long.

'I'm here. What's this about?' He crosses his arms and casually leans against the wall next to Harrison's swivel chair.

'Lara, care to tell us all where you were last night?' Harrison starts.

'Strip club. Sophisticats. Had a great time. Highly recommend it. Ask for Sparkle. She's going places. Mystery, not so much. I suppose the mystery is how she managed to get a job there in the first place.' Lara smiles at Harrison and Christopher.

Christopher and I look at each other, confused. It's not a

destination I would choose or recommendations I'd be taking up, but she's an adult and what she gets up to in her free time is up to her.

'Care to tell them who you were with?'

'A friend?'

No. Please no. I think I know where this is going. I might throw up.

'Does your friend have a name?'

'Yes.'

'Can you tell us that friend's name?'

'Yes.'

Harrison looks like he's about to strangle Lara.

'What is that friend's name?'

'Bamidele.'

I put my head in my hands with an audible sigh. Lara is getting fired. Bamidele is the cutting-edge artist girlfriend of CrimeSpree, one of our more infamous music clients. Lara, when she was supposed to be working for CrimeSpree at a festival last year, met Bamidele. The result of that meeting was a prolonged, secret entanglement between Lara and Bamidele, which, I was assured, ended months ago.

'You knew?' Harrison jumps to me.

'No, she didn't. Do you think I'd be stupid enough to—'

'I knew,' I admit.

'Shit, Aari, no!' For the first time, I hear regret come through from Lara. I feel awful but the best thing to do is to come clean.

'Excuse me, who is Bamidele?' Christopher asks.

'CrimeSpree's fiancée.'

'So?' Christopher isn't getting it.

'Lara here has taken it upon herself to supplement some of CrimeSpree's more intimate duties.' Harrison keeps his eyes on an unrepentant Lara.

'Oh!' Christopher's eyebrows jerk up. 'How did you find out?'

'I was told—'

'You weren't, Harry,' Lara challenges, clearly unaware of the perilous edge she currently occupies between gainful employment and homelessness. She continues, 'While we are all being truthful, yesterday Bamidele posted a picture of me in her bed. I was hiding because I was naked but my gingersnap bum tattoo was on full display. Obviously, Harry and his social media sniffers caught wind of this and followed us using her Insta Live breadcrumbs to Sophisticats, where I got rudely dragged out.'

'I sent you multiple messages to meet me outside, Lara.'

'I obviously didn't see them. As you noticed, I had my hands full at the time.'

'With our client's fiancée!' he said, banging his fist on his table.

'It's not like I can touch the talent! You know what Clive's like, I'd be kicked out.'

'Who's Clive?' I ask quietly.

'The manager,' Lara and Harrison answer in unison, like I should know who Clive is.

'Wait. Wait, wait!' Christopher stops the exchange, waving his hand in the air.

Only now do I realise I've been clenching my fist for most of the conversation.

'Let me wade through the rubble. Firstly, Harry, how the hell do you know Lara has a gingersnap tattoo on her bum?'

'Yeah!' Lara smirks.

'Oh, shut up. You were showing it to everyone at the summer pool party last year.'

'Damn,' Lara whispers under her breath.

Christopher turns to her. 'Lara, how long have you been seeing CrimeSpree's fiancée?'

'I don't know, a couple of weeks maybe... I can't remember... maybe longer? It's difficult to say...' It's obvious Lara is lying. When Christopher's eyes shift to me, I know what's coming. Crumbs.

'How long has this been going on, Ariella?'

'Nine months, but I know Lara ended it ages ago. I didn't know that they were seeing each other again.'

'But you knew the first time,' Christopher pushed.

'Yes.'

'And you didn't say anything.'

'No. Lara said she would end it and she did.'

I want to crawl into a hole and hide when I see the disappointment on Christopher's face.

'Can I just remind everyone that the policy only states no clients...'

'Are you kidding me? You know that starting a relationship with a client is completely forbidden and somehow you think it meets with company approval to destroy a client's relationship instead?' Harrison snaps.

'I'm just saying that it's not exactly specified in the—'

'Are we absolutely positive that CrimeSpree doesn't know?' Christopher interrupts.

'One hundred per cent. If he did, he'd be trying to third-wheel rather than anything else. He's been trying his luck for years,' Lara adds, rolling her eyes.

'You're going to need to start taking this seriously, Lara.' Christopher is measured but forceful.

'I am. I'm just not taking Harry seriously. I know he isn't going to fire me, because this office would already be crawling with HR. Also, I'm not the first. I'm only in here because I'm the first girl—'

'Park the feminist bullshit, Lara. You intentionally broke the rules. Twice, by the sound of it. Those are grounds for immediate dismissal.'

'Yes, but this isn't the first story you've heard about one of us breaking the rules. It's practically celebrated among the boys.

It's a double standard. You still openly joke about the time you got "stratospherically" high with Lady Penelope at her brother's wedding, Harry, which we planned and executed. Drugs are also grounds for immediate dismissal. I know it's your company and you can hardly dismiss yourself immediately, but joking about it with us makes it seem okay. I know I messed up, so punish me, but you can't look the other way for everyone else and then decide that the lesbian is the one that gets it in the neck.'

Lara has a point.

'She's right. We're not firing her.' Christopher turns to Harrison, who is busy narrowing his eyes at a smug-looking Lara. 'But you're moving. You're off CrimeSpree.'

'Fair enough,' Lara concedes.

'You will no longer report to Ariella. For this to have carried on for as long as it has is... disappointing. Ariella, frankly, I expected more from you.'

The fact that I have let Christopher down hurts deeply. I respect and admire him as a boss. I can't look at him right now, so I look at my fidgeting hands.

'That's not fair. She didn't do anything!' Lara leaps to my defence.

'Exactly, she did nothing. You two are too close. It is seriously impeding her judgement as your line— Don't you *dare* growl at me, Lara Scott.'

Lara immediately slumps back in her seat and mumbles a sorry.

'Thank you. As I was saying, we can no longer trust Ariella's judgement when it comes to you, so you have lost the privilege of reporting to her.'

'I'm sorry,' I apologise, still not able to look up.

'I know you are, Ariella, but I am splitting you two up. I think it's time you moved upstairs to our floor.'

'No. I'll move,' Lara volunteers abruptly. 'I'm the one you

need to keep an eye on. Leave her with the team. She needs to be on the main floor. Give me a shitty job up here until I've learned my lesson if you need to.'

'I'd rather have Ariella, to be honest,' Harrison chips in, giving Lara a dirty look.

'Ugh. Come on, Harry. I'm obviously your favourite here. You're just pissed off at me, and I get it. I'm sorry. Let's get some tequila shots, you yell at me all you want, then I'll do something amazing with the clients because they love me, and we'll be pals again. Plus, you know I'll be much more fun up here than Ariella will ever be.'

Harrison looks at Christopher.

'It's your call. Separating them is enough of a consequence for me.' Christopher shrugs.

'Fine. Got anything for her, Chris?'

'We need a music logistics manager for all our gigs to free up project managers. She could take that on?' he suggests.

'That's just cruel, but fine.' Lara sighs.

'Jess can take over client facing.' Harrison smirks.

'I can support,' Lara volunteers.

Lara is taking this all quite well, I notice. There is no way she doesn't have a plan.

'I think we are done here for now?' Christopher asks Harrison.

'Not quite...' Lara adds. 'I take it we are keeping this all quiet because of gossip and all that; so, can we make it look like a promotion? After all, it seems like I will have more responsibility?'

'Sure, we can do that,' Harrison responds, taking his cue from a nodding Christopher.

'Good. Thanks. Cheeky question. Will this promotion be coming with a raise?'

Only Lara.

'No. Get out, Lara.' Harrison shuts her down.

'Can't blame a girl for trying,' Lara responds as she exits the office.

'Once again, I'm sorry I let you both down, guys,' I apologise again before following Lara through Harrison's office door. She is waiting for me by the lift.

'Come here, babe.' She pulls me into a hug. 'I'm sorry you were involved that shit.'

'I'm the one who's sorry I had to tell them the truth.'

'No. You did the right thing. I may not make it back on the floor but they'll be throwing more money at me before they know it. Gig logistics is a doddle, I can do it in my sleep. Jess, however, will be eaten alive by the clients, so I'm going to be permanently supporting her. If I play nice at being Mama Hen, they'll have to give me a raise and more newbies to support. Once they become competent little chicks, our lunches will only get longer. Speaking of which, I am hungry. Fancy a bite? I'm buying.' She winks at me.

Lara couldn't have come out with a better result if she had planned the whole thing. While I am happy for her, she is the only reason I chose to remain on the main floor and now she's leaving.

An uncomfortable feeling settles over me. Things are about to change around here.

NINE

CALEB

I've been awake since three a.m. just watching my girlfriend sleep peacefully. It may be a little creepy, but I don't care.

One of her twisted plaits has come loose and is spreading the grapefruit scent of her shampoo and conditioner all over the pillow. Her face is relaxed with her perfectly shaped mouth parted slightly, but her brows are knitted together and telling me a different story. It's been like that for a couple of weeks, since we told her parents about us. It worries me a little. Not that it has stopped her from taking over the bed, limbs everywhere, leaving me with a sliver of mattress to make the most of, but I don't mind.

I should be enjoying deep nourishing sleep, but instead I'm awake, paranoid that it's all going to fall apart because I don't deserve to be this happy. If karma exists, based on my past behaviour I am due for a vicious kick in the nuts. Yet here I am. I offer a quick prayer to whoever or whatever is listening. 'Please don't punish me with this. Please don't let it be her. Please don't—'

'Hey… are you okay?' Ariella interrupts, blinking sleepily.

'Yeah,' I lie.

'What were you muttering?'

'Was I muttering?'

'Yes, you were.' She pulls in her leg, releasing some bed space, and turns to lie on her tummy while letting out a big yawn. She's awake and interested. Shit. I need to change the subject.

'You've seemed a little sad recently. Are you okay?'

'I am a little. I miss Lara.'

This is exactly the distraction I am looking for. 'Are you going to tell me how and why she got promoted and whisked off the floor so quickly?' I slowly trace my finger up her thigh and I'm rewarded with that smile I adore.

'No, and stop trying to coerce me. You know that I can't tell you unless Lara says it's okay.' She giggles, kicking me lightly with her foot.

'That's not going to happen.' I lean over to my bedside table, grab my phone and open Lara's text to me. 'She's being petty. Look at this.'

> Aari asked me today. I actually don't care if she tells you, but now that I know how badly you want the goss, I'm going to make sure she doesn't. Hopefully you'll bug her into dumping you.

I throw Aari a confused look and all she does is laugh.

'You're going to have to forgive me on this one, Black.'

I melt. We've somehow fallen into fondly calling each other by our last names and I like it.

'I'd forgive you for anything.' I stroke her cheek.

'So would I,' she responds.

'Come here, let's test that theory and try something new.' I pull her into a kiss.

'I feel like I want to know where this is going, Caleb,' she sighs into my mouth. 'But, I like that you're unpredictable.

Either way, I'm in.' We spend the rest of the morning in each other's arms gently exploring our bodies and chatting softly, until the sun joins us.

The quiet bliss of that morning is the very first thing I think of when I walk into work a couple of months later to see Harry, Chris, Aari and Melissa Chang laughing in a conference room. I suddenly feel like I have run full speed, face and chest first, into a brick wall. Maybe I shouldn't have ignored her calls, deleted her texts and 'shuffled' all my trips to Singapore since last year. Casually as I can, I turn into the men's toilets, collect myself for a few minutes, then slip back out of work. I fake illness over the phone and spend the rest of the day pacing the apartment, tortured by what Melissa may be scheming. Ariella was laughing when I saw her, so she definitely doesn't know about us, but for how long?

How stupid was I to think that finishing things with Melissa would be clean and easy? I knew she'd be pissed off at being ghosted, but showing up is next level.

A continuous stream of texts from Melissa starts at around lunchtime, firstly with concerns about my health, followed by comments about the office and then, eventually, urgent demands to meet. I leave them unanswered. At the end of the day, I receive a text from Ariella's phone.

> Awww, the texts you send each other are so cute!

Melissa. That's what does it. I run to the bathroom and vomit everything in my stomach.

'Caleb, you look terrible!' Ariella sheds her coat and drops her bag on the floor as she rushes towards me. 'I'm sorry I haven't been in touch. I would have called but I couldn't find my phone and I was in this crazy meeting all day. How are you?'

'I'm not sure... but I'll live.' I pause for dramatic effect – I am supposed to be ill, after all. She's clearly still in the dark, which means I have some time to deal with Melissa.

'Are you sure? Shall I make you some tea? Is there anything in particular that you'd like to eat?'

She's concerned, and I feel like such a shit.

'No, I could use a cuddle though?' I pull her onto the sofa and across my lap. When she wraps herself around me, she smells so familiar and feels so warm, the fact that I may lose her churns my stomach. Then she plants her usual soft, caring kisses on my face and I want to tell her everything, but I can't.

'Tell me about your crazy meeting?'

'Well!' Her eyes light up. 'I was running out of the rain into the office this morning while you were still drooling in bed, Black. I got stopped by this soaked, shivering, beautiful little lady looking for Ivory Bow. She looked so young and lost, I brought her in with me. She said she had an extremely long interview to sit through, so I made her a cup of tea. We ran downstairs to the magazine, grabbed some clothes for her from Lara's friend, helped her fix her hair and make-up; then we left her wet clothes with the dry-cleaners. I made her comfortable in reception and gave her my work iPad with our brochures open after sharing some pointers on what we look for.

'A little later, I saw her walk in with Harrison and gave her a thumbs-up. Just before ten, Harrison cancelled the daily meeting and asked me to meet him and Christopher in the conference room. Long story short, we weren't interviewing her, she was interviewing us! Caleb, because of all the success you have had in Asia selling Ivory Bow's services, she wants to invest for us to set up a permanent office there. Apparently, talks have been going on for weeks. She wants me to be part of the key team, so we spent the whole day thrashing out how it would work, implications on my projects, timelines and even pay. It was unbelievable. I took what seemed like a zillion toilet breaks to try to find my phone to text you, because she wants you to work on this too. You are the one condition for this to go through.'

'Really?' I knew Melissa was powerful but I didn't know she was a nutcase. She made it abundantly clear that our industry didn't interest her in the slightest and now she's facilitating an expansion into Asia?

Ariella can barely contain her excitement.

'Yes! Really! Caleb, you made this happen.' She squeezes me tighter.

'Does that mean we will be working for her?'

'That's the best part. The day-to-day responsibility for the business would be down to you, the person she hires to be my boss and some other people she hasn't decided on yet. She said she might chime in on major investment decisions but that's it. If I accept, I'll have to head to Singapore in three months to set up and hire base staff and implement policies and key service levels.'

'You're going to move out to Singapore by yourself in three months?' Shit. Melissa is not playing around.

'I won't be alone. She is putting a brand-new team together. She'd like me to create our initial operations plan before I hand it over.'

'Sounds like a massive responsibility.'

'I know. It's still taking shape though. They are thinking of me overseeing the general operations at first, but they will definitely hire a much more competent and knowledgeable COO for me to report to. They can pick at my mistakes, make them shiny and drive the company forward with you.'

'And when do I come in?' I'm trying to have a normal conversation but I know I'm fucked. Melissa's fury is clearly way past what hell has to offer. The only hope I have is to talk her down.

'When we've set up. You're most likely going to be in charge of sales and retention as you already have a client list there.'

'Why you? You're just an event manager.' It sounds more accusatory and insulting than I intend.

'She asked for me.' She smiles her happy smile.

'You've never set up a company before.'

'I know, right? But if I say yes, I will have support. Lawyers, accountants, oh, and also, get this, I will get a home, a house-keeper, a driver and a personal assistant...?' Her eyes round as she laughs with disbelief. I watch her silently with anger rising inside me. *Fuck you, Melissa*. I can't take it any more.

'I'm going for a walk.' I get up abruptly, causing her to topple over on the couch into the space I'd just been occupying.

'I'll come with you! I have too much energy.'

'No. Stay here,' I respond sharply.

She stops laughing and blinks at me.

'I'm sorry. I just don't want you to go away in three months, Aari.'

'You'll join me later. In the meantime, I can come home, you can use your holidays and sales trips to visit. You haven't been out for a few months anyway, so lots of flights to Singapore wouldn't be totally unjustified.' She reaches out for my hand and I step back.

'It sounds like you're ready to pack up and go.'

'Not quite, but why not?'

'Because things have calmed down and we're in a great place. Why are you so keen to blow it up?'

'I'm not!'

'Really? You seem pretty enthusiastic about fucking off to the other side of the world.'

'Caleb!' The pain in Ariella's eyes forces me to pause.

'What's the rush to flee the country?'

'I'm not fleeing. It's a great opportunity to grow. Even Lara is off the floor now and building her own team.'

'You're growing. *We're* growing together. Look how far we have already come! Is that not enough? Am I not enough?' I realise I am shouting but I can't help it.

'No.' She says it so quietly, I barely hear it. 'You're not enough, Caleb.' My heart shatters in the silence that lands between us. She is the last person I expect to hear those words from. She looks like she is on the verge of tears and I know that I will remember this moment as the beginning of the end.

'You've accepted the job?' I ask, quietly seething.

'No. I asked for some time to think about it.'

'It sounds like you have made up your mind.'

Ariella doesn't try to stop me as I walk out of the front door. The minute I hit the street, I unlock my phone to text Melissa. The replies come from 'Do Not Answer', which I changed her name to.

Where are you?

> Have you forgotten your birthday weekend already?

I'll be in the Mandarin Oriental bar in 20 minutes.

> Why? Surely you remember how to get to the Royal Suite.

I don't bother to protect myself from the rain as I walk towards the tube station.

'Caleb.' Melissa smiles, opening her suite door. 'It's so good to see you.' She stands on her tiptoes and wraps her arms around me, before leaning her head against my chest. I stand still with my arms firmly by my sides and try to contain my revulsion until she lets go. The butler takes my coat as soon as I enter, ushers me to a seat and places a glass of white wine next to me. Melissa is crazy if she thinks I am drinking anything within a hundred feet of her ever again.

Melissa takes a seat on the sofa next to me.

'How are you doing? Feeling better?' She smirks.

I don't have time for this shit. 'What do you want, Melissa?'

'Fine. We'll skip the pleasantries. I've decided to diversify and I thought, who is the best person to go into business with?' She smiles into her glass.

'What's really going on here?'

'Maybe if you had picked up your phone, returned an email or acknowledged a text, you'd know. I don't blame you for ghosting, I'll admit I was sensitive for a bit. I've never been cheated on and dumped before.'

'I didn't cheat on you, Melissa. You knew that I was seeing other people.'

'They didn't affect us, she did – don't worry, I am over it.' Melissa finishes her glass and the butler promptly appears with some more white wine. If this is her 'over it', she's deluded.

'If that's the case, can you return her phone?'

'I handed it in to security. You should ask her to change her passcode from 22532. 'Caleb' spelled on her keypad is a bit obvious, isn't it?'

'You found it, did you?'

'Of course.' She smiles sweetly. 'I have to say, I pictured you with someone very different. You've done well. I'm surprised you went for someone so bright. She has a big heart too. I bet that works to your advantage and you get away with all sorts. She let me into your building and left me at her desk to get us some tea. She is so much more trusting than she should be, which probably explains how you have managed to get so far. Thankfully, she is not perfect.'

'How so?'

'She's a bit of a goody-two-shoes, isn't she? No one can deal with that for too long. Also, a little make-up wouldn't kill her; she is in a client-facing role, she could make some effort.'

'She's perfect to me.'

'You'll be bored in six months.'

'Is that why I'm here? To hear that I'll be crawling back in six months?'

'You're here because you're going to help me make a lot of money. I've made your company enough money from the shadows and this friendship needs to have some new benefits.'

'And if I refuse?'

'You're out and your little frenemy Piers is in. That deluded, arrogant, money-grubbing twerp is ravenous for it. Do you have any idea how much he hates your guts? Ariella will come anyway; I'll make her an offer she can't refuse. With her in operations and Piers in sales, I'm guessing your little secrets will be out in ooooh, forty-eight hours?'

'I could just leave Ivory Bow.'

'You could, but you may not want to face trade law and bribery investigations by yourself.'

'What? I haven't broken any laws!'

'Do you really think you just show up and seal contracts worth hundreds of thousands of dollars, only because you're cute and sensational in bed? Did you genuinely think there was a line of corporations just waiting to hand over bags of cash to you? Come on Caleb, we met when you were desperately trying to shed your loser status. You didn't have a single client before you met me.'

'I just thought you put in a good word. How was I to know laws were being broken?'

'Good luck with that, Caleb. Everyone evades imprisonment with the "I didn't know" defence. You'll be fine.' She inspects the back of her hand as if it is more interesting than our conversation. She's bluffing. She has got to be bluffing. I know I'm not going to get any more from her, so I cut to the chase.

'What do you really want, Melissa?'

'For starters, you can stop saying my name in full with such disgust. It wasn't that long ago you were whispering, "I adore you, Mel" under the covers in a pathetic attempt not to use the word "love". Secondly, come and work for me. You're going to make so much money, you may never have to worry about it again.'

'If that's what you really want, why do you need Ariella? Just hire someone else. Like you said, I might be bored of her soon anyway.'

'Initially, entertainment. Now that I have met her, I actually really like her. I think we could be good friends. Aside from that, she is trustworthy, her delivery track record is astonishing, she is focused and I have no doubt in my mind that she will do a spectacular job.'

'Hire someone else, and I'll come with no complaints.'

'Too late, the offer is already on the table. Annoyingly, she is perfect for the job.'

'She is an office-based event manager who doesn't even go on site. She only just got her first big international project last year!'

'I'm not an idiot, Caleb. I know she isn't just an event manager.'

I have no idea what Melissa is talking about but, before I can fake it, she catches it.

'No way. You actually do think that.' Callous laughter explodes from her. 'Caleb, I know you aren't the sharpest tool but...' She bursts out laughing again.

She pulls a file out of the bag next to her, flicks through it and hands me a single sheet of paper with Ivory Bow's organisation chart. Ariella's full title is head of global event operations and lead project director.

'Look who she reports to.' Ariella is on the same seniority level as the CFO, reporting only to Harrison and Christopher. Everyone else at Ivory Bow is beneath her.

'Want to flip over to see how much she gets paid?' Melissa suggests excitedly.

I shove the paper back at her. This is already a mess, I'm not going to compound it by invading Ariella's privacy. Besides, I don't give a shit what she makes.

'I don't care. Revoke the offer.'

'Nope. I want both of you. Don't bother with the "it's me or her" ultimatum. I will pick her, and throw you to the wolves. She is much more deserving.'

'I'll break up with her.'

'Do what you like, she's coming. This isn't about you. You're getting first refusal and a chance to keep your skeletons in the closet because we are old friends.'

'Friends don't threaten each other.'

'I'm making sure Piers doesn't get the job only to find out that you've never met any of your clients. You know it'll happen.'

'You told me I didn't need to meet them!'

'I'm fairly certain they'll want to meet you now you're getting a local office. And how do you think Ariella is going to react when she finds out that those record-smashing sales numbers have nothing to do with how good you are at your job? She called you a sales genius today. Yikes.' Melissa laughs.

'Don't do this, Melissa, invest in something else.'

'No. Besides, this was actually your idea and I like where it's going. It's in your best interest to come along for the ride.'

I've had enough. There is no getting through to her. I stand and make my way to the suite door.

'Caleb?'

I turn around.

'Just in case you were wondering, it's triple your salary before your bonuses kick in.'

'I really don't care how much you intend on paying me.'

'That's not what I am planning to pay you. That's what your girlfriend is taking home currently.'

I don't bother to respond as I leave. I need to think this through with someone. I reach for my phone to find Tim or Jack, only to be greeted by a waiting text.

Hey walking ball-sack! You never fail to impress me. It literally took you five minutes to turn into Jasper! Of course you're not enough. She escaped Jasper's smothering clutches because of the same exact request; that she limits her desires, dreams and needs to just him! I am really going to enjoy watching her dump your arse when she steps out of her blind spot for you and figures it out. Any good places I can pop a webcam at yours?

I click my phone off, walk into the nearest pub and order a neat double whisky from the top shelf.

Let the implosion begin.

TEN

ARIELLA

Caleb's negative reaction to the news came out of nowhere. We've spent so many early mornings in each other's arms talking about countries we would go to if we had the chance to move away and start again. I thought he'd dive for his passport and drag me to the airport without hesitation. Especially as it's Singapore. The clients there love him. It's the perfect scenario.

I really want to put it down to him not feeling well, because his attack was unfair and his demand was completely uncharacteristic of him. Normally, when I ask for guidance, he starts with, 'What do *you* want?'

I expected us to end the evening with our laptops, at opposite ends of the couch, legs intertwined, whizzing fun and interesting Singapore-related web links across to each other and planning a new adventure. Instead, I am standing under my shower, crying.

Today has been strange. One minute I am prepping for the morning meeting and the next I am being offered a job on the other side of the world by a woman I thought was interviewing for an internship. Her wanting Caleb in a business development role makes sense. It's his territory and he'll hit the ground running. I, on the other hand, know that I am good at managing projects and keeping our event operations smooth, but set up an office and build a team? It's an enormous undertaking. But I want it. She makes me want it.

Melissa is awesome. She is lovely and seems kind but is also a firm, hard-nosed businesswoman. I like that. I already know that she will be a tough boss to please, but I am so very excited to work for someone like her.

I like that she confidently opened up about her vulnerabilities; readily admitting she knows nothing about our industry but can see the financial rewards. However, I worry that she clearly stated that she has a plan to 'rectify' my appearance, which makes me uneasy. This was what I was really thinking about when I spoke to Caleb about being unsure. While I want the job, changing the way I look to get it feels like a slippery slope to other changes.

I make Caleb a beetroot and ginger soup for his delicate tummy and grab a bowl for myself before I open my laptop to make a dent in some of the work left incomplete by today's meetings.

Notifications from our internal messaging service flood my screen as soon as I log in. They are mostly from Lara, demanding my attention. I quickly type a response:

amason:
Sorry Lara. Lost my phone. Unbelievable day.

A message comes back immediately.

lscott:
Yes! Finally! What's all this talk about you moving to Singapore?

amason:

Not quite moving yet. Still thinking about it.

lscott:
Oh shit! What direction are you leaning?

amason:
I want to go.

lscott:
Noooo. I will miss you too much!

amason:
Yeah, I'm getting the vibe that it's a terrible idea.

lscott:
Are you nuts? It's a fucking fantastic idea! My selfish needs want you to stay but you have to go! Harry gave me all the goss (and probably added some bits that didn't happen!). It sounds amazing!

amason:
She wants to 'rectify' the way I look. In her words 'a little make-up and much better fashion choices'.

lscott:
So? She's only telling you what I've been saying for ever!

amason:
I can ignore you. She doesn't come across as someone to be ignored.

lscott:
Just think of it as a uniform. Lots of people wear uniforms to

work. This is yours. Has Gollum packed for both of you yet, 'Precious'?

amason:
No. We had a row and he walked out of the flat. I think he just asked me to choose between him and the job.

lscott:
As much as Spotted Dick's demise gives me tingles in my loins, I have to ask. Are you sure? He only leans into his human tendencies when it comes to you.

amason:
His exact words were 'Am I not enough?'

lscott:
While I recognise that Caleb is down and exactly where I want him (only this once, and don't you dare tell him!), I am hesitant to kick him in the stomach. It's unlike him. That idiot will follow you anywhere and do whatever you want. It's the only reason I tolerate him.

amason:
Are you actually mounting a defence for Caleb?

lscott:
Ew. Yuck! I've drunk too much and it's destroying my sense of judgement. We need an extended lunch tomorrow. I am putting in two hours.

amason:
I'm sorry, I can't. I've been asked to clear my day. She's back in.

lscott:

Think she'll give me a job?

amason:
Harrison and Christopher will be the ones to ask.

lscott:
That'll be a 'no' then. Can I have your old job?

amason:
Again, Harrison and Christopher.

lscott:
Fuck. I am going to be in purgatory for ever. Let's have dinner tomorrow. Come with all the gossip. You can start making up for the fact that you're about to abandon me – with my full blessing of course. Gotta dash. Love you!

Having Lara's support is everything. I know I am supposed to be making this decision in a vacuum, but knowing that Lara thinks it's an amazing opportunity is a big boost. The smile returns to my face and I happily work through my tasks before I decide to call it a night.

I am fast asleep when Caleb climbs into bed in the middle of the night. His cold arm snakes around my belly to pull me close to him.

'I'm so sorry, Aari, I'm an arsehole.'

I am taken aback by the desperation in his voice as he plants kisses along the back of my neck. I turn over to kiss my boyfriend and I can tell he has been drinking.

'Your face is wet. Is it raining outside?' I whisper, taking his face in my palms.

'A little. Say you forgive me.' He plants a soft kiss on my

nose.

'Of course I forgive you, but can we talk about why you were so upset earlier?' I lean in to repay my nose kiss with a soft one on his lips.

'I don't want to lose you, Aari.'

'I am not going anywhere. Okay?'

'You're not going to take the job?'

'That isn't what I meant. Caleb, please don't make this hard, I really do need to think about it. Melissa is back in the office tomorrow and she's dying to meet the famous Caleb Black; why don't you come and talk to her?' I run my fingers through his hair to calm him.

'I bet she is.'

I don't understand how he can't see us making this work. I know I am good at my job, but Caleb is beyond exceptional at his. We can do this. I decide to end our conversation.

'I don't want us to fight tonight, Caleb.' I put my mouth on his. 'Want to relieve me of some clothing instead?'

'Maybe tomorrow, if that's okay.' He pulls me closer, puts his head on my chest and wraps himself around me.

My second rejection by Caleb tonight hurts more than the first, but I say nothing because we've closed the conversation for now. I kiss his head and ruminate over my last thoughts as I fall asleep with him holding on to me almost too tightly.

Something tells me that my boyfriend is also holding on to something that is eating away at him, but he has absolutely no plans to share the burden with me.

ELEVEN
CALEB

I try. I do absolutely everything I can to rescue us, but life together deteriorates rapidly. Hugh Mason gave me some hope when we took the same position over Sunday lunch. He, too, thought that she should decline the offer. Unfortunately, Dahlia was in opposition, so I knew I was on the losing team.

'You are not moving halfway across the world with *some person* we barely know,' he said, starting strong.

'Exactly!' I agreed vehemently before it occurred to me that he might be talking about me. Although, at that point I didn't care as long as the end result was achieved.

Dahlia, once again, killed it.

'I was nowhere as old, mature and sensible as she is when I followed *some person* across the Atlantic. I didn't even have the promise of a job, a home, my parents' support or the ease of communication we now have.'

When Hugh Mason grumbled, I knew we'd lost. Valiant but weak effort, sir.

. . .

So, I take the director of sales job. Like I had a choice. Ariella also accepts her role, but is quickly elevated to the chief operating officer she initially thought she'd be reporting to. She claims she was told, not asked, and it's the catalyst for a gargantuan fight and many more quarrels after that. I know this is what Melissa wants as part of her grand manipulative plan, but it is hard not to be angry.

Just when I thought things couldn't get any worse, Melissa happily announced that she was moving Ariella's three-month departure to one month, after two weeks of planning, because everything was going really well. I was so infuriated that she was robbing me of a month and a half with Ariella that I sealed the ring every day that week and took on anyone who was willing to get in with me at Muay Thai. Ariella silently tended to my cuts and bruises all week and didn't ask any questions. By the day before she leaves, our relationship is in pieces, broken by my anger, and thinly held together by history.

I know I have to make things right before Ariella goes, so the night before she flies I wangle a table at one of her favourite restaurants in Knightsbridge to make amends. I am so intent on making this dinner perfect that I leave work early to go home, shower and dress up nicely for her. After I pick up an engraved wallet I ordered last minute from her favourite leather retailer and slip a little photo of us in, I make it to the restaurant early and sit at our table waiting for her.

When Ariella turns up, she is ten minutes late. She rushes her jacket off as she walks through the restaurant, greeting the familiar staff warmly before she sits.

'Hi.' She beams joyfully. 'I'm sorry I'm late. Melissa came into the office and had some bits to go through. We didn't get through them all so she arranged for us to sit next to each other on the flight out tomorrow.'

The words are out of my mouth before I can stop them.

'Why did you bother turning up at all? Melissa finally gave you permission to have a life, did she? How very generous of her.'

Ariella looks like she has been slapped. She stands, silently picks up her jacket and bag, then walks out, waving goodbye to the staff.

I promptly but politely get a zero bill put in front of me.

'Excuse me, I had a beer and—'

The manager puts his hand up with a smile. 'Miss Ariella is a friend of the chef, sir, your money's no good here. Allow me to get your coat.'

I hear Jill Scott singing away in her bedroom, and knock before I walk in. Aside from a small suitcase with a few things in, everything is in its place. I hear her shower running and it saddens me that, just six weeks ago, I wouldn't have thought twice about stripping down and joining her in it. When the water stops, I pray to whatever is listening that I don't mess it up.

'Please leave, Caleb,' she asks softly when she enters her room.

'Ordinarily, I would, but we don't have a lot of time, Aari. I'm sorry I haven't dealt with this whole thing well. I just feel like we are making a huge mistake and I don't know how to stop it.'

'But I don't want you to stop it, Caleb. Not for me.'

'Why are you so keen to go?'

'My reasons haven't changed.'

She looks so sad, for a split second I think about telling her everything, but I can't. I will lose her, Dahlia, Hugh, Zachary, Isszy and even Lara's irritating antics. I have grown to love them as my family. Instead, we just look at each other, until she eventually grabs her nightshirt and disappears back into her bathroom. I collapse backwards onto the bed. How do I tell her that every sale I have had in Asia is down to Melissa and I've never met most of our clients out there? She definitely won't forgive me for having slept with the person who is doing all of this because she is intent on punishing me.

'If I ask you something, will you tell me the truth?' Ariella asks when she returns.

'Of course,' I answer, with my heart in my throat. She knows.

'Are you angry because I am technically going to be your boss? Because I want you to know, I don't see it like that at all. I would never—'

I burst out laughing. Without thinking, I cross the room, hold her face in my hands and kiss her through my laughter. I'd forgotten how sweet Ariella can be under that stubborn, determined, perfect exterior. She starts laughing and kisses me back. We enjoy our first proper kiss since the whole debacle started and it lifts the tension temporarily.

'No, in fact it's quite the opposite. You in a position of authority is a scenario that I could very much get into, recreationally.' I smile.

'Then what is it, Caleb? We aren't going to survive like this. Are we going to try to stay together? Are we done?' She wells up.

'We are absolutely not, by any definition, done, Ariella,' I deliver softly.

'Then why are you behaving like you want us to be?'

'I'm not. It's so gutting to think about not being able to see you, talk to you or have you and whatever weird but delicious thing you're cooking as part of my day. I feel like I've lost you already.'

'You haven't, but we can't carry on like this,' she whispers.

She's right but I don't have the words right now, so I suggest we take a breather and try to reconnect in the only way that can take us back to when things were really good.

'*Sopranos* and ice cream?'

She is asleep in my arms on the couch after two spoonfuls of ice cream and ten minutes after the opening credits. I spend most of the episode watching her curled up, emanating her tiny little snores. When the credits roll, I carry her into my bed, because there is no way that I am going to spend our last night apart. I leap into the shower quickly before I lie down beside her. She snuggles close as I place her head on my arm.

'I love you, my little Mason.' I kiss a sleeping Ariella's forehead and her eyes open slightly.

'Please make love to me, Black.'

I harden immediately. After that, no words are needed. It has been a while; in fact, since just before Melissa resurfaced. I kick myself at how long it has been since I gave Aari a reason to stay. We hadn't even shared a proper kiss until earlier tonight. What have I been doing?

'It's okay if you don't want to—'

Before she finishes her sentence, I cover her mouth with mine and my whole body shivers with pleasure. I'd forgotten her magic, this connection, our dependency on each other. How has this happened?

I am still amazed at how her skin feels under my hands. I take my time and trace the lines of her face, her jaw, her neck, committing it all to memory. She leaves tomorrow. I need to make up for lost time.

'How on earth have we not been doing this every night, Aari?' I mumble.

'I don't know.' I hear her breath choke a little and see the first tear fall.

'I'm sorry, Aari. I really am. I am so sorry,' I repeat, kissing her tears.

'I was scared that you didn't want me any more.'

'You're the only thing, the only one that I want, Aari.' I kiss her face.

'Ooo-ooo-ooo. The one I need, oh yes indeed,' she croaks, attempting to sing. I stop. We both burst out laughing.

'I've missed you, Aari.'

I lift her nightshirt and let the moonlight bathe her body. She is even more exquisite than I remember. I kiss her face, her neck, her chest, and I chuckle as I see my two most loyal fans standing to attention, hoping that I notice them.

'My girls. They are always so ready.' I look up at Aari.

'You are within a million-mile radius, aren't you?' she whispers breathlessly before I keep my girlfriend up all night, revisiting and replaying our greatest, most intimate hits; making the most of her farewell tour and indulging every encore she requests. We rediscover our bodies, remind each other of our deepest desires, share our souls and reconnect our loose, frayed ends. I conclude that I am going to fight for us, whatever it takes.

We wake up at noon, having fallen asleep only four hours earlier from sheer exhaustion. Her flight is at six, so we have about three hours to make the most of the day. I make her grapefruit breakfast with absolute devotion, we condition and comb her hair out from the night before, and I help her finish packing – not that she is taking much.

'I have to get "corporate", apparently. I'm supposed to be in "appropriate attire", whatever that means, so I'm getting a clothing allowance and a stylist. I might as well leave most of my stuff here.'

She seems to have warmed to the idea of being 'fixed'. I don't like it – in my eyes Ariella doesn't need fixing – but I say nothing. I refuse to let anything ruin today. Instead, I pull her close, whisper something dirty I know she'll love in her ear and have my little Mason coming apart fifteen minutes later. I don't let her go until twenty minutes before we absolutely have to leave.

I jump in a nearby Zipcar and drive her to the airport, because I want to spend as much alone time with her as possible. As soon as we check in at the first class bay, Melissa appears.

'Hi, guys!' She smiles.

'Hi!' Ariella beams back.

'Melissa.' I force a smile. She comes over and pinches my cheek. I want to rip her arm out of its socket and beat her with it. I give her a dirty look, and Ariella sees it.

'Awww, he's going to miss his girl.' Melissa leans in to her and whispers loud enough for me to hear, 'Men are so used to getting what they want. Some patience will be good for him.'

I wait for Melissa to check in and go through, so I can have my last few minutes alone with Ariella, but when she's done she beckons Ariella along, effectively cutting our time short. I grab my girlfriend and hope that the kiss that makes her forget herself is still in my arsenal as I plant one on her.

Ariella submits to it more deeply than I expect and pulls me close, pushing herself into me. I absorb every bit of her before I open an eye to see Melissa's fury. In your face. Cow.

'Young love. How cute,' Melissa offers, deadpan. Ariella pulls away immediately, embarrassed. I see her reprimanding look and return a heartfelt smile.

'I love you, Mason,' I declare to her, softly.

'Ready?' Melissa presses.

Ariella nods sadly, adjusting herself.

'Wait.' I grab her hand as she turns away. 'Don't go,' I plead. 'Come home. With me.'

'I love you, Black.' She hugs me tightly. This is her goodbye.

I watch powerlessly as she disappears around the corner towards airport security with that serpent. Suddenly, Melissa re-emerges and makes her way to me. She fixes her eyes on mine and whispers quickly, 'A lot of things can happen over some distance and time, Caleb. Rub my nose in anything again, and I am telling her everything. I can assure you, the way I tell it won't be pretty.'

She adjusts herself and speaks again, loudly. 'Go home and call your girlfriend in sixteen hours. I promise to look after her.'

Ariella pokes her head around the corner just enough for me to see her, blows me a kiss and mouths, 'I love you.'

I watch Melissa catch up and link her arm through Ariella's before they disappear once again, taking any hope I have with me.

Just as I park the hire car back in its bay, I receive a call and accept an invitation from the only person I shouldn't be agreeing to meet for a drink and dinner.

Sitting here now, watching Jasper walk back with a pint in his hand for me, I immediately regret my mistake.

TWELVE

ARIELLA

I am actually in Singapore. If someone had told me, two years ago, that I'd be moving across the world to a country I've never been to, to take a job I've never done, in a city where I know no one, I would have crumpled in sheer panic.

Yet here I am, managing a mixture of fright and excitement. And guilt. This decision was a selfish one. Encouraged by Melissa, I made it outside of external influences. I'm here because I want to be.

When we arrive, we are met by my new PA, Lydia Li. She is imposingly tall and elegant, with bone-straight, long black hair parted precisely in the middle.

As soon as she spots us, she moves with intimidating command and control, choreographing our bags, driver and journey to the car. On the way to the hotel, she is prepared, handing me a phone attached to a local number and a 'Welcome to Singapore' folder containing everything from local laws and customs to hairdressers for my 'almost certainly 3C' hair. She checks me into my hotel with the same speed and efficiency she displayed at the airport, only finally coming to a stop once we are in my room and everyone has been dispatched. She stands, almost at attention, in front of me as if waiting for instructions. I don't give any.

'May I show you around, Miss Mason? The Merlion Suite at the Marina Bay Sands is on the—'

'No, thank you.' I smile kindly. 'Can we talk?' I gesture to one of the plush couches and take a seat in another. For the first time, her confidence disappears and is replaced with worry. She makes her way to stand by the seat I pointed to as I curl into mine.

'Please sit, Lydia.'

She hesitantly sits right at the edge, looking uncomfortable. 'Thank you, Miss Mason.'

'Please call me Ariella.'

Her eyes widen in disbelief. 'I don't think...'

'Would you like some water?' I ask, getting up.

She shoots up immediately. 'I can get you—'

'Please.' I go to the minibar and grab two bottles of water, delivering one to her and then twisting the cap open on the other for myself. I sigh with relief, not just from the hydration the water provides, but also the victory of slowing everything down. It is all happening too fast. 'Are you Singaporean, Lydia?'

'Yes. My mother is Malay and my father is Chinese, so I also speak, read and write Bahasa, Cantonese and Mandarin fluently. I can also—'

'Is it okay if I just get to know you?' I ask. 'We are going to be working really closely together and, while I can see that you're more than competent to support me, it's really important for me to understand how I can support you too.'

'I am here to support you.'

'We can support each other.'

'Why?' The confusion on her face breaks my heart.

'Because I think the world works better that way.' I smile. She looks uncomfortable, so I leave it. I feel exhaustion creeping up on me.

'Thank you for the lovely welcome. If you would like to go home, I can take things from here.'

'I'm supposed to be here with you until you settle in.'

'Thank you, I'm settled. I'm just going to shower and take a nap,' I reassure her.

'Please call if you need me, I'll be in my room.' She stands.

'You're staying in the hotel too?'

'Yes, I'm staying here, in your suite with you.'

'You're not going home?'

'No. According to the agreed plan, I'm to stay with you until you request otherwise.' Lydia taps on her file.

'Please may I take a look at the agreed plan?'

'All of it or just today's?'

'Just today's plan for now, please?'

Lydia opens her folder and passes me a sheet and I scan it. Melissa wasn't joking about hitting the ground running. According to this, Lydia is at my beck and call, twenty-four hours a day. Part of her job is also to diarise my first weeks with photos, as content for both the company and, apparently, my own social media sites. My diary for today has my first engagement at eight tonight: dinner, with a stylist and make-up team arriving at five thirty to get me ready. I start to feel my throat constrict and my breathing turn shallow. I refuse to have a meltdown in front of Lydia, so I excuse myself to go to the bathroom. I draw on everything I have learned over the years to calm myself down. Thankfully, it doesn't take long. I know that I can't be the girl I was in London, and, as much as I want Caleb to be here right now, I don't have that luxury. I need to start to trust myself and my decisions.

'Thanks for this, Lydia,' I start as I step out of the bathroom. 'I don't need you to stay. Please cancel the stylist and make-up team, I will get myself ready for the car at seven thirty. Are your personal belongings up here already?'

'Not yet, my case is with the concierge.'

'Please can you ask the driver to take you home and ask him to collect you for dinner before he comes for me? I do need you and I hope we become a great team, but I don't need twenty-four-hour support. Let's start at nine every morning and aim to finish about six. If we have evening engagements like tonight's, we can look at getting you some time off in lieu. Please let the driver know that I don't need him on standby. How will you get here in the mornings?'

'I get the bus...'

'Okay. Please let the driver know that his day starts and finishes with you. His first job is to collect you and his last job is to return you home, safely.'

'But the car is for you...'

'Yes, and I need you energised and bright in the mornings, and safe at night. Is there anything else I should know about today?'

'No, Miss Ma— Ariella.'

'Thank you. I have a couple of calls to make and I need to take a shower and a nap. Maybe we can catch up on some more of the itinerary items on the way to dinner?'

She nods. 'My number is in your phone if you need anything. Shall I dismiss the butler too?'

'Yes please.'

She nods and leaves the suite. I run to the door as soon as she exits, and bolt it from the inside. I did it. I am so happy that I am calling before I know it.

'I am SO proud of you, my little Mason,' Caleb gushes down the phone after I relay the last few hours to him.

'I am proud of myself too!' I chuckle. 'Want to see my room?' I flip it to video call and we explore the massive suite together. After the tour ends, I flop on the bed in one of the rooms.

'I miss you. I have too much space when I sleep. It feels strange not having to cling to the edge of the bed because you've taken all of it up. I don't know what to do with myself. You, on the other hand, look like you have more space than you know what to do with!' He points at the camera, chuckling.

'I know! It's all a little... excessive!' I stretch out my free arm and rub the empty space.

'Oh, that bed is nothing. Wait until you accidentally wander into the shopping mall downstairs. It's completely enclosed and it goes on for ever with no obvious way out.' He laughs. 'You are not going to be happy. At all!'

The sound of his laughter at my irrational fear of not being able to see an exit makes me happy. It is a sound that has been almost non-existent for the last month and a half. It wakes the desire in me.

'I would give anything to be able to kiss you right now,' I confess.

He exhales, then groans painfully.

'I am not going to ask you to come home, instead I'm going to tell you that I will see you soon, okay?'

'I can't wait.'

'We'll be so busy it will fly by.'

'I hope so. I miss you so much already.'

We sit silently on our phones, looking at each other. Eventually I perk up.

'I'd better go. I should call Mommy and Daddy.'

'You called me first?'

'Yes. Why do you sound so surprised?'

'It's just... Never mind. I love you. Be a good girl and talk later, my little Mason.'

I hang up. While I do want Caleb here, part of me is glad he isn't. I have three months on my own to figure out who I am and what I want, and to focus on building something new. I feel more up for the challenge now that I have had my little victory with the 'agreed plan'.

I call Mommy and Daddy, shoot Zachary, Lara and Jasper each a text and have a quick shower before I crawl into bed for a nap. When I am woken by my alarm, I indulge in a longer shower, then pick a casual, simple grey dress that I purchased a couple of years ago for my interview with Ivory Bow in the UK. I pull it over my head, pop on my Converse and tie my hair into a bun at the top of my head. I put some lip balm on my lips and make an effort by putting a single black line at the top of each of my eyelids the way Lara and Isszy have shown me. I appraise myself and decide that I look chic. Done and dusted in fifteen minutes.

When Lydia turns up at the suite to collect me, I realise that I am far from done. She is wearing a beautifully tailored, figure-hugging red dress that makes her look even longer and sleeker than earlier. She has swapped her court shoes for strappy heels. Her make-up has clearly been done professionally and she looks like she has just stepped out of a photoshoot.

'You look beautiful, Lydia.'

'Thank you, Miss Ma— Ariella. The car is here. How long would you like to get dressed? I will tell the driver to wait.'

'I *am* dressed, Lydia.'

A look of horror crosses her face. 'I am so sorry... I didn't mean to... I am so sorry!'

I laugh to dispel her discomfort. 'It's okay. Shall we?'

On the ride to the restaurant I can't help comparing what Lydia and I are wearing. It's obvious we are both a little uncomfortable. I really am determined to stay who I am in Singapore but I also see that I might need to conform a little. Maybe Converse and dinner just don't go together here. I make a mental note to be more malleable and give the stylist and make-up artists a shot. I don't want to betray myself, but I also don't want to rebelliously swim against the tide.

When we get to the restaurant, Melissa and my other two colleagues are already at the table. I am definitely underdressed. Melissa is wearing a black, sharply cut, angular dress with beautiful detailing around the neck, and both my male colleagues are in suits with open-neck shirts. As I approach they stand up and shake my hand in turn.

'I clearly have some assimilating to do,' I say, trying to laugh to hide my mortification, as I point to my dress and Converse. Melissa offers a kind smile while the gentlemen laugh. Lydia just looks nervous as she waits for me to sit before she does.

We all opt for the tasting menu with matching wines and, once the waiter leaves, Melissa makes the formal introductions.

'Our Aussie powerhouse is Bryce Parsons. He will be head of legal and compliance. I stole Bryce directly from the law firm that my family has used for years. He was their most awarded rising star. Bryce is completely dedicated to this project and has no personal life, so he will be on at all times. Guaranteed. Isn't that right, Bryce?'

She inspires an embarrassed smile. 'Personal life, rejected,' Bryce jokingly agrees in a thick Australian accent, making me chuckle.

'That's what I like to hear.' She smiles before she turns to me.

'Don't let that tall, tanned blond surfer-type laid-backness fool you. I've been in meetings with this guy. Houdini couldn't sneak one past him.' Melissa laughs. 'Thankfully, as you can all probably tell, he is also a thoroughly nice bloke.' She says 'bloke' in an Australian accent, triggering a round of laughter.

'Over to you!' She turns to face the other guy. 'Denzel Washington over here...'

'Not you too!' 'Denzel' groans.

We all laugh.

'Don't you guys think he looks like a young Denzel?' Melissa asks.

She's right, he does. If my mother was here, she'd be having a fit and be halfway to getting divorced right now. Poor Daddy.

'Sorry, she's right,' I say, smiling.

He just shakes his head in happy resignation.

'Denzel's name is actually Devin Cox. He is our chief financial officer. He's going to make sure we are making money and smart strategic financial choices. He's an alum of both Harvard and Stamford and I coerced him to join us when I read about him uncovering a governmental scam and not being afraid to blow the whistle. He's smart and brave, or stupid and reckless, depending on the way you look at it.'

'Stupid. Definitely stupid,' he says in an American accent, making us all laugh.

'Moving on.' She turns to me and I tense.

'Freckles over here is Ariella Mason.'

The guys burst out laughing.

'I like it,' I offer with a raised eyebrow and a smile, trying to be confident.

'Don't laugh too loudly, boys, she may look like a teenager but she is going to be your COO and my right-hand woman. I plan on having as little involvement as possible, so she's in charge. She is the face, the decisions and the fall guy, so she is going to need your support and protection. I was actually looking to hire her boyfriend when I found her.'

'I bet he's pissed,' Bryce adds under his breath with a chuckle. I freeze.

'I think he may have been a little...' Melissa acknowledges. 'But he is joining us in a few months as our director of sales. More about that later. Ariella has a unique ability to build anything, anywhere, to its full vision and, based on her project track record, the level of her delivery is truly incomparable.' She turns to me.

'Having said that, I am yet to see any kind of killer instinct, which you're going to need, so you're going to have to rely on these three.' She points to Devin, Bryce and Lydia.

Thankfully, she then turns to Lydia.

'Lydia Li, who you all have been in contact with, is assigned to Ariella as her personal assistant but can support you gentlemen as an executive assistant before we fill those roles for you. She has an extensive background supporting C-Suite category management and in most cases supporting them all at the same time. She is the best EA you're going to get, anywhere, in the world.'

Lydia blushes and tries to control her smile.

'As you all know, I am Melissa "wannabe Lucy Liu" Chang. You will barely see me or hear from me unless you need me. I am doing this because we can all make a lot of money and build something exceptional, with what I think might be the youngest and most formidable management team in Singapore.'

She raises her glass of champagne. 'Cheers!'

We all clink our glasses and settle into the amuse bouche.

The meal and company are lovely, alleviating some of my fears. I really like the guys; they are gentlemanly, polite, confident, and it is clear that they are competent and ready to go. We are all staying at Marina Bay Sands, where we have a conference suite reserved for the next month while we find an office space.

I sit back and watch the chatter and laughter at the table, knowing that I have done the right thing.

THIRTEEN

CALEB

I hate Jasper. I really hate Jasper.

I should have told him to fuck off when he called.

'Caleb.' I knew his voice immediately.

'What do you want?'

'I caught her just as she was about to take off and she told me you dropped her off.'

'And?'

'And, I thought of you going home to an empty flat. I've been there. It doesn't feel great. Want to grab a beer and a bite?'

That did it. We agreed to meet at a quiet pub we both know in St John's Wood. I spot his neat hair and predictably 'starched-to-straitjacket' blue button-down shirt the second I walk in. He catches my eye and nods to a table where his coat is draped over two stools. I take a stool until he finally joins me with two pints of ale.

'I feel we could have been friends if we didn't both love the same woman,' he starts, extending a hand, once he's put the pints down. I take it.

'You've moved on quite nicely.'

'I wouldn't say I've moved on. I'm making the best of what she left me with.'

'Seems pretty cushy to me – and I wouldn't go around saying that out loud around your new girl. Why are we here, Goldsmith?'

'You make Aari happy and it looks like you're going to be around for a while. I'd like to call a truce because I don't want to lose my best friend.'

'Didn't think I'd make it past Hugh Mason, did you?'

'I didn't. I was wrong.'

'You were. Especially with your bullshit analogy at that Sunday lunch of her being in a sports car and me on a bicycle. We're good as we are.'

'I wasn't wrong about that.' Jasper smiles sadly at me.

'She doesn't give a shit about all that materialistic crap you people put on show.'

'Our friends can be crude and flashy. Real money is mute.'

'I don't care.'

'You don't care, *yet*. Right now, you're enjoying the Bollinger that's a constant in your fridge. Those little meals she cooks with quietly expensive ingredients. But you'll eventually go away for the weekend to celebrate something and you'll realise that you can't put Ariella in a mediocre hotel and dinner reservations are a whole other minefield. You'll feel it then.

'And that's just dating. If this works out, you'll maybe get married. Save for a house. Have kids. That's when it's really going to hit. It'll start with you suggesting that she get a cheaper version of whatever she is buying. Or if you *really* need the champagne in the fridge, a butcher or grocer. Before you know it, you'll resent her for being wasteful, and she'll feel restricted by your impositions.

'The bicycle and sports car analogy isn't about how much money you have. It's about how aggressively protective your relationship with the money you have, is.'

I see what he's saying, but fuck him.

'She makes her own money. She can do what she likes with it.'

Jasper lets out a small, pitying laugh.

'Okay, Caleb.'

'I'll be all right, because she'll never relive the emotional torture she felt being imprisoned by you.'

'That's fair,' Jasper admits, ashamed. 'I don't know how we let it get to that.'

'Not "we". You.'

'You're not wrong. I was neglectful and controlling. If she ever found out some of the things I did, she'd never forgive me.'

There is no way Jasper is going to tell me, of all people, what he did. But I ask anyway.

'Like what?'

'I may have made more than a few persuasive calls to Ivory Bow to guarantee she was bound to her desk at work, knowing she wanted exactly the opposite.' Jasper sighs deeply as he shakes his head and looks down in regret.

'You got her benched? Why?'

'I've always made decisions for us and, at the time, I didn't think I was crossing a line.'

'You long-jumped the line on that one. But I suppose she wouldn't have risen as quickly to head of global operations without your intervention.' Why am I comforting this guy?

'Head of global operations?'

He didn't know either? It doesn't sting as much now.

'Yeah. And she eventually got her wish.'

'You don't sound too thrilled,' Jasper says, curiously.

'I'm not. The investor, Melissa Chang, is a little shady.'

'Why would you think that?'

'She gave Ivory Bow a lot of work. Before Ariella, we... exchanged benefits.'

Jasper's eyebrows shoot up.

'Does Ariella know?'

'She knows that I was never lonely when I was away, but not specifically about her.'

'And you think she's unscrupulous because...'

'I went to see her, to tell her to leave Ariella and me alone. She suggested that the work she was giving us may not have been fully above board.'

'In what way?'

'I don't know. She was pissed off, so I'm not sure if the threat was legit or not. Melissa can be... manipulative.'

Jasper's eyebrows are knitted together with an intensity that can only mean one thing.

'You're going to tell her, aren't you?'

'What makes you think that?' Jasper asks.

'You tell her, she dumps me, you get back together and all of this has just been one sorry elongated mess.'

'I've interfered before. I'm not going to do that again and it is not my story to tell.'

'You'd keep her in the dark and not get involved because it's none of your business?'

'I didn't say I wouldn't get involved.'

'And what would your involvement look like?' I mimic his posh accent but he doesn't rise to it.

'I'd encourage you to tell her the truth after we remove the immediate threat.'

'Melissa?'

'Yes, and I can help. But first, we need to know whether or not her threats are empty, designed to force compliance. Ariella really wants this job and convincing her to leave Singapore without hard, indisputable evidence is not an option. Currently, there is nothing to suggest the new business won't be completely legitimate. Ariella is painfully thorough, and I don't see this sliding past her. We need to find out what we are dealing with, *if* you don't mind me doing this with you.'

'You're offering to help me?'

Jasper sighs. 'Yes. But when you're ready, you have to tell her the truth.'

'That's it?'

'That's it. And if you don't mind, I could use some truth from you on a couple of questions. They might be inappropriate, but they've been keeping me awake at night.'

'I'm listening.'

'When did you first sleep together?'

Shit. I wasn't expecting that. 'Mate, let it go.' Jasper is now just torturing himself and I'm not going to be the bastard who helps him do that.

'I can take it,' he assures me, but I can see that he is already fighting back tears. 'I don't need the how, just the when.'

'It was the day before Zachary dropped everyone in it at Sunday lunch.'

'Only just the day before? I thought I had a problem the night we found her in the rain,' Jasper whispers.

'Not with me. That was all you. She trusted you, but you embarrassed her and abandoned her. Unbelievably, the very next morning she blamed herself for everything and let you off.'

'I messed up.'

'Yes, you did. Big time. After that, I suggested that she shag someone to get over you. Definitely not me. Just anyone else, because that's what I would have done. She agreed in theory, tried, but was absolutely useless. I'd watch her go on dates and come back pissed off because some poor sod tried to just touch her hand or kiss her cheek goodnight. I suppose I started to care. That Friday night, before Sunday lunch, she snuck out of yet another date in the middle of dinner, because the guy asked for a kiss goodnight. We had some gin as she filled me in, and before I knew what was happening I kissed her, because I'd wanted to for a little while – and she didn't pull away.'

I spot Jasper fiddling furiously with the clasp of his Breitling. He's going to lose his shit.

'You should know that she felt absolutely nothing for me. She thought she was having unattached "get under someone to get over someone" sex with someone who wasn't going to judge her. She didn't know that I felt differently. You were the only person who I told how I really felt; although, Dahlia was already on to me.'

'When did she tell you that she loved you?'

'Two and a half months ago. I'd been waiting a while.'

'I think I might owe you an apology. Something happened —' Jasper starts.

'You don't. I know. She told me she slept with you. It's fine. I was hardly keeping it in my pants at the time.'

'What do you mean?'

'I finished things with Melissa that weekend. She didn't take it well. She dropped something in my drink and made it impossible for me not to give her a last goodbye.' I can't believe I just told him that.

'Caleb. I don't think you're to blame...'

'We both fucked up, but I have to ask. Why are you helping me?'

'She's in love with you. Hugh asked me to talk some sense into her when she got the job offer and, when I called, I caught her in the middle of a wobble.'

'A wobble?' Ariella seemed so sure.

'Yeah. We made a quick pros and cons list and let's just say that you taking the job with her was a massive pro. So, instead of trying to change her mind, I congratulated her. You make her happy and I'd like for it to stay that way. For your sake and mine.'

'For your sake?' I laugh.

'My whole house still smells of apples and grapefruit,' he

confesses sadly. He's still nowhere near over her. 'Hopefully, Sophia moving in will help.'

'You'd better watch your back with that one.'

'Good job you're taken.'

There is a short pause before we burst out laughing at the same time.

I actually enjoy shooting the breeze with Jasper for a while longer before we call it a night. As I turn right to walk to the tube station, I hear him call my name before he jogs towards me from his car.

'I forgot to tell you something earlier.'

'What?'

'I think you should think about talking to someone professional about what happened with Melissa.'

'Like a hit man?' I laugh and so does he.

'No, like a counsellor.'

'Why?'

'It sounds like you were sexually assaulted to me.'

It feels like Jasper has smashed me in the face with a ton of bricks. Tim said the same thing. I say nothing, and turn back towards the tube station.

When I get home, it feels too cold, too quiet and too empty. I grab a full bottle of the rum that Ariella loves from the cupboard. I already miss her terribly. I need her between my arms, creating our two-person world that doesn't need anything else. Before I know it, I am halfway through the bottle.

I fall asleep on the couch that night, unable to bear her absence in either of our bedrooms.

FOURTEEN

ARIELLA

I very quickly learned why I'd need a personal assistant, driver, stylist, make-up artist and a housekeeper. My schedule is relentless and our timeline to be up and running is extremely tight. In the last month, I have had to learn all the general legal aspects, policies, parameters and compliance obligations of a Singaporean company from Bryce, who, thankfully, is a patient and excellent teacher.

The financial conduct and tax regulations have also featured heavily on my learning list, but that has been much more challenging to get to grips with. While Devin is highly competent, his knowledge-sharing skills leave a lot to be desired. I know I can depend on him to do an excellent job, but I find that my many requests for clarity and understanding are met with less-than-enthusiastic responses. I understand that I'm a novice, but leaving key operational points that I should be familiar with up to someone else just is not acceptable.

My learning curve is steep, in addition to finding an office, hiring staff, attending the opening of everything luxury- and hospitality-related, joining local business and entrepreneur networks, building a supportive base with women in business groups and cosying up to local meeting, incentive, conference and exhibition associations.

There is still a mountain to climb, but I'm proud of what I have achieved so far. In terms of milestones, I am on track.

The one big deadline I've resigned myself to missing is finding myself a home. It's not going to happen any time soon, so Lydia has extended my hotel stay for another four weeks. I'd be disappointed, but I am getting an average of three hours of sleep a night, so room service and the daily housekeeping go a long way. Eden the stylist and Ruby the make-up artist have also been exceptionally useful for my event attendance. They show up, do whatever they want to me, and release me to the public. Lydia very kindly texts me who I am wearing, what potential clients I should be mentioning, and talking points.

Intense imposter syndrome has me breathing through anxiety attacks numerous times a day but the severe, sweaty, chest-clutching, trachea-closing panic attacks happen around three a.m. Every day.

With my workload, there are just some areas that I am unable to engage in. We have a PR and social media campaign, based on a strategy I can barely grasp, under way. Lydia seemed keen to work with Georgie, our PR specialist, so she is handling that. If you look us up, you will see many pictures of me, the office, Bryce, Devin and Lydia; they paint a very different picture to the reality I currently endure.

I asked Lydia to show me all our sites, once. I can't speak for the others, but my pages show a competent, powerful, energetic, smiley and influential woman who still has time to work out (I showed Lydia a couple of poses in my pyjamas once), eats and adores amazing food (some of the dishes I don't recognise, but you will find me cooing all over them) and socialises with Singapore's elite, all of whom had been introduced by Melissa. I've forgotten all their names and I don't remember half of the pictures being taken, but the captions tell a different story:

'Inspiration!' 'OMG. LOVE HER!' '#humbled' and so on. There are also a lot of subtle references made to the fact that I am single: '#homealone', '#quiettime', '#memyselfandi', '#worknowlovelater', '#marriedtothejob'.

I have no idea who this woman is but I want to be her. Right now, I am a girl way in over her head, desperately alone, functioning on minimal sleep and scrambling for air. All of the time.

Devin and Bryce feature heavily too, and are proving so popular that they will be getting their own pages soon. The shots of Devin, Bryce and me working hard and at various industry functions paints a picture of a united team of go-getters chasing their dreams. There are a few '#femaleboss', '#hangingout' and '#dreamteam' tags in there, making it seem easy and relaxed.

The truth is that it's hard. For all of us. At the moment this is all wildly inaccurate but it seems harmless. However, when my workload lightens, I am going to have to do something about ensuring that we are sharing a more truthful version of our experiences. I also can't help noticing that Bryce and Devin's captions are based around professional, business and curriculum-vitae highlights with a little bit of lifestyle thrown in. My captions seem to be mostly lifestyle. But I park my complaint. As long as I am not damaging what we are building, I can live with it, for now. Lydia is also clearly very proud of what she has achieved so far with our social media presence, and I am hesitant to take that away from her.

We finally sign the lease for a bright, new, twenty-desk office in the Marina Bay office towers in line with Melissa's parameters. She's right. The closer we are to our clients, the better.

Shortly afterwards, Devin and Bryce find a home that has been converted to two self-contained apartments in District 9, and move in swiftly. Thankfully, two days before Lydia has to extend my hotel stay again, Devin finds an apartment at the top of a residential building on Lloyd Road that will double up as a hosting, tasting and sampling space for our clients. Once he approves the higher rental bracket with Melissa, I sign the lease without taking a look. I'm not going to be spending much time there anyway. Before I can ask, Lydia has lined up a handful of housekeepers to interview and arranged to transfer the contents of my hotel room.

When moving day arrives, it doesn't take long to evacuate my hotel room. Devin and Bryce give up their Saturday to help pack up and transfer our makeshift secure boardroom, also known as my suite's dining table and living area. The stylist and make-up artist spent the day before packing and cataloguing their items and, with my personal belongings snugly packed in my single suitcase, we are out in no time. The drive from the hotel to my new home isn't long, and ends in a warm welcome from the apartment's housekeeper. She insists on referring to me as Ms Ariella and introduces herself as Pat. She looks older than my mom, so I apply a Ms to the front of her name too. I like her. Lydia has done a great job.

With Ms Pat's help, it only takes a day to move me into the vast apartment, and by the time we are done, we have set up a home office on the apartment's mezzanine level and all the furniture that was delivered is in place. I move into one of the three immense bedrooms, each of which could easily be large studio apartments. When Ms Pat informs me that the humongous swimming pool has been cleaned, I thank everyone with some champagne and food platters in one of its cabanas before they leave. As soon as Ms Pat finally finishes for the night, I collapse on the gigantic grey wool couch in the middle of my minimalist, expansive living room and cry harder than I have ever cried before.

I desperately want to call Caleb but I don't, because our relationship is in a weird place. When I first arrived, we adopted a good, nightly video call routine. After a few hits and misses at catching each other, we realised that the best time to chat was when I came home after work, which, for a very long time, was at one in the morning. In fact, it still is, most week-nights. It's perfect because that's when he usually finishes at work.

I sometimes got to see the boys from his Muay Thai class. Alfie even got to show me a lost tooth, then encouraged me, with Caleb's help, to enter into negotiations with the Singaporean tooth fairy to extract a bid. Her bid won, payment was fronted by Caleb, but no tooth has shown up to date.

I did everything to make our calls because I knew that if we maintained them, the time would fly by. Just when we found our speed, our conversations got shorter, and sometimes, I fell asleep mid-chat. As time passed, we began speaking every other day, supplementing our phone calls with texts on missed days. Soon, we were replacing all our calls with texts and skipping some of those days too, which brings us to now. The last message I sent was a couple of days ago.

When I have cried to a point much further than exhaustion, I drag myself into my new bedroom, step under the shower and sit on the floor in the corner of the cubicle, letting the water run over me until it turns cold.

The next day, I send Caleb a message to give him my new address. We exchange little bits of news and, by the time he coolly tells me he needs to get a morning run in, I wish I hadn't reached out.

I don't hear from him again until the following Thursday, after I wake up to a text from Mel.

> I hope those boys remained focused and didn't get too distracted moving you in.

She ends it with a winking emoji. I am confused by the text and even more confused that she is sending me emojis, but I text back immediately.

> Yes, they were a great help.

> I am sure they were, just be gentle with them.

This is odd.

> Is one of them hurt?

> Have you looked at the Ivory Bow Instagram today?

> No. Is something wrong?

> No. Well, maybe. You should have a look.

I open up the icon on my phone and there it is. Devin is smiling as he holds my face. My eyes are shut and my lips parted, only a few inches away. I remember this. He was on his knees, plugging the printer in at the socket. I had the other end of the lead and was leaning over the printer, trying to attach it. He'd turned around quickly to get up and we'd bumped heads. All he did was inspect my forehead. This looks like something completely different. Something intensely intimate. The comment below the image reads 'Moving in.' There were over two thousand likes and over a hundred comments. I scroll through quickly. The commenters all came to the same false conclusion. It's been up for two hours. I feel like I might throw up. I call Lydia immediately.

'Lydia. I need you to delete the post of Devin and me.'

'But its performance is—'

'Lydia, please take it down, and can you run any posts like that past me in the future?'

'Yes, of course. I will do it right now.'

'Thank you, Lydia, see you soon.'

I call Mel straight away.

'We have just removed the post. I am so sorry. We are building a company here, not a gossip site!'

'These things happen. You have to admit, you look adorable together. They are calling you Devinella.' Melissa laughs down the phone.

'Oh no.'

'Let's just hope Caleb hasn't seen it.'

My heart stops for a second. Surely he knows that I'd never do anything like that. 'He'll be fine.' I hope he'll be fine.

'Yeah. I'm sure he'll be fine too. Gotta go, but I don't hear from you often enough. Let's change that.'

I spend the morning hoping that Caleb missed it. I'm definitely going to tell him about it at some point; we just don't need this now. As I start to relax early afternoon, my phone starts to buzz incessantly. It's Caleb. It's five in the morning in London and he's phoning. He must have seen it. I pick up my phone and walk out of the office building to sit by the water before I call him back.

'Ariella. What is going on? You're moving in with some guy?'

'You saw the picture? It's not what you think...'

'There's a picture?'

Oh no.

'It was on Ivory Bow's Instagram account, not my personal one. It's been deleted.'

'You have an Instagram account?'

The conversation keeps worsening, so I stay on topics that I know he already is aware of.

'Yes, it's apparently part of the PR plan for the company. I don't control it.'

'Hold on.' I hear Caleb open his laptop and start tapping. This is going to be a long phone call.

'I can't find it. What is it called?'

'AriellaIVB.'

More clicking follows and then silence.

'This isn't you!'

'I know. It's just for a while until things lighten up. After that, I am going to take control of it,' I try to assure him.

'When will that be? Wait. That's not your plate, snails repulse you! Why are you wearing so much make-up? That dress is very see-through, Ariella. Why is that blond guy always standing so close to you?'

I stay on the phone while Caleb goes through not just Ivory Bow and my social media accounts, but also Bryce's, Devin's and even Lydia's. When he is done, he keeps me on the phone while he opens his airline app and purchases a return flight to Singapore.

He arrives next Friday.

FIFTEEN

CALEB

The instant I asked Lara if she wanted to tag along and see Ariella at my expense, I regretted it. She immediately jumped at the chance and, while most would include the word, 'Thanks' somewhere in their response, she, of course, made alternative choices.

'Nice! I get to be there when she dumps your sorry arse for that hunky guy that was staring into her eyes like he was going to eat her alive. I'd totally un-gay for him if given the choice. And that other one. I tell you what, I bet Ariella's eyes aren't complaining. Yum, yum!' She laughs before she pops a fork of salad in her mouth while eyeing up the pasta I've just pushed away.

'How's your salad, Lara?'

'Delicious!' she lies. 'So, have you cheated on her lately with anyone I know?'

'I am not cheating on Ariella, Lara.' This is so typical. She knows I'm not.

'Not with the hot Latina girl at the agency downstairs?'

'Paola? Ariella and I met her in the lift. Together.'

'But you think she's hot and Latina.'

'She's an Argentinian model, Lara.'

Lara goes quiet and then narrows her eyes at me.

'You're such a dick, Black. Just keep it in your pants, okay?'

'Lara. I am about to pay a small fortune for us to spend the weekend with Ariella in Singapore. Do you think I'd do that for someone I'd cheat on?'

'I suppose you're right. Why would any man, with a girl-friend two continents away and little chance of getting caught, attempt to cheat with a lingerie model nearby?'

'I am not cheating, okay?' I complain a little too loudly.

'These expensive girlfriend maintenance flights to Singa-pore are making you cranky, Caleb. Seems like the damage to your bank account may have knocked you off cloud nine.'

'Lara, stop! You can check if you like.' I toss my phone across the table.

'Please. There's nothing more suspicious than someone willing to hand over *one of* their phones.' She snorts. 'Fine. You may not have cheated. This time.'

I've had enough, so I get up, hoping I haven't made a mistake.

'Are you not going to eat that?' Before I can respond, Lara has already had a mouthful of my pasta, shut her eyes, and seems to be moaning at the carbs.

The week is torture. The whole office is abuzz with the 'gorgeous' guy Ariella is apparently moving in with. The specu-lation gets so bad that Christopher and Harrison have to address it; they reiterate that Ariella is a colleague and, while profes-sional support is always welcome, baseless rumours about her personal life diminish the respect that she deserves.

I catch Lara mouthing along to Harrison's speech and I realise she is behind the statement. For a split second, I love Lara Scott. No matter how far away Ariella is, she still has her back. The statement helps, but it doesn't stop my pre-Ariella 'friends' letting me know how pleased they are that Ariella is giving me a taste of my own medicine.

Surprisingly, Nicole, who has been silently nurturing a growing baby bump and a new relationship with some gazillionaire, also weighs in when she pops into my office after the meeting.

'I wanted to come in here to tell you that you deserve this but you look like you're having a really hard time right now, so I won't. Listen, that Barbarella is uptight and boring. It's obvious that she is being styled and handled by people that know exactly what they are doing. They are just pushing her out there. She can't stand in the clothes properly and doesn't even bother to pose. Trust me, she is not cheating on you. I still don't know what you see in her, but you were both very happy. She is not going anywhere.'

Nicole manages to be both offensive and comforting.

'Thank you, Nicole.' I pull out an office chair for her to sit. She nods and takes it, stroking her baby bump.

'What was it about her?' she asks quietly.

'I didn't admit it at the time, but it was her that made sure we had your coffee and pain au chocolat at home. Not me. She gave me a really hard time for treating you badly. She was on your side – until you drugged and tried to kill her. She's kind, and she's sweet and above everyone's bullshit.'

'Basically, she takes your crap.'

'I wish. Far from it.'

Nicole laughs. 'I didn't mean to hurt her, by the way, but you were so different with her and I couldn't understand why.'

'Water under the bridge. How's the baby? Girl or boy?'

She rubs her belly and lights up.

'We don't know. *C'est une surprise.* Anyway, I better get back to work.'

I jump up and open the door for her.

'I hate to admit it but, since you have been seeing Ariella, you are a much nicer person to be around.' She gives me a kiss on my cheek before she leaves.

I hope it's true, because right now everything that is connected to Ariella makes me feel shit. It's not long until I see her and yet I am struggling to find the excitement. As much as she says her social media feed is manufactured, it has convinced me that she's having a blast, while I'm here, delivering her weekly groceries to the shelter and volunteering, to keep myself out of trouble on Saturday nights. Admittedly, I do enjoy the shelter, and sometimes when it's quiet I have good chats with Sue, the resident counsellor.

We've been slowly working through what happened with Melissa and the good news is that my nightmares and panic attacks have significantly decreased. The bad news is that the more I think about it and my current situation, the more trapped, manipulated and angry I feel. My only hope, to get through to the other side of that, is to hold on to what I know and love; but she is six thousand miles away.

This is why I need Ariella to be the girl I remember; and if she's gone, I'm pinning all my hopes on Lara. She's the only person I completely trust, to unapologetically and aggressively, if required, get past everything in the way to find the woman we love and drag her back to us; kicking and screaming if need be.

'You're such a loser, Caleb,' is the first thing I hear at the airport. I turn to see Lara lugging two huge suitcases. I should help, but I don't.

'We're only there for four days!'

'Unlike you, I don't do the sniff test, dimwit. Plus, I'd be more than happy to empty the cases right now and return the stuff you wanted me to take for Ariella. It's illegal, you know. You're supposed to carry your own shit.'

'Hand them over. I'll gladly take them. Four bottles of conditioner and one shampoo doesn't need two huge suitcases,' I challenge.

'I can't believe you turned me into a haircare mule. Just stand back when I check in and try not to breathe loudly.' She shoots me a dirty look before barging past to the check-in desk. I take my place behind her, dreading that I might have to sit next to her for the whole flight.

'Hello... Claire. Lovely name, just like my nan. Are there any upgrades available on this flight?' Lara asks sweetly, while presenting her passport and credit card.

'Yes, Ms Scott,' Claire responds, looking ready to do whatever Lara asks.

Lara upgrades the ticket I bought her to business class right in front of me, knowing I'll be stuck in economy. I'm ticked off but also relieved. At least I'll get some sleep on the flight. After Lara gets her boarding pass, I step up and, before I can hand my passport over, she's gone.

The next time I see Lara is at the luggage carousel, waiting for one of her bags.

'Hairy nuns, Caleb, what in the name of self-pity is going on here? You look like a pile of crap.'

'Thanks.'

We are met at the airport by Ariella's driver, who relieves us of our cases and drives us straight to her home. Ariella's housekeeper, a small but rod-straight, efficient-looking, fast-moving older lady with a razor-sharp bob, introduces herself to us as Ms Pat. She shows us around the massive penthouse duplex that occupies the entire top floor of the building. The living room is huge with high ceilings. The open-plan space is home to a fully kitted-out professional kitchen-dining area that could seat at least twenty, a comfortably plush-looking home entertainment area with a humongous TV and what turns out to be a temperature-controlled glass room with professional gym equipment. A large sparkly outdoor pool runs along the length of the living room, only separated from the inside by glass sliding doors. From where I am standing I can spot a large home office above us, with a single chair at a boardroom table that can easily fit ten. Ariella's home is so huge and so stunning, it looks like it is straight out of an architectural design magazine.

After Ms Pat gives us a quick tour of the living space, she reveals a passageway that presumably leads to even more space. Lara and I follow her down a corridor that splits the new area into two. Ms Pat opens the first door to the right to reveal a beautifully furnished room. It could easily be a luxurious studio apartment, with its own huge bathroom, oversize bed, walk-in wardrobe, book wall, fireplace and living area with floor-to-ceiling glass running along the external wall.

'Mine!' Lara shouts as she rushes past me, leaps on the bed and then rolls around on it childishly to claim it as hers. When she sees there is no contest, she claps her hands with glee. When Ms Pat is satisfied that Lara has stopped acting like a toddler, she shows her where to find towels, bathroom amenities and how to work the TV, and then asks me to follow her. Lara leaves her bags in her new bedroom and follows us to the end of the corridor, where she enters a second bedroom. It is a larger room than Lara's, with a similar layout, fixtures and fittings. It also has floor-to-ceiling glass on the external wall, but comes with an additional sliding door that leads directly to the pool.

'Mine!' Lara calls again, rushing towards the bed.

'Fuck off, Lara,' I declare as I push her out of the way into a huge armchair and throw my bag on the bed, claiming it. I am embarrassed by the look of shock on Ms Pat's face. I immediately feel like an arsehole for swearing in front of her but I figure it's only a matter of time before Ms Pat realises that Lara is feral and only responds to swearing and physically defensive moves.

'Is this Ariella's room?' I ask Ms Pat.

'No. She is next door.' She smiles warmly as she shakes her head.

'Please could you show me where it is? I think I am meant to be staying in there,' I ask as politely as I possibly can.

I follow Ms Pat out of the room. She points to the door next to mine while looking unsure, before she speaks quietly.

'I'm sorry but I can't let you in.'

Lara bursts out laughing hysterically, reminding me that she is still here. 'Caleb! You've been bounced.'

I wait for her laughter to die down, but it doesn't, so I continue. 'It's okay, I'm her boyfriend.' I laugh a little.

Ms Pat looks worried. 'Ms Ariella tell us to respect her privacy and not enter. Not even to clean.'

'It's fine.' I smile as I reach out my hand for the knob.

Ms Pat steps in front me. 'I am really sorry but I must respectfully insist you wait until Miss Ariella return.' She looks so adamant, I back off, and she relaxes.

She escorts us back into the living room and offers us a meal, which we both decline. I settle into the gigantic couch. It feels heavenly but, at the same time, my mind is spinning. There is just no way Ariella would have picked this. It's too much.

'Finally, something I can work with!' Lara exclaims as she flops next to me on to the stylish, light grey wool couch.

'It's a bit flashy for Ariella, isn't it?' I want her to agree. She doesn't.

'Just because it doesn't fit with the Ariella you know doesn't mean she can't become this Ariella, Caleb. Her job has changed. Her life has changed. To be honest, I don't know why she is still hanging on to you.' Lara yawns next to me.

I ignore her dig. 'I understand that, but why would someone

living alone in Singapore need all of this?' I consciously lower my voice. 'I mean, a housekeeper. Really?' Surely Lara can agree that this is not normal.

'You were dropped on your head as a baby, weren't you?' She stares at me, as if waiting on confirmation that she's right. After a few seconds she sighs. 'The apartment isn't for Ariella, you gigantic moron. It's for the COO of Ivory Bow Asia. Do you expect her to invite clients and partners to a tiny shared flat for a soirée where she passes around pineapple and cheese on cocktail sticks? Or have meetings at home around a crusty table with everyone sitting around on bean bags with wine spills on them? Get over yourself, Caleb, and look around. Can you see a single personal item of hers? Or anything, apart from the contents of that office, that relates to her? I suspect all traces of Ariella are confined behind the door Ms Pat blocked you from. Ugh. Honestly, what you have in pervy hotness was taken from your intelligence reserves, thicko.'

Lara is the most annoying person on the face of the planet but she's right. She has to be right. I am praying she is right. The relief I feel transforms my mood. I lunge at her, hold her down and tickle her.

'You think I'm hot!'

'Aaaarrgghh! I'm a lesbian, you animal,' she screams at the top of her voice as she fights to get away from me.

Ms Pat rushes into the living room to find me sprawled across the couch where Lara had been sitting and Lara, looking distressed, standing against the sliding door, clutching her midriff.

'Is everything okay?' she asks cautiously, looking at us like we're children.

'Yes, sorry,' I apologise quietly.

'I'm going out,' Lara huffs, walking out of the door.

Ms Pat and I watch her leave.

'You are brother and sister?' she asks, baffled.

'No. She's Ariella's best friend.' I smile.

'Ah.' Ms Pat chuckles, exiting through the door she emerged from.

I dig out my phone and turn it on. A flurry of texts from Ariella catch my attention and I respond to the last one.

> Welcome (back!) to Singapore Black. I'll be home early. Would you like to go out to dinner or stay in?

I can't help the smile that spreads across my face.

> My little Mason. Let's go out tonight. I got you a little surprise that might make staying in a little difficult. Can't wait to see you.

> I'm so happy you're here! How does East Coast chilli crab sound? I'm smiling from ear to ear and texting (very unprofessionally) during my meeting!

> Get back to your meeting young lady. This warehouse of an apartment isn't going to pay for itself!

> It does actually. Fill you in later. I love you, Black.

Those last four words take the wind out of me. She is delighted I'm here. She is still Ariella. Nothing has changed.

The text exchange makes everything okay. I relax immediately after that, take a shower and indulge in a jet-lagged nap.

When I wake up, it's half past six. Ariella hasn't arrived back from work yet, so I toss on some jeans and a T-shirt, ready to indulge in some messy crab. It isn't long before I hear the front door unlocking, so I head for it and am met by two people. It takes me a second to recognise our earlier driver and it's only when the woman speaks that I realise that it's Ariella standing in front of me.

'Thank you, Matthew.'

'I'll just take your files up to the office, Ariella,' he offers, walking towards the mezzanine.

'It's okay, you can just leave it here—'

'I insist, it will only take a couple of seconds.'

I study her closely as her eyes follow the box up the mezzanine. The woman in front of me is poised, calm and authoritative in a skin-tight, tailored, knee-length grey dress that clings to every curve; not that there is much curve to cling to. Her high grey suede heels finish her outfit off and comple-ment her immaculate waist-length, straight hair, parted sharply in the middle. Her eyes are huge and heavily lined, with unusually thick lashes framing them. Her lips are defined and coloured with a deep red lipstick. She is intimi-dating, sexy and fierce – until she looks at me, relaxes her posture and smiles. Ariella. Ariella is buried under there somewhere.

She straightens when Matthew returns.

'Thank you, Matthew. Have a lovely weekend.'

'You won't need me? You have a couple of engagements,' he whispers cautiously.

'They can come out of your diary. Please ask Lydia to update you.'

He nods and smiles before giving me a quick, unsure look.

'If you need anything, Ariella...'

'I will get in touch. Thank you, Matthew.'

'And goodnight to you, Mr Black.'

Before I can respond, he has left. 'He's a bit intense—' I don't get to finish. Ariella drops her document bag, closes the gap between us, slips her arms around my neck, and her lips are on mine. Yes! This feels amazing. Her lips are soft and familiar, pressing, pulling me closer to her with every breath. She smells the same. Grapefruit and apples. And gin. She has been drinking. I've missed that smell. She pulls away briefly.

'Hi.' She smiles. My heart stops.

'Hi.' Her lips are back on mine but her hands have moved and are undoing my belt.

'Ariella...' It's too fast.

'Shhhh...' she says quietly, smiling and then leaning back into the kiss.

She makes quick work of my zipper. She pulls away again, connects her eyes with mine, chuckles to herself and disappears. Unexpected panic rises in me as crystal-clear images of that night with Melissa resurface rapidly.

'Ariella, wait... stop. No!'

I step back abruptly, causing her to fall forwards and land on her palms from where she is kneeling. Everything goes quiet. After I have done up my trousers, I find the courage to look at where she's sitting, stock-still and silent, staring at the floor. I slowly crouch down so that our eyes will be level when she looks up.

'Aari...'

She looks up at me, ready to listen, but before I can say another word her face begins to crumple.

'Shit. No, no, no...' I scramble, as quickly as I can, across the floor, on my hands and knees towards her. I catch and fold my girlfriend into me just before she bursts into body-shuddering, heartbreaking sobs.

'I'm so sorry, Aari. I love you so much,' I repeat as I hold on to her for as long as it takes for her to quieten. When she eventually does, I suggest the only thing that I know will help.

'Shower?'

She nods, so I pick her up and carry what's left of my little Mason into her bedroom. It's tiny in comparison to the rest of the rooms, and small by normal standards. It is just wide enough to fit a king-sized bed. Two bedside tables covered with framed pictures lit by two warm amber table lamps and a chest of drawers is all she has.

I put her down to find her little bathroom. I have to squeeze past the toilet to open the shower door and turn the water on. By the time I return to the room, satisfied that the water is the right temperature, Ariella has stepped out of her dress. Her bone-thin frame is shocking. Her strong, lean, healthy body with its beautiful curves and soft bits in the most delightful places is now so small and fragile she looks like she could break. She has not been having a nice time, at all. I should have known; instead I abandoned her and prioritised my own emotions.

FUCK YOU, MELISSA.

I grab a towel from her chest of drawers and wrap it around her naked body.

'Thank you, Caleb. I'm really pleased you're here,' she whispers, avoiding my eyes, before walking into her shower room.

SIXTEEN

ARIELLA

I woke up this morning with butterflies, eager to see Caleb. Things have felt quite distant between us, so I'd been thinking about how to effectively press the reset button to take us back to how we were. I wore the dress Eden laid out for today and asked Ruby to make me look a little sexy. I had to repeat myself because she's become used to my reluctant submission. Her answer was an early hairdressing appointment, eyelashes, red lipstick and more of the usual batter she puts on my face daily. Bryce and Devin spent most of the afternoon making fun of my 'eye curtains'. I was about to take them off when Lara walked into our offices being... perfectly Lara.

'Lara!?' I ran out of my office, into her massive laugh and open arms.

'Yes. The one and only.' She swung her arms around and hugged me tightly.

'What are you doing here?' I held on, trying not to cry.

'That misogynistic pig you call a boyfriend bought me a plane ticket and said I was your surprise present. What's surprising is that he didn't wrap my arse up in a bow, brand

"Ariella" on my butt and parade me in here cuffed and naked,' she complained.

I couldn't help laughing. 'Come here!' I gave her another big hug. 'Is Caleb here too?'

She scrunched up her face. 'He's back at the house. He attacked me, so I left.'

'Ah.' Strangely, to hear that nothing had changed in Lara and Caleb's relationship made me feel safe.

'I may have suggested that he wasn't the ugliest bloke on the planet. He got excited, jumped on me and started tickling me. Knobhead.' She started to speak again but stopped, squinted, then took a couple of steps back to look at me.

'You're too, toooo thin. I don't like it. What have you done to your beautiful hair? I don't like that either. And are you wearing make-up? Bloody hell, they've plastered it on. Those eyelashes are going to cause a hurricane somewhere if you don't take them off. You agreed to all of this?'

I nodded yes to everything, sniffling through laughter, and hugged her again. I didn't care what she said, I'd missed her. She hugged me back tightly.

'I can't believe Caleb did this...'

'Yeah, yeah, Mr Promiscuity is a saint. Just blow him and get it over with... Ooooh... hello. Who are you?'

I followed Lara's gaze and found a nervous-looking Bryce trying to leave at the end of it.

'Hi, I'm Bryce...'

'An Aussie! Nice. I'm Lara. You're going to love me.' She winked at him.

'Er, nice to meet you...?' Bryce put his hand out, looking at me, unsure.

'Don't bother looking at her, Bryce. She can't save you. I am her best friend so I am automatically forgiven for everything. Do you have plans tonight? I am new in town and you're not going to leave a girl hanging, are you? Plus, you just got lucky. I'm the best wingwoman on the planet.'

Bryce straightened his back and adjusted himself to rise to the challenge.

'Sure, I'll show you around.' He smiled.

'Good luck, Bryce.' I laughed.

'You're not off the hook yet, Ariella. You're coming for a drink before you bugger off. Also, hand over your house keys. I'm definitely not returning tonight!'

I grabbed my stuff, while Lara invited Devin and Lydia to the closest bar to join us for a drink. When the dancing started, I kissed Lara and headed out.

At some point in the car, I decided to take Lara's advice to 'blow him and get it over with'. If that isn't a reset button, I don't know what is. When Matthew decided to execute the world's slowest package delivery over the shortest distance at home, it weakened my resolve, but I held on. The snarl on Caleb's face was hilarious but I didn't let that deter me. As soon as Matthew left, I could see Caleb was getting ready to have a conversation. I had no doubt it was the exact conversation we have been having over the last two months, and I didn't want to start the weekend by telling him that I'm not coming back home. The gin in my system gave me confidence.

His reaction was as shocking as it was devastating; every time I've felt weak and inadequate since I got here, which has been all the time, came bubbling up to the surface.

'Your shower is tiny,' he says now, leaning against the bathroom door.

It is. When I converted the pool room and outdoor shower into my bedroom, I didn't expect to be showering with company. The apartment is so huge and over the top that I only managed to live in it for a couple of days. Even the bedrooms are immense. Thankfully the pool room, designed as a shaded daybed area to hide from the sun, was slightly smaller than my room at university, so, with a little clever conversion with the help of our production builders, we turned it into a bedroom with a little shower room. It suits me perfectly. It is a nice, small, bright space that I occupy easily, closely surrounded by the pictures of the people that I love. This little room is my home, so it was important to me to have it exactly how I want.

'It is.' I force a smile.

'Scooch over?' he asks, waiting for my nod before he starts to undress.

I look at the space around me. It's going to be tight. As he opens the shower door, I move into the corner until he is in and closes the door. He grabs the shampoo and puts some in my hair.

'I brought you some bottles of your shampoo and conditioner from home. I kept to your magic co-wash ratio. I got six bottles of conditioner for every bottle of shampoo.' He smiles.

His thoughtfulness makes me well up.

'Thank you, Caleb.'

He shrugs and turns me around so he can lather my hair.

'And thank you for bringing Lara. It's the most wonderful thing you could have done. I don't know how to...' I choke up.

'It's okay. Truthfully, the earache I would have got if I had come out by myself would have been unbearable. The peace is worth every penny.' He laughs as he strokes my shoulder to soothe me. I imagine Lara attacking Caleb and I can't help laughing too.

'Before I forget, she told me to tell you that she is refusing to return tonight in order to protect herself from further attacks and preserve her innocence.'

'That girl.'

I catch the laugh in his voice and I want to see his face. I turn around again to kiss him and this time he takes full advantage of it. His hands rise to my face, travel down my neck, over my shoulders, down my back and to the bottom of my spine, where they stop. I want to stay in the shower, with water being the only thing between our bodies, for ever. I've missed Caleb. This Caleb. This kind, caring, attentive, quiet Caleb. These last few months have done their best to suppress him in my memory. I hold on to him under the water tightly with my hair half-shampooed for a little while, before his fingers start to move in different directions all over my back, starting the game we sometimes play in the shower.

I guess it immediately. 'Big Ben!' I laugh, and he laughs right along with me.

'Well done, my little Mason. It's good to see that your soapy Pictionary skills haven't diminished.' He kisses me again. 'Okay, your turn.'

We play a few rounds in the tight space until he loses a best of three, then a five run to me. Again.

'I'm never going to win, am I? Come on, let's rinse you off, this shower is killing me.' He gives me a quick kiss before he rinses me off.

He gets out, grabs a towel, wraps it around himself and holds another out for me to step into.

'I like your room, especially that bit.' He points happily to a picture of us together pulling silly faces. We'd taken it one laughter-filled afternoon at home.

'You don't mind that one?' I whisper, pointing to a picture of Jasper and me.

'Nope. He's way in the back, and he's not all bad actually.'

'Did you just say...'

'I'm not talking about Jasper tonight.' He shuts it down gently while stroking my face. 'Come on, let's stay in and get you fed.'

When Caleb pops next door to get dressed, I pull on some

underwear and a pretty, light cotton, mini yukata Melissa gave me as a moving-in gift before I follow.

'This is new.' He tugs lightly on the belt when I bump into him in the corridor. Seeing him is exactly what I needed. I've been drowning. I could feel myself hardening with the long hours, the challenge, the simple decisions that have been taken away from me and the loneliness. Everyone at work is sweet, but I hardly know them. Caleb being here makes me feel like myself again. Everything on my mind and the weight of carrying Ivory Bow Asia simply falls away with him around. Right now, I just feel like a girl in love with a boy. I watch his every movement as he opens the fridge, checks out the bottles, selects one, finds glasses, fiddles with the drawers trying to find a bottle-opener and figure out where the bin is. I smile to myself. I'm not alone, and when he moves over here I won't feel alone any more. I can't wait.

'What are you laughing at?' He smiles broadly as he makes his way over to the couch.

'You.' I am giddy with happiness despite the rough start to the evening.

'Listen, Lady Big Bucks, we live in a shack back home compared to this. Some awe on my part is allowed.' He plonks the glasses down and concentrates on opening the bottle. I take in every movement he makes and revel in it. 'Stop staring, Ariella. I am here all weekend. Can you find us something to eat? All you have in there are salads and cold cuts. Maybe get us a takeaway?'

I grab the tablet on the house deck and play with the screen, trying to remember how to order in from it.

'You haven't had a takeaway yet?'

'No. Ms Pat usually puts those bits in the fridge and, because I'm out so much, it's usually enough to pick at in between sleeping.'

'Aari, this job is killing you,' he states with quiet concern while stroking my washed hair, which is slowly returning to its original curly state as it dries.

'It's not that bad, I just haven't found the opportunity to go food shopping and use the kitchen, that's all.'

He gently takes the tablet from me, calls up an app, logs in with his details, puts in my address and hands it back to me.

'Here. Now you can order as much as you want. I'd recommend Chinese from Chau's for tonight, at least. They are really good and the delivery service is fast.'

The menu is so huge, after a few minutes I just go into his last orders and hit reorder before I join him, shoulder to shoulder, on the floor to sip the champagne he poured.

'Your TV is obscene, Aari,' he says, laughing, as soon as I take my first sip.

'I know! This whole place is obscene really.'

'Why are you here?'

'It's basically picked to look the part for entertaining clients. The office pays for it so that we can have tastings, meetings and maybe even little drinks receptions for our more exclusive clients. Mel thinks I should be giving them elevated personal attention.'

'As long as attention is all you're expected to give them,' Caleb murmurs. He immediately catches himself. 'I'm sorry, Aari,' he sighs.

'Why do you hate it so much?'

'Look at what it's doing to you. You look exhausted to the point of collapse, which is much more obvious now that all the stuff on your face is gone. You're so skinny, all your muscle tone has disappeared, and I bet you're not sleeping. The question is why are you enjoying this so much?'

'I'm not. It's the most punishing thing I have ever done.'

'Then quit. Come back home.'

'I can't.'

'Why?'

'Because I know I can do this. It's big and frightening and challenging but I want to prove myself and see it to the end.'

'Prove yourself to who?'

'Prove myself to me.'

Caleb, after a small pause, pulls me into a deep, loving kiss. His hand moves slowly up my thigh and it feels good. After a couple of seconds, he pulls away gently and gives my forehead a parting kiss. My heart falls. I want him closer.

'Everything feels off-track, Aari,' he whispers.

'I understand, but I tell myself that it's only for a little while, because you're joining me soon.' I run my hand through his damp, messy hair.

'Yeah.' His response feels non-committal.

I feel distance appear again between us. 'Caleb, what are you worried about?'

He opens his mouth as if to say something, then shuts it again.

'Nothing. Come here, my busy girl.' He playfully lifts me on to his lap so I am straddling him. He's deflecting, but his smile has returned.

'Caleb, is there something bothering you? Anything you want to talk about?' I meet his eyes, concerned.

'No. Like what?' He smiles a little too forcefully. Something is off. Caleb would usually have my underwear between his teeth by now. He's not his usual self. I decide to change the subject and bring him back to me, this time with a little nudge.

'Like how much you have missed me?' I try to flirt.

'Like you wouldn't believe.' He plants his lips on mine. 'I've missed your eyes. Your smell...' He pulls at my silk belt, loosening it but not quite pulling it apart. 'Your skin. Your body. That mouth.'

I feel him harden under me. I lean in to whisper in his ear. 'I've been thinking about the way you touch me all day, and now that you're here—'

The doorbell goes.

'Food,' I announce mid-kiss.

'Tell them to come back...' He smirks. Yup, it's terrible timing. I get off him.

'You did say they were quick!'

'They can wait.'

'Caleb, the one thing we both know you're not, is quick.'

'I'll take that as a compliment... what are you doing?'

'Opening the door?'

'Not dressed like that!'

'Caleb, I have left this apartment and gone to work engagements in much less...' I laugh.

'Disturbingly, I am aware!' he snaps sharply, walking past me to the door. I let it go because I don't want to ruin our night. I grab some plates and let Caleb handle the delivery. I don't realise how hungry I am until he starts to open the little boxes.

'Oh no, they brought us the wrong order!' I say as Caleb unpacks grilled oysters and a dish that looks like chicken livers.

'Don't worry about it. We have rice, noodles, some prawns and chicken.'

'I'll call them. Someone's going to end up missing their order.'

'Don't bother.'

'We should at least tell them they got it wrong and—'

'Aari. Just leave it.'

'Why? It'll save them the aggravation of trying to figure out what happened.'

'Because it's not the wrong order.' He sighs.

'But offal makes you gag, and oysters... oh.'

He doesn't look at me. The last time Chau's delivered, I guess he wasn't alone.

'It was a while ago, Aari.'

'Let's eat.' I force a smile.

We eat quietly with Caleb occasionally sneaking food onto my plate. I ignore him and eat all I can.

'That was good. I've finished.' I rub my belly and get up.

'No, you haven't. Sit.' Caleb motions his chopsticks up and down. 'You had a couple of small spoons of rice, two bits of chicken and a prawn!'

'I'm full.'

'You're worryingly skinny, Ariella, eat some more.'

'Stop being so controlling.'

Caleb is being particularly challenging and I don't like it. I really don't want to fight, but we are both making it a little hard not to. The tension I thought was gone is still here, bubbling under the surface, and straining to come through every bit of mundane conversation. It feels like an ever-present danger that we need to get past.

'You're going to have to tell me what's bothering you at some point, Caleb.'

He looks at me angrily. 'You, this, all of it.' He stares at me hard and accusingly. I move away and cross my arms. I'm going to fight back.

'Go on.' I barely finish before he starts.

'I have no idea who you are. I get that you're working your arse off and building an image but all that make-up, your clothes, your hair... you look cheap, common and desperate, and it's plastered all over the internet, Ariella. For someone that has always been crazy about ensuring that they have total privacy, you're absolutely everywhere. Flirting with this person, smiling with that person... do you even know who they are? Even the move into your... this flat is out there, with you looking like you're about to tongue an employee's face off. You're cosying up to another employee at the many envelope-openings you show up to, wearing barely anything.

'I couldn't wait to see you today, just to have time with you, the real you, but you turn up, rake-thin, caked in make-up –

like... Then you drop to your knees to try to give me a blow job? It almost gave me the ick. I've never been so happy about your obsessive showering. I was so relieved to see it all come off, to make sure you were still under there. And now you won't eat – you love eating. So right now, I want to know: who are you? And what the fuck have you done with Ariella?'

He's shouting by the time he has finished.

I feel a familiar and numbing stillness come over me. It gives me the courage to look at Caleb, right in the eyes.

'Get out, please.' My words are calm and clear but my heart is in my throat, my ears are ringing and I feel like I am about to regurgitate dinner.

'Great. Hello, Icy Ariella. At least I can rely on you showing up to throw me out.'

'Get your stuff, please, and leave.'

Caleb stares hard at me. I stare right back. I am not going to drop my gaze, even though I can feel the tears welling. All I need to do is not blink. He's not going to see my tears. He has been cruel, brutal and unkind; he doesn't deserve them.

'Gladly,' he finally responds, walking into his room. Pregnant with distress, I step outside, shut the sliding door behind me, and make it to the edge of the pool before I let myself howl from the heat of soul-crushing pain under the night sky.

Caleb, carrying his weekend bag, walks to the other side of the pool and stops directly opposite me. 'I think I might be done with us, Ariella.'

'Okay.' At least the uncertainty is gone.

'I'm sorry,' he apologises softly.

'No, you're not. You've been feeling around for an exit since I accepted this job,' I state as a matter of fact.

'Maybe I was just fooling myself that I was happy and this relationship thing was me.' He shrugs.

'Don't be a coward, Caleb. You were in love with me, and I you. You want to finish it? No problem, but don't you dare tell me we didn't make each other feel safe and free.' I seethe. 'You know what the problem was? Your absolute dogged, inexplicable resistance to moving out here. You've somehow convinced yourself that my move to Singapore was all about getting away from you, when in fact it was the opposite. I didn't abandon you, Caleb. I abandoned everything, to start somewhere else with only you. All you have done tonight is prove that you don't even have the courage to try.'

I don't wait for a response. I retreat to my bedroom and lock myself inside. By the time I emerge, broken, the next morning, he's gone.

SEVENTEEN
CALEB

I knew I wasn't ready to return to Singapore when I bought those flights to see Ariella. I was prepared for some discomfort as I wrestled with it internally, but I didn't expect last night to end the way it did. It started sort of weird, but I thought we'd get past it – I'd expected Ariella to have changed a little, of course – but she was too different.

I wasn't myself either. I had to continually remind myself to keep my mouth shut about Melissa because, every time I said anything, I was petrified that it was going to come tumbling out. The gown threw me. I knew Melissa must have given it to her; she had one exactly like it.

The food had been an own goal. Chau's was Melissa's favourite, but I never could have imagined a scenario where Aari wouldn't care what she was eating. She is normally meticulous at making her menu choices.

I wanted to tell her everything – in fact it was the only option I had last night, if we were going to survive whatever Melissa is dreaming up – but there was just too much to tell and too much to lose. Events unfolded so quickly that instinct took over and, in that moment, I chose to break up and suffer the pain of watching helplessly as she walked into her bedroom with my heart.

As soon as I'd checked into the Hyatt, I headed straight to the bar and spent the whole of my first night in there, drinking until I eventually got cut off this morning. I have now spent the day trying to fall asleep in my room. I was hoping the drink would knock me out, but nope, I'm drunk and awake, with nothing to get out of bed for. Eventually, my phone beeps. It is a text from Ariella and my heart leaps.

> Hey Caleb, you left your phone charger and some clothes. I'll get everything cleaned and packed so Lara can bring them to the airport. Aari x.

That's it. Like nothing happened, no hostility, no anger. She even put her usual kiss at the end. I'd purposely left them there so I could have a reason to go back. She has retreated into her shell and is nipping it in the bud. She's not interested in where I am right now and doesn't want me to come back, for anything.

I want to text a million things. I'm sorry. I don't want to lose you. I am a fucking idiot. Let's talk about it. I love you. Forgive me.

Instead, she gets:

> Ta.

Full stop. No kiss, nothing to indicate affection. I didn't even use her name. Just acknowledgement. I am such a shit. I don't deserve to be happy.

I'm lying there deciding whether or not to text something else when my phone buzzes again. I leap at it. I'll do better texting back this time.

> Caleb, what the fuck is going on? I just got
> back to Aari's. Where are you? Are you okay?
> Please let me know you're okay. It sounds like
> we could both use a drink. I'm buying. I will
> meet you wherever you want. Text me back.

This is the nicest Lara has ever been to me. It only solidifies the fact that Ariella and I are well and truly over. I'm not sure what's worse; having drinks with Lara being understanding or Lara being insulting. I can't handle either. I trudge to the shower and stand under some cold water. I catch a whiff of Aari's soap on my skin; I can't escape her in here either. I speed up the process, get dressed, pick up my phone and dial.

'Mel speaking, who is this?'

'You know who it is.'

She lets out a little laugh. 'Hi, Caleb. Are you in town?'

'You know I am. Where are you?'

'Home.'

After all this time, I still don't know where that is.

'We need to talk.'

She giggles. Melissa does not giggle. Ever. 'Marina Bay. Our place. See you in twenty minutes.'

I regret the call and every subsequent step I take until I knock on that door an hour later. She opens it with a big smile.

'It's my favourite employee,' she greets me happily.

'Hello, Melissa.' I do my best to hide my disgust.

'Caleb! Why the miserable face?' She sticks out her bottom lip and pinches my cheek.

'I don't want to be here.'

'Then why did you call?' She smiles insidiously. 'Drink?' She walks to the fridge and pours out two glasses of white wine.

'Where's the butler?' I ask suspiciously.

'Short notice.' She walks over and hands me a glass. I put it down immediately. She laughs as she sinks into her white sofa and crosses her legs. 'Why are we here, Caleb?'

'I just came to tell you that Ariella and I broke up and we are never getting back together, so you can stop whatever you're up to.'

'I don't understand.'

'You've won whatever game you're playing. Ariella and I are done, so you can call your plans off.'

'Why would I do that? Ariella is exceptional and, unsurprisingly, much more impressive than you are. She is intelligent, astute, works unbelievably hard and, I don't say this lightly, is possibly one of the most competent people I have come across. Singapore is in love with her. Even I have fallen in love with her. Her colleagues respect and admire her, she is kind to her subordinates and she is fair.

'The only thing she has going against her is that she is exceptionally private and deafeningly quiet, because she is painfully lonely. I've tried to get us all to reach her on a more personal level but she pulls away every time. That wall is thick and not coming down. So, I decided to move your Singapore start date up. You start in four weeks. Not for you, but for her. Now you're standing here telling me that you've broken up with her. How does that make me happy, exactly?'

'You moved my start date up?'

'I just told you that the only person that managed to chip through that selfish, misogynistic exterior, and bothered to dig really deep to find and excavate some kind of beating heart in there somewhere, is at best worryingly lonely and at worst depressed, but all you ask about is your new start date?'

'I'd rather not be here and you know that!'

'You're still focused on you, Caleb,' Melissa states incredulously.

I sigh and sit down for the first time since I arrived. 'How bad is it?'

'I don't know. I'm a surgeon, not a psychologist, but if we've all noticed, it's not good. Her performance is incredible but she has become very detached. When she first arrived, she fought us on everything. The house, the office, her clothes, make-up, even her PA. Now, she just gives in and doesn't even protest. I fear we may have ground her down.'

'Shit.' I'm such a selfish bastard.

'Yes, shit. Your girlfriend needs you, Caleb.'

I bolt from the room. By the time I get downstairs, Melissa has called the concierge to have a cab waiting. I rush to Ariella's, only to find Lara looking solemn on the couch, opposite a coffee table littered with open snacks, tissues and wine bottles.

'What did you do?' she says, deeply concerned.

'Where is she, Lara?' I demand.

'I can't... she's inconsolable,' Lara says apologetically.

'Where is she?'

'Give her some space, Caleb. Are you okay?' Lara approaches, arms outstretched. I can't do this with her. Not now. I take a chance and tap her name on my phone. She picks up.

'Where are you?' I try to ask gently.

'I'm at work. Is there—'

'I'm coming. Please don't move.' I hang up.

I rush back out, jump in a car, and I am at the Ivory Bow offices in fifteen minutes flat.

'Ariella!?' I call out as I navigate glass cubicles and mirrors, before I walk into a big guy – and recognise him immediately as the guy from the picture.

'You okay, buddy?' He doesn't look remotely concerned about my welfare.

'Is Ariella here?' I look around him and spot her in a glass office tucked into a corner at the back of the room.

'Never mind, I can see her right there.' I move and he steps in front of me.

'I'm not sure this is a good time... it's a little late.'

'It's fine. I'm her friend.'

She looks up, spots me and emerges from her office. She forces a painful smile as she walks towards us. Her eyes are red and swollen, and her face is puffy. It breaks my heart. I want to kick myself in the nuts. I did this to her.

'Hi, Caleb. Devin, meet Caleb; Caleb, Devin.'

I pretend I don't know who he is and shake his hand. 'Aari, can we talk?' I say.

She nods, walking back to her office. I follow.

'Good to meet you, buddy.' Devin intentionally walks into me, hard. I take it; I have bigger problems.

Aari's office is basically an immaculate fishbowl, so there is no getting away from Devin's eyeline. I look around for somewhere to obscure his view. Aside from two large white sofas, a fridge, coffee station and a large white work desk, there is nothing else. Ariella heads straight for her chair. I know she wants to keep a desk between us, but we need privacy. I follow her to her side of her desk and sit on it facing her, with my back to the door.

'How can I help you?' She swivels to look at me, trying to be composed. She's not. She may be trying her best to channel Icy Ariella but her hands are shaking.

'Last night got out of hand, Ariella.'

'You broke up with me, Caleb. It happens,' she states matter-of-factly.

'Only after you told me to get out.'

'Which was after you made it clear that you are repulsed by me.' She has no emotion in her voice or on her face. Fuck. Icy Ariella is firmly back in place. Of all the Ariellas I could be speaking with right now, she is the worst.

'That wasn't what I meant.' I look away, ashamed.

'What did you mean, Caleb?'

'I just meant that you were different.'

'How? Cheap, common and desperate?' she asks.

Oh, bloody hell. If I had time, I would have planned to

handle this better. But then I see a teardrop fall from Ariella's cheek to her hand as she quickly looks away to wipe her face.

'Ariella.' I reach out for her and she rolls her chair out of my touch. I've fucked up. Badly.

'You might want to start thinking about leaving, buddy.' Ugh. Devin. Of course he's in here, he's had front row seats to what is going on.

'Listen, mate, I am here until she asks me to leave. This is none of your business, so if you could just fuck off, that'd be great.' I square up to him.

'It is my business. You're making her cry. It's time to leave.' He takes a threatening step towards me.

Fuck this shit. I escalate the situation by taking all the steps I need to close the gap between us completely. I never throw the first punch but, if he wants to take a swing, I'm ready. There is no point dancing around it. I know I'm being deliberately antagonistic. I've wanted to lay into him since that picture.

'Can both of you just stop it?' Ariella asks tiredly. 'Devin, honestly, I am okay.'

'Are you sure? I can remove him if you want,' he says, narrowing his eyes at me.

'I'd like to see you fucking try,' I goad, staring right back at him.

'It's okay, Devin, please could you give us a minute?'

'Yes, on your bike. She's fine,' I enforce, going back to my original place beside her. She watches him leave and shut the door behind him before she turns to me.

'Caleb, please go home.'

'Let's go together, we can talk—'

'No, I'm sorry. I meant wherever you're staying. It's over, Caleb.'

'Aari, please. I didn't mean to end it last night. I am finding all of this really impossible to deal with. There is so much going on. Can we just talk? Please?'

She's thinking about it. I am getting through.

'Come on, Aari, can we just get out of here? We don't have to go back to yours. Let's just leave, get some air, grab some food, go for a walk, just anywhere but here.'

She looks at me for a good few seconds before she starts packing up her things. I breathe a sigh of relief as I take her laptop from her. I need to get this right.

Devin meets us on our way out. 'Call me if you need anything?'

I cringe when he gives her a hug. She looks extremely uncomfortable being hugged by him. I breathe through it because I can feel my temper creeping to the surface. I relax. It's what he does next that tips me over the edge. The second he holds her face and kisses her forehead, I lose it. I shove him away from her, punch him and, before I know what is happening, he has landed one right back. Then I am on him.

It takes a little while before Ariella, screaming for me to stop, filters through. She has dropped her bag and is trying to pull me off him. I come to my senses and see a bloody and battered face. I stand up and stand back. Fuck.

'Go home, Caleb!' she screams, kneeling by a bleeding Devin, who is attempting to get up to have another go. He lets Ariella hold him down as she rummages in her bag with her free hand. I go straight back to the hotel, pack my bags, head to the airport and get on the very next available flight to Heathrow.

By the time I get back home, I've decided that I am done with Ariella.

Screw this relationship bullshit. I don't need this kind of grief. I don't need anyone. I've managed to drag myself up since I was seven, and I was absolutely fine before she turned up.

The very first thing I do as soon as I get in is clear my bedroom of everything that belongs to her. My drawer with her clothes, her products in my bathroom, and her toothbrush. I put them away in her bedroom before I retrieve everything that is mine.

I box up all her spices from the kitchen and put them away, out of sight. I pick up all her bits around the living room and get rid of the washing powder she keeps next to the washing machine. My adrenaline and I spend the next two hours erasing my home of Ariella.

I put all her possessions neatly in her room. I leave her picture of us on her mantel in her bedroom; she can deal with that herself. The one in my bedroom gets put in the bin. Frame and all.

After that is done, I walk to buy a lockable doorknob, take out her door handle and replace it. I do a thorough sweep to make sure that I got everything. When I am content, I lock the door and separate the four keys. I grab four envelopes, pop a key in each one and get them ready to be posted to her parents, Zachary, Jasper and to the Ivory Bow office in Singapore with a simple note.

'Changed the locks. Ariella's bedroom key spares.' No sign-off.

I block both her UK and Singapore phone numbers. She can tussle with voicemails I don't want to hear, and texts I don't want to read. I can't block her emails because she's going to be my boss. It's fine though, I am happy to keep it strictly professional.

I call her grocer and butcher to change the delivery address of her order, so that it is delivered directly to the shelter. I'm never going there again. Finally, I call an emergency, same-day cleaning service for a full house clean and jump in the shower. As soon as they arrive, I leave the place to them and call Jack to find out where he is.

Caleb Black is back.

EIGHTEEN
ARIELLA

Caleb did so much damage that Devin had to take a week off because of the swelling, the stitches and the loose tooth. I'd never seen that side of Caleb, and it was shocking to witness. He was always so happy, patient and gentle with the kids in his Muay Thai class that I forgot that he was teaching them how to immobilise an attacker quickly and cause damage if it was necessary.

None of this was necessary.

It is easy to blame Caleb for the way he reacted, but Devin had been deliberately provocative since he got on the floor. I saw him walk hard into Caleb when there was no need to, his stance in my office had been excessively threatening, and for him to hug and kiss me like that, regardless of Caleb's presence, was invasive and crossed a huge line.

There is no question he did it to infuriate Caleb. I got the email outlining his intent to take legal action against Caleb the following Monday. He also stated that he was going to ensure that Caleb did not take up the position in Singapore. When talking him down privately didn't work, I had to get Mel involved, which meant informing her that Caleb and I had broken up. Thankfully, she agreed that we need Caleb because his track record in Singapore is remarkable and it would be almost impossible to find someone to match his sales success.

We are already getting some interesting enquiries based on the media we've been generating, but we need a big hitter and closer like Caleb to drag in and lock down those lucrative long-term contracts. My five-year plan and projections centre round Caleb coming in to pull those figures in. We've already hired and are inducting four full-time project managers, so Mel has brought his start date forward to get a jump on our projected sales.

In the end, to satisfy Devin, Ivory Bow Asia assumed Caleb's legal responsibilities and we quietly came to an agreement. Before Devin eventually agreed to let it go, he sent a vindictive and less than truthful email to Ivory Bow UK about Caleb. Thankfully, the team there are bound by bulletproof confidentiality agreements, so whatever happened will stay within the office, meaning that Caleb will be moving out here as planned.

The break-up has been brutal for me. This isn't the sadness and guilt I felt separating from Jasper. This is excruciating, gut-wrenching pain. The grief I feel from the loss of Caleb is sharp and relentless, but knowing that he will be here soon makes me inexplicably happy.

That night, after a long stretch with Devin at one of Mel's family's hospitals, I felt the need to reach out to Caleb, but his phone was off. We did need that talk.

He was right. I'd changed and I wasn't comfortable with the way I was either. I just didn't have the courage to say it to myself, so Caleb said it for me. Harshly. And I reacted by shutting him out. Lara, after listening, feeding, entertaining, wiping my tears, wrapping herself around me and getting me drunk for the rest of the weekend, concluded that we had both been stupid to throw something so 'disgustingly wonderful' away. She pointed out that what Caleb had done, albeit much more severely than necessary, was smack some reality into me.

So, when Lara left, I did what I should have done a long time ago. I moved the make-up artist and the stylist from their permanent roles to freelance contracts, so that they could be called on only when needed. To ensure they had no loss of income, I gave them joint responsibility for the fashion and beauty section of our blog, expanded their service contract to include the entire team and made them collaborate with Lydia on our social media.

They joked that they'd probably never hear from me again; the stylist filled my dressing room with some jeans, fitted shirts, jackets and shoes, while the make-up artist put together three months' worth of skincare products and a regime that would allow me to leave my face bare but nourished and protected.

Now that we have project managers, I delegate most of my evening events to them. They are a passionate, intelligent and vibrant all-girl team, so heightening their profile is a great thing for us, and empowering for them. They enjoy representing Ivory Bow, trying new products, meeting new suppliers, visiting new venues and posting about them.

The time I reclaim by making those changes now allows me to sleep, eat and practise yoga in the mornings. The work is still hard, the learning curve still steep and the days still long, but I am no longer tired all the time and I am having fewer panic attacks.

Maybe Caleb and I can talk things through when he moves here. I miss him terribly. He is obviously keen to get out here too, because he has put locks on all our doors and sweetly mailed keys to me and my family to make sure my things are safe. I have tried to call him to thank him on a couple of occasions but his phone keeps going to voicemail.

. . .

Mel felt that Caleb should arrive from London with some fanfare, so a profile had to be built quickly on all social media platforms to document the transition. I intentionally stayed away from it, because every time I hear his name, it hurts. I knew that he would get the same profile treatment as I did. There will be posts focused on him being out, happily attending different events, and I didn't want my imagination to run away with me. I am doing well until Devin appears one afternoon, tablet in hand.

'You need to see this. We might need to rethink how we position Caleb. He's not what I'd call "on brand" at the moment.'

What I am looking at isn't off brand. It is in an entirely different solar system. While I was going to elegant red-carpet events, exhibition openings and gala dinners, Caleb's profile has him squarely positioned in the late, fast and hard corner of the industry. In almost every image or video, he is partying hard in black faded jeans, plain T-shirts and an array of leather and cut jackets. I don't recognise this person.

Caleb in a packed nightclub doing shots with a vodka brand owner. Caleb hungover in sunglasses on a private plane. Caleb on stage with... is that Stormzy? Caleb leaving a nightclub, pulling a girl behind him, with his other hand covering his face. Caleb looking exaggeratedly helpless while being simultaneously kissed on each cheek by two beautiful women with 'PCD' printed on their tiny tops. Caleb in a huge hot tub, drinking straight out of a champagne bottle, surrounded by people, mostly female. Caleb on a beach, dancing next to a huge bonfire with another girl. Caleb playing guitar with a member of a rock band. Caleb fully clothed in a swimming pool, laughing and pointing at the camera. Caleb at the Grand Prix, in the pit. Caleb with a very familiar-looking brunette sitting on his shoulders at a concert, and seen again, piggybacking her on to a private jet. Caleb drunk, smiling lopsidedly at the camera. Caleb asleep on a couch with a VIP backstage lanyard and pass hanging from his neck. Caleb laughing with band roadies, having a beer, with scantily clad girls in the background. Caleb looking worse for wear stepping out of a cab drunk. Again.

I have to stop because I can't take it any more. When I shut off the tablet, I feel sick. I compose myself before I walk to Devin's desk.

'Thanks, Devin. It's not the direction I would take, but I can see why they would with him. He looks like a rock star. It suits him.' I hand the tablet back before I return to my office.

'I think it threatens the brand. We should set up a call with Mel, Bryce and the PR company to talk about it.'

I go straight to my office and shut the glass door, which is normally left open. I have no idea who is going to be walking into the office in a week's time, but it sure as hell isn't going to be the Caleb I am in love with.

NINETEEN

CALEB

Why I am moving into Ariella's building is beyond me. Not that I care, I am over her. The last few weeks of unrestricted freedom have made sure of that. To build an online media profile suggested by our PR company, I've made it to four continents and sold Ivory Bow all the way.

After our chat in the pub, I sent Jasper everything I had on my clients to identify any suspicious activity while I replaced them with more lucrative accounts. We still hadn't found anything to suggest that I'd broken the law the way Melissa hinted that I may have. If Jasper finds anything remotely questionable about any of our clients, I am going to subtly sabotage the relationship so that they fire Ivory Bow. Even though we are over, Ariella is in this position because of me, and I can't leave her with what I've done.

Surprisingly, Lara provided the springboard to new clients. She texted me one afternoon, warning me that Devin's email describing an 'unprovoked and unexpected wild attack' had landed in Chris and Harry's inboxes. Shortly afterwards, I was asked to clear my desk before the end of the day. It didn't take long. The last thing I did was shred the photo of Ariella and me that I'd moved from my work desk to my bottom drawer.

'Thank Themis you guys aren't together any more!' Lara declared after yet another tequila. We'd been in the pub having my leaving drinks since five and it was now almost eleven.

'Yeah, it's easier this way,' I responded.

'You were so insecure, you let it get the better of you. I always knew that you fucking up was only a matter of time. It's a shame, I'd never seen her that happy.' She poured some more tequila in her glass and knocked it back.

'Can we not talk about—'

'They say you can't polish a turd, but she somehow managed to polish *and* rehabilitate you. How do you, the poster child of misogynistic mediocrity, mess it all up – unsurprisingly, I might add – and still get to fly off to Singapore? Seriously though, am I the only one not failing upwards at this point?' Lara complained.

I decided that I wasn't going down this road with a clearly very drunk Lara, but she continued.

'Do you think that Devin bloke is going to try to slip it in? He's got big hands. I'd a hundred per cent let him get it if I was that way inclined.'

'That's enough, Lara.'

'It's nowhere near enough. You're a coward. She didn't deserve the way you—'

I refuse to take any more of Lara's drunken abuse, so I walk straight out of the bar.

Surprisingly, she called the next day to apologise, only the way Lara could.

'If you're going to Singapore to become some top sales guy, you're going to have to start with some large accounts. I have to work at another music awards thing tomorrow night. If you come with me, I'll get you a VIP pass and introduce you to some heavy hitters.'

'You were bang out of order last night.'

'Whatever. You coming or not?'

'I'll be there, but I don't want to talk about Ariella any more.'

'Sure.' She, however, had one last kick in the nuts. 'But, if you can leave pre-Ariella Caleb at home, that would be great. That guy was a major creep.'

True to her word, Lara made some key introductions, and I took every opportunity handed to me, accelerating my Ivory Bow Asia sales account portfolio.

Now I am here, in my new Singapore flat, talking to a stylist. She is basically revamping my whole wardrobe and is talking suits, jeans, immaculately tailored shirts and edgy jackets. I make a note to invite myself along to some of her industry events when I know her a little better. The fashion industry would be a great sector to attack, especially if we are injecting this amount of lifestyle into the brand. Ariella has warmed them up already by appearing on some best-dressed lists. I wasn't thinking about clothes while I was still in London, so if someone is going to do that thinking for me, they're more than welcome.

I got ahead of my impending workload and hired a fight trainer in London for daily workouts. I've found it difficult to train over the last few weeks because of how busy it has been, and it's only going to get worse out here. Enter the hot, ferocious and absolutely barbaric MMA fighter Honey Kohli. I imagine that I am going to have a lot of fun with her.

She arrives just after dawn the next day. Training is much more brutal than I anticipated; and at the end of the hour she leaves me close to dead next to my swimming pool. This is exactly what I need. When she leaves, I shower and head into work. Everyone is at their desk by the time I get in at eight and I am immediately welcomed by the project team.

'Caleb!' The four ladies crowd around, all happily talking at the same time. I could get used to this. Devin is at his desk, growling. A guy I know is called Bryce approaches and offers a solid handshake.

'Good to meet you, mate, glad you're joining the team.'

I like him and imagine that he'd be a good drinking buddy. I shoot a quick glance at Ariella's office. Her door is open but she is on the phone behind her Mac, typing away. All I can see is the top of her head bobbing.

I am approached by someone who I believe is Lydia, Ariella's PA.

'Hi, Caleb. I'm Lydia.'

'Lydia! Thanks so much for all your help getting me settled.'

'You're welcome.'

'I hear you run the ship and you're the person I really need to keep happy.'

'No, not really...' She smiles before she looks away, embarrassed. I don't delay any longer; I make my way to Devin's desk. He looks up at me coldly.

'Hey, man. I was in a bad place. Let me buy you a beer after work?'

He leans back and looks at me suspiciously before he slowly puts his hand out. 'Sure.' He gives me a firm handshake and returns to his screen. He isn't going to be easy to win over.

I notice that Ariella has finished her call and is packing up her desk. When she stands and I catch a full view of her, my heart almost stops. Shit. She looks gorgeous in the white tee and jeans I am used to seeing her in. Her hair is back to its usual curly mess, piled on the top of her head. Her face looks bare, bright and healthy. She is still a little too skinny but she is filling her clothes and some curves have returned to her body.

She looks like my little Mason as she walks towards me.

I've been preparing for this moment but it was all useless; she still makes my heart leap. I'm going to need much more time to get over her completely.

'Hi, Caleb. I'm glad you're now with us, we've all been excited.' She sticks out her hand and gives me one of her smiles. I forgot about that smile. All my resistance disappears and, when her scent finally hits me, I am transported back to London, walking out of the shower with her. It takes everything I have to resist the urge to reach out and grab her.

'Glad to be here, Ariella.' I use her full name purposely.

'I'm sorry I can't stay this morning, I have some meetings, but maybe we can catch up later? Lydia has your induction plan and she can take you through it. I hope that's okay?'

'Of course.'

'Great. See you later.' She smiles warmly, slides her sunglasses from her hair down to her face and walks out of the door. I force myself to walk to Lydia's workstation just so that I don't watch Ariella leave.

Lydia's desk is minimal and organised neatly, aside from a massive bouquet of large white roses on her desk. It's only then that I realise that there are flowers all over the office. We're probably picking a preferred florist.

'We actually don't have much to do for you today. Bryce has your contract and package waiting, so he just needs some signatures from you. Your iPhone and your MacBook are set up, synced with your UK profile and at your work desk. I've put everyone's contact details in your cell phone and I have synced your diary with mine so I know what you have coming up.'

'The boss wants to keep an eye on me, eh?' I smirk.

'No, Ariella trusts us. I have all senior management's diaries synced with mine so I can plan internal meetings. I assume you will be out of the office a lot, so rather than having to call you I can insert meetings when you're free and put appointments in for you, if you wish.'

'Sounds very organised.'

I get a small smile. 'Devin has your credit cards and will go through your budget. The staff manual and all our policies are in your inbox. That's it.'

'Thanks. Nice flowers, by the way.'

'Erm, thanks.'

I notice she looks uncomfortable but I don't push it.

I make my way to Bryce and Devin, then end up with the project team – Bree, Jess, Sian and Akiko – to find out which projects we are working on, so that I can include them in my client visit schedule. By the end of the day, I have filled my first two and a half weeks with meetings and I am feeling so good I want to celebrate.

'Right. My welcome drinks. Let's go to Sky Park. I'm buying.'

The project girls pack up quickly, with Sian and Jess leading the charge. Bryce and Devin promise to meet us there shortly. Lydia is non-committal because she has to wait for Ariella, who hasn't returned since she left this morning.

At Sky Park, I order some beers and colourful cocktails for the team as we get to know each other. By the time Bryce and Devin show up, we are dancing and I'm selfied out.

'We are going to need them sober for tomorrow, Caleb.' Bryce laughs as he pats me on the back. 'Good to finally meet you, mate.'

Just then Devin walks up.

'Beers and bygones, gentlemen?' I hold my own beer up and hand them a bottle each from the bucket.

'Bygones,' Bryce starts, even though it has nothing to do with him.

'Bygones.' Devin raises his bottle and takes a swig.

.   .   .

I can't help laughing to myself when I am the first to turn up at the office the next morning, just before eight. Lightweights. I like the office. It's nice and bright with lots of space, which I am hoping to fill with worker bees soon. I am whistling to myself as I walk past the kitchen and spot Ariella making herself some tea. I stop but it's too late. She has heard me. I am going to have to talk to her.

'Hi,' I offer quickly, trying to play it cool.

She turns around.

'Hi.' She gives me one of her shy, unsure smiles before turning back to grab her tea. This girl is not going to make it easy for me. She starts to walk out of the kitchen but then stops. 'I got that coffee you like for you, but I think the guys have developed an appreciation for it too. Sorry.' She chuckles.

'Yeah, thanks.' Shit. That came out more dismissively than I intended.

She looks hurt. 'Caleb...'

Just then, Lydia makes her entrance, wearing sunglasses. When she joined our drinks last night, she certainly wasn't shy about ordering.

'Coffee! Please!' she begs as she approaches.

I start a brew for her, chuckling to myself. She really must be suffering. The Lydia I met yesterday seemed like she'd rather die than ask anyone to do anything for her. The project girls join us soon afterwards, playfully insulting me as they come in. One of them is carrying a massive bouquet of flowers that is almost bigger than she is. I immediately know that's Akiko because of how tiny she is.

'Awww... Akiko, are they for me?' I ask.

'Akiko, just leave them...' Lydia instructs, a little too quickly.

'Ooooh, no. I want these ones.' She giggles.

'We have enough flowers in the office. Are we picking a new

florist?' I ask. The office is full of them. Each of the girls has a bouquet on their desk, there are flowers in the kitchen and even in the conference room. The only place where there aren't flowers is Ariella's office.

'No. Ariella gets them every day.' Akiko fills me in.

She has a boyfriend. Clearly Ariella hasn't shared that she only likes three flowers – peonies, ranunculi and – specifically – amnesia roses.

'Devin!' I yell across the office.

'Yo.'

'I'm thinking you need to cut the flower budget and get a real salesman in here.' I laugh, knowing someone is going to fill me in.

'She doesn't buy them, silly.' Akiko giggles. 'She is being wooed.' Her big brown eyes widen as she laughs happily, revealing her deep dimples. She is so tiny and cute, it's hard to be annoyed at anything Akiko says.

'Wooed? By who? Who woos anyone any more?' I ask her playfully.

'We don't know! It's so romantic. For the past couple of weeks, she has been getting different types of roses from a secret admirer. Aren't they beautiful?' She puts her head into the flowers and inhales. Okay. No boyfriend, just a wannabe stalker. I try not to smile.

'Indeed they are.'

I take a sip of my coffee as I subtly watch Akiko deliver the flowers to Ariella from the kitchen. Ariella, looking unimpressed and exasperated, searches unsuccessfully for a card and hands them back to Akiko, who I assume asks Ariella if she can have them. Ariella nods and smiles so lovingly at Akiko, it makes my heart melt. Akiko leaves Ariella's office happy.

'Do you want some flowers?' she asks me.

'No thanks, you have them, Akiko.' I love saying her name.

'Great, Ariella said I could take them home.'

I look towards Ariella's office. She's behind that damn screen again. She's probably dating and just not telling anyone. She has moved on and is happy. Good. Me too.

By afternoon, our photos from the night before are up on social media and PR is already all over it; they're running it in parallel with ones of Ariella looking less celebratory at an industry event. The images of us at the bar having fun already have '#badboyblack' attached to them.

By late afternoon, invitations to various events start trickling into my inbox, but I still haven't had a directional meeting with Ariella, so I ask Lydia to put one in. I just don't expect Lydia, Bryce and Devin to join us in the conference room.

'So, Caleb. What direction would you like to go?' Ariella starts as she sits down.

'I have three different types of accounts. My historic accounts that I need to reach out to, the new Singaporean accounts picked up before I got here and my new drinks, car and music accounts. They are three completely different demographics that I would like to throw client evenings for, but they don't exactly sit side by side.'

'Are you saying you want three different parties?' Devin asks.

'Yes, and I could use some support facing the traditional accounts.'

'Three parties are not going to work,' Devin pushes back.

'Yeah, mate, I agree. We need to find a way to combine them. We need synergy now, especially as the brand personality has been split a bit,' Bryce adds, apologetically.

'Caleb, do you think that if we came up with a holistic concept, all three could come together in one place? We could perhaps fold your clients and goals into the company launch?' Ariella asks, just before she winces silently. It's quick but I catch it. I know what that is, and I glance at the date on my phone just to confirm. Yup. She's going to need her painkillers, a hot-water bottle and her chocolates.

'Will you also be inviting your clients?' I've seen her client list. Snooze fest.

'Yes, it's the launch. We can work with the project team to come up with a common thread.'

'That makes sense – we can also look at getting more value from the budget if you have it at your home and keep it to a hundred and fifty guests.' Devin is taking this to a place I don't like. Ariella's flat? She'll be trying to kick everyone out to get ready for bed before things really start to jump off.

'Caleb, can you work with fifty guests?' Ariella asks.

'No, I'm going to need at least seventy-five.' I need to flood this launch with my guys to prevent it from ending at nine.

'Done. The rest of us will split the other seventy-five. What timeline are you looking at?' Ariella turns up the pressure.

'I'll have all my meetings in for the next month, so I was thinking in a couple of months? When I see them, I can sort the wheat from the chaff and send out a personal invite that suits the demographic.'

'Devin, can we do that financially?'

'Based on Caleb's performance history and the projected sales on the companies we have now, it would be a good investment – as long as at least half of the guests are new clients that are yet to use us and the project sticks to budget.'

'No problem.' I lean back.

'Okay, Caleb, you have your party. Devin, can you email us the budget parameters and maybe we can meet in a couple of days to review expenditure?' Ariella smiles and gets up, signifying the end of the meeting.

'And face-to-face support?' I interject. It's obvious she can't wait to get out of here.

'What do you mean? We will all be at the launch, we just

need to make sure that we know and understand each client's needs,' she responds.

'Some of your clients are on my hit list, Ariella, and I'm going to need to build relationships with their marketing and communication directors. My image is very different to yours, so it would be nice to go to the meetings with someone that can represent that.' It's obvious I mean her. I regret the wording as soon as I use it.

'Devin, Bryce, do you think you could attend some meetings with Caleb?' Ariella asks.

'Sure.' Devin laughs. He knows what I just tried to do. Clearly all isn't forgiven.

'Good.' I shrug. 'I will flag all the ones that we could tag-team on.'

'Is that all?' Ariella takes a step towards the door.

'Yep. Let's get cracking.'

Now that the meeting is over, I open my laptop and fire a message to Lydia.

cblack:

Hey Lydia, please can you get Ms Pat to always have these at home for Ariella?

I attach some links to the products.

lli:

mathez cacao truffles, feminax and a hot water bottle?

cblack:

Yup. Laderach milk chocolate also works. She likes the nutty ones. Can you make it look like it did not come from me?

lli:

Sure. I'll get these ordered and tell Ms Pat to prepare for their delivery tomorrow. The chocolates can be a gift and Ms Pat can mention the other items in passing.

cblack:
Thanks.

I look up to see Ariella working away at her desktop. There. She can handle her own Shark Week from now on.

TWENTY

ARIELLA

Caleb is fantastic for team morale. We went from a focused, quiet, office to a chatty, laughter-filled one. Even Lydia has shed her rigid efficiency and is more relaxed. Hungover mornings have increased exponentially, but client interaction and new business enquiries are up. The PR company was right about Caleb's impact. We've started to get interest from younger brands and the tech industry, which has had a positive impact on the business.

The news about the launch has also boosted the team's energy. The project team came up with some amazing pool party concepts, but worryingly, the more Caleb is involved, the more the launch morphs into a club night in Ibiza. So, apart from some 'Caleb tethering', the plan for the launch is going well.

I, on the other hand, am struggling. Work is great but the challenge of controlling my emotions while sharing a working space with Caleb is a daily battle. He is the life of the office and the pipeline to our clients, so everyone really likes him and they can't do enough for him.

Inside, I am still a mess, and there is no way I am getting

over this boy any time soon. I long for him so much, I moved my desk to obscure my view of the office with my computer screen; because every time I see him, my heart leaps. He, however, is enjoying himself, living his best life, and while I am pleased he is happy, I sometimes wish we could still be on the couch in London watching *The Sopranos* while he plays with my hair, or in bed holding hands while we make love.

My body aches too. The other day, I saw him lick some ketchup off one of his fingers and I felt myself twitch. Down there. But I know it is too late for us. He has been quiet about it but I know he has a new girlfriend living with him. I've seen the stunning, athletic, petite blonde in gym wear leave in the morning to work out quite a few times already. I've always been friendly to her in the lift, as we often catch it at the same time.

One day, the lift stopped on her floor and she got in. I was about to smile my usual 'good morning' to her when I heard Caleb.

'Honey, hold the lift!' He ran out, shirtless, with a hot-water bottle for her. My heart sank as I held back the tears that sprang from knowing exactly what that hot-water bottle represented. Shark Week was hers now.

He spotted me and stopped. 'You're going to need this today,' he said, revealing that smile I love. After giving her a quick kiss on the cheek and promising to see her later, he returned to his apartment. He didn't even say hello.

I spent the rest of the day trying not to fall apart. The good news is, I now know that there is no going back.

Over the past few weeks, Mel and Georgie from the PR company had been strongly suggesting that I start dating, especially with the launch coming. I refused, because they didn't seem to be asking that of the boys – they'd happily pointed out that it was in our best interest for Caleb to be perceived as single, but insisted that dating someone would soften my image and make me more 'real'. Whatever that's supposed to mean. I naturally pushed against it but Mr Anonymous kept sending flowers, and he became the bit between Georgie and Mel's feminism-betraying teeth. When I finally agreed to consider it just to ease the pressure from them, Georgie went digging to find out who he was. It turns out that Dominic Miller the Sixth, a respected entrepreneur, socialite and womanising playboy, is the person who has been sending me the flowers. No, thank you.

'No one is asking you to marry him. Just hang out with him a little and maybe turn up to a couple of things with someone that doesn't have it included in their job description. Show people you have friends. Besides, those flowers scream that he's pretty keen.' Mel chuckles.

'I don't want to lead him on...'

'No one is leading anyone on. Say thank you for the flowers. Make a friend. Let's humanise you. I'll text you his number now.' Georgie backs her up.

'Can't I make a female friend instead? I'd rather not be humanised as arm candy. I'm trying to run a company, not become gossip fodder.'

'You do know that this will happen eventually, right? Your paths will cross. Dominic Miller will eventually put you on the spot when he picks up the phone to call you or, worse still, when he bumps into you at a party in front of people you don't know. You're already in the same social circles, so it's only a matter of time. Why don't you call first and be in control? Maybe take him to dinner somewhere expensive to say thanks?' Mel suggests.

'He sounds unpleasant if he'd do that publicly.'

'Just do it, Ariella. You can't keep showing up alone, or with Bryce or Devin. Caleb is slaughtering you in personality and popularity. It's not a competition, but we need to keep your vision of Ivory Bow out there and remind everyone that you're his boss. We can't do that if you fizzle into obscurity because people have stopped caring. He may have started this with flowers, but think of it as meeting someone in your business network. He's the founder of DMVI and a potential client, for goodness' sake. If you land DMVI as a client, you'll smash Caleb's sales targets for the first year with that one win. You want industry respect and to be seen as a competent and successful COO? Land DMVI. But it starts with a phone call.' Mel sounds frustrated.

I can get behind reaching out to collaborate professionally. 'Fine, I'll call him.' I give up.

'Good. I know it's a strange way to go about it, but Dominic Miller is a great professional contact to have. You have my permission to kick him in the nuts if he makes you uncomfortable in any way.' Mel chuckles, trying to lighten our tense call.

I leave the call and tap in Dominic Miller's number before I lose my nerve. I'm going to hate this.

'Hello, please could you put me through to Dominic Miller?'

'I will try his PA. May I ask who is calling?'

'Ariella Mason, Ivory B—'

'Hold please!' The operator cuts me off.

The phone clicks and goes silent before it starts ringing again.

'Awwww, man! I'm glad you called, but my florist is going to be pissed.' It's him. His voice is friendly, deep, and he has the same accent as my cousin in Chicago. I feel a little more at ease and laugh.

'She's had a good run.'

'My florist is a he and built like an Olympic weightlifter. Thankfully, we have minimal physical contact. You don't want more flowers, do you?'

164

'No thank you, the office is filled with them. They are beautiful though.'

'Did I manage to send your favourite? A little birdie told me you had a favourite rose.'

I laugh. He's easy to talk to. 'I do.' I am surprised he knows and can't imagine who that little bird could be.

'You're going to have to tell me. My florist is desperate to know.'

'Amnesia roses.'

'Shit. I spent a fortune on those Juliets.' He laughs.

'I'm sorry. Can I make it up to you?' It's out before I realise it.

'Ariella Mason.' The minute he says that, my heart jumps. The only person who says my name like that, although in a different accent, is Caleb. 'Are you asking me out on a date?' he suggests cheekily.

'Goodness no!'

'Wow. Don't sound so enthusiastic over there.'

I can hear the smile in his voice and I relax. 'I was going to maybe buy you lunch to say thank you?'

'Dinner tonight sounds great. What am I going to wear? I am going to have to get my hair blow-dried...'

I laugh along with him. 'I know you heard me say lunch, but I can do an early dinner too. Wear jeans, we're going for ramen in some tiny place in the middle of Chinatown. Expect nothing fancy.'

'Great. I'm down. I'll pick you up at eight,' he suggests.

'No, thank you. I'll pick you up at six. Your entourage are still sleeping then.'

'You're such a romantic, Ariella Mason.' He laughs. His voice is dripping with sarcasm.

'I've been told,' I respond, deadpan.

He goes silent for a beat and we both burst out laughing.

'I'll pick you up from work. I'll be appropriately secretive and entourage-free.'

'I can just meet you there?' I definitely don't want him coming into the office. Caleb is out today but I'd like to do this away from questioning eyes. Dominic Miller is not unknown to most.

'I want to see my failed roses. See you at five thirty.'

'Do you ever do as you're asked?'

'Nope. Do *you*? See you at five thirty, Ariella Mason.'

And with a little chuckle, he's gone.

I watch him come through our doors at quarter past five and ask for my office. Everyone looks at him and then, almost at the same time, they look in the direction of my office. I hide behind my screen. He looks very different from the images I asked the internet to provide earlier on this afternoon. In his images he is always in a perfectly fitted suit, with his strawberry-blond hair neatly cut and combed to the side. His challenging eyes are always staring straight and confidently into the camera. Today, his hair is shorter but messier, complementing his light stubble, worn jeans, T-shirt and a biker jacket. I notice he is carrying two motorcycle helmets. Goodness, no.

Lydia sits him down in the reception area and calmly walks into my office before she freaks out.

'Dominic Miller? Ariella! Seriously? Dominic Miller? He's been sending the flowers? Are you going out on a date?'

I'm glad Caleb has been teasing Lydia gently out of her shell, but right now I'm thinking she maybe needs to spend less time with him.

'He sent the flowers, and it's not a date. I'm just taking him out to dinner to thank him.'

'Shall I make a reservation? You're not dressed appropriately!' she scolds.

'He has shown up with two helmets. I think I am appropriately dressed.' I look down at my blue jeans and white Converse sneakers.

'You have to be careful with him. His reputation with women isn't the best.'

'It's just a casual thank-you dinner. Truthfully, my hidden agenda is to see how likely we are to land him as a client.'

'Where are you going?'

'That ramen place you keep telling me about.'

'That place is a dump and they only have six tables. You can't take him there!'

'It's not a date, Lydia.' I laugh.

'You have directions?' Lydia looks unconvinced.

'Yes.'

'Shall I send him in?'

I look over at where he's sitting. Sian, Bree and Akiko are already making friends with him, while Jess is laughing at them from her computer.

'Let's leave him until he's ready to come in.'

When Lydia returns to him, he gets up and confidently strides across the office. I smile and stand when he walks through my open door.

'Dominic Miller the Sixth.'

'Ariella Mason.' He pauses... is he checking me out?

I point to the chair on the other side of my desk. 'You're early.'

'Always.' He focuses his eyes on mine long enough to make me duck behind my computer.

'Goodness, you're beautiful. I thought you were beautiful before but seeing you now, it's taken my breath away.'

'You can't say things like that.' I laugh, reprimanding him lightly.

'Why?'

'Because it's embarrassing.'

'I forgot you Brits don't know how to take a compliment.'

'Exactly. Can we keep it to creative cutting sarcasm, please?'

'Goodness, you're ugly!' he announces, making me laugh.

'Well done, Dominic. You're learning,' I praise. 'Please would you mind giving me ten minutes? I just need to finish this.'

'No problem. I could also use the time.'

He opens up his messenger bag, pulls out a laptop and starts tapping away. He looks surprisingly comfortable.

It's hard to believe that I'd only spoken to him for the first time a few hours earlier. I finish my wrap-up and shut down my computer.

'You done?' he asks, raising an eyebrow.

'Yes.'

'You're going to need to do something with your hair.' He points at the curly hair piled on top of my head, smiling. I take my hair ties out and put two Pippi Longstocking plaits in. My mind goes straight to Caleb. These are his favourites. Just as I think about him, he walks in. Oh no. This is bad. He isn't meant to be in today. I am going to have to walk past him with Dominic. It can't get any worse.

'You are too adorable— I mean, you'll do, I guess,' he corrects himself, chuckling. I'll give it to him, he's charming. He reaches into his messenger bag and pulls out a leather biker jacket. 'You're going to need this.'

I am absolutely not going to wear that jacket to walk out of the office. Even though we have broken up and Caleb has a girl-friend, I don't want to rub the fact that I am going out to dinner with Dominic Miller in his face. I fold the jacket into the smallest possible square I can. I know it's silly, because we're over, but I can't help it.

I leave my bag in the office but put my wallet in my jeans pocket along with my phone and keys.

'Okay, let's go.'

Dominic grabs my hand and pulls me out of my office and through our open-plan space, walking ahead of me. This is a nightmare. Thankfully, Lydia does exactly what I was hoping.

'Ariella, you've left your bag. You'll be back later?'

Thank you, Lydia.

'Yes, I'll be back soon, I have some work to finish off tonight.' I say it loud enough for Caleb to hear, not that he'd care. He doesn't turn away from his computer.

'That's what she thinks,' Dominic says. 'Come on, Ariella Mason.'

Caleb's head moves to the side swiftly and stops. Then he goes back to typing away on his laptop.

As we walk past the project team's desks, Dominic sweetly bends over their cubicles.

'Bye, giiiiirrrlllssss,' he sings.

'Bye, Dooommmiiniiiiic!' they respond in unison and burst into giggles.

'Man, I love your office,' he shares as we step into the elevator.

We get downstairs, and parked there is a beautiful motor-bike. He pulls my leather jacket round me, zips me up, puts my helmet on and helps me onto the bike.

He revs the engine loudly. 'Hold on, okay?'

We whiz through the streets of the city, weaving in and out of traffic, and, I have to admit, the ride is thrilling. We get to the ramen place in twenty minutes, just as they are opening. We descend the stairs and grab a couple of seats. I order whatever they think is the most popular item on their menu.

'You haven't been here before, have you?'

'No.' I shake my head.

'Then why did you pick it?'

'I've been here for four months and all I know are beauti-fully shiny, overly sanitised venues, my home and the office. I

169

have seen nothing of the real beating heart of Singapore. And I kind of don't want to be seen in public with you,' I admit quietly.

He laughs hard, loud and long. 'That's a first. Can I ask why?'

'Well, I wanted to thank you properly but not be caught up in your reputation...'

'And what reputation is that?'

'Womanising playboy.'

'Ah. My favourite. You know, I could just be single, looking for love and making the wrong choices.'

'And love will find you, Dominic. I am sure of it.' I try not to laugh, and fail.

'You have a reputation too, you know.'

I am mortified and all my insecurities rush to the front.

'Don't look so worried. It's bad but it's not *that* bad.'

'I don't believe you.'

'Okay. The first rule of dealing with a reputation is to know that you have one. You're beautiful, obviously hard-working, elegant, trustworthy, but a little cold, definitely unapproachable, perhaps boring, distant and maybe a little lonely?'

I force a smile and try not to look hurt. 'That's me!'

'I also know you've had your heart broken.' His mood changes and he looks directly at me with concern. He isn't smiling.

'Hasn't everyone?'

'Yes, but we all have to let the light back in eventually, and I don't see any cracks yet.'

'We? You've had your heart broken, Dominic Miller the Sixth?'

'Oh yes. A lifetime of rejection has steeled this little muscle here.' He taps his chest with his index finger.

'You, rejection?' I laugh.

'The minute I am certain blackmail is not on your passive

hobbies list, I have a catalogue of frightening high school photos to share with you. I've had enough heartbreak to last me a lifetime, so there's no way I'm having my heart broken again – unless I let it.'

'Don't let it. It sucks.'

'I can imagine. His loss is my gain though.'

'Your gain?'

'If it hadn't ended, you'd be married and answering to Mrs Goldsmith on a completely different continent, and I wouldn't be here, having dinner with you.'

He is out of his mind if he thinks I am going to respond to him flirting right now. 'And how do you know that?'

'Everyone knows that. Your engagement was announced in the *Times*. Twice. Both in New York and the UK. Latest rumour has it you got dumped so you took the job in Singapore to get away from him.' Dominic leans back, looking proud of himself.

'We're done here.' I put my hand up to call the waitress for the bill.

'You're leaving?'

I throw him a disgusted look, because I refuse to respond. He can't be serious. Of course I am leaving. He can keep his DMVI dollars. I'm better than this. My remit does not include being emotionally tortured. Besides, even if I wanted to explain my life to someone, it sure as hell isn't going to be him. I look back to the reception desk to grab someone's attention.

'Ariella.'

I don't bother to look at him. I pick up my phone and push my chair back. If the waitress won't come to me with the bill, I will gladly go to her, on my way out.

'Wait.' He reaches for my hand and I pull it away.

'Domin—'

He cuts me off. 'I ran away too. See this girl?' He unlocks his phone and scrolls through quickly.

I'm not interested. 'I really don't think—'

'I can't believe I'm about to tell you this.' He puts the phone in my line of sight. There's a picture of him, shirtless, holding a coffee on the terrace of what looks like a vineyard, being hugged from behind by an elfin brunette in a man's tuxedo shirt. They both have their eyes blissfully closed with their heads leaning towards each other.

I stop moving.

'Her name is Mack. Well, Mackenzie. This was taken the morning after my wedding. She's now married to my older brother Maximilian. They have kids I'm supposed to love, but I'm struggling.'

He's not lying.

'Stay. Our stories aren't dissimilar.' He reaches out his hand to touch mine and I move it away quickly.

'What do you want, Dominic?' I truly want to know. He takes a deep breath and sighs.

'Full disclosure. You probably don't remember but we bumped into each other at the LVMH party about a month ago. I'd seen pictures of you online at some openings and thought you were kind of cute, but when that blogger at Fashion Week posted that video asking you what you were wearing and you unapologetically, without hesitation, responded that you had absolutely no idea, I knew we'd totally get along. We only managed to say a quick hello walking in because that Australian guy you work with was guarding you like a hawk. I watched you being happy, smiley and fully engaged with everyone that came up to you most of the night; but I also saw you crawl into a corner the first chance you got and silently wipe tears away with a smile still stuck on your face, just in case anyone was looking. You looked so wounded, I couldn't look at you any more after that because I knew exactly what you were feeling. Behind that smile, your heart was screaming in pain. I felt the same for a long time and, sometimes, I still do. So, I started sending you flowers. Just to let you know that someone, somewhere, was thinking about you.'

I calm down. I remember that night. I'd just broken up with Caleb and Bryce got hyper-protective when he heard what had happened with Devin. He decided he was going to come to every one of my evening functions with me and return me home safely. Dominic is telling the truth. I wiped away more than a few tears that night. I start tearing up now.

'Shit. I didn't mean to do this to you. I just thought we'd hang out and get to know each other when you found out it was me. I think I'm kind of inexplicably drawn to you and your war wounds.' He laughs.

'I don't need to be saved, and I don't want a boyfriend.'

'I have no intention of trying to save you – and trust me, the last thing I want is a girlfriend.'

'Any chance of me sleeping with you is also zero.'

'Damn. I was hoping for a little action...' He laughs. I don't. 'I'm joking! I'm joking!'

I try not to break into a smile but I can't help it. 'No, you're not.'

'I did think about it. More than once. In the last fifteen minutes.' He chuckles and I join in. I want to be offended, I really do, but I am struggling.

'No dating,' I clarify.

'No dating, but I do want to hang out with you. I think you might actually be a lot of fun. I could also use your help shaking the womanising playboy image, because my love life is the pits.'

'I am not going to be a fake girlfriend, Dominic.'

'I was thinking of just actual friends.'

'I can do that.'

'Friends?' He extends a palm and I shake it. 'Now, my first friendly duty is to propose we cut through all the bullshit.'

'Gladly.'

'I am going to give Ivory Bow all our events in Asia. You

know, start small. If you guys don't mess our engagement programmes up, we can talk about global contracts. Also, I have some new tech I want to play with, so I'd like to work together to build an Ivory Bow app. If you agree, we'll be seeing a lot of each other at update meetings. Two hours at a time of your choosing...'

'This all sounds good but, if I'm honest, slightly sketchy. If you're serious about Ivory Bow taking on your projects, I'd like for us to go through the tender process and earn it, like anyone else. Every aspect of Ivory Bow must be transparent and should welcome scrutiny. I think an app for us could be exciting but certain restrictions must be applied. For example, access to our client database is a hard no because that would put us in frankly indefensible territory.'

'You're hot as hell, do you know that? Jasper Goldsmith is an idiot.'

'We've had this conversation, Dominic,' I remind him.

'Fine. You've already been through our procurement process. Ivory Bow UK took care of it because you have no trading or execution history as Ivory Bow Asia. The team is more than satisfied. Also, there will be no access requirements, and we can walk through anything else. If you're worried that I am bringing this up after sending you flowers every day for a ridiculous amount of time and that we are doing this at dinner, the process started before we met and you've effectively put a stop to any future romantic shenanigans. Although I must warn you, you could, at any time, fall for me and I can't be held responsible.' He raises an eyebrow at me and it makes me laugh.

'In the spirit of transparency,' he goes on, 'I asked the guys to send a memorandum of understanding to your legal department while I was sitting opposite you in your office. Your project team clinched the deal. They are... irresistible.'

'They are razor sharp, experienced and talented too.'

'So, now that work is out of the way and we're friends, will you let me show you non-shiny Singapore?'

'I'd prefer not to be part of your circus.'

'Give me some credit. I turned up on my Ducati today, didn't I?'

After a delicious meal, I pay and we ride back to the Ivory Bow office, where he drops me off. I try to hand the helmet and jacket back to him.

'Keep them. If you want to outrun my "circus", as you call it, you're going to need them.'

'Thank you, Dominic. I had fun tonight.'

'Me too. There is a lot more fun to be had, Ariella Mason, especially with your birthday coming up, ooooh, next month.'

'How did you know that?'

'Different little birdie. I had to tell you at some point that I was the one sending the flowers and I thought it might be a good day. Now you know, we should do something else.'

'I'm just going to have a quiet one.'

'That's what you think. Now, go into your building before I ride off.'

He waits until I am in, then revs his engine and disappears into the night. It is half past nine before I walk back into the office and everyone has left – apart from Caleb.

When I see him, the butterflies in my tummy take flight before the panic sets in because the safety of additional eyes and schedule constraints is gone. My heart wants to sit on his lap, tell him everything I am feeling and hold him close. I miss his arms around me, his smell, his lips. I miss the way he buries his face in my hair and whispers my name.

'Hi.' I speed past.

'Hi,' he responds, keeping his eyes on his screen.

I make it to my desk and hide behind my monitor to catch my breath. When I start to pack up to go home, I notice he is doing the same, so I stop, giving him the chance to leave first.

175

When he doesn't, I text to ask Matthew to bring the car up front. I spring up from my desk and walk as fast as I can without running towards the elevators, while trying to look casual. I don't want him to think I am trying to stay away from him, which I totally am. Just as I walk past, Caleb shuts his laptop and makes his way to the lifts at the same time.

'Going home?' he asks politely.

'Yes. You? I thought you had a thing tonight.'

'I had a late call, so I'm just going to hit the hay.' He yawns a little.

Don't offer him a ride, I urge myself.

'Can I give you a ride home?' Ugh.

'Sure. Thanks.'

I dive for the corner of the lift when it arrives, and press myself into it. Caleb, however, stands in the middle, feet apart, taking up all the space he wants. We start to descend in silence. When I notice that I have fallen in sync with the way he breathes, I intentionally breathe out of sync and put my hands behind me to keep myself from grabbing him.

I am grateful when the door opens and the lobby air rushes in. The car is waiting outside by the time we exit the building, so my relief is short-lived. We sit silently in the car for a little while and, when I can't take it any more, I excuse myself from Matthew, turn off his microphone and put up the glass partition. Caleb quickly shifts as far away from me as he can. It hurts.

'Caleb, do you think we could try to get past this and be friends?'

'Being friends is not going to work.'

'Can we at least try?'

'No, we can't try, I have seen what happens to your *friends* and I don't fancy listening to you droning on about your love life with Dominic the Ginge.'

I try to hold back the laughter but I can't. Caleb joins in and, for a few seconds, everything feels normal.

'Dominic the Ginge? Caleb! He has nice strawberry-blond hair.'

'Don't give me that strawberry-blond crap, he's ginger. There's nothing wrong with being ginger. Most of the hottest women on the planet are ginger. He just needs to own it and ditch the highlights.'

'He doesn't have highlights. Does he? I can't believe you went there.'

'Yes, I went there.' He smiles at me and I can't breathe. Now is my chance.

'For the record, I'm not dating Dominic. We just went out for ramen,' I explain.

'Ariella, we dated, it ended pretty shittily and we are now in this fucked-up situation. Let's just make the best of it, move on and keep it professional. Whether or not you're dating Singapore's budget version of Jasper makes no difference.'

'Surely there must be a way to salvage our friendship.'

'Um, no. I'm not Jasper, Ariella. I'm never going to be cool with you shagging someone else while I am still pining for you.'

'That's a bit harsh.'

'It is. Welcome to the real world. You were exceptionally lucky to get Jasper. People usually get a bastard like me.'

'You're not a bastard, Caleb.'

'I think you'll find the ladies that kept me company before and after our relationship might disagree. Ariella, I just need you to be my boss and, as my boss, this conversation is kind of inappropriate.'

Silence falls between us for the rest of the journey. I hold back the tears as, in the back of the car, my heart breaks all over again. When we get home, Caleb jumps out before the car has even stopped, so I take my time getting out and walk as slowly as possible to the elevator in the hope that he has caught it and left. Yet, there he is, holding it open for me. I get in and press my floor.

It isn't until we are past his floor that I realise he has forgotten to press his.

'You forgot to press your floor.' I smile tightly.

'I'll come up with you and go down again.'

How could I still be longing for him after what just happened in the car? He was dismissive and horrible. But I still feel the pull that keeps us orbiting. When we reach my floor, I exit but turn around to face him.

'Goodnight, Caleb.' What I actually mean is, 'Come home with me, we can work it out. All you have to do is step out.' I watch the doors shut but the lift doesn't change floors. I wait where I am. Maybe he is thinking about it. In my mind, I beg for the doors to open so he can step out. 'Come out of the lift, Caleb. Come on,' I subliminally message him. Shortly after, I hear a loud thud come from inside the lift, just before it starts to change floors.

I need to come to terms with the fact that it's over.

TWENTY-ONE
CALEB

What the fuck was wrong with me? Seriously?

'I'm never going to be cool with you shagging someone else while I am still pining for you?' Bloody hell. I might as well have showed up with a neon sign, screaming, 'Take me back, Ariella!'

Singapore is not going well for me. Well, that's not strictly true. Work wise, I'm killing it. We are the hottest new company in the city and the enquiries are pouring in. The team is fantastic, bright, fresh and dedicated.

Personally, it's nice to have a fresh start, with a reputation that I'd gladly lean into, rather than push against. I'm having a great time with it. People seem to be lapping up the '#badboyblack' hashtag, which is hilarious because it couldn't be further from the truth.

I may be out almost every night, but I am drinking nowhere as much or having as much fun as people think. I just make sure it looks that way. I have 'getting the party started' down to a fine art. I arrive, introduce myself to the loudest and cockiest crowd, arrange a huge round of drinks, get the DJ to change the music and give it a good hour of intense flirting, opportunistic photographs and theatrical happiness before I sneak off home.

Training with Honey is murder, so I need the sleep. It kills my nights out but it keeps me busy, out of trouble, and dispenses with my, er, let's call it excess energy.

It's not that I am not getting any interest, in fact far from it. I am just focused on what I need to do here. In exact order, I am going to:

1. Legitimise or get Ivory Bow's services terminated from all the relationships with companies that Melissa called in for me. If there is something going on, cutting those ties as soon as possible is the only way to solve the problem. This is my shit and I'm not going to leave it for Ariella to clean up.

2. Make a shitload of money and useful contacts in the next two years before I get out of here for good. However, if by some miracle Ariella quits tomorrow, I'm handing my notice in straight after her. The faster we get out of here, the better.

3. Stay the hell away from Ariella, regardless of whatever I may be feeling, doing or generally thinking about.

So far, I am on track for one and two. Three, on the other hand, is impossible.

My behaviour tonight was shameful. I should have left with everyone at the end of the day. Instead, I cancelled an amazing sales opportunity to make a pretend phone call just so I could stalk Ariella. I just wanted to see when and if she'd come back to the office with that rich prick. I found myself silently cheering when she returned reasonably early, until I noticed the helmet and the biker jacket she'd carried out earlier. There's going to be a next time.

When I caught her yawning out of the corner of my eye, I got hit by a truck of multiple feelings all at once. I wanted to kiss her. I wanted to tell her that I was sorry and that she fucked up too. Taking this job was selfish and allowing it to change her to the extent it did was reckless. I wanted to tell her that I was proud that she's rediscovered who she was. I wanted to grab her by the hand, take her home with me, crawl under the covers, tickle her belly and make her giggle. I wanted to expose the parts of her soul that nobody else saw; that I know still belong to me. Sadly, that wasn't going to happen because she destroyed mine.

'Going home?' That was all it took to get a ride. She ran into the corner of the lift to avoid me, so I spread out in the middle, just to remind her that there was no escape. Unfortunately, there was no escaping her either. I inhaled that smell of Ariella that I loved so much, and, with no Bryce, Devin, Lydia or project girls to keep me in check, it took everything not to reach out for her until the lift doors opened.

It came as a complete surprise when she excused herself from Matthew, pulled up the partition and turned off the driver mic. I had to move away and sit on my hands to stop myself from grabbing her, then I went into panic mode. I redirected all my energy to making sure she couldn't see that I was destroyed because of her. It all went downhill from there.

She wanted to be friends. Hell no. She isn't going to get permission to do what she likes, while I am forced to watch powerlessly and smile, pretending everything is just fine. Didn't she realise that saying yes to being friends was me basically consenting to my own torture? There is no chance she is getting my seal of approval to carry on with that Dominic. I needed to protect myself in the back of that car, so I resorted to childish name-calling. Big mistake. The instant I heard that laugh, my chest exploded. I did everything I could not to join in, but I failed and my guard came down temporarily. I was so pissed at myself, I dragged Jasper into it. I shouldn't have. He has become a friend and I often spend longer than I should talking to him about Ariella. Yes, she is eating, no, I am not going to talk to her. That sort of thing.

When I pretended that I was screwing around and I wanted nothing to do with her outside of work, I saw her blink away the tears as she looked out of the window. What did she expect? I begged her not to take this job. She took it. She told me she would forgive me for anything. Instead, she threw me out of her house and told me to fuck off home. Now she's rubbing my face in it by dating Dominic Miller and displaying the guy's helmet and leather jacket on her office coat rack for all to see? Friends, my arse.

The car had barely stopped before I leapt out. I darted for the lift but, when I got to my floor, I couldn't step out. I had been an arsehole and made her cry, so I took the lift back down to the ground floor and waited. I wanted, more than anything, to follow her out when we got to her floor, but thankfully my head won. As I walked into my apartment, opened a beer and sat on the floor of my kitchen alone in the dark, I was both pleased she was far away and devastated that I wasn't right next to her.

Needless to say, Dominic moved in fast. There he was, in our office pretty much every day that week and the following week, going through the contracts for us to look after his client engagement programmes in Asia. Next thing I knew, he was trying to organise a little surprise party for her birthday. When Lydia told me, I could barely contain my irritation. No doubt he had already secured an invite to the launch party.

I'm not buying the whole Mr Nice Guy routine. Everyone has fallen for the perfect teeth, free lunches, the impromptu trips out and the cakes he brings back for the team when he sometimes pops out. He is almost too at home at Ivory Bow, and specifically in Ariella's office; so much so, he now has a dedicated desk that he steps out to whenever Ariella needs some privacy.

When they are alone in there, he lounges back on her sofa, laptop in lap, apparently working and performing some kind of one-man show, because he won't stop talking to her. He makes her smile often and she's had a good laugh with him a couple of times. The project team thinks it's cute and secretly calls them Dominella. Yuck. Lydia's position is unusually neutral and, the last time I tried to gossip about it with her, she just stated that she likes seeing Ariella happy. Bryce and Devin are, at most, suspicious. It pisses me off no end, so I make sure he catches me scowling at him as often as possible.

This situation with Ariella is a nightmare but the ties to her family make the situation much harder to deal with. I had tried to cut them by declining the Sunday lunches I was invited to, but when Dahlia Mason turned up at the flat after she received Ariella's room key, demanding that I take her to lunch, I jumped at the chance. I didn't want to break the news about Ariella and me to her, but I spilled the beans before they handed us the menus. The last thing I expected was for her to reach for me and ask, with genuine concern, if I was okay. Tears shot to my eyes out of nowhere.

'I'm fine. I'll miss her but I'm fine.'

'You're obviously not. Do you want to fix things, Caleb?'

'It's over. She kicked me out.'

'Did you want to be kicked out?'

I don't answer. Maybe I did.

'Who ended it? I know it wasn't her; but you, Caleb, tend to burn everything down behind you.'

She's not wrong. I got on the plane. I blocked her number. I cleared the apartment of her stuff, then locked and bolted her room. For added finality, I got rid of all the keys so I had no access.

'I see it's dawning on you.' Dahlia took a swig of wine.

Stubbornly, I looked at the menu and changed the subject. 'How is Mr Mason?'

'Hugh is fine. Before I let you change the subject, you lit up around each other, Caleb, but you always gave off this "It's all going to be taken away from me at any moment" vibe. I know she is maddeningly secretive, but it'd be a shame for it to be over.'

It was the last thing she said about our relationship before she ordered the most expensive items on the menu and chose an exorbitantly priced bottle of wine – immediately after she confirmed I was paying. When she was done, she shut the menu and raised a perfect eyebrow at me.

'That's for making my daughter cry.' She smiled at her mild act of vengeance.

'I'd let you order the entire wine list if I could undo that,' I said remorsefully.

'I know.' She smiled warmly at me and reached for my hand. I met her halfway and felt her support come through.

After that, we had a lovely, long, lazy lunch that ended only because the restaurant needed their tables back for their arriving dinner guests. Dahlia unexpectedly picked up the bill with an eye-roll and a simple: 'You're my annoying fourth child now.'

When I walked home that night, it was clear to me that I might, if I really shut my feelings down, be able to move on if it was just Ariella, but I'm not ready to lose Dahlia, Zachary, Isszy and – strangely – Hugh Mason; so, I'll be damned if I let Dominic Miller take that from me. I just need to decide what I want without letting anger get the better of me.

Melissa, of all people, nudges me towards that decision when she shows up at my apartment, uninvited. I thought I'd managed to successfully avoid her, but I suppose she was bound to show up sooner or later; like shit on a shoe.

'Nice apartment.' She walks past me as soon as I open the door. The revulsion I feel at the smell of her familiar perfume is as immediate as it is overwhelming.

'You can't stay. I have a—'

'Landlord's visit in your diary? That's me.' Of course it is. 'It's time we cleared the air.' She takes off her coat, throws it over an armchair and parks herself on the couch in my living room.

'I obviously don't need to ask you to make yourself comfortable.'

'Don't be so combative, Caleb. I came to check in on my favourite employee.' She leans back, crosses her legs and spreads her arms out. She's going to be here for a while.

'I thought that was Ariella.' I close the front door and, repulsed, I find the furthest seat from her.

'You're right!' She laughs. 'You're my second favourite. If it helps, you've proven me wrong, Caleb. I genuinely didn't think you'd be this impressive at your job. We both know how you got here. But you're meeting the challenge and are currently ahead of your targets.'

'You hired me to do a job, and I'm doing it.'

'Surely you're enjoying it too?'

'Not really. I'd rather be back in London, to be honest.'

'Why? You're much better paid here, you have no expenses, you have a home – you keep performing like this and your bonus will be huge. People actually like you here. Let's be honest, you were tolerated, at best, back in the UK. Contrary to what you believe, Caleb, I actually want you to be happy here.'

'I don't believe you, Melissa.'

'What makes you think I'd want you to be unhappy?'

'All of it. This is a game to you.'

'Let's put your narcissism and paranoia aside for a second.

185

If this was purely a business investment, which part of this feels like a game and not a strategically sound decision?'

'Ariella was a risk. You couldn't predict how she was going to perform.'

'I obviously know a lot more about your girlfriend than you do. As I made clear in London, she wasn't a risk at all. The risk was you. My judgement may have been compromised because I still care about you, but you're really in Singapore because she wanted you here too. You were her deal-breaker. I just happened to want the same too.'

My doorbell goes and Melissa stands quickly to get it.

'Perfect timing. I ordered us dinner.'

She meets the food at the door and carries it over to the dining table. After I fetch some plates and cutlery, she beckons me to sit. I pick the furthest seat away from her. All she does is roll her eyes and move closer.

'It's just dinner, Caleb. Everything doesn't need to be a statement of resistance.'

I just need this over and her gone. There is no way I am touching any of that food, so I cross my arms and watch her eat in silence for a little while before she speaks up again.

'How are things between you and Ariella? She's been spending quite a bit of time with Dominic Miller, hasn't she?'

'He's pretty much moved into her office to stalk her at close proximity, but it's none of my business.'

'She did close DMVI and it's a huge contract. It makes sense that there's a lot to iron out.'

'Unless he's allergic to email, there is no reason why it needs to be in person, all the time. We have other clients.'

'You're jealous.'

'Ariella can do whatever she wants with whomever she wants. Like I said, it's none of my business.'

'Rubbish. If it's any consolation, she has "friend-zoned"

him. I hear he's being patient because he knows she's had her heart broken.'

Good girl. She's not giving in to him. I try not to smile.

'I know it's a sore point but, if you're both really over, he's not a bad choice. Dom is a lot of fun and she can calm him down. They can learn a lot from each other and he seems keen. He's already making moves to meet the parents. He has invited them to the little surprise birthday party he's throwing her.'

To keep a lid on the anger building inside, I say nothing.

'Maybe you should move on too, Caleb.' She reaches for my hand and I yank it away.

'I'm all right, thanks.'

'We could—'

'Nope. You're my boss. Not going to happen.'

'I was going to say we could arrange for you to move out of the building if you want.'

'I'm fine. Are we done here?' I abruptly start clearing the table.

'Not quite. I'm marrying Kevin. He has decided he doesn't care about the terms of the prenup. The date has been set. I wanted you to hear it from me.'

The relief that floods through me is unexpectedly intense. 'Congratulations,' I respond without emotion.

'Thanks. So, I promised to give you the Marina Bay apartment. I can no longer honour that. I'm sorry.'

'It's fine, Melissa. Live a happy life with Kevin. I don't need anything from you.' I'm disgusted by that place now anyway.

'We both know Kevin has never made me happy but loving you for two years did. Incredibly so.'

'It happened. It ended.' I am not going down memory lane. Given the slightest chance, I'd set fire to it.

'I want to thank you for that.' Her voice breaks. She is actually emotional. Why she is marrying Kevin Wong, or anyone she doesn't want to, is beyond me. Melissa Chang is a badass. I catch myself softening, and remind myself that she's a monster.

'No need,' is all I say.

She walks to the couch and grabs her coat. 'You'll get your wedding invitation. It's a very long weekend of events. You and Ariella will get your own plus ones but I've put both of you down for one of the two-bedroom cabins. Dominic will be invited because he's friends with Kevin. If you want to make things work—'

'I'm not interested in—'

'Shut up and get out of your own way, Caleb, for goodness' sake,' she snaps, losing her patience. There's the Melissa I know.

'Also, I'm not giving you the apartment in Marina Bay because I'm selling it. The way things turned out during our last night there was beneath me and vile. What I did was unforgivable and I took something that I shouldn't have, just because I knew I could.' Her irritated version of an apology cuts through me. She knows what she did.

I feel the anger, pain, despair and powerlessness in me rise but I swallow it. She currently controls Ariella and my lives out here, and I know the destruction she is capable of. I don't care what she does to me but if Ariella gets hurt by any of my bull-shit, I'll never forgive myself.

I look away to compose myself.

'I'm giving you this one and everything in it instead.' She taps her right foot twice on the hardwood floor and hands me a hard, black box from her coat pocket. 'It's all yours. Ownership is protected until you're ready for it not to be. All the encrypted details have been sent to your private email. That box contains the hard key with the same information. Ivory Bow's rent will be paid directly into a bank account set up for you and held in escrow until you no longer work for the company. I don't want you to have to worry about money again, Caleb. If I can give you that, it will go some way to repaying you for what you've done for me and what I did to you.'

I'm speechless. My mind goes straight to when Jack received a Tesla from his girlfriend Lou; after she'd spent the entirety of their relationship violently taking her anger out on him.

'Hopefully, this wipes the slate clean. However, don't think just because I've done this I'm going to go easy on you. If anything, I plan on working you to exhaustion for the entire duration you're tied into your contract.' She laughs.

'What's the catch?' I ask, but I know the catch. Melissa's bribe is meant to make me forget and carry on, business as usual.

'No catch. You deserve better than you've been handed. Me included. And maybe now you won't feel so inadequate when it comes to Ariella.'

She opens the door and, stunned, I watch her leave.

I immediately call Jasper.

'Hey, Caleb, how's it going out there?'

'Melissa came over, got us a takeaway, apologised and gave me a fucking apartment.'

'Like, she's paying your rent?'

'No, like she bought it, put it in my name and Ivory Bow is renting my apartment from me.'

'Sounds dicey.'

'I have all the details and an encryption key with instructions. If I send it over, can you take a look?'

'Sure. You said she apologised?'

'Yeah. For taking something that didn't belong to her.'

'Wow. That's one way of putting it. What happens now?'

'Nothing. Like I told you, I'm going to shut up, do my time, sell it and get out.'

'You still have the threat of possible criminal activity... did she say anything about that?'

'Nothing. Did you find anything?'

'I'm untangling the web. You're eventually going to tell Ariella the truth, right?'

'Yes, of course, when we know exactly what we are dealing with, if anything. This just takes the pressure off,' I admit.

'It takes the pressure off you, not her. Is "Budget Jasper" still stalking her?' Jasper laughs. I'd given Dominic the name so that I could take the piss with Jasper and Lara.

'Yeah. Pools of drool around the office continue to appear.'

'I looked him up. There's nothing "Budget" about him. He seems very accomplished.'

'Mate, I've had classier farts than him.'

Jasper laughs deep, long and loud. I can't help joining in. I've grown to really like him.

'Jokes aside, are you going to come clean about how you feel to her?'

I sigh. Maybe I've been too honest with Jasper. 'No way. You know what she's like. She'll want to do that friendship nonsense first and there is no way that I'm doing that with Budget Jasper hovering. Dealing with you as original Jasper was bad enough. I have *some* dignity. Best to move on.'

'This is you moving on?' Jasper chuckles.

'Yes. Leave it. By the way, did you know that Budget Jasper asked Hugh and Dahlia out here for Ariella's birthday?'

'Yes, I found out yesterday. Hugh isn't coming, so Dahlia asked me to tag along instead.'

'What did you say?'

'That I'd run it past Sophia.'

'You're not coming then. It's fine, I can look after Dahlia.'

'Not so fast. It'll cost me something big and sparkly but I'll be there.' Jasper laughs.

'Expensive, is she?'

'Like you wouldn't believe, but worth it. She has a good heart.'

'You can crash at mine to save some pennies. And I'll show you my new pad.'

'You're on.'

I hang up and fight the urge to go up to Ariella's and tell her that I'm sorry.

TWENTY-TWO

ARIELLA

'You're not planning on skipping out on me tomorrow, are you?' Dominic asks from my office couch.

I cast my eye at my phone, showing the airline alert inviting me to check in to my flight to Bangkok. 'No...'

'You promised, Ariella!'

I nod and say nothing. Truthfully, I don't know what I am going to do. Dominic makes me laugh, he is professionally inspiring, and I could happily spend all day tomorrow learning how to fish on his boat. We've been almost inseparable the last few weeks because we have been developing an Ivory Bow client app. It started off as a simple engagement app that uses the time and the client's location to suggest unique, instantly available experiences exclusive to Ivory Bow clients.

Thanks to Dominic's support, we became more ambitious and made every service partner commit to donating five per cent of all Ivory Bow booking revenue to a new joint not-for-profit set up by Ivory Bow and DMVI Technology. I've been missing the shelter and being involved with fulfilling projects that give me the opportunity to be of service to the wider community. Volunteering to be on the advisory board of the new project and being actively involved in delivering it also makes me feel like I've reclaimed another small part of me.

We are now jointly leading a separate team, responsible for writing school holiday programmes that provide free tech, creative, entrepreneurial, science and music camps to qualifying eight- to eighteen-year-olds in households below a specific income threshold. The project has given me a real purpose here and I am especially proud of how it is taking shape.

I am pleased that Mel and Georgie made me call Dominic. He pushes me in a way that reminds me of Christopher, because he is just so clever and quick and is constantly brimming with ideas. Funnily enough, the way he stubbornly, authentically and unapologetically stands powerfully in his own space also reminds me of Lara. I made the mistake of telling Lara this and she christened him 'Budget Jasper' and texted him to back off and get his own best friend.

Dominic catches me when I look at my phone.

'You're coming, right?'

The only person who knows that I've arranged for Caleb and me to go away together is Lydia, so there is no way Dominic can be aware. Even Caleb has no idea that there is a flight with his name on it, leaving tomorrow.

'All things being equal...'

'I'm turning up tomorrow morning at ten and dragging you out. It's getting late and I know Matthew's running an errand, so I'll drop you at home. My car is downstairs.'

It's later than I think and everyone left the office hours ago. I pack up as Dominic slings his messenger bag over his shoulder and helps me with my weekend box file. I flip my phone over to hide the screen, a little too quickly. Dominic pauses, scrutinises my face and picks the box up.

'I'm not ready to give up trying to work you out, but I'm

letting this one slide.' He smiles kindly as he leads the way out of the Ivory Bow office. He manages to keep his promise to let it go, until he puts the box down in my home office and is about to leave.

'Can I borrow your phone real quick?' he asks, patting his front and back pockets.

'Sure.' I hand it over. When I realise what Dominic has done, it's too late.

'Firstly, stop handing your phone over to everyone who asks. Secondly, put a passcode on your phone. Most importantly, why is this alert reminding you to check in to a flight to Bangkok?' He shows me the notification I've been trying to hide.

'Hey! That's sneaky.' I grab my phone from him.

'Unbelievable. You were going to quietly jump on a plane?'

'No. Not any more. I booked the flight weeks ago and was hoping I could make the trip work, but it's not going to happen. I'll be here tomorrow. I just need to move the flight.'

Dominic studies my face before sighing with resignation.

'Would you rather go to Bangkok?'

Yes. With Caleb, even though he is being awful and has a girlfriend; because I have somehow become a glutton for punishment and one of those terrible people that tries to move in on someone else's boyfriend. And no, I don't recognise myself either.

'Bangkok can wait. I'll move it.'

'Don't look so sad. It'll be fun taking you out in the boat. You can get some sun, we can stuff our faces with ice cream, drink too much and eat what we caught.'

'Yeah.' I force a smile.

Dominic smiles exaggeratedly at me, showing all his teeth. I know it will be fun. He's solely responsible for my now extensive street hawker and dive bar knowledge of the city.

'I'm hungry,' he announces suddenly. He marches into the

kitchen, opens the fridge and starts taking out the platters Ms Pat has prepared for me.

'Aren't you going out on a date tonight? Buy her dinner.' I walk over and start putting back the salads and meats he took out of the fridge.

'Shit. What's the time?'

'Nine thirty. You have half an hour.'

He gives me a quick hug before darting across the room. 'See you tomorrow? Bright and early?'

'Bright and early,' I confirm quietly as he walks out of my front door.

The apartment feels even more enormous than usual as I lock the door behind Dominic and make my way to my bedroom. I am overwhelmed by loneliness as soon as I sit on my bed.

This isn't how it was supposed to be. Caleb and I are supposed to be packing right now, stealing kisses and laughing as we grab each other's items, with music in the background. I'm supposed to be getting on that plane with him tomorrow and I still want to. I know what I am about to do is a huge risk. He wants to have nothing to do with me and, even though I haven't seen the woman from the lift in a while, she could still be around. I have to try. Dominic will understand; we can go fishing any time. I pick up my phone.

> Hey. I was just wondering if you have plans this weekend?

I get straight to the point so that I don't have the opportunity to chicken out. An answer shoots back almost immediately.

> Why?

His response is short and crushing but I don't want to give up.

I am thinking of skipping town and was going to ask you to join me. I know things aren't great between us but you're the closest friend I have out here.

What about your fishing lesson with your new bestie?

Argh. Caleb is being exceptionally difficult.

I can cancel.

Don't. It's inconsiderate. Anyway, I'm busy.

Why are you being so horrible?

I'm not. You asked me what I am doing this weekend and I told you I am busy.

You just called me inconsiderate. That's horrible.

Only because you're trying to bail, last minute, on the only person that is actually trying to do something nice for you tomorrow.

The only person. It stings.

If I come down, can we talk?

I have company

I know what that means.

Okay.

Go to sleep, Ariella.

No goodnight, just a politely worded 'get lost'.

I walk into my shower, get rid of the day's dirt, climb into bed and cry myself to sleep.

I allow myself to sleep in, and wake at eight to a screen full of calls and texts from family, friends and colleagues. I don't think to look for a text from Caleb until I see the texts from Tim and Em, and Jack and Lou. Nothing. I push it to the back of my mind and respond to each one, trying to rise out of the emptiness I feel. When I finish, I crawl back under my blanket for what seems like seconds before my phone starts to ring. It's Dominic. I don't want to go. I just want to stay under the covers today.

'Morning, Dominic.'

'Happy birthday, Ariella!'

'Thanks, Dominic. Listen, I don't feel like—'

'Let me in. I'm outside. I brought you breakfast.' And he hangs up.

I try to call him back but he doesn't answer. I look at the time. It's half nine. I trudge to the front door and open it to find a happy Dominic standing there, sunglasses on, in navy shorts, a pink shirt and deck shoes. He is holding a brown bag that smells amazing.

'Fresh pretzels,' he announces, walking in and setting the bag down before he takes off his sunglasses.

'Holy crap, Ariella, you look like shit. You haven't got pink-eye, have you?' he asks, taking a step back from me.

'I just woke up.' I grab the bag from the counter and bite into the warm pretzel.

'Thank goodness you shut me down.' He points at my hair with a finger, and retracts it quickly. 'What's going on there?'

'Where? That's my hair.'

'You look like you've been tasered.'

'Are you going to be rude all day?'

'Not intentionally. But for now, get dressed and look human. The fish aren't going to catch themselves and you'll scare them away looking like that. And don't forget to grab your passport just in case we wander into international waters.' He wrestles the pretzel from me and shoos me in the direction of my bedroom.

I jump into the shower, do my teeth and pull my hair into a high, loose bunch. I'm not in the mood to do anything other than put a hair tie around it. I pull on some shorts, a vest top and my Converse, then I toss a swimsuit, a spare underwear set, a sundress, some sunscreen, a hat, a book, my passport and a towel into my large tote.

'Think you could have made less of an effort?' Dominic laughs at me as I walk out.

'It's fishing.'

He just shakes his head. 'Come on.'

We whiz through the busy streets of Singapore on the back of his bike to the yacht club and end up in front of a huge yacht with the name *Her*.

'Here we are.' Dominic smiles.

'This is not a fishing boat, Dominic.' I point at the huge craft next to me.

'It is for some.' He laughs.

'For who? That's a thirty-metre Sunseeker.'

'It is, also, that. You know your boats. Nice. Come on.'

Dominic helps me onboard. 'Happy birthday, Ariella,' he shouts at me, too loudly.

'SURPRISE!'

I jump and turn around to see too many faces behind me, with one in particular standing out.

'Mommy!' I rush to her and almost jump into our hug. She laughs as I feel a tear hit my shoulder.

'Happy birthday, darling!' She holds my face in her hands and plants three of her forceful loving kisses on my face.

The crowd breaks into a huge 'awwww' as some music is cranked up and waiters start to surround us with generously filled champagne flutes. Just then I spot Jasper smiling at me from a distance. I immediately realise how much I have missed my trusted, reliable, steady, best friend. I stop myself from running to him.

'Is Daddy here?' I ask my mom, looking around.

'No, honey, he had to work. He's looking forward to seeing you soon for Zachary's wedding though. He was really disappointed, but I'm not. He would have ruined my chances with Denzel over there.' She nods at Devin, who is sporting a shy smile. She has harassed him already.

'Mommy! I work with him.'

'Oh please. I am an old, decrepit and harmless little old lady who likes Denzel Washington. He is just amusing me.'

'I know exactly what you're up to and I'm telling Daddy.' I laugh.

'Don't you dare ruin my fun. Oooh! Look, he got me a glass of champagne. Let's catch up later.'

Poor Devin. He has no idea. I watch her join a smiley Devin, standing next to Bryce, who was happily beckoning my mother over. That woman is terrible. Devin thinks he's in charge. He's not.

As soon as my mom steps away, I get caught up in a swarm of people wishing me a happy birthday, asking me if I figured out the surprise and how sweet Dominic was to organise it. It's nice. I spot Dominic looking uncomfortable, talking to a relaxed and chatty Jasper. Crumbs. I never thought this would be a fire I'd have to put out. I walk over quickly.

'Jas!' I pull him into a deep hug. 'I am so happy you're here. I've missed you so much.'

He hugs me back tightly. 'I've missed you too. When Dahlia called to tell me she was coming, I knew she wasn't going to let me off the phone until I had purchased the seat right next to her, not that I needed much convincing.' He laughs.

'Sorry. Dominic, this is the infamous Jasper. Jas, this is Dominic, clearly about to become one of my closest friends out here,' I say, teasing, pointing at the boat.

Dominic looks confused but puts out his hand. 'Jasper.'

'Dominic,' Jasper returns, taking Dominic's extended hand.

I pull Dominic into a grateful hug. 'Thank you so much for this,' I whisper into his ear. 'Can we talk later?'

I feel his body relax. 'Could you both excuse me?' he says before stepping away.

'Jasper!' I slap his arm. 'How is the wedding planning going? I've been seriously slacking in my duties.'

'You've been busy.' Jasper sips from his glass happily.

'And how is Sophia?'

'Things are a little tense at the moment but she's all right. How are you doing?'

'It's challenging, but rewarding.'

'Any of those challenges include your good friend Dominic's more than friendly feelings?' Jasper raises an eyebrow at me.

'Nope. He's constantly swiping left and right on his phone and is consequently dating the whole of Singapore. What's going on with you and Sophia?'

'She wants kids.' He sighs.

'But you want kids!'

'Yes, but she wants them right now.'

'Oh.' Mommy predicted this.

'I'm happy, I like her but I just don't know...'

'Have you talked to her about it?'

'Aari, it's your birthday. We shouldn't be talking about this. I should be telling you how amazing this is and how proud I am of you. It's a happy day. Let's keep it that way, okay?' He grabs me into a bear hug and kisses the side of my head through my hair. 'Seeing you happy makes me happy, whether you're with me or... someone else. But today, we are celebrating that you're one more year closer to wrinkles.' He laughs and I punch him in the arm.

'You've seen Mommy. I have nothing to worry about.' I grin.

'Go, have some fun.' He shoos me away. 'We only have an hour of international drinking left before we get to Riau; and someone has to protect Denzel from Dahlia.' He points his nose at my giggling mother, who is having a brilliant time, with Devin hanging on to every word.

'We're going to Riau?'

'You didn't hear it from me.' Jasper puts his index finger to his lips and walks away quickly. I find Dominic, apologise to the people he is talking to and pull him away.

'We're going to Riau?'

'You're having a little island beach party.' He smiles. 'I'm sorry that Jasper is here. When your mom said she had a plus one, I didn't know it was him.'

'You've been speaking to my mom?'

'Lydia has.' He raises an eyebrow at Lydia, who is happily tossing back champagne like there is no tomorrow. 'What's the deal? You don't seem mad at him,' he goes on.

'I'm not. He should be mad at me; and he was, for a very long time.'

'Why?'

'The rumours aren't true. I left. In the worst way. I cleared out my belongings when I knew he was at work and left him three sentences on a sticky note. It was selfish and cruel.'

'But how come...'

'Can I promise to tell you later?'

He nods slowly.

'Thank you for this, Dominic.' Our eyes meet, they hold for a moment and something shifts. I smile quickly and walk away. There is no way Dominic Miller the Sixth is making it out of the friend zone.

The trip to the island ends with us being dropped off on a private beach attached to a magnificent hotel. Our afternoon is filled with a never-ending abundance of colourful canapés, beach games and too many delicious drinks served by encouraging waiting staff. As night falls, the staff start a barbecue and a bonfire while other members of the hotel team walk around giving people keys to their bedrooms for the night.

During the day I found a small cove in the rocks, so I return there when the sun starts to set. The peace from the solitude I feel is welcome and grounding, as I sit on a large smooth rock, listening to the waves crash nearby.

'Hi.' Dominic startles me. 'I saw you slip in here earlier. I wasn't sure whether or not to bother you, but I did anyway.' He climbs gracefully on to a rock and then hops on five more to get closer to the one I am sitting on.

'I like it here.' The truth is, I'm hiding. This party has been a lot to handle.

He makes it to my rock, forcing me to scoot over to make space for him. He smells of a woody soap. It's nice.

'Good birthday so far?'

'Better than I could have imagined, thank you, Dominic.'

'We all pitched in. I just provided the boat.'

'Thank you for providing the boat.' That feeling from earlier comes back. He feels too close and it's uncomfortable.

'So, Jasper…?'

'Jasper and I have history much bigger than dating. He's my best friend.'

'I thought your best friend was some psychotic Scottish

chick called Lara that keeps emailing me to back off and get my own friends?'

'She is too.' I chuckle. Oh Lara.

'History or not, a couple of months ago you were in tears over this guy.'

I want to correct him but I don't. It's too messy. We sit together silently and listen to the waves before I respond.

'It's a little complicated.'

'I hope those complications didn't ruin today?'

'No. This is magical and I don't know how to thank you.'

'You can thank me with that,' he says softly, pointing to my face. 'I like to see you smile.'

'This is too generous.'

'Make it up to me then.' He looks squarely at me and I swallow.

'How?' Dominic cannot leave the friend zone.

'Make me dinner. I overheard today that you're an amazing cook, and I haven't had macaroni cheese since I was back home.'

'You're on,' I agree excitedly. I haven't cooked since I got to Singapore. Ms Pat and I could go shopping for ingredients and walk the markets together. I can start looking for my favourite places to buy groceries. I can walk through food displays, smelling new ingredients, tasting unfamiliar items, learning the local names for my favourites, expanding my palate, maybe even taking some home to experiment—

'Wanna head back?' Dominic interrupts my thoughts, then stands and extends his hand.

'I'd like to stay here a little longer if that's okay.' I hug my knees tighter and hope for some more time alone.

'The tide is coming in and it's getting a little chilly, Ariella.'

It doesn't sound like he is going to leave without me, so I grab his hand.

'You're cold.'

We hop from rock to rock to make our way out and, on the

last rock, Dominic pulls a little too quickly, causing me to lose my balance. Before I can adjust myself, he grabs me as I tumble forward.

'I told you that you'd fall for me.' He laughs.

'It doesn't count if you're trying to kill me, Dominic.'

As we walk back to the beach, I see that a long table has been set and dinner is about to be served. Everyone is relaxed, standing around numerous firepits, drinking and chatting. As Dominic and I walk up, people take their seats. Dominic pulls out a chair for me in the middle of the table, next to my mom, and everyone starts to sing 'Happy Birthday'.

He stands behind the chair on the other side and speaks.

'Thank you very much for coming, especially as most of us haven't known Ariella for very long. The one thing I can say about my newest friend is this: today, we celebrate the fact that she was born, and if she hadn't been, none of us would be here today, in this moment together. I've smiled more in the last month than I have in the last five years because of Ariella, because that's what friendship should be. A source of joy, ridiculousness, challenge, safety and good fun. To Ariella.' He raises his glass and the table responds.

'Speech!' everyone chants. Goodness. This is going to be embarrassing. I get up slowly.

'Thank you, everyone, for coming. Mommy, Jasper, thank you for getting on a plane for me. My Ivory Bow family, thank you for being here. I appreciate you giving up your weekend to spend my birthday with me. Finally, thank you, Dominic. I think the last time I had a birthday party with more than six people was when I was ten and my mom made me.' Everyone laughs and Mommy pitches in.

'It's true. She spent the entire party hiding and it was a nightmare. We couldn't find her for hours. We finally worked out she was switching locations to places we had already checked, because she'd enlisted this one as a lookout.' Mommy points at Jasper and shakes her head. The whole table roars with laughter as he takes a bow from his seat.

'I'm happy you're all here tonight, I feel very... special. Thank you all for making Singapore feel like home.' I raise my glass to clapping, and Dominic encourages everyone to dig in. The table immediately bursts to life with chatter, plates clinking and joy.

'That was a little harsh, Ariella,' my mom whispers as she leans in.

'Harsh? Did I do something wrong, Mommy?'

'I know you're no longer together but a nod to Caleb wouldn't have hurt.'

My heart flutters. 'He's here?'

'You haven't seen Caleb all day?'

I shake my head, hard. I want to see him. 'Where is he?'

My mother leans back and points behind Dominic along our row. There he is, sitting in between two people I don't know, having a quiet conversation with the person to his left.

'He was on the boat?'

My mom nods.

'How did you know that we broke up?'

'We had lunch and, unlike you, he shares.'

I immediately wonder what Caleb has been sharing. 'What did he say?'

'That he said some mean things, you threw him out and, by the time he tried to mend things, you'd moved on.' My mother shrugs as she pops a piece of lobster in her mouth.

'What else did he say?'

'Ask him yourself, baby.'

I plan on doing just that. Mommy turns to Devin, who is already offering to take her to the theatre while she is around. Damn, she works fast.

'Grab some food, Ariella.' Dominic puts a couple of prawns on my plate, then continues to load me up with other items.

'Is this a normal weekend for you?' I ask as I move my plate away.

'Goodness no. I haven't taken off with the boat for a while, so it's just as special for me as it is for you.'

'This is truly extraordinary.' I meet his eyes for longer than I should before I turn away.

'We are going to need to stop doing that, Ariella. It complicates things.'

I shrug, pretending I don't know what he was talking about.

'I know you want to kiss me,' he says a little too loudly as he pokes me in the ribs.

'Shhhhh!' I respond, quickly smacking his hand away while checking that nobody heard. 'You're dreaming.'

'I'm pretty sure I've got this one right. While we are here with you in total denial and me being completely honest, dear friend, I've wanted to kiss you since I first laid eyes on you. Unfortunately, we are both determined to friend-zone each other, so I know it's not going to happen.'

'You guys would have the most beautiful babies!' Dominic's PA delights from where she is sitting, opposite him. I notice Jasper trying to contain a laugh.

'Ariella wishes,' Dominic smoothly defuses. 'These genes are precious.'

'I can assure you of your genes' safety, Dominic.'

'Can you? You don't want to reassess our little friend-zone strategy later?' he whispers.

I shake my head.

Dominic laughs. 'That scared, huh?'

The meal is so sumptuous, we eat and drink until we are full. As the music volume starts to build on the beach, people leave the table to dance between the water's edge and the fire. When

Mommy joins the party with Bryce, Jasper moves up to occupy her seat.

'Did you know Caleb was here?' I ask.

'Yes, why wouldn't he be? I know things are difficult at the moment...'

Of course Jasper knows. Mommy would have given him a thirteen-hour-long catch-up on the flight.

'I had no idea, he's been avoiding me.' I look over to where he is sitting with his back squarely to us.

'He's probably laying low so you can have a good birthday, but you're going to have to talk about it at some point, Aari.'

'I've tried. He has...'

'Shut down?'

'Yes.'

'Being dumped by you isn't easy to bounce back from, even if he did orchestrate his own demise.'

'I didn't dump him; and what do you mean by orchestrating his own demise?'

'Talk to Caleb. I've said more than I should, but you should hear him out before you decide that you're really over.'

'I don't understand.'

'Talk to him. I'm only telling you this because I think you can both work it out. The way Dominic looks at you worries me. I'd hate for him to get his way before you've cleared things up with Caleb.'

'Dominic and I are just friends.'

'That's what you said about me, and then Caleb.' He kisses my head before he gets up.

I scan the party. Caleb's girlfriend isn't here. I want to talk to him right now but I can't in the middle of the party; especially with Dominic still in the dark, and now approaching.

'Hey. Do you have fifteen minutes? I want to show you something,' Dominic says, beckoning.

TWENTY-THREE
CALEB

I had no intention of going to Aari's party, until Jasper and Dahlia turned up to threaten me. Only a select few know our history and I didn't fancy getting their looks of pity while Dominic slobbered all over her.

Her texts the night before made me feel a little better and, if I hadn't been six beers deep by my pool with an increasingly tipsy Jasper, exchanging news about Dominic, Sophia and Melissa, it would have been impossible to resist her.

I was childishly silent on the journey to the boat the next morning, and went straight to the bow to escape as soon as we arrived. The resistant crew eventually relented when they realised that there was no way I was going to join the party.

Ariella hugging Dahlia softened me. I'd forgotten that she was really just a sheltered mummy and daddy's girl who made questionable life choices. If Dominic was trying to give off 'boyfriendy vibes', it all disappeared when he clapped eyes on Jasper. Thankfully, Ariella put a stop to it and sent him on his way; not that he took his eyes off her. Poor fool.

You're wasting your time, mate. You'll be lucky if she lets you touch her. She's just not that into you, I think, and chuckle to myself.

Ariella has put his ass firmly in the friend zone and he isn't getting out any time soon. I've seen him in the office trying to touch her, and her cleverly evading each attempt.

I stayed on the bow and, when drinking with Jasper until six in the morning caught up with me, I retreated to one of the cabins for a nap.

By the time I woke up, everyone was off the boat. I picked up my hotel room key and made it to the dinner table just as Dominic and Ariella were emerging from some rocks – holding hands? What the fuck?

'Caleb. Come on, man,' Jasper reprimanded me for being late.

Why are they holding hands and walking in sync? I'd only been asleep for a few hours. I whispered to the woman next to me, hoping to get an update, 'Those two need to get a room.'

'They are cute, aren't they? Thank goodness he found her.'

'He may still lose her.'

'That's not nice. We were really worried, he had the whole beach looking for her.'

Okay, so they hadn't spent the afternoon together, but something had changed. I tried not to vomit through Dominic's speech. I just needed to get through the meal and get the hell off this beach. Unfortunately, after listening to Dahlia's contribution implicating Jasper, I started to feel like an arsehole. It was Aari's birthday and last night I'd been dismissive. The least I could do was wish her a happy birthday.

Now, when Dominic walks her to the far end of the beach, I follow. Eventually they stop, and Ariella crosses her arms. When he takes her hand, she takes a step back. Good girl. As the wind blows, some of her hair comes loose. Dominic brushes a curl away from her face while they are both laughing, and her body softens. He steps closer, forcing her to tip her face up to look at him, and she goes from defensive to willing. This creep is actively seducing her while pretending to be just friendly. I know those moves. Ariella is going to let this fool kiss her. I can see it. He has broken through.

No fucking way.

'Ariella!' I call out, making them both jump. Good. Dominic has a face like thunder, while Ariella seems to come to her senses, realises what is happening and steps away from him.

'Hey, could you give us a minute?' Dominic growls.

Hell no, I won't give you a minute.

'No, it's okay. Hi, Caleb.' She actually looks relieved.

'I wanted to wish you a happy birthday and have a quick chat?'

'Sure. Dominic, could you give us a few? I'll catch up, we should be heading back anyway.'

Yeah, Dominic, take a hike, I channel through my smile.

'Okay. I'll save you a dance.' He shoves his hands in his pockets and starts walking away. I wait, watching, until I know he is out of earshot before I turn back to Ariella.

'You were going to kiss that arsehole?' I don't realise I'm yelling until I hear myself.

'No!' she yells right back. 'And even if I was, it's none of your business!'

She's pissed off. I'm not prepared for that, so I take my volume down. 'It is, actually. He's a client!'

'Where was all this morality when you were messing around with everything that moved in London, Caleb?'

'Don't turn this around just so you can be with some rich dickhead that collects women like trophies. You're just going to be another notch, Ariella!'

'As opposed to the pedestal you laid out for all those women, before and apparently after me!?'

'This isn't about me, this is about you.'

'Honestly! You're so reliably repetitive. I know it's about

me. You don't need to keep saying it, so just FUCK OFF!' Ariella has never sworn at me before, and she says it so force-fully she has to inhale.

'I gave myself to you, Caleb. Everything I loved, I hated, even everything I was unsure about myself. I gave it to you. And you took it, threw it back at me and told me you didn't want it. So, I am doing my very best to take myself back. Away from you.'

'Ariella, I didn't throw it back—'

'I don't care any more! I've tried and you've repeatedly pushed me away. I know you blocked my number. I know you locked all my stuff away in anger. I know something strange is going on with you. Maybe you cheated, maybe it's something worse. You hurt me but I forgave you. Now I am drawing the line. You've taken everything I was in love with and you have made it miserable. You continue to make me miserable. And it's not okay.'

'You made me miserable too!' I shoot back.

'Well, now you're free.' She starts to walk back towards the party. I panic. I need to stop her, so I toss an accusation that I know will hit way below the belt.

'So you can be free to shag Dominic?'

She stops. It worked.

'Caleb, what exactly is it that you want? I ask because you have made it abundantly clear that you are repulsed by a cheap, common, desperate me,' she snaps back, in utter frustration.

Hearing the words I threw at her come back feels awful. I am disgusted with my behaviour. 'I just wanted to wish you a happy birthday and we have somehow ended up fighting.' I sigh, intentionally lowering my voice and my tone.

'That's because "Happy birthday, Aari" came out as "You were going to kiss that arsehole?"' She mimics my voice, Scouse accent and all. I can't help the smile that breaks across my face and the laugh that escapes.

'Is that meant to be me?' I reach out to tickle her. Who am I kidding? I'm still in love with this woman.

'Caleb, don't, I'm serious!' She fights the smile that starts to creep across her face too. 'You're awful!'

'Can we just sit?' I ask, sitting on the sand.

'No.'

I reach out for her, pull her into me and pull her down anyway. She sits but moves just shy of my arm's reach.

I don't know why or how, but the truth slips out. 'I miss you,' I admit. She looks at me like I have just broken her heart.

'Why are you doing this? Just last night, you basically told me to get lost.'

'It's your birthday and I've been a dick. But I'm mostly doing it because you were about to kiss Budget Jasper.' I exaggerate a disgusted body-shiver.

'You're wrong. The last thing I was thinking was about kissing Dominic.'

'That's not what your body was saying.'

'We're not together any more, Caleb. Why do you care?' She starts drawing on the sand.

'Because I don't want you to kiss Budget Jasper.'

'You and Lara need to stop calling him that. We're friends and he has been really nice to me. You calling him that is not fair.'

'Fine. I don't want you to kiss Dominic Miller.'

'I can kiss whoever I like, Caleb. You don't see me judging you and what you've been getting up to these past few weeks.'

'And what have I been getting up to?'

'I don't know, and I don't care.'

'I think you *do* care.'

'I don't know what you're trying to do but I'm going back to the party.' Aari gets up.

'I'm trying to say that I'm sorry.' I stand and take a step closer to her. I just need to get close enough. I reach out and stroke her arm. Her defences crumble and that soft, open expression that belongs to me returns to her face. She's listening. I get in there quickly before her wall goes up again.

'I am sorry I hurt you. I'm sorry I left a space that Dominic Miller is trying to sneak into. I'm sorry that, because of me, you are stuck on this bloody island at a loud, brash party with a bunch of people you don't know. I am sorry that you are having to put a happy face on for everyone. I'm sorry we are not somewhere far away, alone, in bed naked, laughing and eating ice cream off each other. I am sorry—'

'Hey! You're missing your party.' Ugh. Dominic is back. Before he is on us, I whisper quickly to Ariella.

'Can I find you later?'

It's a small, hesitant nod, but it's there. Progress.

I turn to Dominic. 'Sorry, mate, she's all yours.' I pat him on the back and walk away, knowing full well that Ariella is anything but.

I watch Aari, laughing happily on the beach, all night, but I don't get the chance to grab her again before the party dies down at two in the morning. When I'm about to get into bed after a quick shower, I decide to give it one last try and get the front desk to put me through to her room.

'Hi,' I start.

'Hi.'

'Can I come over to see you for a bit?'

There's a pause. She's thinking about it. Come on, Ariella. I know you want to see me too.

'Beach Villa 7.'

I fly across the resort to her door and she opens it after the first set of knocks. She's in the hotel bathrobe, her hair wet from the shower. She shuts the door quickly behind me, looking uncertain that she is doing the right thing. She pulls her robe together tightly around herself as she faces me. Before I can form a thought, my mouth is on hers, breathing her in. The world, its problems and occupants fall away.

Ariella's arm snakes around my neck, pulling me in as she buries her hand in my hair. I lift her up and into me, resting her legs on my hips, crushing her hammering heart against mine. She is my home. I've been gone so long, it hurts.

We devour each other surrounded by the night's cool breeze rushing through her open terrace door, pouring our longing, our apologies, our fears and our desire into it. With our tongues reacquainting, then settling into their familiar rhythm, I carry her into the suite's bedroom. I sit on the tightly made bed, gently moving her into a straddling position. Intertwining my fingers with hers, I lie back, taking her with me. Our bodies still fit perfectly. She pulls away, lightly panting.

'No, don't go... please,' I whisper, begging, as I lift my head to catch her bottom lip between my teeth. Looking right into her eyes, I pull the belt of her bathrobe apart and place my hands on her waist. She re-engages our kiss immediately. I try to keep my hands in the safe zones of her body – her back, her waist and the base of her spine over her underwear – but I'm finding it hard to stay there. I sit up, bringing her up with me, and gently tease the bathrobe over her shoulders, keeping our mouths connected. The robe pools around her waist, baring the beautiful body I remember. My girls have filled out once again and her soft bits have returned. She's looking after herself. Good.

I break our kiss, flip her over so she is under me and press my body against hers. She lets out that sexy gasp I love so much and, this time, pulls my lips back to hers. I run my hand up her inner thigh, making its way to a destination that we both know is inevitable. Ariella lets out a long low moan as my fingers find their way behind the seam of her underwear. She is delightfully wet. I press my intentions against her.

'I want to make you come so fucking badly, Aari,' I whisper into her ear. Ariella suddenly goes rigid. I know the tension between us has shattered, before she says anything.

'I can't do this, I'm sorry, Caleb.'

I watch the desire drain from her face. 'What's wrong?'

'You can't just come in and do what you like with me. I'm not your sure thing to play with when you're bored and lonely.'

Shit. She thinks it's about the sex.

'I don't think you're a sure thing, Aari...'

'Yes, you do. We both know I will give in, and I almost did. Excuse me.' She retreats into the bathroom while I sit on the bed, trying to think my hard-on away. I can't exactly make the case that it's not about the sex with a boner.

When Ariella eventually emerges with her bathrobe intact, she makes her way to one of the massive couches on her terrace looking out to sea. I don't know what to say because I wasn't expecting any of this. When I left my house this morning, the last thing I expected was to be in Ariella's villa, alone with her naked under a bathrobe.

'Would you like some water?' I ask, grabbing a couple of bottles from her room fridge, and using the opportunity to sit beside her when I return. I see her pulling away already. No. I am not going to let her.

'What is going on, Caleb? What is this secret that everyone seems to know, apart from me?'

'Do you trust me?'

'Actually, no. Not at this moment.'

She has me cornered.

'I think you'd better leave, Caleb, and maybe restrict future advances to your girlfriend?' She yanks the bathrobe tightly around her.

'Wait, what girl—'

Annoyingly, the doorbell to the suite chimes, startling both of us. It's a welcome relief until it dawns on me that it is three in the morning and I know exactly who is on the other side of that door. Infuriated, I march to the door. I am going to handle this once and for all.

'Get back here!' Ariella whispers angrily at me.

'What does he want? It's three!'

'Bedroom, now!' she commands, running past me to get the door. I do as I am told but stand by the door, out of sight, determined to hear it all. She looks through the peephole and sighs before she opens it.

'Hi, Dominic.' I hear the smile in her voice.

'Hey. I was going to go back to the boat to hang out under the sky. I thought you might want to come? I also thought we could have that chat.'

'I'd love to but I am in the middle of—'

'Wait, have you been crying?'

'Don't worry, it's completely self-inflicted.'

'Want me to come back later?'

Later? It's three. It's so late, it's early. And the sky? Really? That's the best he's got?

'I'm a little exhausted, maybe another time?'

'I can...'

I hear the room door shut. Ariella has stepped outside to meet him. I dash to the peephole. She is standing with both arms crossed against her chest holding her bathrobe in place. I can't hear what they are saying but he points at the room a couple of times and she shakes her head, smiling. Eventually he leaves. I launch myself across the room onto the living room couch and try to look like I haven't been spying, as she lets herself back in.

'What did he want?' I try to sound casual.

'Just to hang out.'

'At three? Who wants to hang out at three?'

'You're here, aren't you? Speaking of which, I'd like to go to bed, Caleb.'

'If I promise to keep my hands to myself, can I get in with you? We can chat?'

'Are you joking? No. You have a girlfriend, Caleb.'

'No, I don't.'

'Please don't lie to me. You called her "honey" and handed her a Shark Week hot-water bottle right in front of me. I know she is living with you at home, Caleb. I catch the lift with her most mornings when she's on her way to the gym. You're not this person. She seems really sweet, don't ruin it.'

She isn't going to occupy the moral high ground here.

'That's a bit hypocritical, Ariella – if you knew I had a girl-friend, why did you call me last night asking me to go away with you?'

Embarrassment sweeps across her face. 'I wanted to go away with my friend.'

'Really? Were you going to ask your friend's girlfriend to tag along too?'

'If that was what you wanted.'

Bullshit.

'Think she would have come along, knowing you were letting me undress you a few minutes ago?'

She pulls her bathrobe tighter and has the decency to look away. Exactly. She doesn't get to be holier than thou while she paints me as some cheating bastard.

'I made a mistake and I feel awful about it. Which is why I think you should return to your room and, when you get home, we can pretend this never happened.'

'The way you pretend our relationship never did?'

'That's not fair and it's not true.'

'You seem to have moved on pretty easily.'

'Moved on? Do you have any idea how many times I've

stood outside your door and resisted the urge to knock?' A big, fat tear rolls down her cheek silently.

The fight in me is replaced by an overwhelming desire to hold her close. I reach out, but she moves away as soon as my arms envelop her.

'No, Caleb. You can't push me away, then wonder where I went. You've been so mean.'

'And you've been downright torturous. Budget Jasper is all over you and you're letting him. The whole world thinks you're dating. At least I'm keeping a low profile.'

'You've always kept a low profile, Caleb. You were dating half the building back in London and they didn't know about each other.'

'Not with you! You say you gave me every part of you. What the hell do you think I gave you? I handed parts of me that I didn't know existed over to you and you jumped all over them, said no thanks and threw them out of your apartment. I was vulnerable and being with you was absolutely fucking frightening, Aari. I knew that it would end in this nightmare, where I have lost you and I don't know what to do, because you've opened up this massive gaping hole that I know I won't be able to fill, with anyone, ever again.'

For a minute neither of us moves or says anything, so I decide it is time to leave.

'I'm sorry.' Ariella finally moves closer to me.

'I'm a mess, Aari.'

'What can I do?'

'You can stop talking to me about "getting home" and asking me to "go home". There is no home. Home is you. You're the only home I know and every time you say that, it just reinforces that you don't feel the same. It's annoying.' I can see from her face that I've said too much, so I try to lighten the mood. 'And maybe push Dominic off the boat on the way back?' I laugh a little. It surprises me that she smiles too.

218

'He's just my friend, Caleb.'

'But you know he wants more than that.'

'I know he wants different, not more. I don't think he'd say no if I asked him to spend the night, but you and I know that I can't do that.'

'Does he know that?'

'Of course. I am clear with him – and besides, I need more.'

'More than I gave you?'

'You didn't give me anything. We shared everything, and that was all I wanted. You were my home too.'

She says it so sadly I reach for her again. She lets me pull her in and hug her. I place my chin on her head.

'I'm sorry. I can't believe I let us break up.'

'Maybe we were supposed to. I could use some time on my own to figure myself out. I am intensely jealous, but happy that you found someone to have a quiet relationship with. If you weren't seeing anyone, I'd want to get back together, but this forces me to spend some time on my own and I desperately need that.'

'You know Dominic isn't going to stop trying to swing by at three in the morning?'

'I'll be fine. Still being in love with you helps.'

'Aari. Hearing that makes me want to kiss you.'

'Please don't. We're already teetering on the edge of acceptable behaviour.'

I want to tell her the truth about Honey, but I can't until I've cleared it with her, so I decide to maintain the illusion that Honey is my girlfriend for now. She says that she needs the time, so I am going to give it to her. I can do the friendship thing and spend more time with her, until she is ready to get back together. Until then, I plan to cock-block anyone who comes close, starting with Dominic. He's toast.

I pull Ariella closer on the couch and let her snuggle into me. We talk until she falls asleep, emitting those tiny snores I've missed, breathing deeply against my chest. Just her lying here in my arms, holding on to me, makes me realise that I'd do just about anything to get her back, even if it means sacrificing my own needs. Jasper is right. I have to find the courage to tell her about me, Melissa, Ivory Bow and my old clients. I don't deserve her with everything I am holding on to; and she deserves a better man.

I just need to find a way to step up to the plate.

TWENTY-FOUR

ARIELLA

Waking up in Caleb's arms feels wrong, but I am not about to leave in a hurry.

I do deeply regret taking this job because of what it has done to us. Everything has felt so out of kilter without him. Thankfully, last night's conversation helped. I want my friend back. Well, I want more than my friend back, but he is now with someone else. She's beautiful, confident and always has a polite smile when we see each other. Lying here, my guilt makes me commit to leaving the house fifteen minutes earlier every day to avoid her. I try to stop myself imagining her waking up next to Caleb, running around his apartment with him or cuddling on the sofa watching TV, but it's too late. I bet he tells her to stop wriggling and pulls her close.

'Stop wriggling, Aari,' Caleb whispers as if on cue, and pulls me in.

'I know it's none of my business, but do you tickle her belly?' I feel ashamed for asking.

'No. I don't. It's different with her.' Caleb strokes my hair. 'We're not what one would call affectionate.'

'Calling her honey seems pretty affectionate.'

OLA TUNDUN

'Not if that's her actual name.'

I look up at Caleb to see if he's joking. He isn't.

'Are you just...'

'Let's just say we keep each other out of trouble.'

'Does she know that?'

'She does. She also knows that I still belong to someone else.' He kisses the top of my head.

'And she's fine with that?'

'She's totally fine with it.'

I lie with him for a little while longer, knowing that if I don't kick him out soon, I am going to behave in a way that won't make me proud of myself. It takes everything to extract myself from the warmth of his softly beating chest and sit up.

'Good idea. I better head out.'

I walk him to the door wishing he could stay, but I know he can't.

'I'm glad we talked.' He gives me that slow smile, my slow smile.

'Me too. I'm pleased we are friends again.'

Irritation crosses his face. 'Ariella, please will you stop? I'm not interested in being your friend.'

'But we are friends.'

'Too much has happened. Let's just say we are talking?'

'But—'

Caleb's mouth comes for mine. I should push him away but I don't. His warm hands find their way underneath my robe and stroke my skin. Holding my waist gently, he pulls me close and I let him. His mouth wanders to the base of my neck and I know what's coming. My body responds pleasurably as he brands me with his mouth. I belong to him, he wants to remind me of that; and I want him to. We stay like that, enjoying our closeness for a little while, until his hands start to wander. One's already cupping one of his girls, and the other is slowly making its way past my belly button.

'Okay. We need to stop.' I extract myself from his grasp.

'I think we've just established that you don't want to be friends either.' He smirks.

His self-satisfied smirk makes me want to kiss him again. I clear my throat and pull my robe tighter.

'I'll catch you later.' Caleb sweeps in for a final quick kiss and pinches my bum before he opens the door and walks out of it.

I can't help the smile on my face and the surge of happiness I feel as I hop into the shower and get dressed for breakfast. I even catch myself laughing at nothing a few times. Caleb may be seeing someone, but he still belongs to me and I'm beside myself with glee that we are talking again.

I am still beaming when I grab some fruit and join Jasper and Mommy at their breakfast table. 'Morning!' I almost sing, greeting both of them happily.

Jasper chuckles. 'You look much better than you did last night. You okay?' he asks.

'Yes. Which is more than I can say for you, Mommy. What happened?'

My mother shakes her head slowly behind her huge dark sunglasses.

'Stella here decided to get her groove back by doing tequila shots with people half her age till dawn.'

'Hey, you're supposed to be on my side,' Mommy complains.

'I am. But I haven't been to bed because of you, Dahlia.'

Mummy scowls at an amused Jasper. 'I blame Budget Jasper.'

Ugh. Caleb has clearly been in her ear.

'Things were winding down until he showed up and declared he was in the mood for many, many drinks.' Mommy slides her sunglasses down her nose and gives me a questioning look.

'Did we need to stay though? You were halfway out of the door,' says Jasper.

'Would have been rude not to... especially as it was obvious that he had just clearly been smacked down by madam over here.'

'I did feel a little sorry for Budget Me...'

Jasper too?

'Exactly. He needed us!'

'Did he need us enough to get back on that boat, feeling the way you do now?' Jasper teases. He is enjoying this.

'Listen, you, if I wanted to be moaned at I would have brought Hugh, okay? Ariella...' Mommy attempts to look frail. 'Please can you get your poor old mother some of that juice...'

'There was nothing poor or old about you a few hours ago, Dahlia.'

'You're enjoying this,' she moans at Jasper.

'Budget—'

'Okay, you guys, stop it! You can't keep calling him that!' I reprimand both of them in hushed tones. 'Caleb is the worst and both of you should not be entertaining his childish name-calling.'

Jasper and my mom look at each other with raised eyebrows.

'I don't believe we saw Caleb last night, did we, Jasper?' says Mommy.

'He's usually the life of every party. I wonder where he was?' Jasper joins in, failing to suppress his laugh.

'I have a pretty good idea... Ariella, what's this little fella doing here?' Mommy moves the top of my cardigan away with her teaspoon to reveal my neck.

'You're both so...' I start, relieving Mommy of her teaspoon.

'We just follow the breadcrumbs, or in this case, hickeys.'

My mom points at the base of my neck with her index finger and retracts it quickly.

'We just talked!'

They both look like they don't believe me.

'He came clean and it's fine.'

'Really? I didn't expect this reaction.' Jasper looks surprised.

'I know that I shouldn't be happy about it but at least now I know.'

'So, what do you want to do?'

'Nothing. She's keeping him out of trouble, according to him. Right now, we are just talking again.'

'Who's keeping him out of trouble?'

'Honey. His... I'm not sure what to call her, maybe a girlfriend?'

'Caleb has a girlfriend?'

'I sort of knew but he told me himself this morning.'

'He stayed over last night?'

'Yes, but we just talked until we fell asleep.'

'Was that all he wanted to tell you?'

'As far as I know.'

As if on cue, Caleb shows up at the table. 'Good morning, Ariella. Sleep well?' he teases.

I try to hide the smile that is ripping my face apart. I hate that he has turned me into a schoolgirl with a crush in a blink of an eye.

'Yes, thank you. You?' I giggle. Why am I giggling?

'Best sleep I've had in months. Felt like home.' He winks at me and my butterflies get energetic.

'Did you just sigh?' Jasper asks me, clearly disgusted with my behaviour. I am too, but I can't help it. 'You're both as subtle as an elephant on rollerblades.' He smirks, looking between us.

'I was just saying good morning.' Caleb grins as he tips his sunglasses down from his hair to cover his eyes. I want to bite him so badly.

'Oh really? Then where's my good morning, Caleb?' Jasper teases.

'Good morning, Jasper.'

'Very enthusiastic.' Jasper laughs while Caleb looks straight into the sea with a relaxed, victorious smile on his face. If I don't leave, I am going to grab him in front of everyone.

'I better pack and check out. Are we leaving soon?'

'Yeah, forty minutes.' Jasper looks at his watch.

'I'm good. I've got everything I came with, and so much more.' Caleb beams, still staring out to sea. Embarrassingly, I trip over my chair as I try to leave.

'Try not to trip over your tongue, Ariella.' Jasper laughs, and Caleb joins in. I'm happy that they can sit at a table together, but those two better not become friends. They are bad enough apart.

'Still the lookout?' Dominic asks, walking through the yacht's deserted bow towards Jasper and me. We'd left Mommy and Caleb dangerously close to the champagne, gossiping.

'Always. It's a bit of a lifetime appointment. The pay is non-existent, there are no bathroom breaks, it's permanently anxiety-inducing, murder on the eardrum, but you get some meals. Want to take a shift?'

Jasper doesn't wait for an answer. He gets up, shakes Dominic's hand and leaves.

'I like him,' Dominic declares as he sits next to me.

'Everyone does. I'm a lucky girl.'

'But, if he can't hold on to you, what does it take?'

'Maybe that's the problem. I don't think anyone should be held on to. I think people should just... be.'

'You're a hard one to figure out, Ariella Mason.' He squints at me with the sun in his eyes.

'I know. Sorry.'

'Don't apologise, I like it. But I've got to ask: is it just me or was something else kind of happening between us yesterday?'

'There was a shift.' I keep my eyes out to sea.

'But now it's gone?'

'I think so.'

'What happened between dinner and now? Did someone say something?'

I have to tell him. I grunt, trying to find the words.

'I knew it.'

No, he doesn't know it.

'It was Caleb, wasn't it? When he wanted a chat on the beach? What did he say?'

'Nothing.' I'm not about to tell him about his nickname.

'Ariella, he openly scowls at me at every opportunity, so you're not protecting my feelings or his. I think we both know where we stand.'

I take a deep breath. 'Jasper and I had been over for about a year when you saw me at the party. I wasn't heartbroken over Jasper, I was heartbroken over Caleb. We were together for a little while. It was intense and messy, but beautiful and all-consuming... and then it got hard, for both of us.'

Dominic's eyes widen and his mouth drops open. 'Shit! I did not see that coming.'

'I know. I'm sorry I didn't tell you. I was planning to but I thought it would be a funny revelation over too many drinks once I'd healed rather than... this.'

'That explains why he always looks like he's about to take my head clean off.'

'I'm sorry about that.'

'It's hard to imagine you together. He's so... out there and you're so... not.'

'We weren't a likely pairing, but it worked.'

'And you're still sorting through your feelings?'

I nod.

'You know he's seeing someone, don't you?'

'I've bumped into her a few times. She's very sweet.'

'Sweet? He's dating Honey Kohli!'

I nod.

'You don't know who Honey Kohli is, do you?'

'No.'

'He's a brave man. She's an absolute beast.'

'That's a little rude, Dominic.'

Dominic whips out his phone and starts typing. When he finds what he's looking for, he hands it over to me.

'That's Honey Kohli.'

The five-minute video is of two barefoot women in a cage, wearing shorts, training tops and half-gloves. Dominic reaches over and scrolls the video forward. Caleb's girlfriend is on top of the other girl, with blood everywhere, and is hammering away, until the referee pulls her off her opponent.

Dominic slips his phone out of my loose fingers and into his pocket. 'There are many, many more videos like that. I'd stay away from her if I were you.'

'She's a fighter?'

'She is THE fighter. MMA champion with an unbeaten record. She hasn't fought in about a year but she is still frightening.'

'Oh.'

'How is this news to you? It's all over Ivory Bow and Caleb's social media. You've even commented on how powerful she is!'

'Lydia runs my social media – surprise.' I hear my voice break.

'I'm sorry, Ariella.'

'It's fine.' Everything that I felt last night and this morning shatters all over again. Caleb and Honey are much better matched. She's a fighter too, she's accomplished, she's beautiful and she doesn't come with our complications. I can't help picturing them play-fighting around his apartment. Caleb is in denial if he thinks it's not emotional. They are perfect together.

'Can I see his social media feed?' I ask weakly.

'I don't think you should.' Dominic looks concerned.

'It will help.'

He takes his phone out again and scrolls through. 'This is the first picture of both of them hugging in your lobby as she is leaving your building.'

The picture is granulated but it's clearly them, with the caption 'Loose lips sink ships.'

There are more pictures of them out together at events. They look good together. Her petite frame, dark skin, dark eyes and blond hair next to Caleb, tall, tanned, dark hair and blue eyes – I can't take it, and return his phone.

'Thank you, Dominic.'

'If it helps, they are referring to each other as friends, but obviously no one is buying it,' he says gently.

'Do you mind if I sit here alone for a little while?' I ask him. I just want to be left alone to cry.

'I do. I'm not leaving you alone like this. I'm just going to sit here and I won't say a word. Okay?'

We stay like that, in silence, until the boat gets back to Singapore.

TWENTY-FIVE

CALEB

I wake up with Ariella's thigh across my torso and her hair all over the pillow next to me. I temporarily forget this isn't home and fill my lungs with her scent before I slide my hand up her thigh. It's not until I start pulling her on top of me that reality hits. I sit bolt upright and instinctively push her off me, startling her awake as she falls off the other side of the bed. The loud crack that follows doesn't sound good.

'Aaaarrgghh! Caleb!'

'Sorry.' I jump out of her bed in my boxers and start searching for my clothes. She's annoyed as she gets up off the floor, rubbing her elbow. She is wearing her usual vest and shorts. Okay. She's clothed. Thank goodness. 'What happened last night?'

'You were an absolute nuisance.' Her arms are crossed and she is clearly irritated.

'All I remember is sitting on the floor of my kitchen with some rum. I didn't try to... impose myself, did I?'

'No. Not in that way. In every other way though, you were extremely obtrusive.'

'Phew. Okay, good.'

'No, not good. I've barely had any sleep.' She throws my jogging bottoms at me. I'm slow this morning and it hits me squarely in the face. I feel like I deserve it. She humphs victoriously and stomps out the room. I quickly follow.

'So how did we...?'

'No, not we. You! You came up to my floor, declaring no one could ever love me like you did. I had to coax you back into the lift, take you back to your apartment, which wasn't hard to spot because the door was wide open. I put you into bed and left you there but you were right back up, telling me you didn't want to be alone. You could barely walk. I got some ibuprofen, forced it down your throat with you trying to bite my fingers the entire time because you thought it was funny, and I put you in the spare bedroom. Literally two minutes after I put you in bed, you were in here, tugging at my shorts, saying all you wanted was a cuddle. Then you went into the bathroom, threw up everywhere, had the consciousness to rinse your mouth out with my mouthwash, crawled into bed and fell asleep on top of me.'

'No... I didn't...' I'm horrified at my behaviour.

'Yes. You did. When you eventually fell asleep, I took off your shirt and wiped you down because you got some on you, and cleaned my bathroom. Then I went down, eventually found your keys, grabbed some fresh clothes, locked your apartment and came back into bed to make sure you didn't choke in your sleep.'

'Thank you.' I don't know what else to say.

'Your keys are on the kitchen top. I left a bottle of water by the bed for you with some more painkillers. Your clothes are in the machine. Shut the door after you please.'

I really want to move but my body isn't responding, so when she gets tired of glaring at me, she huffs and leaves, only to return with the painkillers, water and a T-shirt.

'Here!' She shoves them at me. She is so cute when she is

231

angry, with her little v-shaped eyebrows trying to meet in the middle. I move slowly.

'Do you have food at home?'

I think of the Chinese I had with Jasper last Wednesday, the night before he flew back home with Dahlia. It must be five days old.

'Not really.'

'I'll make you some eggs on toast but then you have to go. Do you want coffee or tea?'

'Coffee please.'

'There are new toothbrushes in the cabinet above my sink.'

I can tell Ariella wants to be firm and intolerant this morning. Sadly, she's failing because she is being incredibly sweet. I disappear to take a quick shower and, when I return, she has her back to me, standing with a hand on her hip, balancing one foot on top of the other, stirring some hollandaise while keeping her eye on the poached eggs. She looks so sleepy when she turns around, I feel guilty.

'It will be ready in a minute. Coffee is in the cafetière.' She's not annoyed any more, just tired.

'What's the time?'

She looks at the oven. 'Four forty-seven.'

I can't take my eyes off her as I take a seat at the kitchen counter. I have no idea how I am going to approach this. I thought we'd established a solid holding pattern at her birthday, but since we returned to Singapore she has been cold and distant. First she used Dahlia staying as her excuse not to spend time together, which I can understand. However, since Dahlia and Jasper left, she has been particularly elusive. In fact, I'm certain she has been avoiding me in that confusing, polite, annoying way she does. As she quietly plates up the eggs Benedict she knows I love, all my feelings hit me at once. I take her arm, pull her close and make her eyes meet mine as soon as she puts the plate down in front of me.

'I'm finding it hard to stay away from you,' I confess.

'Caleb. You have a girlfriend. I am assuming you were only here last night because she wasn't at your place; so I think you should eat your breakfast and hop it.'

She tries to move away and I gently hold her in place. 'We talked about this already, we're just...' I want to talk but she starts to wriggle out of my hold, so I let her go.

'I can't do this with you, Caleb, it hurts. Please eat your breakfast and go home.' Ariella quickly retreats into her bedroom without looking back. It kills me when I hear her lock the door behind her. We obviously need another chat but Honey will be here in about an hour, attempting to kill me. I thought I was catching up with her in training until yesterday, when she announced that she feels like it's time to take my training up from basic to a lower intermediary level. I'm going to be broken today at work. I take the plate, mug and cutlery from Ariella's to mine. It'll give me a reason to return.

Aari, as usual, is at her desk by the time I get in, and Dominic is already there too, flirting and making her laugh. I want to smash his face in but not as much as I wanted to when I heard him call her Aari for the first time. She, in turn, now calls him Dom. I haven't actually heard her say it, but I've watched her lips move through the glass often enough to see her mouth the word. Since her birthday, he has become more emboldened. Previously, when I threw him a disapproving look he ignored it. Now, he either smiles back confrontationally or acknowledges it with a nod. I don't like it, but I have no choice but to suck it up. She can hook up with anyone she wants and, although I don't see her hooking up with anyone, Dominic Miller is sneakier and more charming than most mere mortals, so I need to act fast.

I walk into her office unannounced and intentionally step in between her desk and the couch where Budget Jasper is parked.

She leans back, a little surprised. I don't know why. She has an open-door policy. People are bound to walk in from time to time. That's what an open-door policy is, Ariella.

'Hey, Caleb,' she greets me cautiously.

'Hey. Think I could get some time in your diary? I feel like we need a change in direction.'

'Of course, let me have a look.' She directs her attention to her computer.

'Doesn't Lydia usually sort that out for you guys?'

Budget Jasper is trying to make a point and I don't have the patience. I'm not here for him. 'I'm sorry, Dominic – do you work here?' I ask icily.

'Occasionally.' He shrugs and smiles before he winks at Ariella. The fuck?!

Ariella bristles and quickly interrupts. 'I can do four today, Caleb, is that okay?'

'Yep, sure. Thanks.' I leave without acknowledging him any further.

Bryce shakes his head at me when I emerge to return to my desk and, sure enough, when I flip my computer back on, there's a private message from him.

bparsons:
Dude, relax.

He's right but I can't. I am not taking Dominic's invasion lying down. I toss what just happened out of my mind and work on prepping for our monthly PR meeting. It's always a good meeting for me, so I know that Aari will be pleased when we sit down in our video conference with Georgie and Melissa later.

Unfortunately, it turns out not to be a good meeting for her.

'I'm not sure how to say this,' Georgie begins. 'Mel, maybe we should talk to Ariella privately.' She dithers. It's bad. Georgie is not a ditherer.

'We have an open office, Georgie, it's better if everyone knows what's going on,' Ariella gently responds. Georgie clears her throat. Uh-oh.

'Go on, Georgie,' Melissa encourages.

'The bottom is dropping out of Ariella's popularity. The plan was to show two sides of Ivory Bow with the introduction of Caleb, and that worked for a while. Now he has settled in, he is having a bit of an adverse effect on Ariella and the brand is splitting. They are coming across as competitors rather than colleagues.'

Shit.

'In what way?' Ariella pokes, without missing a beat.

'People are picking sides. You're coming off as flat, personality-less and one-dimensional, Ariella. Outfit mentions, supplier support and food posts will only get you so far. In isolation, it's fine, but your social media content is beginning to look really dull in comparison to the content Caleb is pushing out.'

This is not good.

'Why is there such a massive difference?' Melissa asks.

'At the moment, Caleb is coming off as the heart, soul and big personality of the company. He's always out, having a great time with the team and clients. Hanging out with the project girls has given him a really fun, protective, "big brother" boost. Also, this thing going on between him and Honey Kohli is PR gold. She is notoriously private and Caleb is the first guy not on her payroll that she has ever been seen publicly with; so obviously all her followers are jumping on too. His sweaty, shirtless workout posts don't hurt either. We're fans of those ones in particular, here in the office...'

Georgie might as well just nail my coffin shut with Ariella. Everyone knows Lydia controls her social media, so I know for a fact she hasn't seen any of the content I am pushing out, but now, Georgie is delivering a detailed and accurate synopsis. The last thing I need right now is for Ariella to look at my feed.

'Cold shower, Georgie. What's going wrong with Ariella's?' Melissa laughs as she winks at us over the video.

'Ariella, your content has become flat and predictable. You're usually at a gala in formal wear or at some dry business event. When you do have company, it's a member of your team and it looks like you're being escorted more than anything else. The chemistry with your team isn't coming across. You're always perfectly behaved and when they are with you they are the same. You're always pictured leaving early and, if there is ever a picture of you at the event, you have the same "get me out of here" expression. The most interesting thing about you currently is that your skin is always bare but glowing. Also, you do look really chic and a bit rebellious, turning up in jeans to everything aside from your formal events, but that's it. Basically, everyone wants to hang out with Caleb and you're just his uninteresting boss. Ivory Bow has split like we feared and, Ariella, you're losing. Badly. Sorry.'

The entire conference room is silent.

Ariella doesn't miss a beat. 'How do we fix it?' she asks without a hint of emotion in her voice. 'Do I need to attend more fun things?'

'I could go to more formal things with Ariella?' I volunteer, gladly. In fact, it would be the perfect solution.

'No, it will just look like she made you do it.' Georgie shuts me down. 'We need to build a three-dimensional character. We need to push your personality out there because right now, there is none. We need you to stop sitting on your personal stuff. I know you don't want to, but pictures from your birthday might help humanise you, if you release them. Basically, anything that has you looking less "deer in the headlights" with it all. Maybe go to a couple of things with Dominic Miller? A hint of romance could help? We need less fear and more laughter.'

'I have serious concerns that what Ivory Bow is trying to achieve might be overshadowed by my personal life and that is not the goal. I am here to steer the ship and not to entertain the internet.' It's obvious Ariella has had this conversation before.

'Exactly. Ariella doesn't need to be Caleb,' Lydia pitches in a little aggressively. 'No offence to Caleb, but he can afford to be cool, shirtless and fun because the company isn't sitting on his shoulders. Surely the work persona should take precedence over a personal life she has repeatedly requested to keep private? We should respect that. Why can't we work together to deliver more strategic professional content aligned to her role, rather than diminishing her competence by making her a caricature of what you want her to be in relation to Dominic Miller?'

Wow, Lydia has claws? I also like the way she said 'Dominic Miller' with total disgust. Lydia is a keeper.

'I hear you, Lydia,' Georgie starts, 'but we need to build a person, caricature or not. The person pulls the followers in to listen to the strategy.'

'She IS a person! I think it's insulting—'

'Lydia.' Ariella puts her hand on Lydia's arm. 'Send over all the pictures from my birthday, please.'

Then she turns her attention to Georgie. 'I'll go to some things with Dominic but I want to be absolutely clear. We're friends. That's a line I will not cross.' She has given up fighting it. Her single demand, to call Dominic her friend, doesn't mean shit. Honey is actually my friend and people are already creating babies by merging our faces together. I immediately commit to posting lovely things about Ariella – but not too lovely, so the followers don't smell a 'Georgie'.

'We should also leverage the launch,' I add. She's not going to like it, but I have a plan. 'The invitations are stunning but I wonder if instead of it being "Ivory Bow would like to invite you to", it could be "Ariella Mason would like the pleasure of your company at". They can go out with a short letter from Ariella, personally inviting the guests. It can be light and funny. If we set it up right, it will make them feel like they are getting a side of her that no one else sees. Then at the party, she delivers the whole welcome speech. We scrap doing all our individual bits, she carries it all and delivers it all for us. We fall in line behind her. One voice. All eyes. Just her.'

Ariella looks like she is about to pass out. She doesn't like the idea at all. That's fine. I plan on helping her through it, for both altruistic and selfish reasons. I've got you, my little Mason.

'Brilliant idea, Caleb,' Melissa agrees. 'What is the party looking like at the moment?'

Bree, who is leading the launch project, pipes up. 'We are going "Coastal Grecian". The service teams will be in tasteful powder-blue swimwear. We are still working on the amalgamated archer and ribbon bow design concepts for the prints on the suits.'

'When are we thinking?'

'Three weeks. Friday night, so guests can still have their weekends.' Bree takes over.

'That will also give us weekend traction for social media and the Sunday papers,' Georgie adds.

'Georgie, can you catch a flight out?'

'Absolutely, Mel!' Georgie shrieks, delighted.

'What do you think attendance will be like?'

'The RSVPs will come in like that.' Bryce snaps his fingers happily. 'I am constantly being asked when we are going to have a launch party by people I don't know!'

'We should keep it small though.' Devin pulls on the reins. 'We don't want everyone showing up. We said we'd cap it at a hundred and fifty.'

'Have invites gone out yet? I have a few guests—' Georgie starts.

'Sorry, Georgie, Caleb and Ariella have been allocated their invitation numbers and even that is going to be a difficult client cull,' Lydia interrupts. She really doesn't like Georgie. I remind myself to get the gossip from Lydia at our next whisky session.

'PR is an important part—'

'Before we have this conversation, let's see what Caleb and Ariella come back with?' Melissa referees Georgie and Lydia. Ariella has had enough and is about to take charge. I can see it on her face.

'Bree, please can I see the final plans for the party with the updated client journey today? Akiko, please can you get in touch with the designers and let them know that I'd like to see the latest logo options, a revised concept on the invite to allow for a personal message from me and the paper stock choices by the end of the day? Jess, please can you send Lydia a handful of our copywriters with samples of their work for review today, and Sian, please could you get in touch with the speaker coaches and send them over for Lydia to vet? We can look through them tonight.'

The girls nod obediently.

'Lydia, please can you pull a hundred of Caleb and my top contacts for us to sort through?'

Lydia nods and scribbles in her notepad.

'Caleb, do you think you will be prepared enough to run through your preferred invitees at four?'

No chance. Thanks to this new development, I'm going to exploit this little gift and turn our meeting into dinner, alone, at hers, tonight.

'Can we move it to a later time? If you're going through everything at the end of the day, maybe we should meet after that?' I suggest.

'That makes sense. Lydia, please can you make Caleb my last meeting? Whatever time I finish today?'

I air-punch in my mind.

'And can you join us if it's not too late?'

I deflate. There is no such thing as too late for Lydia. Ariella often has to force her to go home.

'Caleb, if you have an opening at four p.m., can you pop over to see me at the hospital?' Melissa requests.

I know she has apologised and is handing me a small fortune, but I'd rather scratch my eyes out with my own finger-nails if there was a choice. 'Sure. Do I need to bring anything or anyone with me?'

'Nope, just your naughty self.'

'Am I in trouble?' I laugh nervously, looking around the room. Melissa has never requested my presence alone, in front of the team, before. This is bold.

'A little bit.'

The whole room laughs with her. They have no idea. 'When is he not in trouble?' Georgie adds joyfully.

'Lydia, please can you get in touch with the stylist and the make-up artist? We should try to soften Ariella's image from now until the party. Please update them on the feedback; they need to keep the jeans and leave her face bare. Let's explore some tiny but fun changes,' Melissa instructs.

Aari shuts her book harder than she normally would. She is not liking the reintroduction of Eden and Ruby.

Lydia has the final say.

'Ariella, I want to speak for all of us. What the internet says about you isn't who you are. We respect you and you're the best boss I have ever worked for. You are kind, generous, stylish and you work incredibly hard. The people that judge you just because they can't be bothered to see who you really are should be ashamed of themselves.'

'Thank you, Lydia. Meeting over,' is all she says. She picks up her notebook and walks out of the room as soon as Melissa and Georgie log off.

After she has left, we all look at each other. The feedback has been brutal. She's miserable, boring and no one likes her. Proving them wrong is a battle I want to fight for her.

'Fuck Georgie!' Lydia slams her hand down on her notepad, before picking it up and walking after Ariella.

'Get in here now! This is all your fault, Caleb!'

This doesn't sound like the 'little bit' of trouble I'm supposed to be in. Not that I care. I ignore her and approach slowly, intentionally.

'How is th—' I start.

'Shut up, Caleb. I told you she was lonely. I told you she was miserable. It was your job to make her happy and you failed, phenomenally.'

'Making Ariella happy is not in my job description, Melissa, and why are you blaming me?'

'Goodness. Why do I keep hoping you're more intelligent than I give you credit for?'

'I'm the first to concede that I was a shitty boyfriend but this is your mess. She's a 26-year-old that did an exceptional job in London because she had steering, support and leadership. Now, she has to learn, on the job, everything about running and delivering a company with the weight and might that you are trying to scale up to. She's miserable because of you. She has met every challenge you've thrown at her, but it has taken everything she has and she's exhausted. The moment she achieves whatever it is you want, you throw another thing at her. The latest is to turn her into your dancing social media puppet.'

Mel studies me, seething. 'I am not turning her into a puppet.'

Fuck you, Melissa. I let rip.

'Yes, you are! You asked her to leave her home, family and friends to move to the other side of the world. She left them. Build a team. She built it. Learn all the legal aspects of running a company. She learned it. Understand all the financial requirements of running a business in Singapore. She understood it. You even tried to make her dress however you want. She gave herself over to you initially, you abused the hell out of it; so, thankfully, she has grabbed some of that control back. Then you make her work and deal with an ex-boyfriend that is a total arsehole. Not only did she do that, she motivated me into actually caring about this business. You're the one person that should be fighting in her corner, not me. Instead, you've now basically asked her to become Dominic Miller's escort, and guess what? She's consented to that too; as long as you don't call it exactly what it is. She can't fucking win!'

I'm shouting so loudly, Melissa, for once, has actually shut up to listen.

'You could help her win, Caleb.'

'I'm not going to toy with her, Melissa.'

'Goodness you're slow. I'm not expecting you to toy with her. Just find the courage to do what you both actually really want and get your relationship back on track.'

'Bollocks. You don't give a shit about what we want.'

'You are only here because Ariella, whether or not she admits it to herself, needs you here. I've even tried to replace you but she's not biting. Irritatingly, I am stuck with you.'

'Is Dominic Miller one of your replacements?'

Melissa mumbles 'stupid' under her breath, clearly referring to me. 'If you're not going to get back together with Ariella, fine, but you're going to start saying yes to the interviews you have been turning down. I'm not asking. You're going to talk about how professional and focused your boss is and you're going to fall in line with messaging. You can keep your whole stupid bad-boy thing, but you make sure that you amplify the fact that it is with her blessing. Do whatever you want about this Honey Kohli thing as long as it doesn't affect Ariella. Obviously, you need to keep quiet about your personal history with her.'

'The minute I speak to someone, they will dig for more and find out.'

'No, they won't. Georgie has briefed *The Singaporean*. You'll like this one. There's a photoshoot and everything.'

'*The Singaporean*? They're as huge and as glossy as it gets!'

'No point starting small. You're the cover. You've been silent for too long. It's time. Now get out. And I am serious about Ariella. If you can't do good, don't do damage.'

'Bloody hell, I hate you, Melissa.'

'That's to be expected.' She shrugs, not the least bit bothered. 'Try to hold on to memories of the times when you liked me, very, very much.'

I wait until I am out of the hospital before I call Lydia.

'Good afternoon, Lydia Li at Ivory Bow. How can I help?' Her voice sparkles down the phone.

'Lydia, it's Caleb.'

'Hi, Caleb.' She audibly relaxes. 'How did your meeting go?'

'I made it out alive.' I laugh.

'Oooooh! Did you get scolded?' Lydia joins in.

'A little. Let's get nightcaps this week and I'll tell you about it.' She's a sucker for a good whisky and a chat, so I know she'll take me up on it.

'Done. So, what do you need?'

'Awkward ask. Do you think you can find a way to not make the meeting with Ariella and me later?'

TWENTY-SIX

ARIELLA

'I am sorry, Ariella, I am not feeling very well...' Lydia admits at the end of the day.

'Oh no. I'll get Matthew to take you home.' Poor Lydia. She's never ill. It was bound to happen. It feels like she has been working non-stop since I arrived in Singapore. I send Matthew a quick text, asking him to bring the car to the front of the building for her.

'Here is everything you requested from the team for the party. I've also emailed you copies.' She hands me a large folder.

'Thank you. If you don't feel great in the morning, let me know and take the day, okay?'

'I should be all right tomorrow. Thanks, Ariella.'

I know the PR meeting was just as hard for her as it was for me. She has total control over my content and posts, because I completely trust her. After the Devin debacle, she put a lot of effort into consulting me on the tone and imagery that she was putting out. It took some scaling back, but she has been getting it right ever since. Or so we thought. It actually doesn't bother me that I am less popular than Caleb. No universe exists where I am more charming and charismatic than he is. My worry is the negative impact on the company, and I can't let that happen. If that means resubmitting to Eden and Ruby tomorrow morning, so be it.

Caleb is doing so well, you'd be forgiven for forgetting how resistant he was to coming. Singapore loves him. Caleb's great edge is that being Caleb will always be enough. Laughing, messy, out-all-night, charming, naughty Caleb. It still hurts that he isn't my Caleb any more, but I hope that will fade with time.

He pops his head into my office just when I am thinking about him.

'Hey! I heard Lydia can't join. Everyone is leaving, so why don't we head home and do it either at yours or mine? We can get sushi, I'm in that mood.' He smiles as he stretches and pats his belly.

I pause to gather as much dignity and self-respect as I can muster to respond, because inside I am screaming a big fat yes. Thankfully, I remind myself that I can't be left with Caleb unsupervised. 'It might be better to do it here,' I suggest, looking out to the office and hoping there is someone else to pull into this meeting. Devin is gone, Bryce is packing up and Jess, Sian, Akiko and Bree are chatting excitedly as they head towards the door. Caleb walks into my office and shuts the door behind him. Please don't do that, I plead silently. Before he opens his mouth, I know I'm going to give in. I'm such a disappointment.

'Come on. We have yelled at each other, you've tossed me out of your home, I've woken up hungover in your bed and shoved you out, I've thrown up all over your bathroom... we've exhausted all possible embarrassing scenarios.'

He's in a good mood, which always disarms me, because this Caleb makes me happy. Now that I've stopped lying to myself about his girlfriend and her irrelevance, maybe it'll be fine. Ugh. Who am I kidding? I'm in trouble.

'Fine. Matthew is dropping Lydia off at home, so we need separate cars back. I don't want your and Honey's fans to send me death threats. I have enough problems.' I put as much fun into that statement as I can, and he buys it.

'I'd snap the neck of anyone that so much as thinks about touching a hair on your head, Aari, so maybe we should avoid that. I'll arrange the cars.'

I watch him walk away, whistling to himself like he doesn't have a care in the world. What am I doing?

By the time the sushi is delivered to mine, we are stuck on the invite list and getting nowhere near our target guests.

'No people with criminal records,' I joke with a mouthful of sushi.

'I have to come to my own company's party; plus, that's like half of my guest list gone!'

'You have a criminal record? I thought you didn't get into trouble because of Jerry?'

'The path to my redemption has been long and rocky,' he hints, smirking at me and shrugging like it's no big deal. I wish he wouldn't smile at me like that. I refocus, and I resist reaching for him. Why did I say yes to being alone with him?

'This is impossible! I am still at fifty-four clients!' I complain, and Caleb laughs.

'I've been at forty clients for a little while, so I'm done. Accounting for people that won't use their plus one, will be out of the country and that simply may not be able to make it, I think I have a pretty secure seventy-five guests.' He throws his pen on the table.

'I'm struggling with who to cut.'

'I'd invite them all,' he suggests.

'What? No.'

'Your flat can take two hundred and fifty guests easily so, if they all show up, which they won't, you will still have tons of space. It's a pool party, on a Friday night. No offence, but as long as we keep the invite non-transferable you will have a huge dropout rate. Most of your list are quite old and traditional. Hanging out with the likes of me is not their scene. If you were invited to this, you wouldn't show up; you'd send me or the girls. Also, if they are not invited, they might be offended, and you don't want to do that. I can afford to offend people because I can just blame you and make it up with beers and chilli crab later. Your list is a lot more complicated than mine. I fully expect my guys to try to crash the party. Yours won't.'

He's right. 'I might just do that. I'll comb through carefully once more to make sure I have everyone.'

With that, Caleb gets up and wanders to the glass sliding door.

'Have you used your pool yet?' He pulls it open, cutting off the apartment's air conditioning.

'No, not yet.'

'What a waste! Mine's only half the size of yours and I swim every morning. I'd never get out if I lived up here.' He tosses his jacket on the floor, takes off his belt and starts unbuttoning his shirt.

'What are you doing?' I call from where I'm sitting.

'Going for a swim. My work is done. You're the one that's stuck.'

I watch him, mesmerised, as he undresses with his beautiful back to me. When he's down to his boxers he disappears around the corner. He re-emerges in a few seconds, wet from a rinse, and dives into the pool. I go to Ms Pat's linen cupboard, grab a big fluffy bath sheet for him and take it outside. Two legs are sticking up through the water as I catch him mid-handstand.

'Towel!' I shout, and point as his head bobs up.

'Come in.'

'No. I still have to check the names.'

'How are you going to have a pool party and you haven't even been in the pool?' He splashes my toes with water and I

247

take a couple of steps back. Caleb wants to play and I really want to join him.

'I don't need to get in the pool to know it's there. Besides, I don't have a swimsuit.' I know it's weak.

'Keep your underwear on. It's not like I haven't seen it all before.'

'No.'

'Here's a little sweetener. Get in, and I'll race you for three wishes.'

Now I'm interested. 'Anything?'

'Anything.'

I take off my clothes, rinse off and step in. Caleb is beside me in a flash. It's nice.

'From this end to the other?' I ask and he nods.

'Ready, s—'

He's off. I can't help smiling. Of course he's going to cheat. What Caleb doesn't know is, I'm fast. I catch up and leave him behind easily. When I get to the end, I hop up and sit on the side to wait for him.

'Draw,' he announces happily, and it makes me laugh.

'Now that my three wishes are secure...' I start.

'Nope. That was just one wish. We have two more to race for. Get back in.' He splashes me. I hop back in, laughing.

'I should have used the pool ages ago. It's nice.'

'Second race?'

'Sure.'

He narrows his eyes at me and smiles as I prepare to swim again.

'First to get out of the pool!'

I've prepped myself for the wrong race and he's quick. I hoist myself up even though he has won, but he pushes me back in just to seal the deal.

'What happened?' He smiles as I bob back up. I don't recognise the laughter that fills the terrace and it takes a second to realise that it's coming from me. Caleb is cracking up too.

'Caleb!'

'I know.' He shrugs, smiling.

I stretch out my hand up for some help, but once he grabs it I push myself back from the side of the pool, bringing him back into it with me. I then force him into a corner with a splash attack. That'll teach him.

'Truce!' He surrenders with his hands up in the air, so I stop.

'Final race?' I ask, getting ready.

'No chance. You could have told me you're a mermaid,' Caleb complains.

'Not quite. But Surrey Sharks Swim Squad Lead, yes.'

'Fine. Final race, but you really should pick on a fish your own size.'

'Want a head start?' I suggest cheekily.

'I have never been more insulted. Ready? Stea—'

I shoot off. I'd forgotten how good this feels, gliding through the water, feeling weightless and strong. I take each stroke and become one with it, as I commit to getting myself a suit and doing this more often. By the time I get to the other end, Caleb is waiting.

'You got out and ran, didn't you?' I laugh.

'You didn't specify what kind of race and there was no way I was going to beat you in the water, sooo...' he explains before he hops back in.

I dive and grab his legs so he loses his balance. I'm cackling when he resurfaces. This is the most fun I've had in Singapore, hands down.

'Bloody hell, I love you,' Caleb declares, laughing.

'At least someone does.'

'Stop it,' Caleb calls as he swims closer and puts his face right up to mine. Oh God, give me strength.

'I've never really cared about being liked or popular. I just wasn't prepared to be told the opposite.'

'I think we both know that I really, *really* like you, and so do the people that know you.' I hold my breath and move away slightly. He's too close.

'Take Dominic, for example. The man stalked you by sending you flowers every day for weeks. This obviously isn't a knicker-invasion exercise for him. Those people out there don't know you.'

That first sentence sounds odd until I realise what it is.

'Did you just call Dominic by his actual name? I didn't even get to use my wish! I'm proud of you, Caleb, you're growing.' I swim around him.

'He's going to be an ever-present character with this new development, isn't he? Plus, you don't need my shit tonight. I never thought I'd see the day where I much preferred it when you were hiding him in your office.' As Caleb floats away on his back, I catch his sad expression. I want to reach out and touch him but I know that, if I do, my resolve will crumble.

'We're just friends, Caleb.'

'Then why have you been avoiding me since your birthday?'

'I found out who Honey is. I know you say it's just physical, but I can't cope with it. You both have so much in common and she's living with you, so I think it's better...'

He immediately turns over and swims back. 'I didn't say that it was physical. I said we were keeping each other out of trouble.'

'Semantics, Caleb.' He's too close again. I need to move but my back is against the side of the pool. I start to submerge but he stops me.

'You cannot tell anyone what I am about to tell you. I'm sorry I didn't tell you in your villa but I needed to check with Honey to make sure it was okay.' Caleb drops to a whisper. 'Honey isn't living with me. She gets to mine at the crack of dawn every morning, fight-trains with me for an hour and leaves me barely breathing. She gets intense back pain when she sits for too long and makes her hot-water bottle herself every day. She'd just left it that day you were in the lift. We've just become really good friends.'

I believe him but I am sceptical. 'Why all the secrecy and why are you having to ask her for permission?' I whisper back.

'Because you're more her type than I am.' He waits to let it sink in. 'Someone she knows is threatening her and she has no intention of emerging from that closet any time soon.'

'That's awful.' In an instant, Honey Kohli goes from frightening potential attacker to someone who must be protected at all costs.

'It was the last thing I expected to hear, especially as I was complaining about you and Lara just before she told me.' He laughs.

'Is she all right?'

'She will be. We are just buying time right now until she decides what she wants to do. I'm quite happy hanging out with her. She's shy, but fun when she comes out of her shell. You'll like her. She thinks you're gorgeous. I've told her to back off, not that I'd be able to do anything if she decides not to. She's ferocious in training, I'd hate to poke her in a real fight.'

'I saw,' I admit.

'Ariella Mason! Did you get jealous and look her up?'

'Dominic showed me one of her fight videos on the way back from my birthday.'

'She's scary, right?'

'I don't believe there is a word in the English dictionary for what she is.' I chuckle. 'Dominic suggested I stay away from you and I had to agree.'

'Please don't.' Caleb closes in and pulls me towards him. 'While we are spilling secrets, I need to come clean. The exact number of women I have kissed since we—'

No. No. No. 'I don't want to know, Caleb.' I really don't.

'Is zero.'

'But you said...'

'I'm an arsehole when you're not around to tame the stupidity.'

This time, I successfully duck under the water and swim away. 'I can't do this with you, Caleb.'

'Do what?' He bobs over.

'This. All this. The I hate you. Let's try. Now I'm blocking your calls. I don't want to be friends, but I'll attack your new ones. I am shagging everyone. You don't exist. I don't care. I love you. I have a girlfriend. Okay, not really, we're just keeping each other out of trouble. By the way, I wasn't really shagging everybody, I just wanted to punish you because I was angry and I am a much better person when you're around.' I am out of breath by the time I finish.

'That's all totally fair.' He's close again. 'What do you want?'

'I just want my friend back.'

'You know we can't do that without everything else, Aari. Everything is a memory. Even just swimming here together. The last time we were by this pool, I broke us.'

'We have no other choice but to try to be friends. Right now, you're parading someone else as your girlfriend to – rightly – protect her from some evil person. I, in addition, am about to reduce everything I have worked for, to be arm candy. Apparently, I have to be coy next to Budget Jasper for people to believe I have a personality! That was an accident! Don't you dare laugh!'

Caleb loses the struggle to control himself and his laugh explodes out of him. I splash him and make my way to the side of the pool to hoist myself out.

'It's time for you to go home.'

'There is no way that is going to happen now.' Caleb swims

in front of me and blocks my route. 'This is what we are going to do. You're going to get your friend back. I'm going to see this thing out with Honey, however long it takes, because I promised. You're going to do the public friendship thing with Dominic. I'll find a way to deal with him, drooling all over you and—'

'I am not lying to Dominic and sneaking around with you. I actually really like him and I respect him.'

'You're going to tell him about us?'

'He already knows we were together, we broke up and I'm still not over you.'

'And now?'

'That we are trying to be friends.'

'Really?' Caleb looks annoyed.

'Yes. That's what is going to have to happen. I don't want you to decide that you hate me again because Dominic is standing too close to me in a photo. I'm tired of the secrecy. If we make it back, I want everyone to know it. I'm done hiding.' And I want to make it back. I really do.

'I understand, but until then can we try to minimise the damage we do to each other? Having people jump to conclusions about you both is not going to be pleasant.'

I know how he feels. I'm there right now with the Honey situation and it's the last thing I want to do to him.

'I promise to do my best. I don't want to lead Dominic on either, so I am going to tell him tomorrow about our PR meeting. That way, he can decide whether or not he wants to join Mel and Georgie's circus.'

'I think it's more Georgie, rather than Melissa. Also, did you get the feeling that Lydia and Georgie have already been at each other's throats?'

Caleb is such a gossip. I love it. 'It did feel a little tense between them, but then again, Lydia is responsible for my social media, so it would have been hard not to take the feedback personally. I should have intervened. I don't want Mel to think that I can't handle conflict.'

'Don't worry about Melissa; right now, she's focused on saving your image. In fact, that was mostly what my meeting with her was about. Full disclosure – she wants us to get back together, but privately.'

'Why?'

'She thinks I make you happy. I didn't tell her that me being a complete bastard to you may have had something to do with you being sad.'

'That was it?'

'That, and you're looking at the front cover of *The Singaporean*.'

It's genius. Putting Caleb in the front seat of traditional media is the better selection out of two of us. He takes it in his stride; in fact, I think he enjoys it.

'*The Singaporean*! That's great, Caleb!'

'Not really. Georgie is trying to make me "Bad Boy Black", but it's just a fun character to play. Maybe I used to be that person but I haven't been for a while.'

'Do you want to get out of it?'

'No, because while it's about me, the article is really about you. I'm supposed to boost your professional profile as the boss who allows me to be my authentic self – which is laughable, considering the article is focused purely on a social media construct. While I don't care what people out there think, it's important for you to know I am not that person, Aari.'

I want to hug him but I don't trust myself, so I busy my hands by making tiny ripples in the water. 'I know you're not. Maybe you should just be yourself and say whatever is on your mind.'

'Can I throw Dominic Miller under the bus?' Caleb smiles slightly. It takes my breath away.

'No, you cannot.' I laugh. 'And please don't harass him in my office any more, okay? He's not a bad guy.'

'I'll try, but when we're alone together like this, Aari, I know that we are going to get through this and choose each other. But then I see Dominic Miller in your office with a ridiculous grin on his face, and I know he is thinking the exact same; only for him it's smooth sailing.'

My mouth is on Caleb's before I can think of it. His tongue finds mine slowly, as if asking permission. I don't have the same uncertainty. I welcome it. He pulls me in, lifting and anchoring my thighs to my hips. He commits to our kiss, holding on to me as if his life depends on it. My heart doubles its pace. I pull myself in to displace any water left between us and he helps by placing his hand on my back to pull me close. When I feel the clasp of my bra release, I end the kiss by swimming a safe distance away to re-hook it.

'I hate that I sit in the palm of your hand and you can do what you like with me,' I confess.

'That's not true. You own me. You leave me alone for five minutes and I'm kicking the shit out of Devin and wind up playing second fiddle to Budget Jasper because I've been a total dick. Life sucks without you. It sucked before you showed up – however, then I didn't know it. Now that I know you exist, it doubly sucks.'

My arms are around him and I'm kissing him again. In this moment, the world feels normal, familiar, safe and complete. Like it always has with Caleb. He softly opens my mouth with his to deepen it. It's not an urgent, needing kiss, but one that re-establishes commitment. He takes a gentle bite of my bottom lip and raises my hands into his hair. I pull away to look in his eyes and tell him the truth.

'It's you, Caleb. It will always be you,' I whisper softly.

'I hope so. I have so much to make up to you.'

Caleb nods his head towards the door that leads to my bedroom.

'If I drag you in there, will it be too soon?'

'Yes.' I hear my own disappointment and Caleb smiles widely. He heard it too.

'I have an alternative strategy to all the dirty things I want to do to you right now. Wanna hear it, or shall we go for Option A?' He chuckles.

'Alternative strategy please,' I miraculously select, even though every part of my body is screaming 'dirty things!'.

'Want to start *The Walking Dead* with me? I've been dying to watch it but I've been saving it for us. It's full of zombies, killing, violence, but apparently it's amazing.'

He raises his eyebrows at me and flashes me that smile. He's irresistible.

'Go on then.'

'Great! Back in twenty!'

We get out of the pool, I clear up the sushi, have a quick shower, change into my pyjamas and turn my TV on for the first time since I moved in. Caleb arrives back shortly after I emerge, carrying our couch blanket from home.

'You didn't!' I squeal.

'I did. Every time I've been in this flat with you, I've made you cry. It's time to make some new memories and separate myself from Dominic in your imaginary pile of friends – the man has no personal space awareness and he keeps farting!'

I can't help the laughter that escapes from me. Oh, Caleb.

Caleb takes the controls and swiftly finds what we are looking for. He then pulls me in on the couch to lean against him as he unfurls the blanket over us. My heart leaps. I am such a fool for him.

'Ready?'

'Ready!' I laugh as an aerial shot of a deserted highway in a dystopian future opens the show.

. . .

'Miss Ariella?'

My eyes slowly open to see Ms Pat standing over me, smiling widely. She raises an eyebrow ever so slightly, looking to my left. I'd fallen asleep on Caleb, who now has both his arms wrapped around me. One of his hands is inappropriately up my top, cupping one of his girls, and his head is balancing on mine.

I sit bolt upright too quickly, smacking him on his chin with my head.

'OW!'

'Sorry... sorry...'

'Aari, what the... oh, morning, Ms Pat.'

'Morning, Mr Caleb.' She smiles at both of us affectionately. 'It's six fifteen and you have guests arriving at seven. Can I make you some breakfast?'

Caleb says yes, as I say no. Ms Pat laughs then. 'Breakfast for Mr Caleb and grapefruit for you, Miss Ariella?'

'No, Mr Caleb was just leaving.' I shoot a dirty look at Caleb, who is finding this just as funny as Ms Pat is.

'No, I am not. I've already missed training. I have time for a bacon sandwich and coffee. I'll be gone before you get out of the shower. Come on, Ms Pat, I want to know all about Mr Pat,' Caleb probes as he follows a chuckling Ms Pat into the kitchen.

I can't believe I slept so deeply and slept in so late. Caleb is still here, chatting away with Ms Pat and munching on a sandwich, when I emerge after my shower.

'You're still here?'

'Bacon sandwich, Miss Ariella? I cut the crusts off?'

'Yes, she'll have the sandwich – and newsflash, the whole crust and curly hair thing is fake news.'

'No doubt spread by straight-haired propagandists.'

'Exactly!' Caleb's eyes are sparkling with mischief. I love him like this, but I don't have the time.

'Listen, I don't have time for you to be adorable right now. You have to go. Ruby and Eden are always early.'

'Did you just call me adorable?'

I ignore him. He knows he's cute.

Just then the doorbell goes. Caleb quickly grabs what is left of his sandwich and coffee and follows Ms Pat to the door.

'Hello, Ms Pat!' they greet her in unison, until they spot a barefoot Caleb in his pyjama bottoms and T-shirt. They both fall suspiciously silent, trying to figure out what is going on.

'Hello, ladies!' he greets them, walking past.

'Mr Caleb, please buy your own groceries. No more free breakfast before seven. I have a lot of work and don't need you pressing the bell at six thirty, looking for food. Miss Ariella starts at seven. You can come for breakfast after that,' Ms Pat calls after him.

'Yes, Ms Pat. Thank you for breakfast. Have a good morning, ladies.'

They wait until Caleb leaves, then: 'I'd gladly cook him breakfast,' Eden the stylist whispers as they approach me.

'And he knows it,' the make-up artist, Ruby, responds, deadpan.

'Shut up, you would too.' Eden nudges her.

'Goodness. I'd cook it to order!' Both of them laugh.

'Morning, ladies!' I call, grabbing their attention. 'Thank you for coming, let's do this,' I declare.

I'm pleased to hear that Ruby and Eden have reformed their idea of my style and have adjusted their recommendations to give me more of what I am already wearing. The only challenge now is for Eden to shred her vison for the launch party, because it sounds like a nightmare.

'I'm going to need you to trust me first,' she starts, 'but you should know that dressing you for the pool party will probably be the point of most resistance. Right now, I am thinking of putting you in a gold bikini, some gold strappy heels and a hand-woven gold kaftan.'

'I am not wearing that, Eden.' There is nothing she can say. I'm not going to the launch half naked.

'I thought you might say that. It's a work in progress.'

We leave it there for the day.

All Ruby does is tidy my eyebrows, replace my skincare products and show me a range of coloured eyeliners that she encourages me to experiment with. Before she can show me how to apply them, my phone springs to life, cutting her off. It's Bryce.

'Morning, Bryce.'

'Hey, Ariella, I know you're home this morning with the stylists, but please can you come in? I've hit an issue with a project.'

'Sure, what issue?'

'A client has cancelled an event and they are demanding a refund.'

'Are they within the cancellation terms?'

'It's not the terms I am worried about; the account they want us to route it to is offshore.'

'Is that where their payment originated?'

'No, it was a domestic transfer. I flagged it with the client as an error but they lost it with me over the phone and demanded I send it as instructed. I called Devin and he said he'd handle it but didn't think it was a big deal, so I called you. Am I being paranoid?'

'If you're worried, I'm worried. Is it a new account?'

'No. It's a historical one from London. Why?'

'I'll be in the office in half an hour, let's meet then?'

'Thanks. See you soon.'

When I get in, a very nervous Bryce follows me into my office.

'This doesn't feel right, Ariella.'

'We'll figure it out. What refunds are due?'

'Seventy-five per cent minus fees.'

'If you think something is fishy, we should give our fees back and suspend any activity we have with them until we've investigated.'

'Caleb is going to be pissed, it's one of his biggest accounts.'

'We'll be gentle. Hopefully we'll clear this up quickly and the client won't be suspended for long.'

'Devin is going to be furious that I went over his head.'

'Better fury than complicity.'

'Are you going to back me up, if it leads us up shit creek?'

'No, I am going to stand in front of you and shield you, regardless of where it may lead.'

'That's a relief. Shall I talk you through it?'

'Yes, please.'

TWENTY-SEVEN

CALEB

I bounce into work that morning, whistling to myself and celebrating last night's small victory with Ariella. It suddenly comes to a halt when I see Bryce's face. He quickly grabs me by the arm, walks into Ariella's office and shuts the door behind us. What now?

'We need to stay calm, Bryce,' Ariella instructs kindly.

'Sorry.'

'We don't have good news, Caleb,' Ariella warns as Bryce looks too worried to speak.

'Okay, shoot.' Whatever it is, can't be that bad.

'We are going to have to suspend the Freight and Ware Industries account.'

Shit. It's bad. She knows. Freight and Ware is one of the accounts Melissa handed to me, so it's already on my list of accounts to annihilate.

'Why?'

'Don't worry, they aren't jumping ship, we've just hit a snag, that's all. Bryce, want to fill him in?'

I listen carefully as Bryce walks me through the problem.

It's not the first time they have started a large project, abandoned it midway and demanded a refund. They did that in the UK. Rerouting the funds to a completely different bank account is news to me, though.

'This stinks, right?' Bryce asks.

Ariella steps in to keep the conversation on track. 'Do you have the original contract from when they were on-boarded in the UK?'

'I don't. Their contract and service point still sits in London.'

'You're their account director though – shouldn't that contract sit with us?'

'It should, but it hasn't been transferred to us yet.'

'We should rectify that, especially as they are now using us as their new service point.'

'I had no idea that they had any live projects with us.'

'They don't. The enquiry came in, got processed and then got cancelled before you joined. Bryce, please can you request the original client contract and their full billing history from London for us to go through?'

'I can do that,' I volunteer. 'It's worth digging into their UK history too, they had lots of cancellations. We'll be able to ascertain whether this is an anomaly or standard practice for them. Who else have you told, Bryce?'

'You and Ariella. Devin blew it off, so we're going to have another word when he comes in.'

'He's going to be hopping mad that you escalated this,' I warn. Devin does not like to be questioned.

'Well, unfortunately, we need answers.' Ariella doesn't even flinch.

'Something is going on, isn't it?' Bryce asks, with certainty.

'I am not sure, so not a word to anyone, for now. This could be an outlier but we have to protect ourselves if not.'

'Gotcha, boss.'

'Thank you, Bryce. Caleb, can you let me know as soon as you get anything from London? Let's see if this financial request has been made before and get some guidance on how to handle it.'

'Sure. Is there anything else I can do?' I swallow nervously.

'No. If this is what Bryce suspects it is, I want you as far away from it as possible.'

I walk out of her office as casually as I can, pretending that my back isn't against the wall. Ariella is going to dig around until she has answers. She's stubborn and relentless like that. Fuck. I step out of the office and call Jasper. I know it's just before two in the morning for him, but I need this.

'Caleb.' Jasper clears his throat as he picks up, on the third ring. I hear him appeasing a pissed-off Sophia back to sleep before his footsteps descend the stairs.

'Sorry, mate.'

'It's fine. I take it that there have been developments.' Jasper yawns.

'Freight and Ware. They are requesting cancellation refunds are routed offshore to a different bank account from the one we were paid by.'

'Good to know. Sounds like the sort of thing that would get one investigated for fraud and money-laundering. I'll look into it in the morning.'

'I'm glad you're just as relaxed about this as I am. Just a quick question, no biggie. Am I going to fucking prison for this shit that had nothing to do with me?'

'Caleb, it's the middle of the night. Give me a break. Besides, it had a little bit to do with you but, no, I don't think so. Did you sign any contracts or paperwork with clients on behalf of the company?'

'No, that was usually Harrison or the CFO.'

'That means nothing leads directly to you. You going to prison is highly unlikely. You have to be careful though, you could still be implicated, which these days is enough to destroy one's reputation.'

'Okay.' I exhale, relieved.

'Chances of Ariella ever trusting you again once she finds out that you've been lying to her, though...'

'I haven't lied to her.'

'You haven't told her the whole truth though, have you?'

'I'm going to tell her.'

'When, Caleb? Asking you to declare your primary contact at Freight and Ware would be a perfectly legitimate request. You'll have to tell her that you didn't close those deals... traditionally.'

'Tonight. I'm going to tell her tonight.'

'Ariella is—'

'Ariella? Again? Really?' I hear Sophia lose her shit in the background.

'No, it's Caleb, he's just—'

'You only just got back from seeing her in Singapore, Jassie! Can we just have one day...'

'Sorry, mate, I owe you a bottle of the good stuff!'

I hang up. Bloody hell. Poor Sophia. She's only just started the hell that I had to go through with Ariella. I'm sure it's not fun for Jasper either. A text comes through from him.

> Maybe stick to office hours from now on?

> Didn't mean to drop you in it mate. Sorry.

I pop back to my desk and submit a formal request for all the files and contracts as promised before I head to my first appointment. My ultimate aim was to get rid of those accounts anyway, so now, more than ever, I need to build up our client list.

When Aari and I leave for a client racing party that I asked her to attend with me, I have every intention of telling her about the accounts, Melissa, everything. She agreed to give the party ten minutes, which is more than I can expect from someone who isn't very good with crowds. It's our first outing together and the last thing I expect is for her to get there and be Little Miss Popular. Ariella is not a natural networker but, then again, she doesn't need to be. When we enter, the party gravitates towards her and I am reduced to the lackey that she came with. The fact that she is one of only about ten women present may have something to do with it; but goodness, she has come a long way. She speaks to everyone who wants to have a conversation, smiles politely and chats in that soft, attentive, calm way that gets me in the chest. If she notices that she's being heavily flirted with, she doesn't show it. Invitations to dinner are met with a swift yes and a simple 'Caleb and I would love to.'

Watching this version of Ariella in action is gobsmacking. She is no longer the shivery little thing that had to be forced to speak at our daily ten a.m. meeting in London. She is quietly confident, engaged and open. Huge parts of her are still walled off, but she has managed to find a place where she can exist comfortably while letting people in. I feel a sudden urge to kick Dominic in the nuts. I missed her evolution, but he has been right by her side through it, no doubt masking his perverted intentions as useful hints and tips. He'd been there when she has tried and failed, questioned herself, taken the risks and moulded this new side to her. I'd been too busy being paranoid and shutting her out. And my bullshit isn't over, as she is going to find out later on tonight. I know she's hopeful for us, and so am I, but watching her now, I'm not sure that there is a way to survive this. I've missed too much. We stay quite a bit longer than either of us intended, but we are back in the car heading back home before ten.

'Have fun, my little Mason?' I tease as I poke her in the ribs.

'I did!' She laughs, slapping my finger away.

'See? It's good to slum it like the rest of us once in a while.'

'It wasn't too bad; the trauma of you pulling me onto the dance floor in front of the whole nightclub at Louisa's birthday set me up for life.'

'Matt, please could you give us a couple of minutes?' I ask before I raise the partition, flick off the car speaker system, pull Ariella over to me and place my mouth over hers. There is absolutely zero resistance. Her legs move to straddle me as I guide her over by her waist. I know I should be focusing on how Ariella and I are going to come out alive after the news I plan on dropping on her later, but keeping my hands to myself feels impossible right now because she tastes amazing. I love the familiar taste of gin on her breath as I inhale her exhales. I relieve her of her jacket and unbutton her oxford shirt. Halfway down, I stop and pull away for a breath.

'Tell me what you told me that night,' I challenge her. She licks her bottom lip and smirks.

'Promising naughty things later cannot be our play right now. Sorry,' she whispers, bringing her lips back down on mine.

I wrap my arms around her, holding the moment so close, it feels impossible to let go. I burn this feeling into my memory.

Matt's voice comes through. 'Sorry to interrupt, but we're here, Ariella.'

'Thank you, Matt,' Ariella responds, scrambling off me and doing up her shirt buttons. Once I've confirmed that she is decent, I open the door, then extend my hand out to her and lead her, fingers interlaced, through the lobby to the lift. Ariella presses both our floor numbers and the lift doors have barely closed when she grabs me by the collar and pulls my face down to hers. She is killing me. She breaks off the kiss as the ding announces that we are at my floor.

'See you tomorrow, Caleb.'

'Can I come up?'

'I don't think that's a good idea. We are going to have a crazy day tomorrow dealing with these payments, I think we need some sleep.'

'I could stay over?'

'Again? Get out of the lift please.' She laughs.

Fuck. I can't tell her. It'll destroy everything. I step out to save myself and watch her immediately press the button that closes the door.

'Ariella, wait—'

'No. You're irresistible,' she responds as the lift doors close.

Like I don't have enough to deal with, you know what comes next don't you? Domi-frikkin'-nella. The project team's porn-sounding name for them is now a thing on the internet. It's especially torturous because Ariella and I are sort of in a good place. Remember her 'I want to be honest with Dominic' declaration in the pool? That apparently came out as 'Caleb and I are communicating and working on moving past everything that has happened.'

Ambiguous, right? I may be keeping my hands to myself, mostly, but I wouldn't call what we are doing communicating. I've been falling asleep almost every night on her couch with her in my arms, after a little TV-watching. We even have our morning routine down: we get up at five thirty and I leave to go and get killed by Honey after I've grabbed the glass pot of porridge Ms Pat leaves in Ariella's fridge for me the day before. Even Ms Pat knows what this is, and it's not 'communicating'.

Dominic is still confidently turning up at the office, looking happy that they are now everywhere together. The only reason I know nothing is going on is that she is always back home early, ready for me to come up with our couch blanket for a chat and a cuddle. Georgie and Dominic, on the other hand, have launched separate social media assaults. The very first image released was one of them leaning against each other on the boat back to Singapore after her birthday. It was black and white and taken from behind, but her curly hair leaning against his buzz-cut was unmistakable.

Their digital and press coverage exploded in Singapore, the UK and the US, where Dominic Miller is, apparently, a big deal. They are everywhere together, laughing, standing too close to each other, and there are a few of her on the back of one of his bloody bikes, holding on to him. For Ariella, the image shift has been almost immediate. Her followers have skyrocketed, with 'Who is Ariella Mason?' '10 facts about Ariella Mason', '5 things you didn't know about Ariella Mason' and 'Style inspiration tips from Ariella Mason' articles popping up everywhere. All because she was photographed with some old-money-inheriting bloke. Humanity is doomed.

Even Lara called to boast about how she accepted a small fortune to dish on Ariella, so she took the money and made up crazy, unverifiable facts about her.

So, when I had my interview with *The Singaporean* a few days after Dominic and Ariella were publicly 'shipped', I was pissed off and destructive, and maybe said a few things that I shouldn't have said. It hits the stands the Monday before the launch party and Ariella is going to lose her shit when she sees it, if the interviewer does his job and keeps all the confrontational jabs in.

Not that the article is at the forefront of my mind. I have other things to worry about. London are taking their sweet time responding to my request for client information and Ariella is getting increasingly frustrated with their slackness. Right now, she has a call scheduled with Harrison and Christopher to side-step the process in order to unravel the issues with Freight and Ware. Her determination to keep tugging stubbornly at this until she sees exactly where it leads is scary.

TWENTY-EIGHT

ARIELLA

The last couple of weeks have been challenging. We are getting no cooperation from London on Caleb's clients. Devin, not that he has ever been the most patient and open of team members, refuses to hire an accounts-payable lead and no longer engages with the rest of us. Bryce's work on this has come to a halt because we aren't getting the documents we need, and I am currently plastered all over the internet for the wrong reasons. Lara, however, has been a light and, while she is loving my commodification, she has also become my eyes and ears in London.

> I'm not sure what you're doing out there but Harrison is fucking furious at you.

> Me? Why?

> Dunno. He called you 'That bitch' a few minutes ago when I was eavesdropping. What did you do?

Nothing. Apart from requesting some files from the CFO and setting up a meeting, I haven't spoken to Harrison. I spoke to Christopher a couple of weeks ago because I needed some operations advice; but that's it.

Whatever it is, Harrison's pissed off. He's planning to fly out for your launch to confront you, so be ready.

That might actually be a good thing. There has obviously been a misunderstanding.

Shall I see if I can find out more?

Thank you, but no. I feel your investigation will go something like 'Harrison! *Expletive* *expletive* *expletive* *expletive* Ariella? *Expletive, expletive*.

Right then, I miss Lara.

How, fucking, dare you, Mason?

Case in point. By the way, I miss you.

Me too. It's nearly nowhere near as sane over here without you. Oooh, they finally managed to replace you!

That took a while. Are they settling in okay?

I bloody well hope so, or I'm fucking firing everyone.

Huh?

How on earth are you running an entire company? They replaced you with me. I took your old job. Well, sort of. I looked at your workload and thought, fuck that. So, I took a pay cut (that's when I found out you were earning a fucking fortune, by the way) and kept the fun stuff like yelling at people and being important. I made them hire two people to deal with your boring paperwork because I'd quite like a life. Might sack them though, they're shit.

I'm surprised you went for it.

Me too! Everyone went for it initially; then they released a more detailed job description and the internal candidates went down to two. Harrison loved them both and Christopher hated them both. Enter me. They both hated me but I figured it out. Haha.

Is Christopher angry with me too?

Definitely not. He won't shut up about how well you're doing but that's unsurprising. You're the Christopher and Caleb is the Harrison of IvB Asia.

Is Christopher coming for the launch too?

Yes! I tried to jump on the trip but I got smacked down. Now that I've mentioned him, I have to ask. How's sexual pandemic doing? I bet you dating the sexy, loaded redhead is driving him nuts!

Dom and I are just friends.

You're still into Caleb, aren't you?

I am.

Fucking hell Aari. Stop. What's wrong with you? You're a total boss, running shit and telling everyone what to do. The second that boy looks at you, you're batting your eyelashes and making sandwiches. Besides, he's dating that total smoke show. No offence, but if you're a 9 on the hotness scale, that Honey Kohli chick is a 56. I say that with love, but also brutal honesty.

> They're just friends.

Is she taking friend requests? I'd very much like to make 'friends' with her too.

> Whenever you make it out, I'm sure he'll be happy to introduce you.

Does this mean that you're back playing with the old CMS?

> CMS?

Caleb's Magic Stick?

> No, Lara. We're just spending time together and figuring things out.

Does Dominic know that you're 'spending time together and figuring things out'?

> He knows we're trying to put the past behind us.

Not what I asked, babe. Besides, when is this time that you're spending together? Both of you look exceptionally busy.

> We watch TV together some evenings.

And does he make it back to his home after that?

> I am NOT playing with Caleb's Magic Stick.

> Again, not what I asked.

> He stays over on the couch, most nights.

> Does 'Dom' know you're cuddling up to Caleb every night and do you think 'Dom' might want to cuddle up every night?

> No. I've been clear with Dominic. We are just friends.

> I'm not too bothered about Dominic's clarity. If you haven't been clear, Caleb will do some stupid shit that will make it clear enough for both of you. You might want to beat him to it.

I had no idea that Lara's joke was a prediction but, when I enter the office on the Tuesday afternoon before the launch, I'm surrounded by whispering and giggling.

'Morning, Lydia. What's going on?'

Lydia swings around in her swivel chair and observes me with a smile on her lips.

'What?' I laugh. Everyone is in a playful mood today, making me happy too.

'Caleb's interview in *The Singaporean*.'

'Tell me.'

'Nope. You should read it.' She closes the magazine and hands it to me. The front cover is a close-up portrait of a smouldering Caleb. He is wearing a slight snarl and staring defiantly at the camera. His dark coat's collar is high and his dark hair messy, making his piercing blue eyes the brightest thing on the page. He looks dangerous and sexy.

'I imagine most women looking at that cover today will have that exact same expression. I caught myself biting my lip too.' Lydia chuckles.

I quickly release it. 'And where is our cover star today?' He didn't make it up last night and I miss him.

'No idea, his diary is empty this morning. He's probably hiding.' Lydia laughs.

'Give me the highlights?'

'Nope. Read.' Lydia turns her chair towards her desk, so I take the magazine into my office with a cup of tea.

The interview starts off tamely, with Caleb giving a severely edited account of his early years and his role within Ivory Bow UK. He dives into his previous deals in the UK, North America and Singapore, talks extensively about client successes and the power of messaging, mentions Mel briefly as an investor and states how grateful he is for the opportunity. They cover style (whatever his hand hits in the morning, with an extensive plug for Eden), Singapore (he has always been in love with the country and he feels privileged to call it home because that's what it feels like) and the office (a thriving hub of laughter, creativity, ideas, fun and considered strategy). All good so far, until the interviewer shifts gears.

Interviewer:
So, we know the professional and the bad boy. What about the man? Is there a special lady out there?

Caleb:
The only special ladies in my life are called Ariella, Lydia, Jess, Sian, Akiko and Bree – the lovely ladies at Ivory Bow and anybody's dream team. Honey Kohli, as you know, is a very dear friend. She is so powerful, it's difficult not to be inspired by her.

Interviewer:
Does Honey Kohli occupy the top spot? It's a bit obvious that you are more than friends.

Caleb:

Honey is greatness personified and an exceptional human being, but the top spot goes to Ariella Mason.

Interviewer:
It is surprising to hear you pick your boss. The rumours suggest that she is struggling to keep you in check.

Caleb:
Ariella Mason struggles at nothing, let me assure you. She is a loyal, committed, honest, generous, hard-working and brilliant woman. It's a shame most aren't interested in looking past the social media posts.

Interviewer:
Dominic Miller seems to have looked past the posts. The word around town is that they are together. She's been on his arm at quite a few functions.

Caleb:
In his dreams. He's punching a bit above his weight, isn't he? Ariella Mason and Dominic Miller are not dating. They are just friends. Ariella would never put the company in an ethically compromising position by dating a client.

Interviewer:
It sounds like you are very protective of your boss.

Caleb:
I am. Very much so. I've seen the 'not so nice' comments and hashtags on the internet. No one wants to see the person. Instead, she gets attached to Dominic Miller because he has money. He's permanently looking for his next conquest, so they think Ariella should be happy or grateful that he might be interested. There are

many more deserving men out there. Dominic Miller isn't fit to carry her shoes.

Interviewer:
Wow. That's fighting talk.

Caleb:
Not at all. I respect the Miller conglomerate as clients. However, the mere suggestion that Ariella would date Dominic Miller cheapens her position, sexualises her role in the industry, diminishes her achievements and compromises her integrity. That rhetoric implies Dominic Miller's superiority, which insultingly reduces her, as you did earlier, to just arm candy; which she most certainly is not. She is a bright, successful 26-year-old woman who runs the fastest-growing client engagement company in Singapore. She has achieved that in just under six months. This whole Dominic Miller and Ariella fantasy romance nonsense is just a lot of noise about nothing.

Interviewer:
Her achievements are impressive. She must struggle to maintain a personal life.

Caleb:
You can ask her yourself. We have our company launch at Ariella's home soon. I'll arrange for you to get an invitation.

Interviewer:
That's very generous. I'll take you up on that. How about your personal life: if you had to describe your perfect woman, what would she be like?

Caleb:
She would pretty much be Ariella Mason.

Interviewer:
You've made that clear professionally. Personally, what sort of woman would do it for you?

Caleb:
Yeah. Still Ariella Mason. She's strong, smart, open, empathetic, owns her path and defines herself on her own terms completely. She looks to no one for validation but is constantly seeking to empower others. She's as close to perfect as you're going to get. That does it, in its entirety, for me.

That's it. I am going to kill Caleb.

'I see Caleb went for it.' Bryce laughs as he walks into my office.

'I am going to murder him, Bryce.'

'Guess who wants a conference call in thirty minutes?'

'Mel and Georgie?'

He laughs again, nodding.

'See you there.' I throw the magazine at the couch on the other side of the room. Caleb has left me a big pile of poo to clean up with that article. I take a deep breath and hit the name in my contact list.

'That took a minute,' Dominic answers, laughing.

'I have only just seen it. I am so sorry, Dominic.'

'Don't worry about it. I expected him to come for me. I just didn't expect him to come for me with the whole country and internet watching. He's got balls. I'll give him that.'

'This is so embarrassing. I'll get him to apologise. I can't have him attacking you and making clients think they are fair game.'

'Aari, breathe. No need for an apology. I'm a big boy and I can look after myself. I've been on the receiving end of much worse. If having too much money at my disposal and not being good enough to carry your shoes is the best he's got, I'm in good shape, even though it hurts a little.'

He is taking this worryingly well. 'You're not annoyed?'

'I'm annoyed enough to let you know you're going to have to make this all up to me.'

I like Dom and I trust him, but I don't like the way that sounds.

'Calm down, Aari, you can take me to dinner.'

I exhale.

'Don't be too relieved, it will be achingly expensive.'

'Consider it done.' That was easy.

'Tonight,' he adds.

'I have a meeting after work but I should be done by nine?'

'I know. I checked with Lydia already. I'll grab you from Raffles.'

'You're lovely, do you know that?'

'I do, but my PA won't think so when she comes back from lunch. The hashtag "defeateddom" is already making the rounds online, and I have pretty good intel that suggests that she started it.'

I send Lydia a quick query for an update on RSVP numbers. We intentionally kept the launch quiet to keep it small but, now it's out there, managing numbers is going to be tricky. The pool party is this Friday and Caleb has just flung the doors wide open, and given anyone who sees an image of the invitation on the internet my home address. All of Caleb's contacts have RSVP'd 'Yes' and, like he predicted, just over half of mine are able to make it. With the rest of the team's RSVPs in, our party for one-fifty is currently at one-seventy-two. Caleb's interview is going to change that.

When the call comes around, Bryce and I are the last to enter the conference room.

'You're not going to believe this,' Georgie starts, excited. 'Since the magazine hit the stands and the article went online last night, Caleb has seen not only a surge in followers but a surge in positive interactions. It looks like he is feeling some feminist love. He has somehow managed to expand his demographic with that interview. Where is he?'

'He's not in yet.' Lydia laughs, glancing sideways at me.

'Probably because he's frightened of Ariella,' Bree chimes in, also laughing, setting the whole conference room off.

I quickly change the subject. 'Has the interview had any impact on the company as a whole?'

'Yes!' Georgie chirps excitedly. 'And not in the way you would think. You also have had a wave of new followers but from entrepreneurs, business magazines and women-in-business groups. Which means we need to tweak your output a bit to what you and Lydia have been saying all along. More business and less lifestyle. I'm keen to see what a fifty-fifty output split would throw back. Also, you now have the largest follower overlap with Caleb. I think it's safe to say the article worked, and we're only about eighteen hours in!'

'What did I miss?' Caleb walks in looking a bit ruffled, with his eyes hidden behind his Ray-Bans. He doesn't look like he has been home. I narrow my eyes at him. Akiko catches my expression and giggles quietly.

'Only that you're a fucking superstar.' Georgie is actually clapping during our video conference. 'My phone has been ringing off the hook with press requesting invites to the launch. Can I have twenty – obviously with no hangers-on?'

'Do you think even more press at a private event is a good idea?' I ask. This is growing at a rate I don't like.

'Ten passes?' Georgie negotiates.

'I am not sure this is the direction we want to go, Georgie, but I could be too close to it. Mel, what are your thoughts?'

'Ariella is right, we don't need the place crawling with the press. But if it isn't covered, did it even happen? Georgie, I think it's fair to allocate six passes, pick them wisely and no plus ones. I'd want to break them down to two weekend papers, two weeklies and two monthlies but that's up to you. *The Singaporean* should have two passes in addition as a thank-you.'

'That's fair,' Georgie concedes.

'Okay, everyone, keep up the good work.' Mel brings the meeting to a close by logging off, which prompts Georgie to do the same.

The things I want to say to Caleb can't be said with an audience. He seems to be of the same mind and stays away from my office all day. I watch him respond with embarrassment and laughter as the office teases him about the article. Eventually, his text comes through as I am on my way to my meeting at Raffles.

> I know I fucked up with DMVI. I'm sorry.

> > Do you think you can lay off him a little?

> Yes.

> > Thank you.

When Dominic turns up at Raffles to pick me up for dinner, he is so noisy everyone can hear him. He has a naughty habit of leaving his motorbike wherever he feels anyway, but parking it right at the hotel entrance in full view of everyone is unnecessarily rebellious. He's hard to miss as he walks into the hotel unzipping his leathers, and it has the desired effect. Everyone is watching. Only then do I realise that Caleb's article *is* going to be expensive, but it's not going to cost me money.

'Hi,' he whispers, leaning in.

'Hi.'

'Ready?' he asks, stroking my face.

'Sure.'

I let him take my hand like he never does and lead me through the busy lobby and out of the hotel. If this is what he needs to do to even the score with Caleb, so be it. His jacket is off and his bike has disappeared by the time we exit.

'Where are we going?'

'Labyrinth. It's only ten minutes that way so we're walking.'

'I need to ask you something.' I retrieve my wallet, tuck it into my jeans, and hand over my laptop and bags to the concierge before leading Dominic away from listening ears.

'Ask away.' He reveals that charming smile.

'This is what it's going to cost me, isn't it? You want us to be seen together. I'm not angry, I just want to know when I am being used as a pawn.'

'It's not—'

'Dom, please be straight with me.'

'I don't need the country and the internet looking at me like I am some perverted stalker forcing myself on you. I don't mind the rest of it, but I need for people to know you're in this too, because you want to be. I'm a privileged, rich, white guy in an Asian country. I can't be controversial. It's disrespectful.'

'Are we being watched right now?'

'I'm pretty sure we are.'

I take Dominic's hand and pull him towards me. Then I slide my arms around his neck, get on my tippy-toes and pull him into a hug, wrapping myself around him. He slides his hands around my waist and pulls me close.

'Dom, don't you ever put me into a situation like this without my knowledge again. It's manipulative and I don't like it,' I whisper into his ear as we hold on to each other.

'I'm sorry.' He sounds like he means it, so we start walking towards the restaurant.

'Did you feel like you couldn't ask me?' I press softly.

'No, I'm just an idiot and I should have trusted you.'

'I agree on both counts.'

We both laugh.

'Is he in trouble?' Dominic asks as we turn the corner and walk towards the war memorial.

'A little bit.'

'Damn. I wish it was a lot. Are you going soft on him because you're still into him?'

'Possibly.'

'Why? While it's obvious that he still loves you, he's also happily running around with Honey Kohli.'

I cannot talk to Dominic about Honey. 'He makes me feel things.'

'Ariella, we all have that thing he makes you feel.' He looks down his torso and then looks back up with a cheeky smile. It takes a beat before we both burst out laughing.

'It's not like that,' I defend myself through laughter. Dominic raises an eyebrow. 'Okay, well, it's partly like that,' I admit.

'Wait. Are you still feeling his "thing"?'

He reminds me so much of Lara just then that I am not remotely offended by the question. 'Of course not!' I laugh. 'I haven't felt anyone's thing since London. I don't like this euphemism, by the way.'

'What is it about him?'

'He makes me feel... awake.'

Caleb has a way of making me operate from my heart and my tummy. He manages to somehow inspire me to do stupid, impractical, inexplicable and illogical things that make me feel really good.

'Care to explain?'

'I've always lived in my head. There, most things are practical and logical, and I was happy, until I wasn't; but I couldn't figure out why.'

'Is this when the "dumping by Post-it" happened?'

'Yes.' I still feel guilty. 'With Caleb, I genuinely don't know what I am doing most of the time, but he makes everything feel in sync. It's completely inexplicable.'

'No one else has ever made you feel like that?' Dom asks quietly.

'Before Caleb, there was only Jasper. I now realise that I made the practical decision to have an emotional response to my best friend because I didn't want to lose him. Our relationship made logical sense and everyone around us happy, so I convinced myself that it had to be right. It wasn't, but I stayed anyway, because I didn't want to hurt him or my family.'

'If cerebral Aari isn't in the driving seat with Caleb, don't you think that might compromise your position as his boss?'

'Of course it does. That's why he's probably happily skipping around the city tonight, consequence-free, while I'm here with you, walking through public parks so that you're not branded as some kind of sex pest.'

'So your decision to come tonight was a practical one?'

'Yes. Caleb was naughty. I'm here to say sorry.'

'Have all your decisions come from your head, when it comes to me?' He's smiling but I know the question is loaded.

'No,' I answer quietly.

'Gosh, you're so hard to read.' Dom chuckles, as he's complaining.

'I know, sorry.' We walk in silence the rest of the way before he pulls me to a stop, facing him, in front of Labyrinth.

'If I were to kiss you right now, what would the response be?' he teases.

'Well, to the casual observer you'd only be doing it to get back at Caleb.'

'It might not be.'

'Maybe not, but we wouldn't be here if that interview hadn't come out today.'

'I do think about kissing you, a little more than I should.'

'That may be, but now most certainly isn't the time, Dominic.'

'Could the time have been your birthday?'

I know what he is asking. I felt it too. There was something there, but I can't entertain it. I'm in love with someone else.

'Maybe if things were different?'

'Good to know.' Dom smiles as he opens the door to the restaurant for me to walk through.

For the rest of the week, images of Dom and me at Raffles, on our walk and even eating and laughing at Labyrinth flood everywhere online. I didn't cross any lines, but the images tell a story that looks like much more than friendship. Dom's satisfaction at us being seen together without resistance is met with Caleb's quiet seething and his declared pretence at understanding. We agree to give each other space for the rest of the week and by Wednesday evening, when I have to move out of the apartment for the space to be dressed, I'm unsure if he and I are on speaking terms.

TWENTY-NINE

CALEB

I expected some blowback from that interview, because I left Dominic Miller no other option but to counter-punch. What I don't expect is a full-on social media assault, with Ariella looking fully complicit. When she comes back that night, the concierge gives me a quick call, so that I am waiting outside her door when she comes up. The exchange is quick.

'I'm tired, Caleb,' she sighs, looking for her keys.

'I was pissed off. He's just all over you all the time.'

'Even if that were true, which it isn't, it would only be an issue if *I* wasn't all over *you*, all the time.'

'You're not all over me!'

'Caleb, I have slept alone in my bedroom maybe four, five times since we went swimming weeks ago. I'm pretty certain the couch now identifies as a bed.'

'That's—'

'Caleb, it's late. Is it okay if you don't come in? I could use the space.' She's serious.

'I'm sorry.'

'I know.' She places a soft chaste kiss on my lips as she lets herself in and shuts the door behind her. I leave and I know that I will have to endure the pictures of them, absolutely every-where together, alone. I try to ignore it all but no matter how hard I try to bury the fury, it is still there, right below the surface, when the launch party arrives.

When I step out of the lift on Ariella's floor, I know I am prepared to do my job. It's a great feeling. All those years being fed easy sales by Melissa left even me questioning whether I was any good at it. Tonight, sixty per cent of the clients in atten-dance are mine. Won through hard graft and persistence since the music awards in London. Proving to myself that I'm bloody good at this job has been one of the very few positives that has come out of moving to Singapore. Having Ariella's more struc-tured approach to sales helps. She made us all painstakingly pull apart and carefully distribute the guest list to each member of the team, with the both of us taking the lion's share. She then made sure we had a strategy to comb through and maximise the opportunities at the party.

The project team were also firing on all cylinders. The final brief settled midway between a cool beach-club night and an elegant soirée. The final sketches looked stunning when they were presented. Ivory-painted columns with marble detailing looked incredible next to the seating alcoves with Ancient Greek-style soft benches. These were paired with accentuating navy, purple and ivory draping to soften the walls. The main living area was to be transformed into what looked like an external courtyard, creating a neutral space between the formal and casual spaces. Her three bedrooms, with their own service teams dressed in navy-blue formal Grecian outfits, would be turned into warmer and softer quiet VIP areas, each with its own mini art exhibition. A Greek historian would be brought in to curate each gallery and give guided tours of the art, rare books, jewellery and antique collection brought in from one of Singapore's oldest and most prestigious auction houses. The lot was exclusive, and it would be the first viewing of the collection due to go up for sale. Yawn. At least there would be the option to eat and drink the boredom away with the themed canapés, champagne, cocktails and spirits.

The pool would, of course, be the main focus, with the dance floor and party focused there. Original-sized Greek statue replicas were to flank the inviting day beds proposed, encouraging a livelier and more hedonistic theme. Here, the service teams would be dressed in navy-blue swimwear with a design incorporating both the ribbon and archer logo concepts. The pool has a decadent Greek feast table planned, next to a live barbecue station to be run by a chef dressed like a butcher. There were also to be ouzo and Greek liquor shot stations. Wines, champagne and spirits would be served by the bottle in the true spirit of opulence and indulgence. With our secret headline DJ booked for the evening, all the willing residents on the four floors are to be evacuated and put into hotel rooms for the night because we're pulling out all the stops for this one.

When I turn up early ready to greet my guests, I am met outside Ariella's flat by two waitresses who both look absolutely stunning. Their purple dresses are long, light, sheer and regal, with touches of gold and what look like ropes used as belts. It's low-key kinky. I am offered the pleasure of champagne or the poison of a shot of ouzo. I select ouzo and promptly get an archer's bow pinned on me. The plan is for the champagne drinkers to get ivory ribbons pinned on them. We thought it would be nice to have a little bit of fun with clients before the party begins to see who opted for what. I pat my guest list in my pocket, even though I know it off by heart. I'm ready.

As soon as I walk in and see Ariella, I know that I am done

for. The restraint I have shown all week is shot to pieces. She looks incredible, standing there in her greeting spot, visibly shaking with fear. I honestly can't see why. Eden has put her in a long, white, flowing Greek column dress with two slits that go right up to the tops of her thighs. While the cut of the fabric is elegant and its texture soft, it's also just see-through enough to make out Ariella's gold bikini underneath. Her hair is up and messy, with simple gold hoops in her ears and some gold bangles around her wrist. Ruby has lined her eyes heavily and left the rest of her face bare. She has a subtle golden glow to her skin that makes her look like a goddess. I'd worship that in a heartbeat.

'Hi, Caleb.' She looks nervous as she tries to tug the slits running up each leg shut with trembling hands. She won't succeed.

'The flat looks great.' I keep my words to a minimum so I don't give anything I am thinking away.

'The girls did a fantastic job. When I walked in, I wasn't sure I was in the same place!' Her voice wavers and I soften.

'You didn't see it being transformed?'

'No, Bree insisted I move out and leave them to it.' She tugs the slits again.

'Eden stitch you up?' I laugh, nodding at her hand on the slit. Shit. No. I need to stay neutral.

She throws me with a worried frown. 'She said it was a long dress with two side slits. She didn't tell me the slits are designed to gape almost up to my bum on both sides.' She tugs again.

I reach out and gently hold both her tugging hands to keep them still.

'Stop fidgeting, Ariella, you look heavenly, but you need to relax.'

She exhales loudly before she looks at me with tears swimming in her eyes.

'I am so scared, Caleb. I've never hosted a party before. I'm usually hidden with the rest of the crew. I feel like everything I practised has disappeared.' Her breath is getting shallow. She's panicking. Shit. Dahlia's training kicks in and I interlace my fingers with hers and look directly in her eyes.

'Look at me. Good, now close your eyes. Can you feel the circles I am making on your hand? I want you to focus on that and breathe with me, okay?' I take her through the counts and we very quickly help her regulate her breathing. When she is calm again, I pull her into me and plant a loving kiss on her temple. I can't help it.

'Don't be scared. I'm here. I've got you, okay? This will be a breeze. We have enough fun, shiny things to distract them and enough booze to speed up the fun. The hard bit is what you do in the office, day in, day out. Yes, you do have to give your speech, but you've nailed it time and time again in the office. I know because I've been watching you. Do you think you can pretend that's where you are? Like it's another rehearsal?'

She looks at me and nods, with complete, unreserved trust. That's when I pull her quickly into the cloakroom close by and place my lips on hers. She doesn't object, in fact she moves closer. When I pull away, she looks sad.

'Stay at mine tonight? When the party is over?' I know it's a risk before I ask. We've intentionally avoided each other all week.

'Yes, please.' She means it. I step forward to kiss her again but she puts a hand on my chest.

'We have company.' She points at the cloakroom team making their way over to their station. The operations briefing is obviously over, so we head back to our original spot. 'Do you want to go and take a look around? The clients aren't due for another twenty minutes,' she offers.

'I'm okay. I'll see it eventually. This is my greeting spot?' I ask, pointing at where I am standing.

'Yes. Bryce goes next to me and Devin next to you.'

'Where are they?'

'The girls are making sure they understand the layout. I volunteered to hold the fort.'

'I'll hold the fort with you.' I don't want to be anywhere else.

'Thank you, Caleb.'

I reach for her hand and stand, hiding our entwined fingers behind me. It feels like it's just us, holding hands and ready to take on whatever is going to come through the door. There and then, everything feels right with the world.

'Would you like some cold water? The ice will help—'

'Caleb!'

Bree squeals as she and the team start to cross the living room to reach us. It is good to see everyone – until I spot Dominic bringing up the rear, chatting with Lydia. I feel my jaw clench and the heat rise from the base of my neck. He's here. I drop Ariella's hand.

'You came together, didn't you?'

She sighs deeply and doesn't answer.

In no time, the launch is heaving, with the event in full swing. The spaces work better than we thought, with some of my guests taking up residence in Ariella's VIP room, trying to meet and network with her guests. Traitors. Having said that, I can spot more of Ariella's guests than expected in the pool area; they're settling into the snugs, with bottles of champagne making their way to them. As a team, we are doing well. Everyone is engaged, exchanging details, and I have already overheard a few live enquiries being tapped into the iPads. Ariella is also hard at work, talking to both her clients and mine; although the racing guys seem to be a permanent fixture in her periphery. Dominic is also stuck to her side throughout the reception and only allows her to be extracted from him by Bryce, just before the speeches.

Ariella takes the stage and stands so close to me that her shoulder is resting against my arm. After she is handed a microphone, the music is lowered.

'Step forward, Ariella,' I remind her in a whisper.

She stays rooted to where she is. Clutching the microphone with both her shaking hands, she has me worried for a second, but then she starts.

'Thank you all for coming. We are so grateful that you have given up your Friday nights to share our launch with us. Tonight, we have old friends, new friends and guests who we hope to become very friendly with.'

Everyone laughs. Her timing is perfect, her delivery flawless. She is doing well.

'I have a few introductions to make. Tonight, Ivory Bow's founders, Harrison Ivory and Christopher Bow, have flown in from London, and we have our lovely chairwoman of Ivory Bow Asia, Melissa Chang, with us.'

The audience claps and whoops. I use the opportunity to tell her to breathe. She takes a deep breath and lets it out just as the noise dies down.

'I'm Ariella—'

A wolf whistle cuts through her speech. No doubt one of my lot. The crowd laughs as Bryce, Devin and I shake our heads while laughing in a jovial reprimand.

'So maybe that's a little too friendly!' Ariella laughs and the crowd joins her. My little Mason has got this.

'I'm a member of the growing fifteen-person team here to look after you and your client experiences. We are here to put your brand up front, your customer engagement above your competitors, and to ensure that your ethos is communicated effectively and with a bit of fun.'

The whistle has thrown her. She has lost track and forgotten to introduce herself. I know because I asked Lydia to send me a copy of her speech and memorised it too, just in case.

'I'd like to introduce Caleb...' Our eyes meet and my heart skips a beat.

The deep whoops and barks from the crowd break through. Definitely my guys. Embarrassing.

Ariella introduces each of us, clearly and carefully, adding little bits of detail that weren't in her original speech, finishing off with Dominic.

'Our final thank-you tonight is reserved for Dominic Miller, from DMVI, who has worked tirelessly around the clock with his team and ours to create our new Conscious Experience app, available for every guest to download tonight. Thank you, Dominic.'

Ariella starts clapping and we all follow, even though I have no idea what she is talking about. Maybe that's why they have been spending so much time together. I find him in the crowd. He is beaming while he blows her a kiss.

Prick.

'So, this is us. This is Ivory Bow and we are here to work with you, for you. I am Ariella Mason, chief operating officer, Ivory Bow Asia. Welcome to a new type of experience.'

The crowd claps and she pulls the microphone away from her mouth and exhales deeply – she has done it. My heart swells with pride and I can't help it. With that, the first few chords of 'Titanium' start to play through the space and the crowd erupts. Formalities are over.

I watch Ariella make her way off the stage and over to a very proud-looking Christopher, who first holds her at arm's length to admire her face and then pulls her into the sort of hug a proud parent would give their graduating child. Harrison, on the other hand, is stand-offish, and gives her a quick but dismissive nod. His mouth is pressed in a firm line. He gives it a couple of seconds before he moves away from the involved, happy conversation Christopher and Ariella seem to be having. I see Dominic Miller spot them and start to make his way over to her. Why is he such a leech? Can't he leave her alone for five seconds?

'That article didn't help you, did it? Did wonders for them though.'

Ugh. It's Melissa.

'Isn't that what you wanted?' I turn to her, exasperated.

'Caleb, when do you think you're going to give up behaving like a child and stop being so contentious?'

'When I am certain you're not using the company to cover up criminal activity with the intent to pin it on the staff.'

'Criminal activity?' Mel smiles innocently.

'You know. Fraud. Money-laundering. That sort of thing...'

'I'd watch what you're saying, Caleb.' Sure enough, her smile morphs into a scowl.

'Or what? What exactly are you going to do?' My eyes narrow. 'Aside from all of us, you included I might add, being led out of here in handcuffs, this is your worst. You have us all exactly where you want us, doing your little dance. Unless you have some new threat, like, I don't know, human trafficking, we're done here. So, go fuck with someone else.'

'Everything good here?' Devin interrupts.

'Yes, why?' I snap.

'Whoa. From a distance it looks like you're arguing with Melissa, and I think you'll agree that's not a good look at our launch, Caleb.'

He nods at a couple of people watching Mel and me closely.

'Everything is fine, Devin, you know what Caleb is like.' Melissa puts her hand on my arm.

I yank it away. 'Get the fuck off me,' I whisper as I leave.

'Caleb!' Georgie calls out, walking up with champagne swilling in one hand and the other arm laced through Honey's.

'Hey, Georgie...' I gently guide Honey out of Georgie's hold and over to me by her waist before giving her a kiss on the cheek. I keep my arm protectively around Honey, because we really do not need Georgie 'PR-ing' both of us.

'Friends, my derrière!' Georgie is almost orgasming with glee.

'Nothing to see here, Georgie.' I laugh. I do like Georgie. She's fun, bubbly, chatty, likeable and very good at what she does; which makes her exceptionally dangerous.

'I disagree. There is plenty to see. You have to meet Dan.' Georgie quickly scans the crowd and shouts for him to come over.

'Do you think you could give Dan fifteen minutes? Preferably with Honey present?' she says to me.

Dan approaches with a mouth full of canapé, then extends his hand for a shake. I take it.

'Hello, Caleb. I had a couple of questions I was hoping to ask you tonight...' he manages. As he is speaking, I catch Ariella out of the corner of my eye, chatting with Dominic and a couple of guests.

'I'd really love to, Dan, but unfortunately I have scheduled meetings during the party tonight. But we can grab a coffee one lunchtime?' It's the best I can do. 'Georgie, would you mind taking Dan's questions pertaining to tonight? Thank you!'

I escort Honey over to Ariella's group and join in the conversation politely until there is a natural pause.

'Ariella, I thought I'd introduce you to Honey.'

'Hi, Ariella.' Honey steps forward and gives Ariella a kiss on each cheek.

'Hello, Honey. It is such a pleasure to finally be introduced to you. You are such a phenomenal athlete! How long have you been fighting professionally?'

I see Honey beam and I tune out of the conversation while I throw a massive fuck-you smirk at Dominic. He knew exactly what he was doing when he showed Ariella the videos of Honey fighting.

'It's also finally good to meet you, Caleb,' the lady to my left remarks and extends a delicate hand.

'Lovely to meet you too.'

'You've never met?' Dominic asks, confused, and then follows it with an intentionally audible 'Interesting.'

'No.' I smile light-heartedly at the lady.

'Kimberley Teh...' The minute I hear her name I know I've fucked up. She is one of Melissa's introductions. My calendar indicates that, officially, I have met her at least twice since the move to Singapore and many times before that; but in reality, despite my numerous actual attempts to meet her by showing up at the Skin Skill Systems head office without an appointment, I never have.

'CMO, Skin Skill Systems,' Dominic goes on.

I think quickly. 'Kimberley! Of course, so sorry.'

Dominic is not buying it. I can almost hear the cogs in his brain turning.

'There is someone I'd love you to meet!' I tap Ariella's shoulder to signal that I am leaving with Kimberly, before I start guiding her towards Georgie.

'I'm so happy we have finally met! I've been trying to take you to lunch for a while,' I reveal.

'I know, but your image is a little problematic for us.' She laughs.

'How so?' I smile.

'Going anywhere with you inspires the suggestion that it's more than lunch.' One eyebrow shoots up. 'We may all be too polite to mention it, but you do know that what is going on between you and Melissa is no secret?'

She is kind in her delivery. There is no point in denying it, so I come clean.

'That's fair. You should know, though, that we ended things last year.'

'I expected you to deny it. Thank you for being honest.'

'Does everyone know?'

'Not everyone, but unfortunately the people that matter do, so it's hard to take you seriously. Your boss, however, we like.'

'I have no chance of leaving my reputation behind and proving myself, do I?' Shit.

'No,' she responds sadly.

'Thank you for telling me. At least now I know— Excuse me a second, here is the person I wanted to introduce you to.' I tap Georgie's shoulder. I may not have met my contacts but I know each company back to front.

'Georgie! I'd like you to meet Kimberley. She's the CMO of Skin Skill Systems. Is Dan still around? They have just launched a product that not only cuts burn-healing time down by thirty per cent but also reduces scarring by as much as seventy. Kimberley also sits on a board that awards scholarships to underprivileged young women across the globe with an interest in using science and technology to improve their local living standards; with a specific focus on skill-sharing.'

'Oh wow!'

I know Georgie sees a potential new client, and she doesn't waste any time unloading her charm offensive. Before long, Kimberley Teh is in fits of laughter. When I excuse myself, Kimberley reaches out to stop me.

'Tea. In the lobby of my office building. Leave the flirting at home and come with a proper pitch and some real solutions for us. We'll give you a proper shot.'

The party has only been going for an hour, and I've already had three conversations that could have ended in disaster and I'm tense. I need a drink. Thankfully, I spot the guys from

Ochuka Distilleries debating what neat spirits to put through the luge. It's time to turn my night around.

'Oi! Waiter! Fix me a drink now!'

I feel three hard pokes on my shoulder. I recognise that Scottish accent and whip around.

'LARA!' I lift her into a hug. It feels fantastic to see a friendly face. Lara and I may not be the best of buddies, but I trust her. Besides, underneath all that rudeness and unnecessary savagery, I know she actually thinks we were friends.

'Yuck! Stop! Ew! Gross! I don't want to catch anything!' She laughs as she pretends she wants to be let go.

'Why the hell are you here?' I realise I haven't been this happy in a while.

'Chlamydia. Singaporean outreach programme. Getting the female population to stay away from you. Have you managed to get that seen to yet?' She crosses her hands against her chest and regards me suspiciously.

'Oh, come here!' I pull her into another hug.

'Still a lesbian, Caleb. When did you get so huggy?' She comedically slaps my body away. 'Where is Aari? I want to surprise her and make her feel guilty that I volunteered to be Chris and Harry's lackey just to come and see you two ingrates. It's not all bad, we're staying at the Shangri La so avoiding them until we fly back on Monday night is going to be a breeze!'

'She's in the VIP area, I think,' I offer.

'Are you guys still fighting?' She rolls her eyes like we are being idiots.

'We're not fighting. We're not together, as you know, but we're not fighting.'

'Good. You may be like a disgusting rabid stray animal she rescued from the bins behind the local kebab shop, but I'm used to you now. Let's get a drink.'

As we make our way to the pool, Honey intercepts our journey. She has grabbed her coat from the cloakroom and is leaving.

'Thanks for the invitation, Caleb. I'm going to head home.'

Lara pushes in front of me and extends her hand, wearing a massive smile. 'I'm Lara.'

Honey slowly takes her hand. She knows exactly who Lara is.

'You're Lara?' She looks surprised.

'Yes.' Lara turns to me, in full victim mode. 'For fuck's sake, Caleb! What have you been saying to people about me?'

'Nothing. Just that you're crazy and violent. Basically, the truth!' I defend. Honey bursts out laughing.

'Caleb! I'm going to wait until you're asleep, then I'm going to stab you in the eyes with toothpicks!' Lara complains and kicks me in the shin, hard. I grunt in pain before she turns to Honey. 'I'm not crazy and violent.'

Honey looks like she is having a hard time believing Lara.

'Really! I'm not.'

Honey is trying not to laugh.

'Right. You're not going home. Let's have your coat. Come on,' Lara demands. Honey looks unsure as she takes off her coat and hands it to Lara. 'Be right back!' Lara says, stomping off with the coat.

'You can pretend to go to the loo and take off when she isn't looking,' I offer.

'I like her. She's funny.'

'Oh no.'

I start to head to the pool once more, only to be cornered by a furious and already inebriated Harrison. Great.

'Was that Lara?' he asks, tripping over those three basic words. This is not good. The man cannot hold his liquor.

'Yeah...'

'I knew we shouldn't have let her come. She's supposed to

be coordinating our diaries and meetings but we haven't seen her since we checked in. She has also put herself down as a woman travelling alone, so they won't even tell us her room number. Instead, our PAs are working odd hours back home. I don't know why the fuck we gave her Ariella's old job.' Harrison grabs a cocktail making its way past.

How Lara still manages to be employed is beyond me, and now she has convinced them to give her Ariella's old job? I can only imagine that Ivory Bow has more than a few metaphorical bodies (almost all Harrison's, I'm sure), and she knows exactly where they are buried.

'How are things back in the office? Do they miss me yet?' I say, attempting to change the subject.

'Nobody gives a shit. Well, apart from Piers. He's pissed off because I have taken over your clients and he's failing miserably with Africa. He wanted the continent, I gave him the continent and now he's bitching about the continent. I might sack him. He is bloody useless.' Harrison places his glass on a passing tray and grabs a glass of champagne.

'I warned you about him.'

'He's the least of my problems. What is this shit about Ariella demanding all the files of your Asian clients?'

'We hit a snag and they haven't been transferred over...'

'Fuck off with the innocent act. Do you *really* want them sent over? I'm responsible for those accounts now, so I know that most of them have no idea who you are. What were you doing in Singapore on all those business trips? You sure as hell were not having meetings with potential clients. More importantly, how were you landing these accounts if none of them have met you?' Harrison places the empty champagne glass on a poseur table nearby, looking around for a drink.

'You're getting drunk.' I step back.

'Not drunk enough to miss that you've just gone as white as a sheet. What aren't you telling us, Caleb? I know what I'm not telling you.' Harrison smiles. I don't like it. He grabs another cocktail from a passing tray.

'What's that?'

'I'm keeping your accounts. Every last one. Nothing is coming over. You're going to have to start from scratch over here. Sorry, mate, I can't afford to lose the revenue. You'll get some sort of reduced bonus, we just need to figure out what that is. Besides, those cancellations are worth a fortune. It's easy money for essentially doing nothing.' He winks at me. And, in an instant, I know. Harrison knows that the payments are all wrong and there is something to be found.

'Keep them. I don't give a shit.'

Harrison has no idea he has just handed me a gift. I was planning to legitimise or lose them anyway, and now I don't have to think about them any more. If Melissa wants them, she can deal with Harrison directly. I have enough new clients to keep me busy and I can use the time I allocated previously to focus on bringing in more business. I may be behind on my projected targets because I have now lost all my historic accounts to Harrison, but DMVI will more than make up for Ivory Bow's overall target shortfall. Besides, I know that I can build the lost revenue back up.

'That's what I thought you'd say.' He thinks he's won. It's best to let him think that way. That's what Harrison has always been about. 'While I'm feeling lucky,' he continues, 'Ariella has grown up a bit, hasn't she?'

I step closer to him. 'If you touch her, I will break every single finger you lay on her, before I beat you to a pulp. Do you understand me?'

He laughs in my face. 'It may be worth it. That gold bikini, wowzers.' He shivers exaggeratedly before he walks away. I want to go after him, because he is a ticking bomb. Instead, I go over to one of the many members of the security team and point Harrison out as he grabs another drink. I explain that he is inebriated and has made a suggested threat at Ariella. I also take great pains to explain that, while we don't want a lawsuit, he should be extracted from the party by any means necessary.

When I'm finally working on my guest list, laughing and doing shots by the pool, I see two security guards silently escort a subdued Harrison out of the party. It turns out his removal is the exact pick-me-up I need.

Things are starting to look up.

THIRTY

ARIELLA

When I wake up the next morning in Caleb's apartment with my head in Lara's lap while she snores away, I can't contain the joy I feel. We did it.

Every single action, plan, decision, mistake, conversation and challenge built up to last night. It was better than I could have dreamed. Our guests turned up happy, receptive and, most importantly, engaged. It felt good to be the COO I hoped to be for a few hours. Being able to finally talk about nothing but Ivory Bow, our vision, delivery process and successes was such a relief. For once, I didn't get a question about what I was wearing, Dominic Miller, or whether I was single. For the first time in Singapore, I finally felt that I was being seen as I wanted to be: hard-working and dedicated.

When I sent the team home at the end of the night, after giving them all Monday off work, Caleb and I sat by the pool taking it all in.

'You did it, Aari.' He looked so proud.

'*We* did it.'

'I've never seen Christopher dance before.' Caleb chuckled.

'It was so good to see him! I might stay in London for a bit longer to shadow him when I return for Zachary's wedding. Are you still happy to be my plus one?'

'Of course. Besides, I miss Dahlia,' Caleb admitted softly.

'Did you see Harrison? I was hoping to catch up with him.'

'Nope.' Caleb shook his head. 'Anyway, it's late. Want to get anything from your room?'

'Nah, I have everything at the hotel.'

'Remember, you're not going to the hotel tonight. You're staying at mine,' he reminded me.

'Caleb, I know I said so earlier but...'

'Come back to mine, just for a few minutes. If you still want to go to your hotel, I'll put you in a car myself.' I knew the power this boy wielded over me. I could be convinced in a few minutes.

'One minute,' I conceded. He couldn't do *that* much damage in one minute. I caught him smiling. Ugh. He could do plenty of damage in one minute. I grabbed a toothbrush from my room before we left. 'Just in case,' I whispered in the lift, without meeting his eyes. I heard him softly laugh to himself.

Just when I thought the night couldn't get any better, Caleb opened the door to his apartment and I saw Lara in his kitchen buttering some toast. I was running into her arms before I knew it.

'Whoa!' she exclaimed as I threw myself at her and burst into tears. She held on to me tightly. 'I've missed you terribly but more importantly, I am so fucking proud of you,' she whispered into my ear.

It just made me weep harder. I felt every hurt, every pain, every discomfort and frustration that I'd been carrying around the last few months drain away. It took a little while for me to let go.

'Hey! Is that my shirt you're getting butter all over? That's bloody Savile Row!' Caleb pointed at Lara, annoyed.

'You. Why are you here?' Lara threw back.

'It's my apartment, Lara!'

'You said make yourself feel at home, so I did!' Lara complained.

'Honey looks at home, and she's not in my clothes. Are those my boxers?'

'Fresh out of one of your brand-new packets. Everything else is guaranteed to be hygienically dicey.' She wrinkled her nose in disgust.

I hadn't noticed Honey until then, sitting in his living area in her party dress, laughing at Caleb and Lara. I offered a little wave and went over.

'Are they always like this?' She was enjoying watching Lara and Caleb going at it.

'Always. Secretly though, I think they love each other.' I smiled.

'I did tell her not to rummage through his stuff.'

Caleb was right. I really do like Honey.

'Nice try. Did the party get a little noisy?'

'A little. I was going to leave before I was abducted by Lara and held hostage by the pool. By the time I looked up, it was really late. I'm training Caleb in the morning, so he said I could stay. I hope that's okay?' She looked concerned.

'I am so glad you're here. If I have to give a police report tonight, I'm going to need someone to be on Caleb's side.'

'She's a bit mad, isn't she?'

'Yup, and unapologetically so. That's why I love her.' I smiled at my best friend, who was making stabbing motions in Caleb's direction with a fork. 'Need something to sleep in?' I asked Honey as we watched them go at it.

'That'd be great.'

'Come on, let's grab a couple of T-shirts and those new boxers Lara found.'

By the time I emerged from Caleb's shower in his clothes, Honey was chatting and laughing with Lara and Caleb while finishing some toast.

'Want some, Aari?' Lara asked, pointing at the bread.

'No thanks. I have too much adrenaline coursing through me still. That's the fastest shower I have ever had.'

'Well, I'm absolutely knackered.' Caleb yawned. 'If you ladies want my bed, I'll take the couch. Honey, the spare room is yours.'

'I'm buzzing too! Shall we stay up, get sozzled on Caleb's booze, eat his crisps and watch something scary?' Lara suggested.

It's not a bad idea. 'Yes! Caleb, you can have your bed. Honey, wanna join Lara and me?' I said, extending an invitation.

'No, scary films really freak me out. It's ridiculous really. I'll watch a true crime special about an actual serial killer on the prowl and sleep like a baby.'

We all burst out laughing. 'I'm going to get some sleep,' Honey went on. 'I need to be on my game to train tomorrow. Caleb, want to start a little later if you don't have anywhere you need to be?'

'Yes. Ten?' Caleb suggested.

Lara and I grabbed some blankets, turned off the lights and made a little bed for ourselves on the couch before we picked the spookiest film on Caleb's streaming service.

'It's all been a bit shit out here for you, hasn't it?' Lara asked, taking a sip out of her gin and tonic as we watched the opening credits.

'Just a little bit,' I responded, catching her eye, before we both burst out laughing. She pulled me into a hug.

'Don't you dare come home. You're killing it.'

'I'm trying.'

'Aaaargh!' we both screamed as something swished across the screen, making us jump.

'Morning. Hibiscus?' Caleb whispers, as he pops a pot of tea and a cup down before quietly clearing the glasses and crisp packets in front of us.

'Morning, thank you,' I whisper, trying not to wake a still-sleeping Lara.

'You look happy. It's nice,' he observes.

'I feel happy.'

'Bloody hell, get a room!' Lara complains as she moves my head off her lap and stands up. 'I smell coffee. Where?'

Caleb laughs and heads back into the kitchen. He is shirt-less this morning, with his soft navy joggers hanging low on his hips. I catch myself licking my bottom lip as I watch him walk away.

'Have you been training?' I ask in the direction of the kitchen, trying to sound nonchalant.

'No, Honey is still sleeping. I didn't want to wake her.'

'What time is it?' Lara asks.

'About ten to eleven?'

'Ah, I was supposed to have a meeting with Christopher and Harrison at ten. Oh well. Sooooo, I swiped a bag of those swimsuits and your merch yesterday...'

'Lara, those were supposed to go on our online store!'

'They will, once I've helped myself to the bits I want. How about we ditch our mobile phones, like properly lock them away, lounge by the pool all day, swimming, drinking, gossiping, falling asleep and eating stuff that is terrible for us?'

I could definitely stop and shut the world out for a day.

'What about Christopher and Harrison?' I ask, worried.

'They can't fire me for having food poisoning, can they?'

'How are you still employed?' Caleb asks, just as surprised as I am.

'Funny, I was thinking the same about you,' Lara counters as Honey emerges.

'Ready, Caleb?' she asks. 'I don't have my kit but we can do some sequence work today?'

'Sure. Espresso and start?'

'This, I've got to see.' Lara runs towards Caleb's cloakroom, pulls out a bag, then tosses me a swimsuit and some sunglasses. 'Come on, Aari. Let's get the good seats!'

I quickly grab the items, making a mental note to pay for them.

Twenty minutes later, Lara and I are on Caleb's sun loungers watching him train by the pool with Honey. It looks dangerous, intense and really hard work.

I'd have been more frightened if Lara wasn't running a detailed sports commentary peppered with phrases like 'Beat his ass! Go on, choke him! Break his arm!' Even Honey has stopped a couple of times because she's laughing so hard at some of Lara's comments. At one point, when Honey has Caleb in a floor lock, Lara gets up and stretches out her hand, yelling, 'Tag me in! Tag me in! Please tag me in!' Honey bursts out laughing so hard, she loses her grip and Caleb takes advantage.

Honey easily has the upper hand for the whole hour but it's hard not to be impressed by Caleb. Watching his body move, getting up again and again, blocking, countering and sweating with the lean muscles in his back moving just under his skin. At one point, I get busted by Lara.

'Aari! Can you try not to look so thirsty? Honestly!'

Caleb wasn't lying when he said Honey often left him for dead by the pool floor. After the cool-down stretches, I watch Caleb collapse on his back with his chest heaving heavily while Honey casually steps over him to get them some water. Even I realise how disgracefully lusty I am when Caleb finally drags himself into the outdoor shower, emerges in his swim shorts and dives into the pool. I get in shortly after him.

'Ariella Mason, have some self-respect!' Lara calls, just before she joins Honey in the kitchen.

'Are you okay?' I ask, approaching him as he floats on his back.

'I will be. Being weightless for a few seconds helps.'

'I'm sorry. You did really well though.' I pour some water on his chest and stroke the hair on his head. Caleb immediately stops floating and looks at me weirdly.

'Mason, are you flirting with me?'

'Maybe, a little.'

I plant a kiss on Caleb that is meant to be suggestive but quick, but it soon turns into something slow and sensual. The longer it goes on, the more it feels like the kiss is coming from a place I can't shut out any longer.

'I should get my arse handed to me in front of you more often.' Caleb laughs into our kiss and I feel his body come alive underneath me.

'Hey! Hey! Hey!' Lara interrupts, throwing ice cubes at us from the jugs of water she and Honey have brought out. 'Honey is staying, can we keep it PG?'

Honey is looking anywhere but at Caleb and me.

'Right. I've ordered a ton of food from different places on your delivery app, Caleb. Now, who wants to play Marco Polo?' Lara places the tray carefully on the table by the pool and dive-bombs in.

'I don't know how to play,' Honey admits, shyly.

'Doesn't matter. Grab a swimsuit from the bag and jump in, I'll try to avoid you the first couple of rounds. MARCO!' Lara shouts without counting as she submerges suddenly, causing Caleb and me to scramble instantly.

. . .

'I had the best day. You guys are really cool. It's been a while since I've laughed so much,' Honey says to Lara and me as she steps out of the taxi.

'We should hang out again before I go on Tuesday. Ariella, you up for it?' Lara nudges.

'Sure.'

We wait until she gets into her home safely before we pull away.

'I like her.'

'Do you now?' I raise my eyebrow at Lara.

'Oh no. I like her as a person. Did you know that she's Sri Lankan and her family had to flee the civil war?'

'No, I didn't.'

'Yup. She's just cool, you know? Besides, I learned my lesson with Bamidele. I won't be flirting with any more straight chicks looking to experiment any time soon. She's easy to be around. And did you see her beat the shit out of Caleb? That's going to keep me in gleeful orgasms for a while.'

I really want to tell Lara about Honey but I don't. Honey should be the one to do that, not me. 'I like her too. She's a lot calmer and quieter than I expected her to be – especially after watching her fight. Are you coming over to Raffles with me or going back to the Shangri La?'

'Shangri La. I have a flood of angry texts from Harry threatening not to pay my hotel bill. I'm not too worried though, he hasn't got a legal leg to stand on, but Chris has called a breakfast meeting for tomorrow, so I need to arrive looking food-poisoned.'

How Lara is going to get away with explaining a three-day disappearance is beyond me. I'll leave her to it.

'Want to cruise around on a bumboat tomorrow evening and get some hawker food for dinner?' I offer.

'If I'm alive and not chained to the toilet in my room, sure.

Okay, this is me. I love you.' Lara gives me a big hug before she steps out of the car.

'I love you too.'

I really should go back to my hotel, take a shower and go to sleep, but I don't. Fifteen minutes later, I'm standing outside Caleb's door, in his T-shirt and tracksuit bottoms, not touching his bell. If I do, it's going to change everything. We've been at the cusp of tipping over for a while. I'm still standing outside making up my mind when my phone buzzes.

> You and Lara get back to your hotel okay?

> > Lara went back to the Shangri La.

I don't want to lie to him, but I don't want to give away the fact that I am outside his apartment behaving like a stalker right now.

> I thought she was avoiding Christopher and Harrison?

> > Christopher called a breakfast meeting.

> Yikes! That doesn't sound good.

> > Nope.

> I had fun today. I've missed wasting days with you.

> > Me too.

> I miss spending nights with you too.

> > Me too.

> I want to come over there so badly.

Don't.

That does it. I press his doorbell.

Caleb's mouth is on mine as soon as he opens his front door.

'Caleb, CCTV.' I point to the camera. Keeping his mouth on mine, he drags me into his apartment and closes the door behind us.

I remember this feeling. My head is light, my heart is thumping and everything in my tummy is somersaulting. I breathe Caleb in and feel him envelop me from my head to my toes.

'Aari...' Caleb pulls away, panting. 'I feel like we should set some boundaries so we don't go too far; because right now, I'm really struggling.'

'I don't want to set boundaries tonight, Caleb.' We can pick up the pieces tomorrow morning.

He lets out a low moan as his body pushes into mine against the bedroom door, and I feel his prominent response to me. Keeping me pinned under him, his thumb travels from my face, down my neck and between my collarbone to circle one of his girls over my bra. My back arches, welcoming his touch. When Caleb hears my sharp inhale, he brings his other hand up to the other and does the same. It feels sensational.

'Look at me,' he asks as I try to regulate my breathing as he teases my nipples. I open my eyes and see a curious-looking Caleb observe me like he is seeing me for the first time.

'I've missed this look on your face. I've missed the way your mouth parts as you try to breathe, the way your eyebrows knit together as you're surrendering to me, and mostly the determination in your eyes. Like you're desperately trying to figure out where you end and I begin.'

The feeling intensifies to the point at which I can't take it any more. Holding his gaze, I gently put my hands on his.

'If I don't get a break, I think I might explode, and I'm not ready yet,' I explain between laboured breaths. I've missed the dirty smile he gives me. I pull his shirt over his head, toss it on the floor and pull him into a kiss as I run my nails down his back. It's his turn to close his eyes and moan.

'Caleb?' I whisper to get his attention.

'Hmmm?'

'Please don't push me away this time, I can't take it,' I plead, resigned to it. Caleb reaches over silently and flips the light switch near my arm, allowing the moon to illuminate the room.

'I want you to know we have all night, okay? But I feel like we need this right now.' I know that I will do whatever he asks.

Caleb takes off his tracksuit bottoms and helps me out of my underwear before leading me to the bed. He arranges himself in the lotus position without letting go of my hand. 'Come here.'

I comply and Caleb guides me gently as I straddle him. He engages our kiss immediately and desire shoots through me as he adjusts my hips, encouraging my legs to wrap around him, allowing me to safely rub against him between our kisses.

'You've been too far away from me for too long, Aari, and I know it's my fault. I'm sorry,' he whispers with our foreheads touching.

'I'm sorry too. I lost myself for a little bit there.'

'I'm so glad you came back tonight.' He looks into my eyes.

'So am I.' I press my chest against his, wanting to be closer, needing to be closer.

'I need you to stay. Everything is wrong and nothing fits without you.'

'This is where I belong, Black. I don't think I ever left, I just tried to convince myself that I did.' Feeling myself move against Caleb is beginning to get me to that point.

'Are you saying that this whole time, you've wanted me as

much as I have wanted you?' Caleb asks softly, unsure, searching my face. I close my eyes as my hips move harder against him.

'Much, much, more.' I exhale, trying to find the breath to contain all the feelings overwhelming me.

'Do you think you're ready for me?'

I nod and stop for Caleb to put the condom in place. When he slides into me, I don't recognise the sound I make. He wraps me into a hug and I do the same with my legs, pulling him closer and further in. We immediately fall into sync as we start to move together.

All our words are gone as I melt into my boyfriend.

'You're the love of my life, Aari. I've never loved anything other than you. Ever.'

I feel a tear from Caleb hit my shoulder and it's too much. Soon I'm crying too. The last few months have been hard but I don't want anyone or anything else.

We hold each other tightly through our orgasms as they build, detonate, overlap and ebb, with our sweaty chests inseparably pressed together.

'I'm yours, Caleb,' I whisper as I let my body go limp against his.

THIRTY-ONE

CALEB

Last night was completely unexpected. When Aari left with Lara and Honey, it took everything in me not to jump into a car and wait for her in the Raffles lobby. I knew the way she kissed me in the pool had meaning; I just didn't realise how much. The party was good for her. It was a significant milestone that just reconfirmed she was on the right track, and I think she had needed that for a while. Maybe she just needed to get that out of the way.

I watch her lying next to me as the sun comes up, her head buried in the pillow. I've missed teetering on the edge because she has taken over the bed. Thankfully, these beds are huge compared to our standard kings in London, so I have a little more space to play with. She deserves the rest; it has been a long road.

We kept each other up all night, talking, laughing and making love. We promised each other to leave the bigger conversations until morning; which was absolutely fine with me. I look at my girlfriend and admire the three little hickeys I've already placed on her because she admitted she has missed them. She's too far away. I gently rearrange her arms and legs, straightening them out. When I succeed, I pull her into my chest so that we can be closer. I struggle to contain my emotions as I breathe her in and hold her tightly. Eventually, I shut my eyes and I let myself fall back asleep.

I am woken up a few hours later by the sound of the shower stopping, followed by Ariella re-entering the room in one of my huge, fluffy towels. I make a note to get her the tiny towels she, and I, are used to.

'Morning!' She wanders over to my side of the bed and plants a kiss on my lips.

'Hi,' I whisper into it, walking my fingers up her thigh. 'What are your plans for today?'

'I was thinking of taking a bumboat tour with Lara, eating in Chinatown and doing very little.'

'I take it I'm not invited?'

'No, sorry.'

My fingers reach their destination and Ariella swallows and shifts a little.

'What time is all this meant to be happening?'

'Some time early evening. I should… call to make sure… she hasn't been marched onto a plane. Her meeting should, um, be over by now and, um, she hasn't left me any messages.' She's trying hard to ignore my fingers. She has forgotten what I'm like. That's all right, I'll remind her.

'It won't have been a pleasant meeting.'

'No – erm, but it's Lara, she… she'll be fine.' The word 'fine' emerges as a whisper.

'You okay there, Aari? You seem to be struggling to get your words out.' I snigger.

'That's because you insist on doing naughty things to me under my towel.'

'Why don't I stop doing naughty things to you underneath your towel and get rid of the towel altogether?'

I pull her on top of me, flip her over on her back, open up her towel and bury my face between her thighs.

The day unfolds like we are back home. We shower, eat, swim, laugh and spend the day together, knowing that the world outside will wait. Dominic interrupts once with a text, asking Aari to give him a ring. She ignores it, with a 'I'll call him on Tuesday.'

It's good news for me when Lara cancels their plans, citing abuse of power. I don't blame Christopher and Harrison – she did disappear for three days after they paid for her flight and hotel in exchange for her doing some actual work. It's not until I mention it that Ariella remembers that she was due to check out of *her* hotel today. The time she takes rushing over there, packing up and returning to me feels like for ever; but by the time she returns, dinner has been delivered and I've set up a little picnic by the pool.

'This is lovely, Caleb.'

Good. I wanted to do a good job. We're halfway through the meal before I ask. 'So... how do you want to handle this?'

'Handle what?' She pops a piece of cheese in her mouth.

'Us. You said you didn't want to hide.'

'Oh.'

I've caught her off guard.

'If you want to take more time or change your mind, it's okay. We've gone from a standing start to lightning speed. We can hit the brakes while we figure it out.'

I watch her relax. My girlfriend crawls over on her hands and knees and plants a small, tender kiss on my lips. I like these types of kisses too.

'Thank you. I'd like to tell Dominic on Tuesday and I think

it's only fair to let the project team know, especially as Bryce, Devin and Lydia already do.'

It's more than I was expecting.

'Do we keep things quiet outside of work?'

'Yes, Honey still needs you, but I'm drawing a hard line under the Dominic and Ariella circus. I still want to hang out with him as my friend, but I refuse to feed that narrative any more.'

It's not the time to fight the Dominic fight. She has already committed to telling him. I don't need to light the 'I want to stay friends' fire yet. 'I was thinking we could pop to the market tomorrow, get some ingredients and we could cook together? Maybe invite Lara over if she manages to escape?' I know I have just laid out all of Ariella's favourite things. I've been thinking about them all day.

'You mean I cook and you hover around being distracting?'

'Yes.' I beam.

'I'd love to but I have a lunch meeting at noon tomorrow with Christopher and Harrison. Maybe after? Around two?'

'That works. Do you need to prepare for your meeting tonight?' I ask, worried that the answer is yes.

'No. I'm ready and anything else can be done in the morning, but I should have an early night. Besides, I'll be going with Lydia and she's always just as prepared as I am.'

'Let's get you that early night!' I encourage her, standing to take the food tray with me.

'To sleep, Caleb!' she reinforces.

'Of course to sleep!' I look offended.

'It's just that I haven't slept properly since Thursday night.'

'Me too. We'll go to bed and just sleep.'

And that's exactly what we do; after I dish out a couple of orgasms and add a few more hickeys to my new collection.

.   .   .

I send her off after a little morning surprise on Monday before she leaves me with Honey.

'I like your friends,' Honey starts as we warm up.

'Lara's more like one of those cute but barky puppies you keep around to deter intruders.'

'Yeah. She's very different from anyone I've ever met, that's for sure.'

Lara is that.

'It looks like you sorted things out with Ariella?'

'We're spending time together.' I smile so widely, Honey stops the warm-up.

'Right now, you are so different to the guy that's all over my social media feed,' she teases.

'True, but we still need that guy and I'm not going to bail on you.'

'Are you sure that's okay with Ariella?'

'Her exact words were, "You can't let Honey down, she still needs you".' Honey looks emotional at my words. 'Don't worry, it takes as long as it takes.' She nods. 'Have you thought any more about how you're going to handle your issue?' I go on.

'I don't know. Lara invited me to London. I thought I might take some time out and get some space to think about it.'

'Was it a flirty invite or just a friendly one?'

'Just a friendly one. Nothing like that.'

'Does she know?'

'No. I didn't want things to be weird and culturally...'

'Fair point, I'm an idiot – it's not like straight people go around announcing their straightness to everyone.'

'She's really pretty though.' Honey stands back, ready to start an attack drill.

'Lara? She's fucking hot.'

Honey comes for me and quickly puts me in a headlock. 'She is,' she agrees as I immediately start to tap out of the hold.

Honey destroys me as usual. After some breakfast I settle

into my hit list from the party. If Ariella and I are going to do this, now more than ever I need to pull those figures in and smash my sales records; so, I start with each contact, and pull their actionable items, requirements and business values apart, piece by piece, while I wait for her.

I send a quick message just before her meeting.

> Good luck, boss.

She responds immediately.

> It has been painful being away from you this morning. See you later. I love you x

I feel those words and it takes a little while for me to respond.

> I bet it wasn't as painful as what Honey just put me through. I love you my little Mason, finish quickly.

> As quickly as possible.

When 2 p.m. comes around, I can hardly sit still, but I don't hear from Ariella so I give it another hour. Harrison can be distracting, so she is probably overrunning. It's what I tell myself until 5 p.m. strikes and I have heard nothing; so I send her a text.

> Just checking you're okay. Long meeting!

I get nothing for ten minutes so I text again.

> Are you okay my little Mason?

Nothing. At six, I text Lydia.

> Are you guys still in the meeting?

Lydia shoots a text back immediately.

No.

> I've been trying to get hold of Ariella. Is everything all right?

No.

Panic immediately sets in and I call Ariella's phone. It rings to voicemail. I try again and it does the same. I call Lydia and the ringing is cut short.

> What is going on?

Download Signal and give me a minute. I will message you from my private phone. Delete this.

I do as I am told and I wait for what feels like for ever. Finally, I get a text from an unrecognised number.

Caleb, it's me Lydia.

> What's going on? Why all the clandestine moves?

I REALLY shouldn't be doing this.

> Doing what?

Ariella knows that most of your UK–Singaporean clients have no idea who you are. Harrison told her at lunch because he's convinced you had him thrown out of the party.

Everything holding me up drains away.

> Harrison doesn't know what he's talking about.

She made me pull your diary from when you started and we've both been at the apartment, calling them, all afternoon, asking when last they saw you and when next to put an appointment in. We've gone through them all and it falls in line with what Harrison told her.

> Are you upstairs now?

Yes, but I'd advise you to stay downstairs. I'll text you when I am leaving. She is not coping well.

> I can come up and clear it up.

No, you can't. The only thing you can do right now is tell her the truth about EVERYTHING. Before I was Ariella's PA, I led Melissa's administrative team. I know, Caleb. About all of it. I organised your cars, your rooms, paid your bills and even made some of your phone calls. Right now, I'm only violating my contract because you're my friend and because you need to tell her everything. She is determined to find out; and, from what I have seen these past few months, she will. I suggest it all comes from you.

Shit. Fuck.

> Thanks Lydia. How is she?

Not good. I've got to go. I told her I needed to pee. For what it's worth, I was hoping you would get a fresh start too. I'm sorry. I'll text you when I'm about to leave but you should know, she doesn't want to see you.

My legs can't hold me up any more so I lie flat on the floor of my apartment and feel the weight of it all come crashing down. I do the only thing I can.

> She knows.

Thank goodness. What made you finally tell her? Big points for texting during office hours by the way!

> I didn't. She found out. Long story. I have to go and face her, man, and I don't know if I can.

If it helps, I'm fairly certain you're not going to prison.

> I don't care about that. It's the other stuff.

That'll be difficult to tackle. Let me know if you need me. Call/text, I'll back you up the best I can.

For the very first time, I see it. I see why everyone thought she was making the biggest mistake by leaving him. I finally saw what all their friends saw and what I refused to acknowledge. With all his faults, when it comes to Ariella he is always going to put himself second. Even now. Not like me. It kills me to write the next text.

> She deserves to be with you, not me.

Jasper texts back immediately.

She doesn't want me, does she? She wants you. Why don't we try to fix this and give her what she wants?

I stay on the floor until I hear from Lydia at nine thirty.

Get the lift now. Tell her concierge told you she was back. I'll tell them on my way out. Tell her all of it, Caleb.

I grab my keys and my phone and fly up there, without

knowing what I am going to say. I wait patiently outside the door and, true to her word, I don't have to wait long.

'Oh, hi, Caleb!' Lydia calls, louder than usual. 'Ariella?' she calls next, winking at me and tilting her head for me to go in. I mouth a quick 'Thank you.'

'Ariella?' she calls again. 'Shall I drop Ms Pat off at home?'

Ms Pat emerges out of nowhere with nothing but kindness and sympathy on her face. Shit. Ms Pat knows too. Fuck.

Ariella finally appears and her face reminds me of the night Jasper and I collected her from a rainy bus stop in Kilburn. She has been crying. Really hard.

'Yes, please take Ms Pat with you, and "Caleb" too.' She air-quotes my name with her fingers.

'Aari?' I pretend I don't know what is going on to hide Lydia's help.

Lydia and Ms Pat beat a hasty retreat and leave us in the flat alone. I stand by the door while Ariella stands at the end of the walkway to the bedrooms.

'Aari—' I walk towards her.

'Stop!' she shouts, crying. 'Don't come any closer!'

I do as she asks. From this distance, I can see that she is shaking badly, and I don't know what to do.

'Aari—'

'Ari-ELLA!' she shouts once again. 'Stay there!'

I plant my feet firmly and put my hands up. Shit. She is frightened of me. My little Mason is scared... of me. It destroys me but I hold back the tears.

'Who are you?' she demands.

'It's me, Caleb,' I answer, unsure of what she is asking.

'No!' She steps forward carefully towards her couch and throws me a stapled stack of papers before stepping back quickly to the end of the walkway. 'Who ARE you? And what do you want from me?' She is crying hard, frightened and, as far as I can see, on the verge of a panic attack.

I pick up the papers she threw. On there is every single diarised lie I have told since I started in Singapore, highlighted in bright yellow and orange. She has been through every single entry, line by line.

'Please, Aari...' I start to cry.

'Who ARE YOU?' she repeats, shouting at the top of her lungs and knocking the breath out of herself. She looks terrified of me.

I can't believe that I am standing at the opposite end of her living room, trying to convince her that I am not going to hurt her. The emotional damage is already done. 'Please, Aari, let me explain—'

'It's ARI-ELLA!' she screams at me with everything she has. 'Oh my God, no, pleeeaaaseee, no...' is the last thing I hear her say before she crumples in a heap and passes out across the room in front of me.

THIRTY-TWO

ARIELLA

'If she's breathing, you're fine.'

'She is.'

'Good. I'll stay on the line. What happened?'

I hear them before I open my eyes and, when I do, I am on the couch in my living room. My legs are elevated and the button and zip of my jeans have been undone. It's dark. The small amber light from the coffee table and the moon are responsible for lighting the entire room. I am groggy but I find the energy to roll off the couch and crawl to the opposite end of the room.

'Aari... ella.'

It's him. I try to move away from the direction of his voice but my back is against the wall.

'Please try not to move too quickly.' Caleb has crouched down to my eye level, far away by my sliding doors, holding both his palms up. 'Jasper, can I call you back?' he says to the phone on the floor as he lowers a hand slowly to cut the call off.

'No! Jasper to stay on the line!' I panic.

I don't know who this person is. All the clients serviced in the UK, who made the region a success for Ivory Bow, either hadn't met him before Friday night or had no idea who he was. Some were irritated about being repeatedly asked about the same person. 'The other guy that phoned' had been pushy. Until he moved here from London, Caleb Black didn't exist. There is no evidence of him going to meetings with anyone, despite logging at least three flights a year to Singapore.

When Harrison told Christopher and me that the UK was going to keep the original Singaporean clients, I was ready with the defence I'd prepared over the last few days. I even had a strategy to ensure both locations benefited from these accounts. As far as I knew, Caleb had brought those accounts in. He deserved to keep them and I was prepared to fight for his right to do so. I knew it was going to be tough, especially as Harrison had just baselessly accused Caleb of getting security to throw him out of our launch party.

'I am not prepared to take such a massive hit to our revenue, Ariella,' Harrison argued.

'I think I might have a solution to minimise that,' I countered softly.

'You can draw up as many solutions as you want, we are keeping those accounts.' Harrison dug his heels in.

'Harrison, those are Caleb's accounts. He worked hard to grow them. You can't just take them away and give them to someone else!' I reasoned.

'I'll be looking after the clients he left behind personally.'

'He hasn't left them behind; if anything, he has moved closer to them in order to provide better service and support.'

'That would be true, but they don't know Caleb Black.' Harrison made a show of sitting back.

'Personal attacks on his character are not the way to go here, Harrison,' Christopher chimed in.

'It's not a personal attack. I've spent the last month reaching out to his clients. Half of them know who he is but have never met him. The other half have never even heard his name.'

'Harrison, that simply cannot be true,' I challenged. I know Harrison is a founder, but I couldn't let him get away with what he said.

'It's true. I don't know who is responsible for Ivory Bow's success in Asia, but I can categorically say it is not Caleb Black. He didn't exist in Singapore until he moved out here.'

'Christopher...' I started to address a perplexed-looking Christopher.

'I pulled all his flight and hotel receipts since he started working in the region. Initially, it all looked fine, just the usual piss-taking room service, bar receipts and taxis at two in the morning, but then on his fourth trip in, it got strange. Caleb's flights were normal but his expenses went down to zero overnight. He didn't claim a penny, not even for the taxi to or from Changi, for two and a half years. The hotel room bill for the last few trips are just a bunch of no-show charges.' Harrison picked up his phone. 'I've sent all his expenses, or lack thereof, to your inbox.'

Christopher looked as stunned as I felt.

'I question if he was in the country at all. So, if Caleb wasn't coming to Singapore, where was he going? How was he sealing huge deals with people that don't know he exists? Most importantly, is Caleb Black who he says he is?'

That was the point when I excused myself to find somewhere quiet to breathe. When I got back, Christopher and Harrison were having a heated discussion. I left them to it. I had to know if it was true. Lydia and I went back to mine, printed off Caleb's entire appointment schedule since he had joined and called every single contact. Harrison was right. The only clients who knew Caleb were the ones he'd landed after he moved to Singapore. So I dived into the expenses. The last forty-eight hours kept invading my thoughts, the revulsion that arrived with them intensifying each time.

· · ·

'You don't need me on this call, Aari,' Jasper responds softly after a while. 'Just hear him out.'

'You know?'

'Yes, I know. Call me if you need me, but hear him out first.'

Jasper hangs up without waiting for a response. The fact that Jasper knows and is not freaking out makes me a little calmer. I watch Caleb carefully as he leans back against the sliding door and sits on the floor.

'I want to come over there and hold you while I tell you this. I should have done this months ago, the day you came home with news about Singapore. In fact, I should have told you long before that, but I couldn't find the courage. I can't begin to tell you how much you have changed the entire landscape of the person I want to be, Aari... Ariella – and losing you, Dahlia, Zachary, Isszy, Hugh... even Lara; losing all of that was terrifying.'

Caleb wipes his eyes with the heel of his palms and I soften enough to crawl back and sit on the couch, but as far away from him as possible. A deep sigh escapes from his chest.

'I took the role at Ivory Bow because I just wanted a fresh start. My last job in the City fired a load of us in one day and I needed an income. It seemed simple enough. Travel and sell our services. Initially I got some small sales, which were good but not great. At the time, there was someone else looking after North America, but I had great old contacts in Singapore, so I convinced Harrison that I could make Asia work. The first three trips out here were complete failures. Just when I was going to give up on having a fourth trip, I got invited to the Tech Awards, got a little drunk and met someone. We spent the night together and I didn't realise it at the time but she was really well-connected. She made a few phone calls and the sales came flooding in. In almost all cases, I would just get the enquiries and not meet the contacts. I became a star at work. We were billing more in Asia than everywhere else put together. A direct result of that was that I spent all my time out here with her, which suited both of us fine. She was engaged to someone else and she knew the last thing I wanted were attachments; so, I got to live my life as I wished everywhere else, but out here I was hers.'

I feel sick but, at the same time, exceptionally calm. I speak slowly so he hears every word I need him to.

'You slept with this woman because of what she could do for you. That's why you weren't logging expenses or staying at your hotel. You were here, staying with her, every single time.' I hear the hard disgust in my voice.

Caleb looks away.

'Is that why you've been doing so well since you moved over? Are you still sleeping with her?'

'No. Everything I've done since I got here has been all me. It's been over since last year, Aari. I ended it during my last work trip to Singapore when you and Jasper... that trip. I told her about you as soon as I got in. Stupidly, we agreed we could remain friends, but eventually... you basically weren't the only person sleeping with someone else that week. I know I gave you a hard time about Jasper but hearing that you "thought" you wanted me after I'd burned everything to the ground for you made me lose it a little.'

I silently watch Caleb wipe the tears streaming down his face with his hands. Part of me wants to go to him, but I stay put.

'You made me so, *so* happy and I thought it was all behind me. Then she started calling and wouldn't stop. I ignored her for months. In one voicemail she'd offer me the world and in the next she would promise to take it all away because I'd stopped all my trips to Singapore. I stupidly thought I could handle it and genuinely thought she would get over it eventually. I wanted to tell you, but I felt that I had finally found my corner in this world that belonged to just me and I didn't want to destroy it. Then out of nowhere you got the job offer in Singapore and I was too cowardly, too scared to tell you; and now we are here and it's all turned to shit. Oh God, Ariella. I'm so sorry.'

He was stupid. He'd made a colossal mistake, but it's clear it's been destroying him from inside.

'I thought breaking up with you would be easier. Or pushing you away so, when you found out, you wouldn't hate me as much as I can see that you do right now.'

I move towards Caleb and kneel in front of him. I can't help it. I can see how broken he has been by all of this.

'Caleb, I don't hate you, but you can't blame her. You're here because of your choices; and now you have to face the consequences. Harrison isn't giving up those accounts and, to be honest, I'm happy he is keeping them because they are tainted. This is a good opportunity to move forward.'

'I want to, I really do. That's all I have been trying to do ever since you came home and told me about the job offer, but things got so bad that seeing how we would get through it was impossible. I am so sorry. I really am. Please believe me.'

'I believe you. Whatever happens, we can figure it out together, but you have to be truthful. I will stand by you.'

'No, you won't.' Caleb shakes his head tearfully.

'Yes, I will. I will face whatever challenges there are with you.' I bring my palm forward and stroke his cheek.

'You won't.'

'Caleb, I promise I—'

'It was Melissa. I was seeing Melissa.'

I back away from him in an instant.

'I'm sorry. I am so SO sorry...' he sobs uncontrollably.

I struggle to take a breath I can't find.

THIRTY-THREE

CALEB

It's out there. I can tell from Ariella's face that a massive jigsaw has just put itself together in front of her. I don't want to tell her any more tonight because I know I've dragged her right to the edge of her tolerance, but she needed to know the truth. Ariella's face darkens in rising anger. Shit. I have never seen that before. Eventually, she speaks coldly, clearly and calmly.

'I'm going to call Melissa.' She gets up without warning and starts to walk out of the room. Shit. It's the last reaction I was expecting. I get up and chase after her.

'Wait, Aari! Don't!' I catch her by her hand and she yanks it away. 'There's something else.'

'More?' Ariella turns towards me and pushes me away at the centre of my chest, hard. 'Tonight, you've admitted to being a hypocrite. A cheat. A liar. A fraud. And a whore.' Each word does exactly what it is intended to and I find myself backing away. 'What more could there possibly be?'

She drops to her knees, sobbing. 'What more?' she growls through tears. I drop beside her to hold her and she uses everything she has to fight me off. Hard. I hold on.

'I am really sorry, Aari...'

The harder she fights, the harder I hold her, until she exhausts herself and we are both weeping uncontrollably.

'I'm sorry, I am so *so* sorry...' I just keep repeating, over and over again. The minute her body softens, I loosen my hold.

'Please let me go, Caleb,' she whispers calmly, and I do. She arranges herself opposite me and looks in my eyes with her puffy, bloodshot ones.

'What else?' she asks, composed and focused.

'Since I started, I've been trying to ditch those original accounts Harrison is taking because I think the suspicious payments Bryce found were intentionally set up that way, and I'm almost certain Devin is involved.'

'When did you know?'

'When you left, Jasper reached out and I basically told him everything about Melissa. I was probably destructively hoping he would tell you so I didn't have to. I shared what I thought was an empty threat from her, but it worried him, so he asked me to pull the client files and contracts. I handed them to him. As a precaution, we decided that I needed to start severing ties with those companies and discouraging others from springing up in their place.'

'And you're sure Devin knows about this?'

'Devin is the money guy. I am almost certain he knows this shit is going on. Bryce flagged that payment, but a couple of accounts Devin has brought in and passed over to you might be worth looking at. I think we should have a call with Jasper tomorrow, just so he can give you more detail. He's been in the trenches with me on this.'

She gets up and looks at me. Really looks at me. 'Anything else? Is that everything?'

I could tell her about Melissa spiking my drink, but it has nothing to do with what we are battling right now. I desperately need her forgiveness, but manipulating her by becoming Melissa's victim would be disgusting and I don't need anyone's pity.

'The apartment downstairs. Melissa came to see me one evening and told me that it was mine. She bought it and put it in my name. I haven't looked into it, I sent all the information over to Jasper.'

She nods and says nothing. She has shut down. Fuck.

'I am going to bed. Goodnight, Caleb.' She walks to her bedroom and shuts the door.

I want to leave her alone. I want to give her some space, but I can't. I follow her and knock before I crack it open a little. Her head and body are under the covers in bed.

'Aari, can I come in?'

'No.'

I sit on the floor just outside her room.

'I did this. I am so sorry. I will do whatever it takes. I promise you I will fix this. I love you more than anything. Please, please say you will try to forgive me. Please.'

She sits up with no emotion on her face. 'Do you mind sleeping in the guest bedroom? I know this is excruciating for you too, and you're not going to go home even if I ask, but I need to look after myself tonight.'

'Please don't make me leave. Is it okay if I just sleep here in the doorway?'

'I'd rather you sleep somewhere more comfortable than the floor, but if that's what you feel you need to do, I don't have the energy or the fight in me to try to convince you otherwise.' She shrugs, before getting out of bed and walking over to me.

'Go to sleep, okay? Let's talk in the morning.' Then Ariella places her hand on the handle of her bedroom door and closes it slowly, shutting me out.

After she does that, I go to the closest guest bedroom, grab a couple of pillows and a blanket, then return to her door to make a bed on the floor outside it.

. . .

I don't sleep. I can't. I lie there trying not to throw caution to the wind, enter her bedroom and hold her as I listen to her crying most of the night. I can't believe I have done this to her. Before Ariella stepped into my office that day to irritate me about not renting my room to her because she was female, I realise I wasn't dissimilar to Melissa. I was cold and selfishly using people to make myself feel better. All those one-night stands where I went over my 'let's just have fun' talk. I was such an idiot. I grew up detached, used, tired, angry and lonely and it was the only way I knew. Taking what I wanted without thinking about the scars I left behind.

When Ariella moved in, I remember thinking how weak, vulnerable and foolish she was; leaving someone who gave her comfort, security and all the crap women wanted, for no reason, then moping about it. If I was being honest, the only real reason I didn't try it on with her was because she was paying way over what the room was worth, and I kind of felt sorry for her, which should have been the first warning sign. I didn't feel sorry for anyone.

I tried to stay away from her, but she was relentless in just being lovable. Her innocent perspective, her easy laugh, her brutal honesty and her unreserved ease at being and laughing at herself captivated me – and captivate me still.

And now I've ruined it. I should have trusted that she would have forgiven me. She had seen every side of me. She knew the reputation that followed me around. She had met my family, for goodness' sake; she knew how I grew up and she still stayed. Copping to what happened with Melissa when we had our last encounter would have been risky but we definitely wouldn't be here today. I've fucked up the best thing that has ever happened to me.

I remember looking at her just before we left the house for Zachary's engagement party and thinking how great it would be if we had children and how beautiful they would be, if they were just like her.

'Caleb?'

I must have fallen asleep at some point. She is squatting next to me with a mug of coffee. I love this woman.

'Running into her in London was no accident, was it?' Ariella admits to herself.

'No, I don't think so.'

'This job. I didn't earn it, did I?'

'I don't know but you are so amazing at it.'

'That night we had a fight back in London and you left, you went to see her, didn't you?'

'Yes. I'm sorry.'

'What happened?'

'I asked her to leave you alone. To leave us alone. At the time, I thought I could control it.'

'Not control it, control me,' she corrects me.

She's wrong.

'No. Not at all. I know that there is no stopping or controlling you. As you so accurately put it last night, I was trying to find a way that didn't expose me as a fraud, and I definitely didn't want you finding out that I was only doing well because I was someone's whore.'

She moves closer and places her hand on my cheek. 'I'm sorry I called you those names and I regret the way I did,' she apologises, before silently walking away.

I grab my phone and look at the time: five twelve. I text Honey to cancel this morning, set my status to 'Work from Home' and request to dial in on our weekly meeting. I fire off a quick text to Jasper.

Thanks for last night

He replies immediately.

> Well done. That took some courage. You ok?

> Hanging on. Everything is fucked.

> Have you checked in with her this morning?

> Not really, she didn't say much when she brought me coffee.

> You're still at Aari's?

> Yeah.

> Wow. Ok. If you're still at Aari's and she is bringing you coffee, you're doing much better than you think.

If someone had told me that I would come to depend on the guy she left when she moved into my flat, I would have laughed in their face.

I head into the kitchen. Aari loves her grapefruit and tea in the mornings and I want to do everything I can to say sorry. I know Ms Pat is going to turn up soon, so I get busy. It takes no time to prep, so, once I've displayed it nicely on the counter, I fill the kettle with water and flip the button on. I am contemplating what the hell to do when Ariella walks in.

'What are you doing, Caleb?'

'I'm making breakfast.'

'I'm not sure if breakfast—'

'Aari, please let me do this one normal thing for you. After that we can get back to how much I have fucked up the best thing that has ever happened to me. But please just have breakfast with me.'

She sits. I pick the song I have been thinking about all night on my phone and press play. When 'ROS' starts to play, her eyes narrow as she looks at me.

She knows it's my song for her.

She watches me make her tea as she starts on her grapefruit.

'Thank you, Caleb,' she says as I move her tea in front of her.

'How are you feeling?'

'Manipulated. Betrayed. Lied to. Hurt. Used. Puppeted. Unworthy. Mocked.' She shrugs sadly. 'I know you're sorry. I know it wasn't intentional. I know you think you did everything you could to extract yourself from this situation you put yourself in. I'm just bitterly disappointed that you didn't do the one thing that would have put a stop to it, which was to tell me the truth.' She sighs and it feels like I have just been punched in the stomach. She's absolutely right.

'Tell me what to do, Ariella, and I will do it.'

'Who else knows all of it?'

'Just Jasper.'

She shuts her eyes for a few seconds. 'My turn to pick a track,' she says softly as she picks up my phone.

She stops the current song midway and puts her song on. Her selection devastates me but also gives me hope. She picks up her mug of tea and walks back to her bedroom, leaving Stevie Wonder's 'I Don't Know Why I Love You' blasting at top volume from my phone.

I let the track finish because I deserve it, then knock on her bedroom door.

'Yes?'

I walk in sheepishly. 'We need to talk about DMVI. He knows Melissa. She'd waved the account in front of me in the past, but then everything went quiet.'

'Dominic can't be doing this.'

'I don't know. I just think it's worth checking out.'

Ariella straightens herself. 'I'm going to work.'

'Jasper has information that might be useful – he is expecting us to call.'

She agrees without hesitation. After we set her laptop up in her living room, I send Jasper a quick text with the call link and password.

'Hey, Jasper. Thanks for doing this. Tell me what you know,' Ariella starts. Her voice is cold; she's pissed off with him too.

'Aari, are you okay?' a very concerned Jasper asks into the screen.

'Yes, I am fine. Let's see if we can stop everyone from Ivory Bow being implicated in a crime.'

'We are going to figure it out, okay?' he assures her as he shares his screen.

'Sure,' Ariella responds, not sounding sure at all. As soon as she looks away to get a notebook and pen from her bag, Jasper motions for me to calm down.

'It's important before I start, Aari, that what I am about to tell you could have happened to anyone. It could easily have happened to you and you wouldn't have a clue. In fact, I am having some guys look into whether or not it is happening right now.'

'No need to look. It is.'

'Caleb told me what happened the night you flew out there. Some of the things he said made me a little uncomfortable and I asked if I could do a little digging. With his help, I have all the details he could get of all the Ivory Bow activity with Melissa's contacts. The run-of-the-mill meetings and parties were fine, but most of the really complicated ones that didn't happen were really fishy. The contract was signed, Ivory Bow got paid for the project in full, and then it went on to pay the suppliers and the venue.

'But in absolutely all of the cases of events where four hundred thousand Singaporean Dollars or more was spent, the events didn't take place. They would cancel with the suppliers, who in turn would return the money via bank transfer, not to

Ivory Bow but to a bank account Ivory Bow nominated. It is always the same five suppliers. Ivory Bow also refunded a nominated account and not the originating account. It didn't make any sense until Caleb told me that they insisted on which suppliers to use, so I looked a little harder and found out that the suppliers were not only paid within a couple of days the client payment came in, they were also tied to offshore companies that had nothing to do with whatever services they were providing. This shows the event was always meant to be cancelled, and someone internally knew. In all cases, money left with Ivory Bow was always your full management and onsite support fee. To the exact penny.'

Ariella sighs.

'I know I said this earlier, but it's important for you to understand that Caleb couldn't have known. The way your company is set up is perfect for this kind of thing. One person goes out, seals the deal and hands it over to wonderfully separated logistics and payment teams. Then another team picks it up and runs the job on the day. It's perfectly disjointed and fragmented with handovers. Quite frankly, we wouldn't know any of this if it wasn't for Melissa threatening him. By the time we started to scratch the surface, you were already there, and our suspicions were confirmed when I got back from your birthday. It has taken a while.'

'We need to report this, Jasper.' Ariella throws her pen on the table.

'That's what Caleb said, but we have no idea how far or deep this runs. If we are going to do that, we need a plan. We know Ivory Bow UK is complicit but these are huge, powerful, international companies we are talking about.'

'Right,' is all Ariella says. Jasper is silent to let her speak, and then hurriedly continues when she doesn't.

'I'd like to take a look at the financial reports of the contracts you are currently pulling in.'

'Okay.' Ariella going down to one-word answers is making Jasper panic. I can see it all over his face.

'Be careful, Aari, you got given this company and you didn't pick your chief financial officer. You wouldn't know how to. He was already here, waiting for you; selected by someone that knows what they are doing. What if your CFO is in on it? Unlike Caleb, your signature is on everything. You will have read through the contracts and noticed nothing. Little clauses like "clients will have final approval of supplier choice" would mean the client gets to pick whoever gets paid if they want to. You wouldn't think your client would come up with their own supplier suggestions, would you? Then after they have put their supplier choice in once...'

'It becomes part of their profile and we don't look anywhere else until the yearly review.' She finishes the sentence.

'It's not all bad news – you can trust your chief legal officer, and he will be able to help you get through this, quietly.'

This time, she doesn't even respond.

'I can take you through the flagged companies, telltale signs and clauses to look out for? There's a definite pattern and I think that if you can easily identify these, then you can isolate and eradicate any issues before it causes any major problems.'

'Please,' Ariella says as she grabs her pen from the table and opens her notebook again.

Jasper opens another folder on the screen and patiently takes us through the network Ivory Bow had been feeding. When he finishes, Ariella looks completely numb. I put her in this position. This is all me. When the call is over, she closes her laptop and takes a long, silent look at me. I can feel the devastating disappointment emanating from her.

Without a word, she packs up her laptop bag like I am not there and leaves me sitting on the couch by myself as she walks out of the apartment.

THIRTY-FOUR

ARIELLA

I press the bell repeatedly and knock as hard as I can. I'm not going anywhere. I am on my own with this and I have to get to the bottom of it. I feel so stupid. The job offer. Believing everything and everyone. Enough. The last few months, I have been stuck in a carefully constructed maze, with me, the mouse, ignorantly wandering around in the dark, stupidly following tiny bits of cheese laid out for me. It has been hard work but, when I really look at it, everything has been served to me on a platter. It had all been constructed too carefully. Not any more. I've woken up.

'Okay, okay, I'm coming!'

The door opens, and a messy-haired, straight-from-bed Dominic shades his eyes from the sun.

'What is your relationship with Melissa?' I ask, straight to the point.

'Do you want to come in, Ariella?' He opens the huge door as wide as it can go.

'What is your relationship with Melissa? Both of you had a lot to say to each other quietly at the launch. I want to know.'

'I was going to tell you.'

'Dominic, please tell me you are not attempting to launder money through Ivory Bow?'

'What?'

'I said, are you attempting to launder money through Ivory Bow?'

'What?! No! What are you talking about? She was canvassing the launch for investors and I told her not to bother, that I'd take everything she's selling. It was enough to become a majority shareholder with a controlling interest and she didn't want that, so we got into the terms a little.'

'How do you know Melissa?' I don't have time for this.

'I know Kevin, her fiancé, really well. Kevin and I collaborated on some projects and we got along. Melissa and I bump into each other because of that, and she mentioned I should take a look at Ivory Bow.'

'You initially contracted with Ivory Bow because you "bump" into each other?' That's rubbish and he knows it.

'Please come in, I have neighbours.'

'I want to know, now.'

'She approached me ages ago about Ivory Bow. I told her I'd think about it. She told me to get in touch if I wanted better tax breaks than I was getting. Unfortunately, I am a massive fan of the many tax breaks I'm already getting as a domiciled business owner here. I also thoroughly enjoy the many benefits of not being imprisoned.'

'If you knew that, why did you hand it all over to us?'

'Because of you. I met you.'

'That's ridiculous. You didn't even know me.'

'No, but you guys passed our checks and I did my homework on you. I also really wanted to get to know you.'

I believe him, but I don't trust my instincts any more. I turn around and start walking to my waiting cab.

'Ariella, what's going on? Please come in.'

I don't respond. I need to get to the office right now.

I fire a text message to Lydia.

> Morning. I need all full-time Ivory Bow staff in the conference room at 8 am. Anything in the diary for today must be cancelled and everyone must be present.

I get a text message back immediately.

> Ok. Is everything all right?

> No. Also, I want Devin locked out of everything. Emails, his laptop, his access keys, everything. Send him a text about the meeting.

I open another message box, this time to Jasper.

> I need your help.

> What do you need?

> I'm stripping Devin of access and tossing him out of Ivory Bow. I need help finding a clean and competent new CFO that is qualified enough to pick apart what he has done and put new systems in place.

> How long do you think it will take to get Devin out? I imagine that'll be a lengthy internal process.

> It'll be done in an hour.

> I'll be with you tomorrow night.

I arrive at the office and get to work. This needs to be handled quickly.

We are now six months into the business; we have only just had our launch but we have a good roster of new clients who can carry us through. I look at our historical client list from

London and start to put lines through the businesses and subsidiaries that Jasper identified. I put them in a red alert email to Bryce to be blacklisted. They are Harrison's problem, but I don't want them slipping through the cracks should they decide to jump ship of their own accord.

It's not long before I see everyone start to pile in with tired faces and cups of coffee. The mood is frantic and unsettled. I want to reassure them but I can't. Caleb, hiding behind his Wayfarers, knocks on my office door and moves his sunglasses into the dark thick curly mess on top of his head. He is pale, with sunken, red and tired eyes. I quickly look at the papers in front of me and keep sorting them. He is obviously in pain, but so am I.

'How can I help you, Caleb?'

'I just wanted to make sure you're...' He reaches his hand out and touches mine. The moment he makes physical contact, I feel like I am going to cry. I move my hand away.

'I'm fine. Do you need anything?'

'The guys are wondering what the meeting is about and I didn't know if...'

'What do you really want?'

I am aware that I am being particularly cold but I can't deal with anything other than getting us out of this mess.

'I just wanted to say I am so sorry, Aari.'

'Please get out of my office.'

He looks like he has just been slapped. I don't care. I have the debris from his mayhem to deal with.

'Okay. We're ready for you in the conference room,' he whispers before he leaves. I hear the choke in his voice and I want to cry too. I pull myself together.

'Thank you. I will be in shortly.'

The second he leaves, I hold on to my desk and take as many deep breaths as I can to get myself to some degree of calm. I push the desire to cry, the hurt, the fear, and the need to be held and comforted, deep down and bury it. I make a quick call to the building's concierge, straighten myself, grab my notebook and make my way into the conference room.

'Good morning, everyone.' I stand at the head of our boardroom table. 'Thank you for coming.' I turn to Bryce, who is sitting next to Devin.

'Bryce, please can you relieve Devin of his laptop and phone?'

'Wait, what?' Devin, who had been looking bored, perks up.

'Devin, I am suspending you, with full pay, starting immediately.'

A collective gasp from the team seems to shake the conference room. Bryce, not meeting Devin's eyes, slowly and apologetically slides Devin's phone and laptop over to himself.

I watch six of the building security team, arriving right on time, walk into our office and stand in front of the conference room.

'Lydia will collect and send any personal effects to you, and your suspension will, of course, remain confidential. Please allow these gentlemen to escort you out quietly.'

'Why am I being suspended?' Devin says, rising to his full height.

'Bryce will be in touch.' I meet his angry stare with a bored one. I am not scared of you, I repeat to myself internally as I hold his look.

Devin straightens his suit and walks out of the meeting room silently, with his head held high. Two members of the security team meet him at the door to escort him out of the office. After he is gone, I collect my thoughts and deliver them to the shocked team sitting at the table looking up at me.

'Anyone who feels particular loyalty to Devin is also invited to leave now. You will also be suspended with full pay until further notice.'

The room is so still and silent, I can hear my heart hammering in my chest.

'Good. I would like to take this opportunity to remind you all that you are bound by iron-clad non-disclosure and confidentiality agreements.'

I have their attention. Here goes.

'We have evidence that suggests that Ivory Bow UK may be involved in money-laundering for some clients, and Ivory Bow Asia may have had a brush with this. Devin has been suspended because at worst he is involved and at best he has been negligent. We have information that suggests that this is not an error but an intentional construction by our chairwoman. I intend to excavate the truth from every contract, client project and financial transaction this company has been involved with. My intention is to annihilate this cancer to save Ivory Bow Asia.

'If you prefer not to be involved in rooting this out and dealing with it, now is the time to say so. You will be suspended with pay, and, regardless of what the findings are, at the close of the investigation you will be dismissed without prejudice. There is no coming back to Ivory Bow for you. So, I need to know who is in and who isn't right now.'

I wait for the whole room to start leaving. No one moves.

'If you have decided to strap in, this is what is going to happen. One. Bryce will draft an email that you must send, personalised, to all your work contacts. It will be dressed as routine because we are going for a financial transparency award, which is essentially true. This email will soften them to the fact that they may be contacted by a consultant.

'Two. We are going to go through each project, supplier and company contact to do a full financial check. If there is anything less than above board going on there, find Bryce or myself and talk to us confidentially. You will not be punished, but you will be required to put a stop to it and that person, company or supplier will be blacklisted.

'Three. You do not speak to anyone, and I mean *anyone*, including Devin or Melissa, about what has happened in this room this morning. Talk among yourselves as much as you like – gossip, speculate, cry, hug each other – do whatever you need to do within the confines of this office. That means all client visits are cancelled until further notice. Security downstairs will not let anyone through unless they are on a pre-approved list that has been provided by Lydia. The only voice I want to hear "out there" about this is Devin's. If or when he speaks about this, I want to make sure that voice is singular. Anyone calls you for comment, forward that call to me or Bryce.

'Four. There will be a freeze on taking on new clients, because all our current contracts, memorandums of understanding and general services agreements need to drastically change. All our existing clients will get these to sign regardless of what we find. Any client that does not sign this will no longer be a client. There will be no room for negotiation.

'Five. We will be engaging the help of outside consultants to support Bryce, so please cooperate. The team will be very small but effective.

'Six. DMVI will be our test case as they are currently our largest domestic client. Dominic Miller knows the bare bones about this but is largely in the dark about the details. He does not need to know any more than he does already. Let's keep it that way. We will run through our processes with DMVI first and, if it passes the sniff test with their lawyers and accountants, we will be rolling this out very quickly.

'Last and not least, if anyone knows anything that might jeopardise us righting this ship, find me and tell me. There will be no consequences for the truth in this company. Does anyone have any questions?'

Bree puts her hand up. 'What do we say when people start asking questions?'

'Tell them the truth. We are overhauling the system and you can't talk about it until it's done. If they give you any hassle, direct them to me.'

Caleb lifts his head for the first time during the meeting, catches my eye and mouths, 'thank you'. I ignore him. I answer all the questions that come at me and, when no more questions surface, I close the meeting. Nobody looks anywhere near as scared as I feel.

'Thank you very much for coming in early. Let's beat this beast. Bryce, my office please?'

I grab my notebook and walk out of the conference room, leaving them to ruminate in the gutter of corruption in which they have just found themselves.

'Melissa might be involved? Holy shit.' Bryce follows me, shutting my office door behind him. 'How?'

'Ask Caleb. We need to draft these statements and we have to go through every single purchase, right down to tea bags. I'll obviously be hands on, but we are going to need help. Jasper will be in Singapore in a couple of days and he's going to help us hire a team to pick this apart quickly so you can focus on legal.'

'Is that a good idea?'

'What?'

'Your ex-fiancé and your ex-boyfriend working together to help create something that a guy that wants to bang you approves of, to save the company where you are COO? Isn't that going to get a little... awkward?'

'Apparently, Caleb and Jasper have been in their own little bromance for a while now, not that anyone bothered to tell me... and for the record, Dominic and I are just friends. There will be no banging of any kind. Now, can we draft these statements please?'

'Yes, boss.' Bryce smiles. It helps me relax a little as we focus on drafting the letter to Devin with our HR consultant, then the first draft to the clients. Once that's done, we start going through our standard contracts with Jasper's flags, with Bryce talking me through his points of concern. Dominic somehow slips past Lydia and our security controls to arrive with lunch for the office at about one.

'Are you okay? You scared the shit out of me this morning,' he asks, standing in front of my desk.

'I'm going to grab some lunch...' Bryce excuses himself quickly. Dominic takes the chair Bryce just vacated and leans in.

'Devin approved some highly suspicious transactions. He's been suspended. Now we are poking at what increasingly looks like a house of cards.'

'Wow. You said that like you just told me what you had for breakfast.'

'The facts are the facts.'

Dominic comes closer.

'Don't!' I stop him. 'Please don't touch me, don't be nice to me, don't feel sorry for me or I will burst into tears, and I can't. I have too much to do. I cannot be scared, or an emotional wreck right now. I just need to get this done.'

The pity in Dominic's eyes almost breaks me. He returns to the seat, adjusts himself and sits down. He thankfully switches into practical mode.

'Aari, I want to assure you that I'd never put you in this position. We are squeaky clean. If you find anything that seems the tiniest bit ambiguous, we will change it. You will get no resistance from us.'

I nod because if I try to speak, I will sob.

'What can I do?'

'Bryce is going to need all the help he can get and I am no lawyer, so we could use a couple of people from your legal department?'

'I've got you. Want me to move them in here for a few days when you're ready?'

'Can Bryce come to you instead?' I don't want anyone in here who can overhear anything. The team needs our office to be a safe space right now.

'I can make that happen. We'll find him an office.'

'Thank you.'

'What about the finance? I can get my hands on a couple of forensic accountants if you like?'

'Jasper is looking at the finance for us. I need someone completely out of it and he's been playing with Ivory Bow files for a while, it seems.'

'Jasper and Caleb are going to be working together in the same space? I might give this place a wide berth...' He chuckles, looking at me in utter disbelief. He suddenly brings his fingers to his mouth and pulls an exaggerated frightened face. I can't help chuckling myself.

'Okay good, you're still in there. Can I get you something to eat? It's from the Japanese place you love. I brought enough to feed an army and two salmon and seaweed salads for you. I got the restaurant to put your name on them.'

'You're too good to me.'

'Haven't you heard? I'm trying to get into your pants and, according to social media, I am failing badly. Hashtag Desperate Dominic and all that.'

I can't help another chuckle escaping.

'I'm glad I can still make you smile.'

'Dominic, stop making me laugh. I am in the middle of a crisis.' I shoo him and he breaks out his smile before he gets up.

'I'll send Bryce back in with both your salads. Eat them.'

'Thank you, Dominic. For everything.' I watch him leave, not quite sure that I can trust him.

I eventually force Bryce to go home at nine, then get up at ten to head out for the night. It is only when Lydia knocks on my office door that I realise that she is still at work.

'Go home, Lydia. We are going to have some challenging days and I need you to get home at a decent time.'

'Ariella, I have written my resignation and I hope you will accept it.'

'No, Lydia, not you! Why are you resigning? Is it because of Devin? I know you were good friends. Let's chat and after that, if you decide to do this, I'll suspend you with pay until we are done here.'

'It's not Devin. I've done something unforgivable.'

Not another problem. I find the unopened bottle of whisky in my desk, pour some into two of my water glasses, hand her one and gesture towards the couch. I flop in myself.

'You have whisky in here?'

'It was a welcome gift, I've just never opened it. Today seems like a good day to do that though.' I take a sip and wait for her to do the same. 'Nothing is unforgivable, Lydia. Why don't you tell me and maybe we can figure it out?'

She sighs. I let her quietness sit between us until she is ready.

'I get copies of all your incoming and outgoing email.'

'That's not worrying, but you're privy to everything, so—'

'And once a week or whenever she asks for it, I forward what you've been doing to Melissa.'

That, I was not expecting. The betrayal makes me shrink back.

Lydia bursts into tears. 'I also pass on Matt's logs of all the places you go, and who you go to those places with. He's been asked to record it and send it to me.'

'And Matt has been doing this?'

She nods as she takes a swig from her glass.

'Who else has been keeping an eye on me?'

'Ms Pat. But ever since you threatened to fire her the week after you moved into your apartment, she sends us what she can.'

My heart breaks. I adore Ms Pat. 'I've never threatened to fire her.'

'I knew she was lying, but I didn't say anything. She told us that you said if she was in the apartment when you came home from work, she'd be gone. All she ever sends over is that you wake up alone, have bran every morning for breakfast and never acknowledge her apart from "Where is my breakfast?" and "I'm leaving." She clearly manipulated her hours so she wouldn't have any information to pass on, and has been making up her reports since.'

I am relieved. I trust Ms Pat. But I also trusted Lydia and Matt.

'Is there something Melissa knows that I should be concerned about?'

'I don't know. She and Devin spoke all the time, but for me, she only seems to be interested in you and Caleb, sometimes Dominic. She knew when you broke up, she knows you fought on the way home once, she knows that you had sex in the back of Matt's car after the racing party...'

'I didn't have sex with Caleb in the back of Matt's car!'

'That's not what Matt's little porno report says.' She rolls her eyes and I can't help laughing. The whole thing is unbelievable. She allows herself to join in.

'Is there anything specific you've done that I should know about?'

'I told her about your date with Dominic, how often he is

353

here, whenever he takes us all somewhere or brings in lunch. She is constantly pushing for me to find something, but there has been nothing. Even if there was, I maybe would have passed it on in that first month before I got to know you, but I never would have since then. I promise you.'

'Is there anything else?'

She shifts in her seat uncomfortably. 'Yes.'

'Tell me.'

'She exchanged a lot of emails with Caleb before he joined.'

'Are you monitoring his emails too?'

'No, when I was setting up and migrating his emails on his new laptop, I saw them. She sent him some pretty hateful and threatening emails before you joined, but none after that.'

I push thoughts of Caleb to the side. I have no space for him today. I bring my attention back to Lydia.

'Do you really want to leave?'

'No, but I don't see how I can stay.'

'Then stay – but it's going to take some courage on your part.'

'What do I need to do? I can see if I can turn the tables...'

'No. It needs to stop. If Melissa asks for any more reports, I want you to tell her that I know.'

Real fear crosses Lydia's face. I grab the bottle of the Ichiro Queen of Clubs Whisky from my desk and hand it to her.

'I can't. It costs a fortune!'

'Think of it as a gift. Thank you for the truth and, if you decide to leave, thank you for everything. I'm glad I got to open it with you, Lydia.' I hug her.

I let Matt know I'll be down in five minutes, grab my case and make my way to the car. He is standing by the back door to let me in as usual and I wait until we start our journey.

'Matt?'

'Yes, Ariella?' His smiling eyes meet mine in his mirror.

'Have you been telling someone about where I go?'

'No, of course not, Ariella.'

'You haven't been logging and reporting my movements?'

'I would never do that! Who is telling you—'

'Now would be the time to tell me the truth, Matt. I promise there will be no consequences.'

'No. Never. You can trust me, Ariella.'

'Okay. Could you pull into the Ritz Carlton please?'

Matt keeps flicking nervous glances at me in the mirror as he navigates his way into the hotel driveway. The doormen open the door.

'I will wait—'

'No thank you, Matt. In the morning, we'll be terminating the contract with your car service company. You will get a glowing reference but a strong recommendation that all the drivers sign non-disclosure and confidentiality agreements. We won't say any more. I'll also arrange a bonus of one month's service fees and fare averages to be paid directly to you. Thank you for the last six months.'

I step out and ask the gentlemen at the door to call me a cab.

The day has been long, challenging and hard. I just want to go home, get under the covers and cry. I make my way home and up in the lift thinking of how brutal the day has been, but feeling proud that I've survived it. My bones feel shattered and my body is exhausted.

As soon as the lift door opens, I see Caleb sitting on the floor in front of my apartment door. I really don't need this.

'Aari, please hear me out. I just want to say—'

'Caleb, please, I can't. Thirty hours ago, I found out your ex-girlfriend recruited me and you didn't say a word. She convinced me to leave my life in London to move halfway across the world and you didn't say a word. You knew that she was furious with you and you didn't say a word. She literally made me responsible for a company that you were suspicious of and you didn't say a word. She threatened both of us to you and you didn't say a word. You suspected she was laundering money through the company she gave me to run and you didn't say a word. She owns our company, our homes, and she is having me spied on. All because of you. Yet I am here. Fighting to make sure we all don't end up as convicted criminals. I don't have the space to hear what you have to say now, because you should have said it all nine months ago!' I fight back the tears.

'Aari, please.' He reaches out and I flinch. 'Oh God. What have I done?'

I see the tears well up before he quickly pinches the top of his nose with his thumb and index finger, and I crumble inside.

'Come in.'

Caleb goes straight for the corner he occupied last night; far away from me, on the floor with his back against the sliding door. I will myself not to, but I can't help sitting next to him, leaning my back against the comforting, cool glass. We sit silently next to each other in the dark room with our shoulders touching.

'You've broken my heart, Caleb,' I tell him quietly.

'I know.' He sounds so wounded, I clasp my hands to prevent myself from reaching out to him.

'Were you ever going to tell me about Melissa?'

'Honestly? No. Because I didn't want you to look at me the way you looked at me last night and I didn't think it would matter once the accounts were gone.'

'It matters. Lydia has been sending her my emails, Matt has been recounting our fights and feeding her fantasy back-seat-sex stories, and she put Ms Pat in here to spy on me.'

'Not Ms Pat?'

'No, not Ms Pat; she's been painting me as a cold, quiet, grumpy bran-eater that always wakes up alone in the mornings for the last six months.'

'How are you going to handle it?'

'Lydia came to me with it and tried to resign, but I gave her the night to think about it. I'll keep her if she decides to stay. Matt's been fired. Ms Pat, I'll deal with tomorrow.'

I feel the guilt and self-loathing radiate from him as we sit there silently.

'I just want the truth, Caleb. Is there anything else?'

'No.'

I sigh with relief.

'I really screwed things up, didn't I?'

'Yes, and it hurts. Like absolute hell.'

'Please forgive me, Aari.'

'I already have.' He was stupid and handled it badly, but I could see how he could have felt he had no choice.

'Really?'

'Yes. Of course I have, Caleb. I love you so much but this thing we have, it's done. We're finished. I'm—'

Caleb's lips on mine catches me by surprise. I am more surprised to find my own lips parting to welcome him. For the first time since last night, my loud, busy, anxious mind is silent and calm. His kiss is soft and delicate, full of apology and yearning; absorbing the day's fear and pain from me. I pull him closer, lacing my fingers through his messy hair, unchanged from my floor this morning, and our kiss becomes more demanding. The hunger for him overwhelms me. Caleb pulls away abruptly, his breathing laboured. My heart is slamming against my chest. I say it before I think it.

'Let's talk in the morning.'

In one swoop, Caleb is up, carrying me into one of the spare bedrooms. He chooses neutral territory. He knows we aren't out of the woods. He lays me down and undresses me, stopping at my underwear to take off his shirt. He grabs my ankles, pulls me roughly towards him to the edge of the bed, gets on his knees, pulls my underwear to the side and buries his head between my legs. My body, my mind, my spirit and my soul surrender to him. As he buries his face deeper, it doesn't take long for my body to shudder. My orgasm builds to a new high as he buries his mouth in me, deeper still. I explode with his mouth on me and as it ebbs he gently guides me down.

Caleb slowly joins me on the bed with his body hovering over mine.

'Aari, please look at me.'

I open my eyes to look straight into his deep blue ones.

'I love you. I'm sorry. Please don't leave me.' His tear hits my cheek and I pull his lips onto mine. I don't want to but I know I have to. Pleasure runs through me as Caleb's mouth hits my neck. My hands develop a life of their own as they caress the ridges on his back, following the lean muscles I know and love as they move. My legs open themselves up to him as I feel his hardness press against my abdomen. The feeling almost makes me unravel again. I turn both our bodies to the side, facing each other so that I can stroke him. I am unprepared for the audible exhale that escapes him.

'I didn't think you'd ever touch me like that again, Aari.' He sighs. It flips a switch in me. I lay him on his back, travel down his body, taking his jeans with me, and put him in my mouth.

He responds in that way that makes me feel powerful and invincible. I take him further into my mouth and the groan he produces is guttural. When we're like this, I own him. Not Melissa, not anyone else, me.

'I'm going to...'

'Don't.' I stop.

A confused Caleb half-sits up and I can see the pain in his face as he tries to obey my command. I walk into my bedroom to find the box I'd bought just before he came to visit the first time. When I return, I take off my bra and step out of my knickers, slide the condom on him gently, climb on the bed and lower myself onto him.

'Are you sure this is okay?' Caleb whispers as he sits up to kiss me. After I nod, I meet his kiss and hold him close before he lies back down. I love him so much. I lean forward on top of him to hold hands and interlace our fingers. I rock back and forth, pushing him in as far as I can. It doesn't take long for me to come apart, his face to change, my legs to tremble and for him to follow immediately after. We ride our waves together, with them becoming one. As the feeling tails off for me, I keep going for him to come to the end of his, then collapse on him, sweating and exhausted. He leaves himself in me as he crushes my chest against his, kissing my head. We stay like that and, for once, I don't feel the need to be clean straight away. I am going to miss his warmth, his smell, his arms, the almost supernatural force that binds us when I make love to him, and sleepily chatting with him afterwards, with his body perfectly curled around mine.

'Want to jump in the shower?' he asks, starting to move.

'Not tonight,' I respond as I move on to my side and curl, as deeply as I can, into him. Caleb puts his arm out for my head and pulls me in with his hand snaked over my waist before resting it on my belly to begin the little familiar belly tickles that I love. It always makes me laugh initially and, once I get used to it, it puts me to sleep effectively.

Tonight, is no different.

THIRTY-FIVE

CALEB

I spend my second consecutive night wide awake. I refuse to let myself fall asleep lying here naked next to Ariella, listening to her tiny snores with the entire length of her body pressed against mine. If I could freeze time I would, right now. I want to keep her here as long as possible.

Panic sets in just before four when she stirs, asking what the time was. I dance around an answer, then make that lazy, half-asleep love that she likes to her, and she goes back to sleep. I'm throwing everything I have at her because I know that when she wakes up, has a shower and remembers where we were last night, she is going to dump me. I lie frozen, knowing I am on borrowed time. She often jokes that great sex is my superpower; but determination is hers. When Ariella makes up her mind about something, that is it. My only option here is to leave a door open for myself; which means giving up everything, including her.

'Hey,' I whisper as I stroke her belly and kiss the back of her head. 'It's seven, we slept in a little. I'll turn on the shower and get your stuff.'

She groans as I extract myself from her. I turn on the

shower, then collect her shower gel, body glove, conditioner and body cream. By the time I return she is in the steam. I hand them to her.

'Thank you.'

'Can I join you?'

She steps aside to make room for me. We slip into our shower routine silently. I help co-wash by putting her conditioner through her hair. She washes me, we rinse her hair out and then I wash her. I steal kisses from her throughout but keep it functional. I get out first, wrap a towel around myself and have two waiting, for her body and her hair. In the bedroom I help her with her body cream on her back, her bottom and her legs while she does the rest. After we are done, we stand there in our towels looking at each other, neither knowing what to say next. Ariella breaks the silence.

'I have clothes in my room for you.'

We pick our clothes up from the floor and, as we walk across the corridor in our towels, Ms Pat comes through from the living room. She smiles warmly at us, turns around and leaves the corridor as we enter Aari's room. Ariella says nothing, just opens her bottom drawer to reveal five white T-shirts and five white boxer briefs.

'How did they get here?'

'I brought them from London with me; I sometimes slept in them when I missed you.' She lifts them all out, stacks them on top of each other and shuts the drawer. 'You should have them back.' She manages to finish the sentence before she bursts into tears.

I pull her into me and I let her tears fall on my chest.

'We can't go on like this any more, Caleb... we have to...'

'Please don't do this, Aari. I know how bad this is, but please, don't take your love away from me. Give me some time to be the person I know you deserve, because you certainly don't deserve this. Give me a chance to come back and to earn you. Please don't decide now. I can't lose the best part of me.'

I lift her face to mine, wipe her tears with my thumb and kiss her deeply. I have given everything up for the hope I can come back. It's all I can do. I know she is still in love with me and by doing this she is hurting herself too.

'Caleb, we can't—'

'Please, Aari. Please tell me what you want me to do. Please.'

She's in tears herself. I hold her as she cries against me, and give her the time to get it out. I stand there, praying to anything that can hear me. Please not her. Punish me with anything else, not her.

'I am going to need you to commit to a few things and I don't think you can.'

'Let me try. Please.'

'I need you to be nice, you were horrible to me when we broke up. You can't be grumpy when you don't get your way. You can't block me. No emotional blackmail, and no blowing hot and cold. I also need you to be civil to Dominic, and not make me feel awful that we are friends. And no flirting with me in front of him to piss him off. I am no longer a conduit for your anger, Caleb.'

'I can do that,' I whisper as I kiss her again. I help her lose her towel and find her nipples, hard and wanting. I circle them as our tongues meet. I trace a finger down her belly and into her underwear. She lets out a gasp and breaks away slowly.

'Slight revision, no flirting period. And no sex. It's... distracting. I want us to have a platonic relationship before we consider anything else.'

I can't help the smile that crosses my face. 'Okay.' I place my hands on her hips and pull her towards mine. 'However, you should know that you can call on me whenever you want,

362

should that change,' I whisper in her ear before placing my mouth on her neck.

'Caleb. What did I just say?' She fights to control a laugh but she loses.

I let her go. I don't want to ruin where we are. It could still go either way.

'Okay, I will respect your boundaries, but please can you put my clothes back?'

She leaves a T-shirt and a pair of briefs on the side and puts the rest back into her drawer. I cheer inside.

The mood is much lighter as we both get dressed, and I feel that I am almost out of the woods. I don't have her answer yet but I know that I have done all I can for now. In the living room, Ms Pat has a bacon sandwich and coffee for me, next to a prepped grapefruit and hibiscus tea for Ariella.

'Thank you, Ms Pat,' I say as I sit down, while Ariella stands at the kitchen island.

'Ms Pat, I know you, Matt and Lydia were hired by Melissa to keep an eye on me.'

'Oh, Miss Ariella!' Ms Pat tears up. 'I tell them nothing. You are like daughter to me but they keep saying talk, talk, talk so I made you little bit bitch and give them the same story every week. I changed my work time with lie so I don't see anything. I promise I tell them nothing.'

'I believe you, Ms Pat. Lydia told me. Matt has been fired. Lydia needs to decide if she wants to stay. I would like to give you the same chance. You can leave and I will pay you until you find another job, or you can stay but the lying has to stop. You need to tell them that I know.'

'I want to stay. I tell them. I like looking after you... and Mr Caleb. It's easy work with good pay.'

'Ms Pat, are you supposed to be telling them about me too?' I ask.

'No, but the plenty cleaning and grocery shopping I do for

you, I should tell, for free. I don't even get pay for you.' Even with the tears in her eyes she frowns and gives me a dirty look.

'You've been cleaning my apartment?'

'Of course! You think you have magic fairy or something? Laundry doesn't just do, iron and fold itself, Mr Caleb. Why you think you always have coffee, milk and sugar?'

'That's you?' The three of us burst out laughing. 'I thought the building just had daily housekeeping staff.'

'Good luck with this one, Miss Ariella, he is not genius.' Ms Pat points at me, chuckles to herself and leaves us at breakfast.

Aari sits next to me and we eat in a comfortable silence.

'I think you might need to start leaving Ms Pat a big cash envelope every week.' Ariella smiles at me as she gets up to put our dirty dishes in the sink.

'For sure. Ms Pat is going nowhere,' I confirm. 'Am I?' I ask nervously as I sip my coffee. I hear her sigh, and wait.

'No, but I need distance. I am absolutely destroyed by this and I'm furious with you, Caleb. You've done this devastatingly horrific thing to me – but I can't stop thinking about how much I love you and how much I want *you* to be okay. That's not normal. I can't give you what you need right now because I need whatever I have for myself and the team. We have this huge mountain to climb and it's going to take everything I have.'

I get my stay of execution. That is all I need because I know I am going to do everything possible to dismantle that mountain.

'Thank you. I will do whatever it takes to get us out of this, I promise.'

'I know.' Ariella looks at me sadly.

I get up, walk to her and kiss her tenderly, pouring all my feelings into it. She meets my kiss with hers.

'You are so much more than I deserve. I am so sorry, Aari.'

Just then my phone begins to buzz. I know who it is. She has been calling since Ariella threw Devin out of the company.

I show Ariella the screen. Her stance completely changes. I watch my soft little Mason's face harden, see her cross her arms against her chest and step out to occupy more floor space. Shit. I watch Ariella prepare to face the battle against Melissa that I was unable to fight for myself.

'Answer it,' she instructs without emotion.

I hit the green button and flip the sound to speaker. 'Melissa,' I answer.

'Want to tell me what the fuck is going on?'

'Allow me, Melissa,' Aari says. 'Devin got removed from his position because he is under investigation for gross negligence at best, and it turns out you're a criminal.'

'You're going to reinstate Devin.'

'I'd love to see you try to make me.'

'You silly, stupid little girl... you have no idea what you're toying with.'

'Tax evasion, money-laundering, fraud, conspiracy to defraud, document falsification, criminal facilitation, evasion of duty, offshore evasion enablement, cheating public revenue, intimidation, blackmail and being an indecorous human being. How am I doing?'

'Caleb—'

'Don't bother, Melissa. She knows everything.'

'Everything?'

'Yes. You, me, the apartment, Lydia, Matt and Ms Pat. All of it.'

There is silence at the other end of the phone. Ariella tightens her stance and narrows her eyes at the phone. Holy shit, the rules just changed. Melissa is no longer in charge.

'Melissa, why don't you find some time in your diary today to come into the office for a cup of tea? We should negotiate the terms of your removal as chairwoman.'

Still, silence. Melissa clearly doesn't like being talked to like a child; Ariella clearly doesn't give a shit what Melissa likes.

'I understand. It's a lot to take in. Let me know when and I will clear my diary for you.'

Ariella reaches out, hits the red phone icon on my screen, turns around and walks into her bedroom without another word.

I have no idea who was just standing next to me having a conversation on my phone, but if I were Melissa, I'd be very, very afraid.

THIRTY-SIX

ARIELLA

Melissa comes back almost immediately and we agree on an eight o'clock meeting at Ivory Bow. Once I've sent the additional invitations to Christopher, Harrison, Dominic and Bryce, I head into the office and I am delighted to be greeted by Lydia.

'You're staying?'

'Yes, and I'm going to make it up to you.'

'Let's just start afresh. And on that note, I have a task already – please would you mind putting a daily briefing in for all of us every morning at ten, starting today?'

'Absolutely.'

'Thank you, I'm so glad you're back; I'm not sure I can get through this without you.'

It's not long before I have to take my place at the top of the boardroom table at the briefing.

'Thank you very much for coming to our first daily briefing hour, everyone. Every day, Bryce and I will take five to ten minutes at the top of the hour to give you daily updates about where we are in terms of progress. The rest of the meeting is yours to ask or challenge anything and tell us what issues or problems you are facing. You have the power to invoke our presence for the whole hour if you need to; this is your time. So, without further ado, Bryce, want to kick us off on where we are in terms of changing our company documents?'

'Sure! Thanks, Ariella.'

I take a seat and let Bryce take the floor. While I see his lips moving, I don't hear a word he says, because I have never had so much noise in my head and I have never been more frightened. The faces around the room are trained on Bryce, paying attention with an intensity that starts to fill me with courage. They all want to fight for this. Even soft, adorable Akiko has her eyebrows furrowed as she wears a look of pure concentration on her sweet face. Failing them just isn't an option but it's going to be gruelling.

'Ariella?' Bryce brings me back into the room and I get back on my feet.

'Thank you, Bryce. I have a bit of additional news. The office will be closed tonight from seven p.m. to midnight. We have a management meeting with Ivory Bow UK and Asia to discuss and negotiate the removal of Melissa as our chairwoman.'

The whole room gasps. I completely understand the reaction.

'I'd rather not take any questions about the meeting tonight because all my responses will be vague, speculative and possibly more accusatory than I would like. However, I hope to fill you in on the hard outcomes from the meeting tomorrow morning. If you want to work late tonight, please take your laptops home. My personal recommendation would be to spend the time with people who love you instead.'

I pause to breathe.

'Questions?'

Everyone's hands shoot up, so Bryce and I start to tackle the questions, one at a time.

. . .

Lydia and Caleb barge into my office, one immediately after the other, as soon as I make it back after the briefing.

'Both of you are coming in a little hot, so I'm going to need you to calm down,' I request as I lean against my desk to face them.

'We want to be there tonight,' Lydia demands.

'I know, but you can't be. Only people directly affected by her removal are attending.'

'We're directly affected,' Lydia pushes.

'Yes, but in the same way everyone employed here is – and they aren't coming.'

'Ariella, Melissa can be... dangerous.' Lydia looks nervously at Caleb.

'I have reserved a team from building security to be stationed on the floor from seven to midnight. Their job will be to control access, so please don't turn up and make things more difficult for them.'

Just then Bryce joins us.

'They want to come tonight,' I fill him in.

'Ah. Melissa only agreed to Harrison, Christopher, Ariella, Dominic and me. She'd have to approve you both, and I'm guessing the answer will be no.'

'Dominic is going to be there?' Caleb challenges. 'I can take his place.'

'No, you can't. Your mere presence is a trigger for Melissa. You have history and I can't rely on you to be impartial. Plus, I can't use you to press my terms. Melissa was canvassing the launch for investors. Dominic expressed an interest in picking up whatever Melissa was putting on the table. Problem is, if he does that he will have a controlling interest. He needs to know what he is getting involved in.'

'So, Dominic is going to be our boss,' Caleb sneers.

'It'll be unlikely after tonight, but he might,' I clarify.

'What happened to "he does not need to know any more than he does already"?' he counters.

'I'm working on sealing the minutes of the meeting – everyone attending tonight is about to receive their paperwork. Dominic won't be able to walk past the office without wondering whether or not he has broken the agreement,' Bryce explains.

'I'm concerned that neither of you really understand who you're dealing with,' Lydia adds.

'You're right, I don't think we do, but we need to face it. She has been doing this all her life with several organisations, while I am still figuring out what I am doing with this one. We will basically be taking on an experienced professional who doesn't have the same reservations we do when it comes to committing crimes. Chances of failure are high; but if that ends up being the case, we are going to fail while giving it everything we have. Surely you both knew, once I found out what was going on, this day was always going to arrive.'

Lydia and Caleb settle into silence for the first time. I don't mean to be accusatory, but they have both contributed to this situation.

'Caleb, I need you on Jasper duty anyway. If you can fill him in on the last forty-eight hours when you pick him up, I'd be really grateful. Lydia, please get in touch with security, get the right guys for the job tonight and send them our standard non-disclosure and confidentiality agreements. Also, reach out to Georgie and ask her to halt all PR and media activity, without exception. If she won't get off the phone, put a meeting in for next week. Please get in touch with Ruby and Eden and ask whether they'd be open to returning to a full-time contract. If the answer is yes, dig out their old contracts, update them and send them to them. They need to be signed and returned before my meeting tonight. I can only protect them if they are full-time employees.'

They both nod, unsure.

'I think that's it. Please can I have some silence for the rest of the day?'

And that is what I get. As the day progresses, my anxiety and fear increase. It becomes unbearable at five, so I head home to stand under the shower for a little while. When I emerge, I find Caleb sitting patiently in my living room. He looks up with a face full of regret.

'What's up?'

'I just wanted to check that you don't need anything before I pick Jasper up.'

'No, I'm fine. Thank you.'

'Please don't take any risks with Melissa. If anything bad happens, I don't think I'd be able to live in this world without you.'

'Nothing is going to happen to me, Caleb.' I close the gap between us and plant a quick but reassuring kiss on his nose. 'I have to go.'

I place my wallet and keys in my back pocket and pick my phone up. It's time.

Dominic, Bryce and I are in the conference room at eight sharp, so I hit the button on the phone in the middle of the table and our screens light up with Christopher and Harrison's tired faces. Christopher looks exhausted, while Harrison is wearing a look of defiance.

'Hello, Harrison and Christopher, thank you very much for joining us.'

'No problem, but can we get on with it? We only just got off the plane a few hours ago,' Harrison complains as he yawns at the camera.

'We are just waiting for Melissa.'

'Good. Now we've exchanged pleasantries, when you see

Lara you can tell her that she's fucking fired!' Harrison growls. Bryce chuckles behind me.

'Can we park that for another day?' Christopher asks, exasperated.

'No. She can't just disappear in Singapore and not show up for the flight!' Harrison spits.

'Are you sure? Something could have happened to her...' I start to panic and grab my phone.

'Nothing has happened to her. First of all, it's Lara. She's like a fucking cockroach, she will always survive. Secondly, she checked out, drew the middle finger on the hotel bill she got delivered to my room at four a.m. and got them to transfer her entire bill to my room. This was after she emptied the minibar and either bought the whole hotel drinks or went on a massive bender. Lara is fucking fine.' Harrison throws his pen at the wall.

'You don't know where she is?' Christopher asks gently.

'No. The last time I heard from her was Sunday night, I think you guys had her working on something? I can text her to make sure she's okay...'

'She was running up her hotel bill all of Monday and was sane enough to move her flight on Tuesday, so she's okay.'

Lara clearly knows how to get under Harrison's skin.

'Let us know when she gets in contact, okay? We're not happy with her and we probably will be letting her go, but let's just all be—'

'Sorry to interrupt, Christopher, but Melissa is here.'

Melissa appears, escorted by the security team. It's a quarter past eight.

'This is all a bit much isn't it?' she jokes, taking a seat.

'Hello, Melissa. Would you like a drink?' I offer.

'Yes. White wine please,' she instructs, relaxing in her chair.

'I'll get it,' Bryce volunteers.

I make quick introductions of everyone around the table and get right to it.

'We have a strong suspicion based on reliable evidence that Ivory Bow UK has been laundering money for the following companies that are about to come up on screen.' I hit the button on my laptop.

'Wait, what?' Christopher exclaims, looking at Harrison.

Melissa just rolls her eyes, and the shock on Harrison's face is almost laughable.

'For the last couple of years, we've been accepting funds from companies that Melissa has fed us and redistributed those funds to various offshore accounts minus Ivory Bow's management fees. They are mimicking the lifecycle of an interrupted, cancelled or suspended event.'

'Those companies account for more than half of our revenue!' Christopher exclaims. I did not expect this to be news to him and the fact that it is restores him to the position of the mentor I thought he was.

'I believe so. I think you and Harrison are going to have to launch an internal investigation to gain more clarity. I have some information I can send over to help but, unfortunately, things don't look good for you over there.'

'Harrison, did you know about this?' Christopher is shouting now.

'This is all news—' Harrison starts unconvincingly.

'Harrison knew,' I interrupt. 'Harrison has known for a long time, and so has Preston.'

'Is this why you insisted we make your uncle CFO?' Christopher slams his fist down on the table. 'What the hell were you thinking, Harrison? We will lose everything! We could go to prison!'

I let Christopher express his rage at a meek-looking Harrison while I take stock of the room. Bryce is watching quietly, Dominic looks perplexed and Melissa is the picture of bored relaxation as she sips her wine. I try to keep the meeting on track.

'As you know, while we are a separate entity out here, our existence has only come to be because of Melissa. So, it is not a reach to assume that we were set up to expand on what has been essentially a success for her in the UK.'

'It's happening over there as well?' Christopher stares angrily into the camera.

'Bryce caught a similar pattern over here a few weeks ago and we assumed it was an error, so we attempted to put new systems in place to ensure that it isn't a situation that repeats itself. Unfortunately, our CFO over here has always been a little subversive, and those practices have not been put in place. After our lunch on Monday, I verified the status of the historic accounts that Harrison mentioned and an eerily similar pattern was established. I suspended our CFO yesterday, pending a full internal investigation.'

'She's nothing if not quick,' Melissa whispers under her breath before taking another sip. Bryce and Dominic shoot her fiery looks. I ignore her and continue.

'I thought it would be wise to have a conversation about my intentions to remove Melissa as our chairwoman and the impact, if any, that will have on Ivory Bow UK. I don't know what the investment profile is for you but I know that she basically owns us out here.'

'Well, as far as I understand it it's more like a franchise agreement, so we won't be affected by her removal aside from the yearly fees – but, as I am sure you can all tell, I clearly don't have a clue what's going on in my own company. So, Harrison?' Christopher demands.

'That's correct, it's largely based on a franchise agreement,' Harrison confirms quietly.

'Okay. In which case, I am emailing over my terms for Melissa's removal as our chairwoman.' I walk back over to my laptop and press send. I breathe as I watch everyone grab their phones and open the email before I continue.

'In broad terms, the email I just sent contains an option to dissolve Ivory Bow Asia and an option to continue operating – both of which will implicate and make me complicit in your crimes.'

Bryce starts shaking his head.

'No, Ariella...'

'Yes, Bryce. I have intentionally left you out of the agreement.'

'There has to be a better way...' he argues as he scrolls up his screen.

'There isn't.'

I breathe before I continue.

'I introduced Dominic Miller briefly earlier. He is our biggest client out here and has been in discussions with Melissa to take over a controlling interest in the company. After tonight, that's a decision he will need to make, knowing exactly what he will be inheriting. Ivory Bow's value is currently grossly inflated and has supported criminal activity perpetuated by the chair-woman of Ivory Bow Asia. This is a sinking ship that needs rescue at the moment, not the glamorous global agency everyone believes it is.'

Dominic's eyes are trained squarely on my email.

'If Dominic chooses not to invest in Ivory Bow Asia, which, in my opinion, would be the sensible decision to make, Ivory Bow Asia will simply dissolve. You will have the freedom to spin it any way you like, as long as none of the staff are impli-cated. In exchange for not reporting this to the UK and Singa-porean authorities, which is a crime in itself, I am requesting a full year's pay for each member of staff, now to include Ruby and Eden who, as of this afternoon, were reinstated as full-time members of staff. I'd also like signed statements or affidavits confirming that they knew nothing about this, and were not involved, excluding myself and Devin, who must be terminated immediately.'

'Ariella, you can't do that. It's blackmail. Extortion. It's—'

I cut Bryce off. I need to get to the end.

'I know. In addition to this, Ivory Bow UK must terminate all trading and business relationships with Melissa and her contacts within the next sixty days. If not, the authorities in both locations will receive everything I know and have.

'If Dominic chooses to take the immense risk to invest, Melissa must find a way to dispose of her remaining interest and shares in Ivory Bow. I will commit to staying on at Ivory Bow for the next two years starting on completion day, but all the other members of the team will be released from their current contracts with six months' pay and given the option to leave or stay. For those that choose to stay, they will receive a six-month pay equivalent as a bonus after their first year of employment.'

I take another breath.

'I will no longer be the face of Ivory Bow, and will be demoted once a competent and qualified COO has been employed; a position that I have always been immensely inadequate for. Dominic's interim team and Bryce, should he choose to stay, will be responsible for hiring a new CFO and putting financial processes in place that will not leave Ivory Bow Asia exposed to this sort of activity in the future. Again, you will only be able to take advantage of these terms if all relationships with Melissa and her contacts cease. If not, the same steps will be taken.'

I walk over to help myself to a bottle of water, then take a seat again to brace myself for whatever is coming.

'There is a lot about this that's dicey, Ariella,' Bryce whispers.

'That's why you are sealing this meeting,' I whisper back.

'I notice Caleb gets off scot-free in your little scenarios,' Melissa observes condescendingly.

'He's covered under the staff clause,' I respond as I take a sip of water. I expected her to do this and I cannot be rattled.

'Why is Caleb being singled out?' Dominic asks his first question of the night.

'Caleb was Melissa's conduit to Ivory Bow. He thought he was making legitimate sales but—' I start.

'Let's tell the whole truth, Ariella. I was screwing your boyfriend and feeding him clients that he happily hopped over to England for me. He was very, very grateful at the time, I seem to recall.' Melissa laughs. She's enjoying this. I hold my nerve.

'Is this true?' Dominic and Christopher ask at the same time.

'Yes, unfortunately. However, he was under the impression he was dealing with legitimate companies with actual business enquiries,' I defend him.

'I don't know if I'd want to keep him, knowing that.' Dominic looks at me sincerely.

'He has pulled in enough clients to see us through a year of trading without DMVI and they trust him. Whether we like it or not, he is the face of Ivory Bow and I am not going to do this without him. He gets the same treatment as all the other members of the team and I am not bending on that.' I hold firm. I'm still angry with Caleb but he doesn't deserve to be hung out to dry.

'Cute,' Melissa snarls. I ignore her and try to breathe as intentionally and as quietly as I can while everyone continues to read through my document.

'Can I suggest we reconvene on Monday?' An exhausted Christopher breaks the silence. 'Ariella, there is no question we will be terminating all of this activity, consider that done. We need some time to clean house and decide whether or not keeping the agreement with Asia is something that we still should be doing.'

'Our business will shrink immensely – we need the franchise funds,' Harrison argues.

'Harrison, if you say one more word, I am going to throw you through the fucking window,' Christopher threatens without missing a beat.

'No need to reconvene for me. I don't intend to push back. I never understood the industry anyway.' Melissa clicks her phone to lock it.

'I need the time. When would you like to have my decision, Ariella?' Dominic asks.

'Does Monday work for you too?' I suggest.

'I can give you a decision by then, but the paperwork might take considerably longer.'

'That's fine. In the meantime, I have Jasper coming in tonight to help so we have a clearer picture of where we are financially.'

I look at the time. It's not even ten yet. I expected much more conflict.

'We have a plan. Thank you for making yourselves available. Let's catch up on Monday?' I say to no one in particular as I cut the video link out.

'Everyone here knows how to get paperwork to me, so let me know what is decided.' With that, Melissa walks out without a care in the world.

'Wow. Ariella.' Dominic sighs as he sits back in his chair.

'I know.' I shrug.

'You look shattered. Want me to give you a ride home?'

'It's fine, you go. I'm going to have a quick meeting with Bryce.'

'I have a couple of calls to make, so I can do that while I wait.'

'Thanks, Dominic.'

'I'll be downstairs.'

I wait for him to grab his jacket and both our helmets from my office before I turn to Bryce.

'I don't like how easily that went.' Bryce looks worried.

'It did feel a bit too easy, didn't it?' I agree.

'We could just be paranoid because the last couple of days have been so hard,' he suggests.

'Maybe.' But I know what he means. Something doesn't feel right.

'Is it okay if we leave the recap till tomorrow? Today has been a lot and I'm fried,' Bryce asks.

'Sure. Thank you for being there. Are you heading home?'

'Nope. Off to go and get the right side of drunk, so I might be late tomorrow.'

'I wouldn't blame you if you don't show up at all,' I say sadly.

'You may have blindsided me tonight, but I'm showing up, don't you worry. You're not alone in this, especially now that we are going to have a new boss.'

'I don't think so. I brought him in to show him the carnage he'd be inheriting. No one in their right mind will touch us after that.'

'For your sake, I hope you're right, but you might be in for a surprise. Let's get out of here. I'm calling a cab to take me to all the drinks.'

Dominic is by his bike when Bryce and I exit the building. He looks happy and relaxed, so I shake the intensity of the meeting off too.

'I have to ask, how much in parking fines do you accumulate in the average week?' I laugh as I approach.

'Not as many as you'd think, but I am for sure a repeat offender. You okay?' He's particularly chirpy for someone who has just been in the same meeting I have.

'Yeah. Just exhausted. You?'

'I'm good. Let's get you home.'

There is a freedom and peace I have come to enjoy being behind Dominic on his bike. I try to empty my head as we whiz through the city. I like to drown my thoughts out with the noise of the wind and blur of the lights. Just as I'm managing to succeed, we come to a stop in front of my building and Dominic pulls into a parking spot. I get off the bike, remove my helmet and start to say goodbye, only to find him shutting off the engine and doing the same.

'I'm in Ariella. I'm investing in Ivory Bow,' he informs me, dismounting.

'Are you sure? You should really think about this. It's a huge risk and we are more a circus of criminals than a business right now.'

He laughs that laugh that makes me want to laugh along too, and I do.

'I know, but I've worked in close proximity with you for a few weeks now and you're... astounding. You've built something really interesting and it's such good fun.'

'Interesting is a hilarious word to use.' I smile.

'I know. Let me come up and I'll tell you more.' He takes a few steps before he realises that I am not following.

'I don't think that's a good idea,' I say quietly.

'Why?' Dominic smiles like he has just told himself a private joke.

'It's late and—'

'That's not why. It's because of this.' He moves his index finger back and forth between us as he walks back towards me. 'Something is going on here and every so often we both feel it. If anybody else had given you a ride home, you'd be inviting them upstairs for a drink of some sort. I, on the other hand, am out here, being held at a distance.'

'Dom, I don't think this is the time...'

'I don't think this is the time either, but you've made it the time, Ariella. I know you're trying to do the best you can with this shitty situation you find yourself in, but tonight, you've pushed me up against the wall for a decision that forces me to choose between losing you or buying us some time.'

'The decision to invest shouldn't be personal, you should be making it based on the business case.'

'Ariella? Really?' He laughs kindly. 'Come on. Be honest with yourself.'

I don't say anything.

'If I don't do this with Ivory Bow, you'll be out of here the first chance you get and, let's face it, you're never coming back to Singapore. I would never force myself on you, but I would like to see what could happen, because I know you feel it too. Besides, even with Melissa's inflated valuation, Ivory Bow isn't asking for that much money, so two years to see if this could go somewhere sounds like a good idea.'

'Dom, I am definitely not worth the gamble. I don't trust myself or my judgement at the moment. Lara has been silent for two days and I didn't realise. She's supposed to be my best friend and I have no idea where she is. I also stupidly and selfishly kind of asked Jasper to come out to Singapore even though I knew it would cause quite a bit of conflict between him and his girlfriend. How terrible is that?'

'Ariella, I can completely understand—'

'No, you can't. I slept with Caleb last night even though I am completely devastated by what he has done. I am so furious with him, I can't think straight. I am leaping from emotion to emotion without looking and everything I am feeling is so intertwined, I can't pull them apart. I can't separate the love from the fury, the pain from the desire, the betrayal from the deep loneliness I am terrified of feeling again. Right now, I am a walking disaster!'

'You're not. You're just human. I've watched you the last

few months take everything thrown at you and contain it all. Your problem is, you're an expert at looking like you're thriving when you're actually falling apart inside. I still think about those silent tears you shed, the first time I saw you.'

Dominic holds my face in his hands.

'Lara is fine. Jasper is an adult capable of making his own choices and Caleb... well, I can't help you with Caleb – but I can show you that, if you want one, you have a choice.'

Dominic lowers his face to mine and kisses me gently. His kiss is soft and reassuring. It gives me the space to pull away but also, with each moment that passes, gives me a reason to stay. I lose myself in it, as the contents of my mind fall away and I breathe him in. He pulls away as softly as he brought us together and leans his forehead against mine.

'I know my timing sucks and this may never happen again, but please can you stay a little longer so we can find out? I know you don't trust your judgement at the moment, so I won't do that again until I know you're sure but for that to happen I am asking you to stay. I have no—'

A loud cackle of laughter cuts through the night air around us.

'Ariella Mason! Budget Jasper? Really? Guuurl, you are such a ho'! I fucking love it!'

I break away and turn around to see Lara laughing hysterically, next to a worried-looking Jasper, while Caleb stands next to her with his eyes cast downward, looking visibly pained.

This cannot get any worse.

A LETTER FROM THE AUTHOR

It's an absolute privilege to share *Complicated* with you and I hope you enjoyed your journey with Ariella and Caleb. If you would like to join my reader community to have exclusive access to new releases, bonus content and other little surprises, please sign up for my newsletter!

www.stormpublishing.co/ola-tundun

For an author, a short review can make all the difference in encouraging a reader to discover my book for the first time. If you enjoyed my book and can spare a few moments to leave a review, I'd be immensely grateful. Thank you so much!

I'm drawn to exploring characters who the reader recognises and finds hard to judge and who are rarely truly guilty or innocent of their less-than-honourable acts. I enjoy finding the beauty in the messiness of life, encouraging the reader to reconsider where they stand on a series of modern issues while enjoying a fast and fun read.

Thank you once again for being part of this unbelievable journey with me and I hope we can stay in touch – there is so much more to come!

Ola x

KEEP IN TOUCH WITH THE AUTHOR

www.olatundunx.com

f facebook.com/olatundunx

X x.com/olatundunx

O instagram.com/olatundunx

♪ tiktok.com/@olatundun_x

ACKNOWLEDGEMENTS

To my wonderful Fairy God Agent Emily Glenister at DHH Literary Agency, I am so incredibly lucky to have you as my warrior, champion and friend. To the best editor that I could have hoped for, Emily Gowers. Thank you for consistently meeting me with passion, life and a genius I wouldn't be able to touch on my own.

To the Storm Publishing and DHH Literary Agency teams and author families. Thank you for creating such warm, welcoming industry homes for me, and for your continued support.

For all the people that keep life beautiful:

Debola (still my ride or die for LYFE lol), Ashley, Myriam and Els; thank you for literally carrying me through this second book.

Diana, Oriton, Lola, Natalie, Mon, Saskia, Sara, Seun, Huma, Mr J, Ayomi, Jeannette, Nicky, Jane, Angela, Kate, Neema, Yael, Beejal, Kay, Zainab, Bisola, Matthew, Sarveen, Esther, Dave and Segun – thank you for consistently showing up and staying up. Your love and support in the quiet, away from the noise, when I am riddled with doubt and feel that I have nothing left to give, is the reason I am here, doing this.

Dominic, what would I do without you? You're still stuck with me.

Jacqui, Liz and Alex, thank you for saving me from myself, again. Elke and Anna, thank you for all you do to amplify these stories.

To my husband and daughter, you are the most important beings in the world to me. I hope I continue to make you proud.

Most importantly to God. I remain still, because I know. I continue to trust and surrender to your will.